The Flavor of Hearts

CAROL MILAZZO

Copyright © 2012 Carol Milazzo

Cover Art: Carol Milazzo

All rights reserved.

This is a work of fiction.
Any similarity to actual people or places is purely coincidental.

ISBN-13: 978-0615594507
(Carol Milazzo)
ISBN-10: 0615594506

THIS BOOK IS DEDICATED TO:

MY SISTER
VIRGINIA MILAZZO
AND MY MOTHER AND FATHER
JOSEPH AND DOROTHY MILAZZO

*Without their invaluable support
the fruits of my creativity
would be non-existent.*

1

Itzi climbed the stairs to the rooftop terrace; it was humid but the steady sea breeze cooled the night air. He settled his tiny frame into a lounge chair and turned his eyes skyward; a thing he'd done nightly longer than any man alive.

In a blink he mentally notated every visible star and its place, detecting the slightest movement from the night before. No man has ever known the sky like Itzi. A photographic memory and extraordinary recall of detail made him the ultimate astronomer. His celestial predictions were legendary.

"Itzamna has flown among the stars."

Itzi could hear his older sisters saying it.

"Itzamna has flown among the stars."

This night he tried not to think of his two older sisters, so long gone from his life. The little man could see in his mind's eye every sky he had ever seen. He could lay these mental images one on top of another; the slightest difference had a sound; somehow Itzi heard space moving and he was never wrong.

He refocused on the sky above. Picturing the discovered galaxies beyond the visible stars Itzi smiled. The state of the art telescope looming on the roof behind him had given him sight beyond his eyes, an amazing gift. Now Itzi saw space in three dimensions; he had eons of light years in his vast memory and he soared through the mental pictures.

"Itzamna has flown among the stars."

Again Itzi tried not to think of his two older sisters. He would not appear ungrateful to the great god Chac; the god who had provided this amazing journey across time. Yes, Itzi would continue to fulfill his part of their bargain.

The little man closed his eyes. Itzi pictured the sacred calendar; in his mind he watched the wheels turning. No society in history had measured time more accurately than the Maya and Itzi was celebrated among them.

The ancient calendar rolled in his head; wheels inside wheels: the inner ring turning to the left and the outer ring turning to the right. The glyphs lined up to state the day and month: HOO CIB; July eleventh.

Itzi smiled slightly. After all these years he still translated time. He still thought first in his ancient tongue; translating the Mayan to the modern. He had spoken so many languages over the years, sometimes words were a mish mash, but the language of time had never changed for the brilliant astronomer.

HOO CIB; Itzi smiled again. It was his birthday. The calendar wheels whirred in his computer like brain. He immediately began calculating the Mayan Long count. The little man shook his head in disbelief. Today he was 1088 years old.

He certainly didn't feel or look his age. As the great god promised for every BAKTUN Itzi had aged one TUN; one year older every 394 years. Itzi smiled broadly; all the knowledge of 1088 years stored in his brain and his body was barely 33 years old.

"Saku'un...."

Itzi's eyes flew open at the sound of his brother's voice. It was unthinkable that anyone would interrupt the astronomer's meditations and study of the night sky.

THE FLAVOR OF HEARTS

"SSSaku'un'...." Bartolomeo stammered; he used the Mayan term for older brother. The family addressed Itzi this way when they wanted to show him the utmost respect.

"mmm..Mama was hoping you could come down a little early. She has made your birthday dinner..."

Bartolomeo was suddenly afraid; to interrupt a High Priest during his communion with the sky was unforgivable; an act sometimes punished in ancient times with death. Bartolomeo was very aware of his older brother's status; though many things had changed over the years, Chac the great god of thunder and rain had surely chosen Itzi. The miracles and blessings their family had experienced over the last century were solid proof of that. Long ago Itzi was venerated by the people of Uxmal as a god on earth and Bartolomeo was positive the reverence was well deserved.

"Of course, I'll come now," the little man agreed rising to his full four feet in height.

Sensing his sibling's nervousness Itzi reached up and placed his hand on his younger brother's shoulder.

"Tolo, do you think she made a turkey?" the tiny man asked pleasantly.

"Could be," the younger man relaxed.

Bartolomeo grinned as they headed for the stairs. He could picture the gold serving platter waiting below: turkey stuffed with ground beef and boiled eggs, simmered in burnt pepper sauce; definitely his older brother's favorite food, cooked his favorite way.

2

Their mother was standing at the dining room entrance. A powerful healer and spirit woman in her own right, she leaned down and kissed her eldest son on his forehead.

"Itzamna, happy birthday."

"Mamatzil."

Itzi addressed his mother in their old tongue; the literal translation was revered mother. The little man smiled at his four younger siblings. They had decorated the room with his favorite flowering plants and wore their finest clothes and jewelry for this special occasion.

The ornately carved dining room table was set with the family's most precious service, solid gold plates and utensils glimmered in muted candlelight. Jade and gold serving dishes lined the table and two sideboards holding an interesting array of Itzi's favorite foods.

The juxtaposition of the modern with the ancient was almost comical. Next to an enormous pile of Salbutes, Mayan tortillas stuffed with turkey, sat a steaming pepperoni pizza. Cochinita Pibil, marinated pork wrapped in banana leaves shared space with a bulging tray of deep fried peanut butter and banana sandwiches.

Mayan desserts and chocolate in every form lined one sideboard. Itzi grinned when he saw the pyramid made from a dozen boxes of Drake's Ring Dings. His taste for chocolate had never diminished over the many years and the cream filled cake was easily his favorite modern snack.

Once the little man took his place at the table's head his mother circled the room with a carved jade pitcher; she filled a goblet at each place setting with chocolatl, the sacred Mayan drink made from crushed roasted cocoa beans, water and spices.

Raising her portion she looked skyward and began the celebration dinner with a prayer.

"All honor and blessings to our lord Chac, for the life he has given us," she intoned. Lowering her eyes she faced her oldest son at the opposite end of the table. Holding the goblet at a slightly lower elevation she went on,

"Blessings to Izamna, our beloved light on earth, favored servant of the great lord Chac."

As she drank from her goblet the rest of the family did the same. This day the drink was made the traditional way, unsweetened. Itzi smiled at his younger sisters' reaction to the bitter taste; it was clear they now preferred their chocolate with sugar.

"Happy Birthday, Itzamna, my dearly loved first son," his mother's face softened with a tender smile.

"Happy birthday, Itzi," the family spoke in unison then drained the goblets of the chocolatl.

Itzi spoke, happiness coloring his words,

"Praise to the great lord Chac, for all he has given us."

The tiny man smiled as he looked around the table, "and from my heart I give you thanks, my precious family. Without all of you my service to our god would be unbearable."

The two brothers and two sisters eyed each other quizzically; Itzamna rarely spoke this way. Through him the god had favored their whole family with unnaturally long lives and immense wealth, they certainly did not feel worthy of their great brother's gratitude.

Itzi could sense their unease; they loved him as their brother but still feared him as a High Priest. Though he abandoned his official religious titles the night he left the great pyramid, the family would never forget Itzi's exalted status.

The little man grinned from ear to ear and motioned toward the huge stuffed turkey on the platter in front of his place.

"Let us eat this wonderful meal, I think I will finish this whole bird myself!"

Laughter filled the room and drastically lightened the mood. The family tore into the multitude of serving trays. Itzi's mother watched her tiny son with great joy. Itzamna had a miniature body, but his appetite was huge; it was always a pleasure to watch him eat so heartily.

She thought back to the night of his birth. The midwife had gasped when the baby appeared. He was perfect in everyway except for his stature; he was easily one quarter the size of a normal Mayan newborn. The ladies in attendance had knelt before the spirit woman with her first born son at her breast; they called him a miracle, surely a gift from the gods.

Word spread like wild fire through the neighboring villages of the Yucatan: a healthy baby boy, born no bigger than a bird. The spirit woman smiled. Legends still persisted that her oldest son was hatched full grown from an egg!

She remembered her pride at his naming ceremony; the High Priest called her son Itzamna, after the creator god of the Mayan universe. The temple priests sensed great things for the tiny boy, later Itzi's enormous intellect and amazing memory would prove their predictions more than correct.

When Itzamna became High Priest and ruler of Uxmal his mother thought he had fulfilled his destiny; today she shook her head, little had she known.

3

Itzi's sisters cleared the entrees from the table and replaced them with the array of sweets and desserts. Bartolomeo filled jade shot glasses with Xtabentun, a modern Mayan liqueur made of honey, anise and rum. The family toasted with many rounds; a festive atmosphere prevailed.

Itzi teased his younger sisters, "No chocolate martinis? No Cosmopolitans?"

Itzi's little sisters were almost his age, they too had existed over a century. Presently they lived just as they looked; as singles in their mid-twenties, enjoying everything the modern world had to offer two beautiful girls of wealth and privilege.

"You'd be surprised to know that they're drinking this in the best clubs now, Itzi," his youngest sister informed him with mock offense.

It was true, Mayan culture was now "hot"; it was all over the media, especially with doomsday predictions centering on the upcoming end of the Mayan Long Count Calendar in the year 2012.

"Anyway," she continued far more sincerely, "we're going traditional tonight, for your birthday."

Bartolomeo turned toward their youngest brother and slapped him on the shoulder,

"Give it to him, Fonso." he instructed motioning toward Itzi.

Ildefonso stood. The spirit woman craned her neck to look up at her youngest son. Fonso stood six foot five. He was born at nearly twelve pounds; her last born son was the physical opposite of her first!

Itzi," the big man began, "I know we're not supposed to get you anything, but we couldn't resist this…"

He passed an oversized envelope to the head of the table. The suspense was palpable as Itzi examined the contents. Cyrillic writing covered the top of the first paper; the body of the letter was in English.

It welcomed Itzamna Cenotes as an international civilian space traveler. It spoke of training sessions and medical examinations to be held in Star City in Russia. The letter instructed Mr. Cenotes to honestly fill out the enclosed questionnaire. A photograph of a space craft on a launch pad fell from the packet.

"Fonso," Itzi sounded perplexed, "what is this?"

"The Russians are sending civilians, regular people into space. We got you a ticket, Itzi! They will bring you above the clouds into space!"

Itzi was thunderstruck. The ancient astronomer followed the news stories of space exploration very closely; he had been awed by the films of men walking on the moon and the photos of our planet they sent back. He avidly collected the NASA photographs taken with the Hubble Space Telescope.

Itzi remained speechless.

"I don't know, Fonso…" the little man finally spoke, still staring at the picture of the space craft.

He and Ildefonso had witnessed a US Space Shuttle launch in Florida, the ground shook from those rockets a mile away! Though Itzi had none of the fears of mortal men, frankly he was floored by the idea of riding on a rocket.

Sheepishly Itzi grinned at his gigantic youngest brother,

"Fonso, I'm nervous enough riding in your automobile…"

"You don't want to go, Itzi?" Ildefonso was incredulous.

THE FLAVOR OF HEARTS

Bartolomeo was shocked as well by their older brother's reaction. "You will see our planet as our first ancestors saw it!" Tolo chimed in excitedly, "You have to go, Itzi!"

"Bartolomeo!"

All five of her children turned toward the spirit woman. "Itzamna will lead us, as he should!"

She put a sharp emphasis on the words "lead us".

Tolo became wide eyed at his mother's rebuke. He had meant no disrespect; his words had come out like a directive, but he never meant to give his older brother an order.

"Saku'un," the younger man stammered an apology for the second time that evening, "I would never presume to—"

"Tolo, it's fine," Itzi interrupted, "it's fine. Everybody, it's fine."

"Mama," the little man smiled at his mother, "it's fine."

"Tolo," Itzi turned to face his chastised brother, "fill the glasses again. We must toast this gift. I will seriously consider riding in the spaceship," Itzamna reassured his siblings, "I appreciate all of you and your wonderful gift."

Thankfully Itzi could feel the sudden tension dissipating. As the family drank another round of the sweet Mayan liqueur the little man spoke again, "But if I decide not to go, I think you should go, Fonso."

Every eye turned toward the family giant, shock was all over his large handsome face.

"Me?" his usually baritone voice sounded three times higher in pitch.

"Yes," Itzi laughed as he answered, "In fact, even if I decide to go aboard the space ship, I think you should go too."

All the siblings broke out into huge smiles. Ildefonso was easily the most adventurous of all of them.

The alcohol had made Itzi playful and he continued,

"In fact, I think we should all go," the little man stole a glance at his sainted mother as he declared, "yes, I think we will all be blasted into space."

The spirit woman's eyes grew as wide as hard boiled eggs. Her first son watched in amusement as a half hearted protest sputtered from her lips.

"Itzamna, I-I-I don't think I- I could---"

The spirit woman would never go against her son's plans; surely he was the great god's chosen, but panic dripped from her words. Their mother was uncomfortable in any transportation beyond the horse and buggy.

A manic grin broke out across Itzi's little face.

"I'm kidding, Mama," Itzi laughed out loud at her obvious relief.

Peals of laughter filled the room as the spirit woman threw her napkin at her oldest boy.

"I am serious about the rest of you," Itzamna gestured toward his siblings when the mirth died down, "any of you who would like to see the earth as our first ancestors did, Fonso will make the arrangements. I will seriously consider taking a ride into space and all of you should now do the same."

The brothers and sisters eyed each other excitedly. They murmured sincere thanks to their oldest brother. Once again he was providing an adventure beyond their wildest dreams.

Satisfied Itzamna pushed his chair back from the table and rose.

"I think I will go to my room and rest before work this evening." he patted his tiny stomach, "I have eaten so much I am stuffed tighter than Mama's delicious turkey."

The family stood as their exalted brother headed toward the dining room door. As he passed the side board he took two boxes of Ring Dings and placed one under each arm.

"Itzamna," his mother called to him, "it you eat all those cakes at once you will feel sick."

"Yes, Mama," the little man replied, again laughing out loud. He was 1088 year old man in a 33 year old body; with one sentence his beloved mother could still make him feel like a 7 year old child.

4

Itzi was still smiling when he entered his bedroom. His mother always found a way to make him feel normal, to make him feel human.

He placed the Ring Dings on his dresser and leaned the envelope from the Russian Space agency against the mirror. Amazing, the little man thought eyeing his unexpected birthday present; the gifts of the great lord Chac grew more and more wondrous with each passing year.

Itzi turned on the ceiling fan and stretched out on the king sized bed. His mind immediately traveled back to his 30th birthday in ancient Uxmal.

In much the same way he had stuffed himself at his mother's dinner and returned to his house to rest. In his bedchamber atop the imposing temple pyramid he fell into sound sleep. Awakened by a noise Itzamna had been shocked to see a figure inside his quarters, at first he was sure he was dreaming; death surely awaited any man who dared come unbidden to the House of the Magician.

Itzi had sprang from his bed and moved toward the intruder. At closer inspection he could see it was an old man with a long narrow face and pointed snakelike teeth.

Surprisingly the trespasser was barely taller than Itzamna himself.

"Who are you, old man?" Itzi demanded in the fierce tone he used during the Sacrificial Rites.

"I am Chac, Itzamna," the old man's voice was deep and resonant, a surprise coming from his skinny reptilian face.

For the first time Itzi noticed the axe the old man carried. The tiny High Priest drew in breath to call for his temple's guards; he would gladly take this trespasser's blood and offer it to the great god this old man dared to impersonate.

"I am Chac, Itzamna," the old man repeated.

This time the words echoed in a most unnatural way, his voice sounded like thunder. Itzi froze.

The old man cradled the axe in the crook of his elbow and extended his forearms, turning his palms toward the floor. Immediately water dripped from his hands; a plinking sound filled the room as the drops hit the floor.

Water pooled at the old man's feet as rain continued to fall from his wrinkled extremities. Itzi watched in amazement as the stone floor became soaked. In a minute the wetness reached Itzi's bare feet. When he felt the liquid on his toes the tiny High Priest was sure he was not dreaming.

Itzamna dropped to his knees and pressed his forehead to the floor, now feeling the wetness on his face and legs. Itzi heard the miraculous indoor rain stop but he dared not move a muscle. Prostrated before the god Itzi waited for the axe to sever his neck, surely the great god of rain and thunder had come this night to claim his High Priest's blood.

"Rise, Itzamna," the voice still sounded like thunder.

Itzi obeyed, but averted his gaze from the figure before him.

"Look into my eyes," the old man commanded.

Again Itzi obeyed. In the large black pupils two tiny lightning bolts lit the old man's deep eye sockets, like lightning lights the summer night. The tiny High Priest gasped, his own eyes wide with wonder.

"Do you now believe I am your lord god Chac?" the old man asked.

"I do, great lord," Itzi bowed his head to the Mayan deity of thunder and rain.

"Walk with me," the god commanded.

They left the bedchamber and stepped into the night outside Itzi's home atop the pyramid. The god led the little High Priest to the eastern corner. With a wave of Chac's wrinkled hand a mist appeared and pictures filled the gray cloud.

"Do you know this place, Itzamna?" the god asked.

The High Priest squinted at the vision: a step pyramid, uncared for and overgrown. Looking more closely Itzi suddenly had recognition.

"Chichen Itza?" the tiny man asked horror-struck.

He was appalled by the condition of the Temple of Kukulkan. It looked as though it had been abandoned for a thousand years.

"What has happened to our great ally?" Itzi asked softly, concerned for the people of the great Mayan city state to the east.

"Nothing yet," Chac answered grimly, "but it will happen."

If the great Chichen Itza would fall...Itzamna shuddered.

"What of my city? Your city," Itzi corrected himself, "what of Uxmal?"

"The same," Uxmal's patron god replied.

A tear sprang to Itzi's eye and rolled down his tanned cheek. With a wan smile the god touched Itzi's face and claimed the droplet.

Lying on his king sized bed over a thousand years later the little man still shuddered at the memory; the god's touch had been as cold as the dead.

"I have a request of you, Itzamna,"

Itzi could hear the voice of Chac today as if it was yesterday.

"Anything, lord," the tiny High Priest had answered immediately.

"Hear my request first and I grant you the right to refuse me."

The last part sent a chill up Itzi's spine.

5

Chac pointed a bent finger toward the sky, "Do you know what happens at the end of the 13th BAKTUN?"

"Yes, great lord, the union of First Mother with First Father."

Itzi spoke of a celestial event. The Maya called the sun of the winter solstice First Father; they called the dark cloud constellations in the Milky Way First Mother.

Itzi's answer described a predicted celestial event: on a certain date, the first sun of the New Year would line up with the dark rift in the center of the Milky Way. This rare alignment occurs once every 26,000 years. Modern astronomers call this the alignment of our sun with galactic center.

The god smiled. Yes, it was true; no mortal man knew the sky like tiny Itzamna.

"Exactly. Our universe will be reborn," the god spoke cryptically, "not only ours, but worlds you cannot imagine."

The date the lord spoke of was far in the future. Itzi wondered what this date could mean to him personally; his bones would surely be dust by then.

"Much power is needed to fuel this rebirth," the god began to explain, "oceans of life's sacred liquid, the solid beats of a mountain of hearts."

Itzi's eyes opened wide. The warriors of Uxmal were powerful, but how many could they bring to the altar? The little man wasn't sure that many people even existed. Itzamna had an amazing grasp of numbers, quickly he multiplied the days; what the god asked was impossible, no priest could harvest a mountain of hearts, even in a lifetime.

Again the god was amused; he could hear the brilliant calculations in the High Priest's tiny head.

"It is possible, Itzamna," Chac said softly. "But you cannot do it here, and you cannot do it in the way you have done it."

"How can I give you what you ask, great lord?" suddenly the High Priest feared the answer.

"It is a much larger world than you imagine, Itzamna. You know much of the sky above, but you know nothing of the world we stand upon. Many, many cities exist, many much greater than the ones you have seen. Men of all colors live in ways you cannot envision. I need you to visit these places and harvest many hearts, many flavors of hearts."

Itzi struggled to make sense of these words. Could a man be the color of the sky, the color of the leaves of trees? He would visit the places where these strange men lived? How? The numbers still staggered the tiny High Priest. Questions flooded his brain, but Itzi remained silent.

Chac laughed out loud at the green and blue men of Itzi's imagination.

"No men are the colors of the sky or the leaves of the jungle. There are those with white skin, pale as sun bleached sea shells, there are others as dark as a roasted cocoa bean, with every shade in between. There are men with golden hair, hair the color of your finest maize; there are some with hair as orange as the hottest flame. Men exist in many varieties like the birds that fly above."

Itzi was amazed, but still didn't speak.

THE FLAVOR OF HEARTS

"Each year, starting this year, on the night of First Father I will move you from place to place," the deity promised, "and all you will need, I will provide."

"Great lord," Itzi finally responded, "I believe you will provide, for you always have…but I could hold the Sacrificial Rites every day from now until the skin falls from my bones and not accumulate half the hearts you need for your glory."

"You can fulfill my needs, Itzamna, I can give the Gift of Time," Chac explained, "I cannot promise you eternal life as that is reserved for the gods, but I can slow the rate at which you age. For every BAKTUN you will grow one TUN older."

Itzi's computer like brain whirred with calculations. With such an extended life he could harvest a mountain of hearts for the great rebirth!

Suddenly the High Priest realized the further implications, he would watch everyone he loved wither and die, his beloved mother, his brothers and sisters…he would live alone through turns and turns of the sacred calendar…better Chac should cast him into Xibalba now, the little man would take his chances in the Underworld's torturous hell.

"Great lord god," Itzi carefully measured the last words he would probably speak, "I have been your humble servant…"

Chac held up a bony hand, interrupting what he sensed as the High Priest's refusal. He felt the tiny man's anguish and fear of never ending loneliness; frankly the great god was glad to hear Itzamna still felt love. So many High Priests grew callous from the rivers of blood they had spilled.

"I will extend the lives of your family as well," the god offered graciously, "They will travel from place to place with you. I wish you to be happy in my service, Itzamna. I will provide you and your family with perfect health and wealth beyond your dreams. You will all have experiences far greater than you can imagine."

Chac paused to hear Itzi's thoughts, but the tiny man was awestruck; though the little man was brilliant this was already too much for him to assimilate.

"Do not give me your answer tonight, Itzamna," the god spoke reassuringly. "Speak to no one of my visit tonight, no man or any other entity. You may tell your family, as they too now have the choice to come on this journey or not. I will return in twenty days for your decision. At that time I will explain how you will begin this new life in my service."

The god placed the axe he held at Itzi's feet.

"I leave my weapon with you, Itzamna, as a gift," Chac smiled, "It will help you remember this evening as it happened."

The god faded away like smoke over a fire. Itzi stared at the axe for a long time that night before he picked it up.

Itzi opened his eyes and rose from the huge bed. He walked to a glass cabinet on the wall of his room. The axe was prominently displayed along with the personal artifacts Itzi had taken on the night of the first Move.

The little man smiled when he recalled his family's faces when they heard his story and saw Chac's weapon. The blade was gold...no Mayan had ever seen metal. It truly was something from another world.

Itzi looked below the axe; the little man opened the cabinet and removed his ceremonial knife. The obsidian blade still felt razor sharp. He ran his fingers over the inlaid jade on the ornately carved bone handle.

It had been a long time since Itzi held the ceremonial knife; he closed his eyes remembering how effortlessly it pierced a human chest. He could still easily recall the feel of a human heart beating in his hand, the warmth of the sacred blood dripping down his arm as he raised the precious offering to the gods.

Itzi replaced the knife and closed the cabinet. Frankly he did not miss the smell of the blood and the death. Marking the humans for the great god was much easier.

The little man turned to look at the clock on the opposite wall; it was past midnight. Ildefonso and Bartolomeo would be waiting to open the shop, it was time for work.

6

Emily dialed one, then ten more numbers. She imagined the call flying through the air all the way into Manhattan. If only the pulses would transport all of her instead of only her voice.

"Satchi and Satchi"

"Emily Hoyle for Joan DeMeter"

Emily figured her old friend was still at the office. It was late Friday, a sweltering July afternoon. Any Manhattan resident with the means had probably reached Martha's Vineyard by now but Emily knew Joan's habits. Her ex-coworker would wait for the sun to set and travel in the late evening avoiding the rush and the mass exodus.

"Emily!" Joan's voice sounded pleased, "How are you? How's Tim?"

"I'm fine, Tim's great. Yourself?"

"Great, busy as always."

Time was always at a premium on Madison Avenue so Emily approached the subject at hand.

"Joanie," she said, addressing her sorority sister with her old college nickname, "you said to call by the end of the month about the Ford account."

Up until eighteen months ago the two women worked side by side at Manhattan's most successful advertising agency producing some of the biggest ad campaigns in the country. Emily's resignation and move to Philadelphia left a gaping hole in both women's lives personally as well as professionally.

"Oh, Em, I'm so sorry," Joan's voice took on a softer tone, "I should've called you. Bob thought it was too big to involve anybody out of house. It's huge, everything's revamping; he was afraid of stuff falling thru the cracks...you know how it is..."

As her friend's voice trailed off Emily's heart sank. Another campaign gone with the wind, the former New Yorker was close to despair.

When her husband Tim was presented the position as assistant curator at the Philadelphia Museum of Art he generously offered to turn it down. Even though it was a mammoth opportunity for him, he knew the necessary move from Manhattan would throw a monkey wrench into his wife's already highly successful career.

As Joan's assistant, the two women headed the A Team at Satchi and Satchi, handling the best and most high profile accounts. Emily was on the fast track to take full leadership once Joan was promoted.

Ironically, it was this high level of success that even let Emily consider leaving Satchi and Satchi. She wanted the same for Tim. His job in Manhattan, assistant manager of European acquisitions at the Guggenheim was pretty much a dead end. There was no sign of advancement there.

The museum in Philly was old and respected. She knew if Tim worked there for even a few years, bigger and better doors would fly open for him in the New York museums.

"Em...Emily, are you there?" concern colored her old friend's voice.

"Yeah, yeah, I'm here." She tried to conceal her disappointment.

"Look, next week I'll have something for you, I promise. We're getting the John Deere account, high end riding lawnmowers. We're aiming the whole push at women. I'll definitely call you in on it. Definitely. Hey, why don't you and Tim come up for a long weekend? We can all go out to the Vineyard, what do you say?"

"I'll see, sounds good. I'll talk to Tim." Emily tried to end on an upbeat tone, "Well, I'll let you go. Great to talk to you, Joanie."

"You too, Em, let's do the weekend thing. I miss you."

"Same here," the transplanted New Yorker replied as she cradled the phone.

Emily removed her reading glasses and sat at her desk staring into space. She thought of Tim's expression the night she broke the news. Over dinner at Benito One, their favorite restaurant in little Italy, she told her husband she planned to resign. He was astounded; his mouth agape and his gray blue eyes as wide as saucers. If it wasn't so painful now, she'd laugh at the memory.

That night she wound up convincing her husband they should move. Over delicious tortellini and clams Emily told Tim of Satchi and Satchi's offer of freelance work. She grimaced, recalling her stupid optimism.

"Besides," she remembered saying, "I won a Clio for God's sake. How hard will it be to find work in Philadelphia?"

She looked up at the advertising business's highest award, gleaming on the shelf above her computer monitor. Today it gave her a sick feeling in the pit of her stomach.

How ludicrous. It was actually her decision to live in this backwater excuse for a city. God, the way things turned out. Extracting her long legs from under the desk she rose and headed toward the bar in the living room.

Uncorking a bottle of Merlot she berated herself. How could I have been so stupid? The agencies here were so provincial. The menial positions offered....a joke. She poured the wine and took a swig before the blood red liquid settled in the goblet.

At first Satchi and Satchi was true to its word; Emily's former employer sent some pretty good freelance work her way. As time wore on though, the flow of assignments had dried to a trickle. Emily could hardly blame them, the "out of sight, out of mind" attitude was highly prevalent in New York advertising. As she raised the goblet to her lips she tried to remember the last campaign she received.

The donut chain...that was it. Emily drained the oversized wine glass and refilled it. That campaign turned out to be a monster. With her slogan, "America runs on Dunkin" and the new faster paced TV spots, the older company no longer feared the threat of Starbucks: the powerful new kid on the block.

Her former agency was thrilled with the outcome, the co-owner Bob Satchi phoned her personally. Dunkin Donuts numbers were massive, the response to Emily's campaign brought unprecedented sales to the chain. She remembered him gushing.

"Tying athleticism to donuts and coffee...using a jogging icon ...genius, pure genius, Emily. Congratulations, fine, fine work"

The brown haired woman drained her second glass of Merlot; God that was six months ago and no work since. Today's meeting was solid proof of the lack of freelance opportunities in Philly. If despair had a deeper level, she was there.

Filling the wine glass almost to the brim Emily crossed the spacious living room and headed toward the balcony. Sliding back the heavy glass door she entered the well appointed terrace and stood at the rail.

The waterfront high rise, looming high above the Delaware River, was one of Philadelphia's most desirable new addresses. The view from the twenty second floor was stunning by any standards. Two magnificent bridges gracefully connected Pennsylvania to the distant greenery of southern New Jersey: the Walt Whitman in the distance to the right and its counterpart closer on the left: the older Ben Franklin. The boat filled harbor and string of waterfront clubs at Penns Landing below were colorful dots from this vantage.

Any other person would have been soothed by such a vista, but not the homesick New Yorker; not today anyway.

Suddenly Emily took a deep breath and spit over the balcony; an act miles out of character for a woman of her refinement. Her wealthy upbringing had instilled all the perfect manners prep schools and afternoon teas could provide.

Taking full advantage of her solitude the lady reared up and spit again, propelling the clear bodily fluid in a high arch above the ground below.

"Fuck you, Philadelphia."

She said it out loud; the crude obscenity highly out of character as well.

After a large gulp of Merlot she turned and settled into one of the overstuffed patio chairs. She wanted to cry, but no tears came.

Timothy Hoyle parked his car in its assigned spot in the apartment building's underground garage. Noticing Emily's Mercedes nestled in the adjacent space the lanky blond man felt a tinge of worry. She was home a little too early from her afternoon meeting for things to have gone well.

Sighing he entered the elevator. He was never happier professionally; his job in Philly was far more than he ever hoped for. Totally in charge of the museum's new annex Tim had all the powers and duties of the curator, even though his official title included the prefix "assistant".

Overseeing the restoration of the historic building and selecting its contents; it was everything he dreamed of when he earned his doctorate in European Renaissance art.

As the elevator shot him skyward he wished something nearly as great would happen for his amazing wife. More than a tinge of guilt engulfed him. Emily had given up a lot to further his career, and hers was clearly languishing.

The ding of the elevator interrupted his reverie. Tim made his way down the plush hallway and turned his key in the door labeled 2202. Striding through the spacious living room he glanced down the hallway toward the bedrooms; no light in the spare one Emily used as an office. Still walking he looked to his left: the kitchen and its attached dining room were also unoccupied.

Hoping his wife was changing or taking a nap, Tim decided to go down the hall to their bedroom. Turning back toward the living room he noticed the terrace door was open.

Oh man, the young man thought with trepidation, she's out on the balcony. Lately when Emily was in the worst of moods that's where he'd find her. The loving couple rarely fought, but they had some groundbreaking rows out there.

Resisting a juvenile urge to run the other way, Tim laid his brief case on the couch and went out to find his wife.

"Hey, Em," he said softly, afraid to startle her.

Sliding into the chair next to hers he went on,

"How was the meeting with the pizza guy?"

Raising her hand to halt the topic of conversation, Emily's head turned toward her husband.

"He was an idiot," there was a slight slur in her usually melodic voice.

Emily saw Tim take notice of the wine goblet; half full in her other hand. She held the glass out to him, slightly askew.

"Want some?"

The man quickly accepted the offer for two reasons: he didn't want his beautiful wife spilling the deep red wine on her favorite silk blouse, and more importantly he needed some immediate fortification.

Tim drained the remaining Merlot in three big gulps.

"I talked to Joan," his wife blurted out. "They're not using me on Ford."

Waves of guilt engulfed Tim. Jesus, what could he say?

"I'm really sorry, Em. Really."

The words came out sounding so lame. Again Emily held her hand up.

"Not your fault." she sighed out the forgiveness.

Guilt drowned Tim now; basically it was his fault, and he knew it.

The young couple sat in silence.

"Let's go down to Rock Lobster," he finally suggested. "We'll eat and get trashed."

He didn't expect her to agree, but was thrilled when she did.

The club on the waterfront was close enough to walk. Located on a pier that extended out onto the Delaware, Rock Lobster was a summer hot spot for the younger set. It was a lively place and the food was always excellent.

Tim and Emily enjoyed a savory Shrimp Scampi and too many Strawberry Pina Coladas. Tasty food and abundant drinks did wonders for both their sour moods.

To preserve energy Tim hailed a cab to take them home.

In the cool air of their apartment, Tim scooped his slim wife up in his arms. He carried her to the bedroom and laid her softly on the king sized bed. Gently he removed her blouse and bra, exposing her perfect breasts. He kissed every inch of her.

Knowing Emily's love of foreplay he gave her all he could imagine. Finally entering her, he began slowly; gradually increasing his speed and force. They came simultaneously, and slept soundly in each other's arms.

7

The weekend went too fast Emily thought over Monday morning coffee. Tim had been so attentive, making sure they did a lot of her favorite things. She knew how bad he felt about her professional situation, even offering to let her move back to Manhattan, where he would join her every Friday night.

As much as she missed the hectic pace at Satchi and Satchi and the city that never slept, she was positive that daily life without her blond haired partner would be unbearable. Facing the truth was one of her strengths; she loved her career, but unequivocally she loved her husband more.

Emily picked up the phone and speed dialed Dana. The friendship with her neighbor was the only good thing in this backwoods burg.

Dana Torroni answered on the second ring.

"Yo, Em. What's up?"

Dana had such an infectious personality. Four little words and Emily's mood improved dramatically.

"Are you doing anything today?" the New Yorker asked her girlfriend, knowing that she probably was.

Her pal had boundless energy; like a whirlwind always on the go. A native Philadelphian, Dana knew the area like the back of her hand. Insatiable curiosity made her the perfect companion; she was always full of ideas and things to do. In their year long friendship, Emily couldn't think of a single day that Dana Torroni stayed home.

"I was thinking of going to the Franklin Institute. I wanna catch that Tutankhamun show. Wanna go?" the reply was a little breathless.

Emily knew her friend was probably on the treadmill. Dana was a stickler for regular exercise. A full blooded Sicilian, Dana called workouts necessary torture; she claimed otherwise she'd succumb to her Mediterranean genes and grow to the size of a Volkswagen.

"Don't I need a ticket?" Emily knew the show was a popular attraction.

"No. My cousin Jay works there. He's gonna let me in. He'll let you in too."

That was another great thing about Dana, her endless army of cousins; good for anything from free pizza to wholesale designer shoes. You could practically name an occupation or service and Dana had a cousin who would gladly help you out.

"Sounds good. What time?"

"Come down in an hour and we'll go." Dana was even more out of breath.

Emily agreed and headed for the shower as she turned off the phone.

The two friends reached the top of the steps of the world renowned science museum on the Logan Circle. Standing under a huge banner announcing the Treasures of Tutankhamun Dana pulled a pink cell phone from her purse and dialed.

"JayJay, we're here."

She hung up the phone without another word. Almost immediately a tall young man with a shock of curly black hair and Dana's laughing eyes appeared. Hugging her cousin Dana introduced her girlfriend.

Jay hugged Emily warmly as well, speaking to the top of her head.

"Glad to meet you. Any friend of Dane's is a friend of mine."

True to his word Jay led the girls past a huge line of people in the cavernous lobby waiting to buy tickets. He escorted them through another doorway and past another long line of ticket holders waiting for admission. Marching them right to the entrance of the exhibit, he spoke to the ticket taker.

"Hi ya, Marko. These are the reporters I told you about. I'll leave them in your capable hands."

With that Jay turned and sauntered off.

The ticket taker gave the girls a VIP greeting and motioned for them to enter.

Emily always enjoyed the Egyptian galleries in the New York museums. Dana was captivated with the ancient culture since her eighth birthday when her Dad took her to see a real mummy at the Museum of the University of Pennsylvania. The ladies spent a little over an hour looking at the priceless treasure buried with the boy king, impressed by the workmanship and beauty of each object.

At the end of the exhibit the girls got in line to purchase the companion book to the show.

"Do you want to look around in here?" Dana asked her friend, unsure if Emily had ever visited the Franklin Institute before today.

"Tim and I spent a Saturday here when we first moved to town," her friend replied. "The planetarium was cool. We came back another night for a Pink Floyd laser show."

"Yeah, Lou loves those light shows too," Dana said speaking of her husband. The dark haired beauty leaned over and whispered into her gal pal's ear, "Lou gave me my first hickee in the giant heart on our eighth grade school trip."

Emily laughed out loud. She would probably never view the Franklin Institute's famous walk-through replica of the human heart the same way again.

Once the girls paid the cashier and made their way outside they decided on a late lunch. Over springroll appetizers at Susanna Foo, Philadelphia's premier Chinese restaurant, Dana asked her friend,

"Did you know there were two mummified babies buried in King Tut's tomb with him?"

"Really?" Emily replied, dipping her springroll into the sweet sauce.

"Yeah, Ankhsetamun, his wife, she miscarried twice. She was only fourteen. Can you imagine? Pregnant twice, by the time you're fourteen?"

Dana sounded like she was repeating the neighborhood's latest gossip rather than events that happened over 2000 years ago.

"Wow," the vivacious Sicilian's tone turned to amazement, "I said the word pregnant without getting all misty eyed. Lou said time would help me get over it, I didn't think so but now look at me…"

As her voice trailed off Dana munched her Shanghai spring roll and shrugged.

Emily could see the surprise on her friend's face; frankly she was surprised too. Five months previously Dana was devastated to learn she could not conceive. The gynecologist had always attributed the energetic woman's sporadic menstrual periods to strenuous physical exercise but when months of attempts at parenthood were fruitless Dana and Lou sought answers. Basically the fertility doctor said Dana had limited to non-existent egg production.

At first, with the door slammed shut on the prospect of naturally becoming a mother, Dana couldn't walk by a lady with a stroller or see a newborn on TV without bursting into tears. Through the months to follow, poor Dana avoided even saying the word baby, her mouth would choke around it; and though she no longer sobbed, her eyes will fill to the brim with tears at the mention of anything to do with children.

That was until today. Emily raised her glass and held it out to toast her dear friend's important milestone.

"Way to go, Dana. Way to go."

With clear brown eyes and a huge smile the pretty Philadelphian raised her glass and tapped it on her friend's. As if on cue a waiter appeared with two steaming plates; the girls tore into the beef lo mein with shiitake mushrooms. Emily silently thanked God for a great friend like Dana and for her pal's emotional improvement.

"You're gonna have to roll me down the street, I'm stuffed," the shapely Sicilian lamented as the pair exited the popular restaurant.

Both girls were laughing as they approached Dana's silver Mini Cooper.

"I might not fit in the car," Emily commiserated; rubbing her stomach and pointing to the tiny British import.

Threading their way through the first hint of rush hour traffic Dana asked Emily about the upcoming week.

"You guys doing anything Thursday?"

Emily was glad to hear the question.

"We don't have anything specific planned, to be honest, I think we're running out of places to go. I know it's me. Lately every time Tim suggests something I think 'not again'. I know it's me...." Her voice trailed off; the frustration evident.

"How about a ball game? Lou gets great seats from work. The new park is really nice, what d'ya say?"

Emily wasn't much for sports but the idea sounded good: definitely something different. People were raving about the new Citizens Bank Park and Tim loved baseball. With her own twinge of guilt she realized Tim probably only suggested things he knew she'd enjoy.

"Thanks, we would love to," she gratefully agreed. With the utmost sincerity she went on, "Thanks, Dane, you're the best. I don't know what I'd do without you; you're such a good friend."

"Awww, you make me blush."

It was true; Dana's olive skin was tinged with pink. The Philadelphian racked her brain for new ideas for her transplanted friend.

"You and Tim ever been to the Jersey shore?"

"Yeah," Emily replied with a sigh. "We've been for weekends at the Borgata a few times. They have a pretty nice spa there. We stayed at Caesars' on the beach a few weekends too. I liked the beach, the water was nice. I'm not much of a gambler...."

"Have you ever been to Wildwood?"

"No. Is it near Atlantic City?" Emily's interest was piqued; she'd never heard of the place.

"It's down the coast farther, toward the tip of New Jersey."

As Dana pulled into the high rise's garage she went on,

"It's a real old time shore town; it's got a great boardwalk. Real retro now because most of it hasn't changed in 40 years." She laughed but went on more seriously, "You'd love the beach there, it's big and clean...the clubs too, a lot of clubs, great nightlife...that's it we're going. Let's talk to the boys over dinner tomorrow. Me and Lou haven't been to Wildwood in quite a few years...oooh, I'm so excited."

Emily laughed as the girls extracted themselves from the tiny car. That's precisely why she loved Dana Torroni so much. Buoyed by her friend's infectious excitement she readily agreed to dinner, a ballgame and a weekend in Wildwood, New Jersey.

8

"Ladies and gentlemen of the jury,"
Lou's voice rang out clearly over the courtroom's humming ceiling fans. As he approached the jury box every eye was drawn to the well built man in the Brooks Brothers suit.
"I have only a few things to say before you deliberate."
Louis Torroni was a bear of a man. Six foot eight with the muscular body of a longshoreman he looked nothing like most of his fellow lawyers. High school and college wrestling gave the big man well developed arms and powerful legs. Summers spent working with his dad as a bricklayer built Lou's massive shoulders and legendary strength.
"When Mrs. Hopkins bought a baby carrier she shopped carefully; her main concern the safety of her first baby. You heard in her testimony that she read many magazine articles and searched the internet for the safest, not the cheapest...not the lightest...not the prettiest... the safest baby carrier. She relied on the company's description of its product and the countless testimonials that Beechwood Industries had on record."
The classic description tall dark and handsome fit Lou Torroni to a tee; only few small things gave a hint that the man was nearly forty; a small paunch developing around his

previously rock hard waistline and two tiny patches of gray that sprinkled his curly black hair over each temple. The charismatic attorney went on,

"Mrs. Hopkins believed the brochure she received from Beechwood Industries that stated the carrier was made in America to the highest standards. She believed Beechwood Industries when they boasted that no baby carrier was ever returned as defective. As, you know now, ladies and gentleman, the Beechwood PickMeUp was made in China to little or no standards and over three thousand units were returned with defective handles."

Lou's presence loomed large at Carbine and Horowitz, Philadelphia's largest law firm. His easy going personality and quick wit made him everybody's favorite co-worker; his fierce litigation skills and head for detail made him the firm's most successful product liability attorney. At least five landmark decisions were credited to the native Philadelphian and most of his colleagues thought a full partnership at the prestigious firm was certainly in the big man's future.

Lou looked each juror in the eye as he walked along the rail of the jury box. Twenty four eyes followed him as he turned and walked back toward the plaintiff's table. The handsome attorney picked up a pile of multi-colored folders and facing the jury once again he went on,

"In fifteen cases the handles came off and the PickMeUp's precious cargo spilled to the floor. Fifteen babies fell to the floor,"

Lou paused and held up the pile of multi-colored folders.

"Fifteen babies hit the ground and Beechwood Industries' official statement is:"

Lou read from a paper on top of the folders, " 'the handles dislodged and in some cases the passenger was relocated.' Relocated," a tinge of disgust colored Lou's voice as he looked up and repeated the word.

With a clear even tone the attorney continued,

"Beechwood Industries was aware of the problem and did nothing to fix their design defect. According to Beechwood

Industries, fifteen babies hitting the floor is," he read from the paper again:

" 'An allowable percentage considering the many thousands of babies carried daily in PickMeUp carriers.' "

"You heard the testimony of our expert, Thomas Sloan; professor of product engineering at MIT, a thirty cent washer would have avoided the bumps and bruises on fourteen innocent passengers haplessly riding in the Beechwood PickMeUp."

Lou went for the pay dirt,

"A thirty cent rubber washer would have saved the life of Alexandra Hopkins, but Beechwood Industries preferred not to address their product's obvious design flaw, and why should they? Alexandra Hopkins was in the allowable percentage of babies hurt."

Again a whiff of disgust colored Lou Torroni's voice,

"Beechwood Industries preferred not to consider the worst case scenario."

He motioned toward his client seated at the plaintiff's table,

"The scenario we have here today, a tall woman walking down Broad Street carrying her two month old baby in a brand new Beechwood PickMeUp when the handles stayed here,"

Lou pointed toward his thigh, "and the baby wound up here."

Boom!

The lawyer stomped his foot forcefully on the floor, loudly punctuating the word "here". The sound echoed like a gunshot in the cavernous courtroom. Some of the jurors actually cringed.

"Ladies and Gentlemen," every person hung on Lou's words, "I don't consider any injury to any baby allowable. Beechwood Industries thinks differently. Please consider the allowable percentages of babies hurt when you enter the jury room today.

Our expert, Dr. Randall Powers of Children's Hospital, testified that little Alexandra Hopkins died from bleeding to her brain, caused by wounds to her neck and head from

THE FLAVOR OF HEARTS

sudden impact trauma. Let me ask you, Ladies and Gentleme just how much sudden impact trauma should Beechwoo Industries consider allowable? Just how many young lives should Beechwood Industries be allowed to count as expendable? My opinion is none. We will wait, Ladies and Gentlemen, to hear your opinion. Thank you the effort you have taken to hear the facts and for the time you have generously given to be here."

Lou heard the judge giving the jury instructions as he made his way back to the plaintiff's table. As he sat down he faced his client. Andrea Hopkins was crying. Louis Torroni felt sad anytime he saw a woman sobbing, but the lawyer inside the man felt unabashedly glad. Lou could hear the voice of his mentor Joseph Carbine,

"Real tears mean real money."

Lou patted his client's hand and gave her a confident nod. He felt good about this one and he was usually right. His Sicilian grandmother on his father's side was supposedly gifted. She knew the future and she always said Lou did too. Lou smiled inside, yeah, he felt good about this one.

The jury deliberated one hour and awarded Andrea Hopkins 12.5 million dollars for the untimely death of her two month old daughter Alexandra; Lou T's sixth landmark decision. He accepted the congratulations of his fellow attorneys at Carbine and Horowitz in his usual manner; he blushed as he told them sincerely that it was nothing they couldn't have done. He congratulated Ginger, his brilliant secretary/paralegal for her excellent work on the Hopkins case and promised her a fat bonus when the fee came in. Then he hid in his office from any further accolades.

Lou celebrated the successful morning in his own way. Leaving the office a few hours early, he stopped to buy a box of chocolate covered cherries at the lobby gift shop then drove out of the city toward the suburbs.

Traffic was light on I95. Lou merged onto Route 476 and was at the Wayne exit in no time. He hit every light green to St. Michael's, a sprawling complex of buildings on manicured lawns and gardens. The nursing home was immaculate and pleasantly decorated. Lou wound his way through the familiar hallways and stopped at room 128. The brass door plaque was engraved: Katerina Torroni.

The handsome lawyer entered the room and smiled as the little lady in the overstuffed chair by the window looked up from her needle work.

"Tony," she said brightly, "you're home!"

Lou leaned down and kissed his mom's cheek. She still mistook him for his father. Altzheimers had muddled most of his mother's memories.

"Hi, Mama." The big man said pleasantly; love filled his voice. "I brought you some candy."

He gently placed the box of chocolates on her lap on top of her latest expertly tatted lace. The little lady's full lips formed into a circle as she expressed her delight,

"Ooooh," she cooed ripping off the colored wrapping and opening the box.

Most people thought Lou Torroni was full bred Sicilian; but sitting beside his mother the handsome man's Greek side was more than apparent. Katerina had passed her prominent nose, full well formed lips and thick curly hair to her son; a lot of Lou's easy going personality was a gift from the Papalakis side as well.

Lou smiled at the look of ecstasy on his mother's face as she munched the first of the sweets; Katerina Torroni loved all candy but chocolate covered cherries were her favorite.

"Oh, Tony," she said excitedly, "they're so good. Eat one."

She held the box out to Lou; he took a candy and popped it into his mouth, "Where's little Louie, Tony? Call him, let's give him a cherry." Katerina looked up at her son still mistaking him for her departed husband.

"I'm Louie, Mama." Lou said softly.

Confusion immediately clouded her voluminous brown eyes so Lou went along as he usually did hoping to make his mother happy again.

"Louie's outside playing, we'll save him some. Let's eat more, they're really good."

Lou took another chocolate and motioned for her to do the same. The mother and son sat side by side enjoying the sweets and the pleasant view of the gardens from Katerina's window. He was glad to hear she was feeling fine when he asked. Poor circulation, a result of her advanced diabetes, sometimes caused her legs to swell but today she was the picture of health.

Lou complimented his mom's beautiful lace work and heard the latest developments in her stories, Katerina's name for the TV soap operas she watched faithfully every afternoon. After about an hour Lou kissed his mother's forehead and told her he'd be back on Sunday.

"Have a good day at work, Tony." Katerina told her son as he left.

There was a spring in the attorney's step as he wound his way through the hallways and back to the entrance. His mother looked great that day. Lou had finally gotten used to his mother not recognizing him; he took solace in the fact the she mistook him for his father. Lou idolized his dad and missed him terribly. When bone cancer took the life of Anthony Torroni a few years back it was the hardest thing Lou ever lived through.

The tall man waved at the nurses as he passed their station; all the staff at St. Michael's loved Lou. He visited his mother like clockwork every Sunday, many weeks more often. With so many of the patients at the nursing home all but abandoned by their families, Lou Torroni's devotion to his mother was refreshing.

Traffic back into Philadelphia was heavy but moving at a good pace. Lou decided to make one more stop before he joined his wife for dinner.

Margaret was ready to lock the front door of Olde City Florist when she saw Lou Torroni's Cadillac pull up to the curb. The owner waved and waited for him to enter.

"Two large bouquets?" Margaret asked the attorney. Lou was a regular and valued customer at the little flower shop.

"Two large." he answered grinning. His smile lit up the room.

Lou complimented the florist on the beautiful arrangements and ran his American Express card through the machine. With a bouquet under each arm he headed for home.

Margaret locked the door and watched the handsome attorney drive off. She said what many women said behind Lou Torroni's back,

"Where do you find a guy like that?"

Balancing the two bouquets Lou unlocked the door marked 2102. As soon as it swung open luscious aromas filled his nose. The sweet smell of tomato gravy intensified as he got closer to the kitchen; now he could hear the sound of sausage frying.

Dana Torroni was seated at the counter looking through a fat book titled The Treasures of Tutankhamun. Lou snuck up behind his beautiful wife and held the flowers in front of her face.

"Oh, Lou, they're beautiful." Accepting the gift Dana turned and embraced her husband of ten years.

Lou kissed his wife and winked as he headed across the kitchen toward an older woman busy at the stove.

"For you, Mrs. Genardi."

Lou held out the second bouquet to the plump little lady responsible for the mouthwatering aromas filling the apartment. She turned her head from her frying pan and bubbling pots, eying the man of the house with the colorful blooms.

"Mr. Lou, you're not supposed to buy me flowers."

"Why not, Mrs. G? You're my girl too." Lou gave the same answer for probably the thousandth time. Mrs. Genardi protested every time he brought her a bouquet.

THE FLAVOR OF HEARTS

Lou went on in a more mischievous tone, "Besides, if it wasn't for you I'd starve to death, I'd waste away."

Dana Torroni never cooked. An oddity for her nationality, many times she introduced herself as the only Sicilian woman you'll ever meet who never made a pot of spaghetti.

Growing up, Dana's grandparents did all the cooking at her house; the rest of the family spent long hours at Corelli Meats, the family's business on Ninth Street.

Tomaso Corelli was considered progressive; he encouraged his children to develop their individual talents, the girls equal with the boys. Little Dana ran the cash register at the butcher shop since she was barely tall enough to see over the counter. Her gift for numbers was legendary. By the time she was in high school Dana kept the books for the family's string of butcher shops and their burgeoning sausage business. Nobody was more proud than Tomaso Corelli when his daughter graduated from Temple University with a degree in accounting. He often reassured his wife Angelina that a man would come along that would appreciate Dana.

Lou Torroni took a seat at the counter beside his wife.

"How was court?" Dana asked closing her book.

Lou hesitated to give Dana any details of the Hopkin's trial. A baby was such a sore subject for his poor wife, let alone a baby that died.

"Good," he answered guardedly, "It went in our favor."

Dana stood up and walked around the counter into the kitchen. She faced Lou as she pulled a vase from a cupboard.

"How much did they give her for her baby?"

Lou was shocked. Dana's voice was clear and even.

He replied with obvious surprise, "Twelve and half million; they gave her twelve and half million."

Dana could tell Lou was astonished at her lack of tears.

"I'm feeling better, Lou. You were right; I guess time helped me out, like you said."

Lou practically jumped over the counter. He took his wife in his arm and kissed her passionately. He loved Dana so much; he wanted to give her everything she dreamed of. He wished so many times over the last year that he could zap some eggs into her ovaries. With elation he danced her across the kitchen; thrilled that she was over the worst of her disappointment.

"Okay, you two, sit down to eat." Mrs. Genardi said turning from the stove. She tried to look stern, but her love and happiness for the young couple was easy to see.

9

Early Tuesday the uniformed guard watched Timothy Hoyle approach the back stairs. The assistant curator was a good looking man; at first the single women who worked at the Philadelphia Museum were disappointed to find he was happily married.

"Morning, Dr. Hoyle."

"Tim, Enrico, call me Tim," the blond man answered as he entered the rear entrance.

"Sure, Doc." Enrico replied trying to sound a little less formal.

The newest assistant curator had made the same request of all the guards the first day he met with the security staff. God, that was over a year ago Enrico thought, remembering that meeting like it was yesterday.

Timothy Hoyle told them he didn't want anybody to stand on formality; saying he wanted the guards to know him and he wanted to know each of them. They were surprised to hear that the new assistant curator believed that the guards were the glue that held the museum together, protecting the priceless art and the museum's patrons.

He told them to call him Tim, and not to be afraid to approach him with any concerns they might have. The guards were slightly amused by the enthusiasm of this fresh faced new addition to the museum's staff. He was certainly different than his pickle pussed predecessor.

Today, true to his word Dr. Timothy Hoyle knew every guard by name, and took seriously any suggestions they made regarding the museum's operation.

Personally, Enrico would love to call Dr. Hoyle by his given name, but he knew such informality would incur the wrath of Edward Jordan, the museum's curator. Dr. Jordan was a real stickler for detail; the head man at the museum felt each employee deserved their proper respect, especially the big muckety mucks. Any peon who didn't act accordingly could be bounced out quick and this was definitely a job worth keeping.

Tim entered his office and greeted his secretary.

"Dr. Hoyle," Carla sounded breathless, unusual for her. She was always calm, cool and collected.

"Marv called three times," she went on, "he wants you to call him right away, it's about the tiles."

Tim's main job was overseeing the Philadelphia Museum's newest addition, a new annex on the Benjamin Franklin Parkway. Currently the restoration of the historic building was half complete. Marvin Healy was the foreman in charge of the annex, a competent man in every way. An early morning call from Marv was probably bad news. Tim dialed the burly man's cell phone.

"Tim," the foreman got right to the point as he always did, "the travertine got delivered twice. I called the importer, even talked to the owner there. He treated me like jerk off..."

Tim Hoyle smiled, the union guys never stood on formality.

"He says there's no way we got double," Marv went on, "but I got boxes on the dock up to my ass. I checked the manifest three times, we definitely got double here."

The imported marble tiles were a huge expense in the restoration. Cheaper ceramic tiles were considered, but quality was paramount. The annex had to look every bit as good as the main museum. Marv's voice took on a more conspiratorial tone,

"Tim, let's keep it. They insist we didn't get it, later we'll insist the same thing."

The assistant curator wasn't even tempted to take advantage of the mistake.

"No, Marv, we can't accept twice the travertine. I'll make them come and get it."

"Tim," Marv tried to convince the assistant curator, "That guy's an asshole, when I called him the last time he said I was bothering him, he says he's sure the order is right, I even checked the price with him, he's got the right price and the wrong amount. Let's keep it. We could do the whole downstairs with all this."

Tim explained he wasn't about to let the masons lay tile the museum hadn't paid for and travertine marble was not in the budget for the basement.

"Come on, Tim," now the foreman sounded like he was talking to a child. "The owner says it isn't here. It's a gift, let's lay it downstairs."

Tim was almost amused by Marv's attitude but honesty was always the best policy. He told the foreman to leave the additional crates on the loading dock

It took an hour on the phone to straighten out the order. Tim was amazed how hard it was to return $200,000 worth of marble delivered by mistake. Marv was right about one thing, the arrogance of the owner at Worldwide Imports was hard to believe; that man deserved to find a huge deficit down the road. Tim smiled. Yeah, the asshole deserved a lesson, but Tim wasn't about to steal nearly a quarter of a million dollars worth of tile to give him one.

Tim spent the rest of the day in his favorite place in the Philadelphia Museum of Art; the storerooms in the basement were loaded with treasures of every kind. Overseeing construction on the annex was sometimes a hassle, but the selection of the art that would eventually reside there was a dream job. The day flew by as Tim compared inventory lists with the museum's vast holdings. A growling stomach was the first sign that the day was over; checking his watch for the first time Tim realized he missed lunch again.

Entering Dave and Buster's Tim easily spotted the Torronis. Even sitting down Lou towered over everybody else seated in the popular restaurant. Tim pulled out a chair for Emily and took the last seat at the table.

The four friends ordered drinks and appetizers. Over crab stuffed mushrooms and baby back ribs Tim told Lou, Dana and Emily the story of the travertine marble.

"How could anybody send an order like that out twice?" Dana was incredulous. As an accountant, a $200,000 mistake sent a shiver up her spine.

"I'm shocked the foreman wanted to keep it." Emily chimed in, amazement in her voice as well.

Lou Torroni was more than familiar with building sites. Up until he passed the bar exam Lou worked construction every summer with his dad. Tony Torroni was a legendary mason and Lou had seen miles of marble floors expertly laid.

"Hey, I'm shocked you even heard about it."

The beefy attorney took a long sip of iced tea and went on, "Those guys must really like you, Timmie Boy. A load of marble like that, it's a wonder it didn't disappear."

The assistant curator shuddered. He never even considered that possibility. He could just imagine that asshole from Worldwide Importers calling irate about $200,000 worth of missing marble; if Tim wasn't so hungry and the food so good, he might've lost his appetite.

Lou could tell by Tim's expression that the idea never occurred to his friend. Even though they were the same age Lou looked at Tim like a little brother; the guy was so innocent.

"Wow," Tim's eyes were wide. "I never thought of that."

That was another reason Lou liked Tim Hoyle so much. The man was so candid about everything, even his own shortcomings. Tim was the definition of likable, probably the exact reason nobody shady made off with that marble.

Lou pulled an envelope from his breast pocket.

"I got the tickets for the ballgame tomorrow. You're gonna love these, Timmie Boy, right behind homeplate."

Lou dangled the Phillies envelope in front of his buddy, yanking it out of the way every time Tim reached for it.

Dana and Emily laughed. Their husbands looked like two kids fighting over a baseball card.

The waiter delivered the entrées and the two couples ate ravenously. Over dessert and coffee Dana mentioned the trip to Wildwood. Lou readily agreed. He loved Wildwood and thought the Hoyles would feel the same; well, he was sure Tim would. Hedging their bets Lou asked Emily,

"Have you ever been to Cape May? We could take a side trip down there too."

Emily admitted that she hadn't, but she had definitely heard of the Victorian town on New Jersey's tip.

"You'll love Cape May too, Em," Dana offered, "great antique shops."

"Good it's settled. I'll check on reservations tomorrow," the attorney offered, "if I can book it for this weekend, I will."

Tim could tell Emily was excited. Lately it was hard to find places to take her; she seemed so bored with everything. Philadelphia was really a wonderful city; sometimes he wished his wife would give it more of a chance.

10

Lou called the Blue Palms on Wednesday morning. He knew the owner of the Wildwood hotel since they were grade school classmates in South Philly. Though it was the height of the season Lou's old friend promised two rooms for that weekend.

Lou called Dana and told her the hotel was booked. On the way out to a deposition the handsome attorney told Ginger to keep his schedule free Friday afternoon. Lou realized he was excited over the trip to Wildwood. Hah, he thought, like a kid again.

Every Wednesday Dana and Emily took a yoga class. When Dana suggested the Indian form of exercise the New Yorker was skeptical. Not one for exercise in general Emily was surprised how much she enjoyed yoga and the physical benefits she felt from it.

The lanky New Yorker hopped in the elevator and pushed the button for the floor below. When the Emily met Dana in a store the year before the girls hit it off right away. They were surprised to find they lived in the same building; even more shocking, they lived a floor apart, their luxury apartments were one on top of the other: the Torronis in 2102 and the Hoyles above in 2202. Their strong friendship blossomed quickly.

Lou often joked that the girls spent too much time in the elevator; he wanted to install a fireman's pole in the Hoyle's living room that would deposit Emily directly in the Torroni's kitchen. Emily smiled on the short ride down; she'd never been on a fireman's pole; maybe it would be fun.

Dana swung the door open before Emily was done knocking.

"Lou got us reservations for this weekend in Wildwood!" she exclaimed. "I can't believe that, I thought for sure we'd have to wait till the end of the summer!"

As the friends rode down in the elevator Dana told Emily of the great clubs and crazy boardwalk attractions. She told her New York friend some of the wild things they'd done as kids at the shore town. Wildwood was the Mecca for summer partying for all the local high schools and colleges. Emily found herself genuinely looking forward to the weekend.

The girls took Dana's car to the yoga center on South 24th Street. The studio was unusually crowded but the class was stimulating as always.

"Wild bunch in there today, huh?" Dana commented afterwards as the girls settled into the Mini Cooper, "usually the wild ones don't show up until fall, when the college kids hit town."

Emily had to agree, yoga class usually had a surprising mix of age groups but today the center city studio was packed with a new crop of young neo hippies and pale tattooed goths.

"That one girl had a big spike through her nose, did you see that thing?" the shapely Sicilian asked, "that had to hurt, can you imagine?"

Once again the New Yorker had to agree; it was hard to imagine voluntarily letting someone stick a half inch metal spike through your nose.

"What about the one with the stretched out earlobes, my God, did you see her?" Emily asked as they motored down Market Street. "I must be getting old. Huge rings stretching a big hollow hole in your earlobe; I mean, does she really think that looks good?"

"I guess she does; Lou says he thinks people do it for attention." Dana shuddered, "To me it looks like pain big time."

As the girls crossed 8th street, Emily suggested stopping at The Gallery, Philadelphia's multi-tiered mall.

"What do you say? I'd like to get a new bathing suit for the weekend." Emily went on candidly, "I'm afraid my old one might not fit me anymore. I think the yoga has tightened me up some, especially my butt."

Dana Torroni preferred dental appointments to clothes shopping; in her opinion pawing through racks of clothes and trying them on was the height of boredom. That day she put her feelings aside.

"Sure thing, Em," she said steering the Mini Cooper into the shopping center's underground garage, "I wouldn't want you coming out of the ocean half undressed!"

The girls went from store to store in the cavernous Galleria. Emily was shocked at the prices on bathing suits.

"Look at this," she exclaimed holding up a tropical print bikini, "it's $140!"

Dana admitted her current bathing suit was probably five years old and she bought it on sale for $9.99.

Money wasn't an issue for either woman. Lou did extremely well and Dana's share of Corelli Sausage was highly profitable. Emily's family went back three generations in New York real estate; the interest on her trust fund was enough for anyone to live more than comfortably. Realistically both girls could purchase thirty $140 bathing suits and not feel a pinch at the bank but ridiculous extravagance was not in either of them.

It took an hour but finally the girlfriends found bathing suits to their liking; fashionable with somewhat reasonable price tags. As often happens shopping: one item turned into two, then three, then four. By mid afternoon the girls were lugging four new beach towels, two new beach bags, two pairs

THE FLAVOR OF HEARTS

of sandals, two bathing suits and two cover-ups through the mall.

Dana eyed the shopping bags in her hand and giggled as she confessed,

"I haven't bought new clothes in almost a year. Every fall my cousin Rita drags me out shopping so I'm not an embarrassment at family functions. Last fall she left me in a bookstore while she picked out all the clothes."

Emily shook her head laughing; now that she thought of it, she'd been hundreds of places with Dana but this was their first time clothes shopping.

"One more stop if you can handle it," Emily pointed toward the sporting goods store near the exit. "I wanna get Tim some new bathing trunks."

"Oh, it'll be hard," Dana answered feigning weakness, "but I'll make it."

Emily easily found a new bathing suit for her husband; long baggy shorts with a Hawaiian print. Dana bought a set for Lou as well. On the way to the checkout Dana spotted a rack of Phillies jerseys,

"Yo, Em," she said pointing toward the display of pristine white shirts with the distinctive red lettering, "let's surprise the boys."

Lou Torroni wiped the remnants of shaving cream from near his ears and splashed on some Calvin Klein aftershave. He eyed his sexy wife through the mirror standing next to him at the double sink. He reached out to grab her, maybe they had a few minutes…

A water bug ran across the marble vanity top. Lou froze in his tracks. Dana squashed the insect instantly. She faced her husband, his hand still outstretched but not moving,

"Got it for ya, tough guy."

Dana's voice was soft and playful. Lou gave her a mock sour look.

Lou told Dana one of his deepest darkest secrets on their wedding night. He hated to kill bugs. Sure, at the office, if the girls were screaming and asking him to be the man, he squashed a spider with the best of them. He maintained his macho status on construction sites swatting flies and killing other vermin but he confessed to Dana that it always gave him a stomach ache. Feeling the life squash out, it made Lou sick since he was a little kid.

Touched by the vulnerable revelation, Dana silently vowed that night to swat any bug that came within a foot of Lou Torroni; now it was a secret they both kept.

Lou scooped his loving wife up in his arms; he kissed her neck and buried his head in her sweet smelling chest just as the doorbell rang.

Tim was ready for a ball game; all last summer he meant to make his way to the new park and see a Phillies game. When Lou threw open the door at 2102 it was apparent he too was in the mood for a baseball game.

"Are you ready for some baseball?"

The big man was doing his best Hank Williams Jr. impression, reworking the words of the Monday Night Football song. He was pantomiming batting and catching as he sang. Emily and Tim laughed out loud.

The well built attorney was a big sports fan; he loved the Phillies, the Eagles, and the Flyers. No matter how badly a season might go Lou was loyal to his hometown's teams.

"Louie," Dana called sweetly from the bedroom, "go down and put the AC on in the car, OK, honey? We'll meet you down there. Em, could you help me in here?"

Emily shrugged innocently as she headed for the bedroom.

"Let's get the chariot ready for the princesses, Timmie Boy."

The men headed for the door, as he closed it Lou yelled back to his wife,

"Shake a leg, Dane, I wanna see the first pitch."

When the girls stepped out of the elevator into the downstairs garage they heard Lou's Cadillac purring.

THE FLAVOR OF HEARTS

Approaching the car the girls heard the expected hoots and hollers. Lou was hanging out the driver's window, cold air streaming around him,

"Woo, Dana Baby, you look hot!"

Dana's Phillie's jersey was form fit. The girls were surprised to find authentic baseball jerseys sized for women. Dana bought a tight one because she knew it would have just this effect on Lou. The little red shorts were an afterthought but she could tell her husband loved the outfit.

Tim was surprised to see Emily dressed like that. The white Phillies Jersey complimented her trim figure and she was all legs in the bright red shorts.

"Woo hoo, Baby", Tim whistled his approval. "Ryan Howard doesn't do that jersey justice!"

It was a short ride across town but as the couples approached the baseball stadium in South Philadelphia traffic began crawling. Lou waited in line bumper to bumper to make the turn onto Pattison Ave.

"Oh brother," the big man said, quickly lowering his window. In a more threatening voice he yelled at the man approaching the Cadillac. "Yo, Buddy, don't touch my car."

The homeless window washer lowered his spray bottle and rag. A little fearful he stayed two arms length from Lou, but took a shot,

"Hey, ya got any spare change? I'm a veteran, Brother."

Before Lou could reply a noise from behind distracted them both.

From the back seat Emily hit the electric window and stuck out a $10 bill. The homeless man dove on the cash and in a split second took off down the street.

Fearing Lou Torroni the window washer gushed thanks to Emily over his shoulder as he ran,

"Thank you, Miss! God bless you, Miss!"

Lou raised both windows from the front seat,

"Em," he said incredulously, "you shouldn't give those guys money. They're mostly con men. It's even dangerous..."

Tim interrupted.

"I tell her all the time, I can't stop her."

Turning to his wife in almost a pleading tone Tim went on, "He's only gonna drink himself silly, Em"

"I know, I know,"

Emily knew they were both right. She heard it from her parents all her life as well. Dana said the same thing a million times too. Deep inside Emily knew it exacerbated the problem of the homeless in the cities but for some reason she couldn't help herself. When she had a wallet full of money and a little would make somebody happy even temporarily; well, she couldn't help herself.

Lou was glad the traffic started moving. That panhandler would tell every compatriot in a three block radius there was a real soft touch in the silver caddie. He was relieved to park the car in the VIP lot.

It was a beautiful night for a ball game, warm and breezy. Lou's law firm owned a lot of great seats at Citizens Bank Park; that night the two couples took advantage of four of the best. The action was so close from the first row behind home plate; the girls were mesmerized. Tim was enthralled; he never had a better seat at a baseball game.

In the bottom of the seventh with the bases loaded Ryan Howard, the Phillies young power hitter came to bat. It sounded like a cannon shot when he connected with the pitch. The fans rose to their feet as the ball sailed over the center field wall; a standing ovation continued as all four players crossed home plate.

Lou reached behind the girls standing between them and hit Tim on the shoulder. He drew his friend's attention to the ball park's jumbo screen. The camera was focused on their beautiful wives, celebrating the grand slam in their form fit Ryan Howard jerseys.

Dana and Emily looked so sexy it appeared the continuing standing ovation might be for them; and though it had been a perfect night at the ball park suddenly Lou and Tim couldn't wait to go home.

11

Late Friday afternoon the two couples left Philadelphia, heading to New Jersey over the Ben Franklin Bridge. Leisurely they drove down the Atlantic City Expressway and on to the Garden State Parkway. Surprisingly, Emily was enchanted with Wildwood with its newly burgeoning condos and picturesque harbor. She loved the retro architecture. The adwoman laughed out loud at the decorations that gave the Blue Palms hotel its name. Full size royal palm trees faithfully rendered in plastic with bright blue fronds dotted the corner property.

The couples dined at Uries, a popular restaurant and bar nestled on the Wildwood harbor. They thoroughly enjoyed the fresh seafood and frozen drinks. Tim was ecstatic; Emily was so relaxed, it was the nicest dinner the couple had in six months.

The four friends headed back toward the hotel and decided to "walk the boards" as the locals called it. The Philadelphians enjoyed all the Wildwood boardwalk had to offer: the games of chance and skill for prizes, the frozen custards, pizza and Greek gyros. They revisited childhood on wild amusement rides, screaming and yelling like kids.

Eventually the crowds thinned out and for the first time all evening Emily checked the time. The night had flown by; she was shocked to see it was after one am.

The bright moon, sea air and cool ocean breeze created a romantic atmosphere. The four friends continued down the wooden walkway; in what seemed like no time they reached the northern end.

Standing at the metal railing the couples paused for an impromptu make out session. They kissed and snuggled like teenagers would; then strolled arm in arm back toward their hotel.

As they walked Tim noticed a line of people outside a tiny storefront on a street adjacent to the boardwalk. He glanced at his watch. It was after two in the morning. What would ten people be doing in a line at this hour? The Wildwood night club scene kicked into high gear in the wee morning hours, but that obviously was no night club. Tim expressed his curiosity to his companions and they left the boardwalk for a look see.

The hand painted sign said Buena Suerte Tattoos in bright orange letters shadowed in yellow. The tiny store front had a mural painted across the front that looked like a beach scene.

It was strange to see a line of people waiting at this hour to get into a tattoo parlor. Even more strange was the type of people in that line, not the ink covered, spiky haired types that you would expect.

"Look at them," Emily said to her husband, gesturing with her head toward a couple halfway down the line.

"They have to be in their 70's," she said incredulously. From across the street the four friends could see it was quite a mixed bag of people waiting outside Buena Suerte. The old couple, four very clean cut college students, two fat women in their forties and two other couples that looked like they stepped from the pages of an Abercrombie and Fitch catalogue; certainly a far cry from what you see outside the tattoo parlors in Philadelphia.

"Let's go in" Dana suggested.

"No way-" Emily said, but before she could finish the sentence Lou and Dana crossed the street. Tim shrugged and the Hoyles followed.

Approaching the end of the line Emily heard Dana ask the last couple, "What's going on? Is this really a tattoo place?"

"It's magic" the last girl in line replied.

The girl's boyfriend shot her a withering look.

"Magic?" asked Dana.

"Yeah," the girl replied. "Buena Suerte, get a tattoo here and have good luck forever."

The last girl in line sighed and leaned into her male companion. He gave her another withering look.

"Shut up, Tina." There was a slight slur in his voice.

At closer look the last couple in line seemed a little tipsy. "Well what do you know?" Dana said turning to Tim and Emily, "It's a magic tattoo parlor."

Now Tina's boyfriend gave Dana the withering look.

"Let's go, it's late," Emily said walking back toward the ramp that led to the boardwalk.

Thankfully the other three followed. She glanced back down the street from the top of the ramp. More people were in line, now there were about twenty. Wildwood is really wild she thought to herself.

12

Saturday morning after a late breakfast the four Philadelphians stopped at a corner store. They loaded a cooler with ice and drinks for an afternoon on the beach.

At first Emily scoffed at the signs that claimed Wildwood's beach was world famous. Today, eyeing a half mile of pristine white sand gleaming in the brilliant sun, her mind started to change. From their vantage at the boardwalk rail the Atlantic Ocean was a deep navy blue, with crisp white breakers heard as a distant roar. The multicolored beach umbrellas already staked near the shoreline and the echoing caws of seagulls gave the scene before them dreamlike quality.

"Wow," Tim was grinning like a twelve year old boy. He charged down the stairs and headed toward the water, his three companions quickly following.

They spread a blanket and set up two beach chairs halfway between the ocean and the boardwalk. The sun was already high in the sky, bouncing waves of heat off the sand.

"Louie, let's go in," Tim said motioning toward the water.

The girls were already settling in for sunbathing, sitting side by side on the blanket. Dana rifled through her beach bag, extracting her Spray On Coppertone lotion.

"Be careful out there, Lou." Dana shaded her eyes as she looked up at her husband. "You're not a kid anymore."

"Who says?" he called over his shoulder as the two men headed for the shore.

The girls watched their husbands get smaller and smaller as they approached the horizon.

"When we were in high school Lou would go out so far in the water the lifeguards would go crazy. They would blow the whistles and Lou would ignore them. Once they went out in the boat and took him in…they almost called the police."

Emily heard a small tinge of worry in her friend's voice.

"Wasn't Lou a lifeguard in college?" Emily asked.

"Yeah, but that was at a pool. He's a great swimmer, but he never exercises anymore…he's not in the shape he thinks he is."

They watched their husbands in the distance diving into the breaking waves.

"Don't worry. Tim can be crazy too, but he would never let Lou ignore the lifeguard. Here, let me get that," Emily took Dana's sun tan lotion and sprayed it liberally on her friend's back. When Dana had retuned the favor the girls laid down and let the warm sun begin to bake them.

Emily closed her eyes. The piercing sun created a warm orange glow behind her eyelids. She could hear the pounding surf, hypnotic in its steady rhythm. Emily had never jogged long enough to feel a runner's high, or experienced the out of body feeling some of the girls at yoga class had talked about.

With the heat of the sun, the sea air and the drum like waves she reached a state of relaxation unknown to her. The seagulls sounded farther and farther away, their bird songs echoing. Nirvana or New Jersey? She laughed in her head.

Her body felt weightless. The crashing waves in the distance; she could feel them, a steady beat in the sand below her back. She was floating; it was glorious. The ocean's pulse was rising up her legs, throbbing into her thighs. Her breathing was long and deep, in a fog she pictured Tim on top of her, pounding like the surf, her breath quickened...she was...she was...

Emily bolted upright so quickly she was lightheaded for a second. She did not almost orgasm on a public beach! She rubbed her eyes, coming back to Earth and getting her bearings. She looked down at Dana lying face down on the blanket. Thank God, her friend was dozing. I bet I was dreaming too she thought. Emily reached under the folded towel she was using as a pillow and pulled out her watch. It was a shock to see that three hours had passed. Time does fly in Wildwood, New Jersey she thought.

She peered down the beach looking for Tim and Lou. With a small sense of alarm she blocked the blazing sun with her hand and scanned the shoreline. It was way more crowded than when they got there. Ready to bolt to her feet and run toward the water, she spotted them 20 yards away with about fifty kids in a beach volleyball game.

She sighed, releasing the tension that had tried to over take her. Opening the cooler nestled in the sand beside her; she chose a bottled apple juice from the frigid slurry. It was ice cold, the sweetness danced on her taste buds. She closed her eyes and savored it. It was the best she had ever tasted. Reading the label, it was nothing unusual, maybe it was the surroundings.

Turning her attention back to the volleyball game she caught a spectacular sight: her husband, jumping high in the air spiking the ball over the net. The ball hit the sand with Lou on top of it. Tim's team erupted in cheers and high fives. She watched her husband reach down and gently slap the hand of a tiny little girl.

He is such a good man, she thought. I haven't been too good to him this last year. She winced, recalling her almost constant complaining. I gotta be better. Almost as if he had heard her promise telepathically, Tim turned his attention from his ecstatic teammates and saw her watching him. He waved and a huge grin took over his face. He peeled away from the still cheering throng of kids and headed her way.

THE FLAVOR OF HEARTS

Tim's new swim trunks, riding low on his hips, gave a full view of his six pack abs shining with sweat. He was lean but had a far better body than one would expect of a museum curator. The sun had made his blond hair blonder and he was as beautiful today as the day she married him.

"Did you see that?" he asked her plopping into the closest beach chair. A second later Lou lowered himself into the next one.

"Lucky shot, Timmie Boy, I was blinded by the sun."

Emily handed them each a Gatorade.

"Amazing athletic prowess, boys." She raised her apple juice in a mock toast.

Dana stirred on the blanket. Flipping onto her back she sat up.

"Wow, what time is it?"

Glancing down at her watch Emily told her friend it was almost four o'clock.

"Man, I was out like a light." Dana gingerly felt her thighs. "I should've bought a higher SPF."

For the first time Emily checked the condition of her own sun drenched skin. It was pinker than she expected so when Dana suggested they leave the beach Emily readily agreed. The men hefted the blanket and beach chairs.

The little group wound up running the last stretch of beach, the sun had heated the sand to an almost unbearable temperature for unshod human feet. Breathless they crossed the boardwalk and ambled down Lincoln Avenue to the Blue Palms.

Sitting on the hotel's upper deck the Philadelphians watched the steady stream of people coming and going from the beach and boardwalk. Emily was surprised by the mixed demographic; people of all ages passed in the street below. Wildwood's festive atmosphere was contagious; the adwoman had never felt better.

The friends agreed to meet in the same spot at seven for dinner.

13

Dana suggested Alfred's for dinner; a family run restaurant long known in Wildwood for great Italian food. The parking lot was full when the Lou steered his Caddie into the last space. The building was unassuming from the outside, but pleasantly decorated inside.

Emily expressed misgivings; every table was occupied. Dana approached the man at the cash register. It was a scene Emily had watched many times in the last year. In a second the cashier was hugging Dana like a long lost sister and motioning for all of them to follow him.

The man led the two couples to a luxuriously decorated private dining room off the main one. Settling into a table for four Emily commented on the ultra elegant décor.

"Wow, this is amazing. The dining room outside was nice but this..." she looked up at the crystal chandelier above their table, "this is really something."

Tim agreed, highly unexpected at a little sea side restaurant. The little dining room seated twelve and the atmosphere was remarkable; it was every bit as nice as the most upscale New York restaurants.

"Yeah," Dana said, looking around the intimate room, "I'm surprised myself...he said it was nice."

"Was he your cousin too?" Emily asked.

As an only child Emily was in awe of her girlfriend's huge extended family.

"No, no..." the little Sicilian laughed. "My father's an old friend of the owner; we've sent meat and sausage down here for as long as I can remember."

As if on cue a round man with a jet black moustache came through a cleverly disguised door from the kitchen holding a bottle of wine and four stem glasses.

"Dana Corelli, I was wondering when you'd finally make it back to your Uncle Al's."

Dana hugged the roly-poly owner. She introduced her companions as Al Bonacorso circled the table and placed a glass before each of them. The man was the epitome of old world charm; he apologized to Lou for using Dana's maiden name. He warned the four Philadelphians that their money was no good in his restaurant as he filled each of their goblets with a ruby red homemade zinfandel.

A waiter distributed four thick leather bound menus and Alfred assured his guests that if they wanted something not listed it would be made special for them. The jovial owner left them to make their choices, asking Dana to pass on his regards to all of her family.

Tim laughed as he began perusing the giant menu. "Not listed?"

Everyone laughed. Alfred's menu was at least ten pages long; every Italian delicacy was present and then some. Emily closed her menu and turned to her husband.

"Tim, pick something for me would you? I left my glasses in the beach bag. I can see the names of the dishes but the type's too small for me to read the descriptions...."

Tim made a few suggestions from the seafood section. The Hoyles ordered the Ravioli Pesci, cheese ravioli in a pink cream sauce topped with jumbo lump crabmeat. Lou and Dana chose stuffed eggplant Alfredo on a bed of linguini.

Lou ordered iced tea and poured his wine into Dana's glass.

"No drinks tonite, Louie?" she asked.

Lou Torroni wasn't a teetotaler but he rarely touched alcohol. All his life he watched his favorite uncle battle alcoholism. Seeing the destruction caused by unbridled drinking Lou imbibed very cautiously.

"I'm pacing myself," he winked at his pretty spouse.

Waiters began filling every inch of the table with food: fried hot green peppers, roasted red peppers in olive oil, fresh baked Italian bread; crusty on the outside and warm and soft on the inside. The entrées were expertly prepared. Over frothy cappuccinos Emily moaned,

"I ate too much. I'm stuffed."

Her friends nodded in agreement; Alfred's fine reputation was certainly well deserved.

"Well, we'll dance it off," Dana declared.

She turned to Lou and went on.

"What d'ya say? The Fairview?"

For a second Lou wished he'd drank a glass of wine or two; dancing was not the ex-wrestler's forte.

"OK, Dane," he agreed "since you got us this great dinner, the Fairview it is."

The dance floor was already crowded at the legendary Wildwood dance club; later it would be packed tighter than the proverbial sardines. The girls went to freshen up and Tim and Lou approached the bar for drinks.

"Dancing sucks," Lou confided to his friend. "Slow dancing is hard enough but this..."

The big man pointed toward the people gyrating wildly on the dance floor.

"I feel like an asshole."

Tim looked up at his buddy.

"Louie, you're looking at dancing all wrong."

Tim passed on the invaluable advice a senior gave him as a freshman at his first high school dance.

"When a hot girl wants to dance, you dance! Hell, a hot girl wants to shake her body up and down and all around right in front of you. Right in front of you, Bud! Close enough so you can smell her! All you gotta do is,"

Tim's voice took on a more conspiratorial tone, as the senior's had so many years ago.

"Put your weight on the right foot and stick your same arm out a little like this,"

Tim demonstrated. He let his arms hang loosely at his sides. As he shifted his weight onto the right foot he let his right hand travel out in a semi-circle thigh high in front of him,

"Then you put your weight on the left foot and stick your left hand out; over and over, in time to the music."

Tim's shoulders swayed back and forth as he moved his weight from foot to foot and let his arm naturally swing out.

"Then you watch the show in front of you."

Tim raised his eyebrows as he stopped his impromptu dance demonstration. Out of respect for Lou's lovely wife Tim left out the senior's last pearl of wisdom: try to sway close enough to look down her blouse. Instead he ended with:

"I could watch Emily dance in front of me all night long. She shakes her boobs and her ass, oh my God..."

Tim's voice trailed off. Lou had to admit that this crazy advice made sense; he should concentrate less on himself and more on Dana out there dancing.

"All right, Timmie Boy," the handsome attorney laughed. "You might have something there."

Tim was glad to help his pal in any way. Lou had become a great friend over the last year. After the girls met Tim remembered his trepidation meeting Dana's husband. Funny now, from the first minute the men felt like old friends.

Lou was surprised how well Tim's whacky advice worked. He forgot himself altogether, swaying to the music watching Dana. She was an amazing dancer, moving effortlessly like a cat. As the Fairview filled, revelers packed the dance floor tighter and tighter; a humid heat emanated from the pulsating bodies. Dana glistened in the colored lights; Lou had never been so turned on.

The couples danced every dance. Dana was shocked, this was a new Lou. Three hours want by like twenty minutes. Nearly exhausted the two couples took a much needed break, walking down the street to The Shamrock.

Wildwood's long standing Irish pub was packed to the rafters. Eventually they found seats and took a much needed rest. A singer in the center of the huge oval bar led the crowd in wild sing alongs. Beer flowed freely in the friendly atmosphere.

Dana mentioned Hill 16, a dance club she heard girls discussing in the ladies room. She was thrilled and surprised that Lou was up for more dancing.

The four Philadelphians walked three blocks to the new club; the pulsating beat could be heard in the street. Inside the mammoth dance floor was jammed with people undulating like one organism to the infectious music.

The two couples eagerly joined the crowd and danced feverishly for about an hour. Repairing to the bar for a much needed rest they surveyed the crowd; Hill 16 was certainly a hot spot for the young and beautiful. Everyone was half naked. Dana subltly pointed to a couple down the bar; the man was so far on top of the girl next to him there might have been a sex act happening.

Emily pointed with her head toward the edge of the dance floor: two stunning girls, obviously sisters, tightly pressed up against one another thrusting their hips in perfect synchronicity. Their filmy green bra tops and matching hip hugging mini-sarongs barely covered their private parts. One rested her head on her sister's shoulder, the other had her head slightly back; both had their eyes closed; seemingly transfixed by the music and the movement. Many people eyed the girls and their slightly taboo display.

"Wild!" Emily yelled into Dana's ear above the din.

The two couples turned back toward the bar when the drinks came.

"Crazy, huh?" Lou yelled as they quenched their thirsts.

THE FLAVOR OF HEARTS

All three nodded in agreement; draining their drinks almost simultaneously.

Turning back toward the dance floor the four friends were shocked to see that the crowd had more that doubled; it was now wall to wall people in Hill 16.

"What do ya say we go?" Tim yelled above the cacophony.

Three heads nodded in agreement and the couples started to press their way through the throng to the door.

Dana held Lou's hand as they threaded their way through the hoards of people. She turned around when she felt him stop. Her mouth dropped open; she saw a blur of green, tanned flesh and jet black hair with Lou's head sticking up out of the middle. The dirty dancing sisters were all over Lou like a cheap suit!

Lou was wide eyed with surprise, in a split second they attached themselves to him from either side like two barnacles. The girls were on tiptoes to reach him, one was kissing his neck and the other was kissing his cheek.

Sweet expensive perfume filled his nostrils, soft silky hair caressed his neck and chest; Lou immediately shook his body like a dog that runs from a bathtub and dislodged both girls. He put a hand on each of their shoulders and pushed them away from him as far as the crushing crowd would allow.

Disbelief showed identically on both beautiful faces; the girls were probably never rebuffed. The deafening music allowed no words for explanation; Lou reached between the sisters and swept Dana in his arms. He passionately kissed his beautiful wife, making out with her for a good long minute. The crowd crushing in upon them roared with approval.

When the Torroni's came up for air, Lou grinned as he heard the applause and the catcalls. The sea of people parted a little for the Philadelphians and gratefully they wound their way outside.

"Oh my God!" Emily exclaimed, "Could you believe those girls?"

Tim and Lou looked at each other and laughed.

Dana held up her fist and with mock anger she said, "You're lucky you got rid of them so quick, Louie! I would have fought both of them!"

Lou leaned down and kissed her again, "That's why you're my girl, Dane. You and only you."

Lou and Dana grew up in the same neighborhood; Dana Corelli was his first girlfriend way back in the eighth grade. Through high school and college they were friends but dated others. Lou thanked his lucky stars every day for the chance meeting that rekindled their puppy love; all the girls he'd ever had rolled into a ball wouldn't equal one Dana.

The couples walked arm and arm down Pacific Avenue toward Lou's car; boisterous club hoppers filled the street. Emily and Tim expressed their amazement on the short ride back to the hotel.

"I haven't seen people going this crazy since Em and I went to Mardi Gras." Tim commented as they drove by two people having sex in a doorway.

"Some of that was tame compared to this." Emily chimed in, watching a dozen motorcycles riding in pairs traveling in the opposite direction.

"This goes on every night down here," Dana said, "all summer long."

"Yeah," Lou agreed as he pulled the Cadillac into the parking lot at the Blue Palms.

"Weeknights are even wilder, the clubs have Beat the Clock nights. They practically give the booze away; people really go nuts."

Wildwood Emily thought. In her professional capacity she couldn't have named this place better.

14

Exiting the car Dana suggested a walk before bed. As on the night before they strolled to the end of the famous boardwalk; and again on the way back they spotted Buena Suerte, the magic tattoo parlor.

This time there were three people in line, another odd mix of people. The four Philadelphians leaned on the boardwalk rail and watched the action down the block

Even though the building looked ancient, the front door slid open sideways, disappearing into the wall; futuristically, like a Star Trek door. The first in line entered, a shirtless man in a denim vest, jeans and biker boots. The door slid shut behind him.

In about a minute the door again disappeared into the wall. A stunning young woman dressed in Jimmy Choo shoes and a revealing Versace dress came out. Crossing the street she joined an equally well dressed man waiting. She smiled and showed him a small bandage on her forearm. He leaned down and gently kissed her forehead. They walked off arm in arm toward a Porsche parked at the corner.

Ten minutes passed and the pocket door reopened. This time a fat man in Bermuda shorts entered, with the door sliding shut behind him as well. Again, in about a minute, the door opened. The shirtless man in the denim vest exited with a small bandage on his upper left arm.

Eventually one person was left, a man, maybe in his 50's with long a graying ponytail.

Made bold by alcohol, Dana suggested commemorating the wonderful weekend with a tattoo. Tim and Lou were thrilled with the prospect. Emily was appalled. In all of her 29 years she had never even considered such a thing.

"Tim", she exclaimed to her husband, "you've gone all these years without marking yourself up. Are you crazy?"

"I've always wanted a tattoo. Come on, Em, let's do something wild."

Tim never talked to her that way, it sounded more like a challenge than a request.

"I love Lou's tattoos," Dana said, hugging her husband and resting her head on his ample chest. "I definitely want one."

"You sure, Dana?" he laughed, encircling his dark haired spouse with his muscular arms, "It hurts a little. What about your mother?"

She answered with her head still resting on him,

"Now that Mom and Dad live in Boca, she'll never see it. Even when we visit, she never sees me undressed. Hey, I'm a big girl anyhow."

Suddenly Dana turned and faced her girlfriend.

"Come on, Emily, let's get something small. You can get it somewhere nobody will see," she giggled, "except Tim."

Sensing her friend was still unconvinced Dana dropped the gauntlet, "You're not scared, are you?"

Afraid to seem like a stick in the mud, Emily caved in to this adult form of teenage peer pressure.

The four friends left the boardwalk and lined up behind the pony tailed man. They got a closer look at the mural on the store front as they waited outside: a sparkling aquamarine ocean flanked by a pristine beach and a craggy cliff. Tim noticed a small square structure at the summit of the rock face. It was clearly the Mayan ruins at Tulum; Tim had visited the ancient site in college on a trip to Mexico.

THE FLAVOR OF HEARTS

He recalled the breathtaking view from that cliff and the subtle power of the Temple of the Frescoes. The students visited other Mayan ruins that summer, but Tulum with its breathtaking view of the azure Caribbean was easily Tim's favorite.

The subject matter was highly unexpected for a New Jersey shore town but the quality of the mural frankly shocked Tim. It was painted with as much skill as anything in the museum; very unusual for a storefront decoration.

Suddenly, with a whooshing sound the door slid open, allowing the man with the gray ponytail to enter. The door quickly whooshed shut, with a slight metallic clang.

Now first in line, Tim stood before the entrance. The screen door was an ornate cast iron frame with a tightly woven mesh screen; nothing could be seen of the interior. Unbidden the door slid open.

The large man in Bermuda shorts reappeared; the door immediately clanged shut as he exited. The assistant curator saw no way to open the door; no handle or anything to step on to activate an electronic sensor. As he mused on the business sense of a store with such puzzling access, the door slid open by itself.

When Tim motioned to his wife to go first, she refused.

"You first," she said, increasingly shy about this dubious adventure.

Tim stepped through the opening. Hearing the door closing behind him he turned to hold it open for Emily.

A huge man stepped between Tim and the entrance.

"One at a time, sir. Only one."

The baritone voice had a slight accent, hard to place. He was well over six feet tall, muscular, with short black hair and deep set brown eyes. His white T-shirt made his tanned skin appear even more bronze.

"One at a time," the man said addressing Emily through the screen door.

Tim saw an oversized wrought iron handle welded to the inside of the doorframe. So that's how it opens, he thought.

The doorman motioned toward the opposite side of the miniscule lobby. There was a smaller man seated behind a counter that spanned the width of the tiny room.

With two steps to his left, Tim was in front of the counter man. God, he thought, no wonder this place is one at a time. By his estimate the room was no bigger than a closet; it was barely eight feet long and definitely no more than four feet wide.

"Sir, please fill out the card".

The counter man extracted a brown oversized index card from a carved wooden box on his right and placed it in front of Tim with a pen. The date was already printed at the top as part of a border of light blue Mayan Glyphs. There were lines for the usual info: name, address, phone and email. At the bottom there was a statement declaring the applicant in good health and lacking any physical conditions that would prohibit the application of a tattoo. There was a line for a signature.

Tim looked up from the card and eyed the counter man. He too had a broad face, brown deep set eyes and leathery tanned skin. Funny, he seemed like a smaller version of the door keeper. The counterman again motioned toward the card.

Tim glanced over his shoulder; the giant doorman looked like a statue in an alcove. The little space on the other side of the door barely contained him. Tim was intrigued by the tiny room's décor. Relief carving covered the wall surrounding the front door. Definitely Mayan, Tim thought, very authentic too. Colorful mosaics covered the other walls.

"Sir, please fill in the card now."

Tim's attention was yanked back to the counter. This man's accent was heavier than his large partner, Spanish or South American maybe.

This was certainly different than any tattoo parlor Tim had ever seen. There were no frames of artwork on the walls for your choice, no photos of satisfied customers.

Again the young man's attention was hijacked by a wall decoration. Behind the counter the Mayan calendar was exquisitely inlaid with thousands of pieces of colored glass. Tim was astonished; such meticulous work.

"Where do I pick my tattoo?" Tim asked curiously, still mesmerized by the fine mosaic.

"Inside," the counter man answered, "Inside you will see your tattoo. Please, sir, you will now fill out the card."

The voice had a musical quality; the accent was pleasant and somehow seemed reassuring. Tim decided to go with the flow and wrote down the required information. The man slid the finished card into a slot in the wall to his left.

Now smiling, showing perfect ivory white teeth, the counter man said enter and gestured toward Tim's right.

For a second Tim was taken aback. There, parallel to the front entrance, was a six foot passage beautifully inlaid with the same Mayan tiles as the lobby walls. He definitely didn't notice it when he first walked in. How could he have missed it?

Perfectly formed Mayan glyphs encircled an arch above the tiled corridor. Impossible, Tim thought, this was definitely not there when I...

Again the counterman spoke, "Enter now, sir. Buena Suerte."

The sing song voice put the accent on "now".

Tim's curiosity grew as strong as his amazement and he entered the passageway.

15

Tim felt cool air as he reached the end of the walkway. He audibly gasped at the room he entered. As small and claustrophobic as the lobby was, this was its polar opposite. It seemed gigantic. For a second Tim thought he was outside. Soft diffused lighting gave the room the feeling of night, yet there was more than enough illumination to see clearly.

On the wall opposite the entrance a huge South American pyramid loomed above the potted palms and cactus that dotted the interior and lined the walls. Drawn by the stunning artwork, Tim strode across the room for a closer look. Peering over the greenery he realized it was a fresco, easily two stories high. Its workmanship was astounding. He had not seen a fresco of this quality anywhere in Europe. God, he thought, this is the pinnacle of a dying art. He was floored; a million questions flooded his brain.

The tap on his shoulder pulled him violently back to earth. He wheeled around to find a tiny man dressed in loose white linen clothing. His broad face, deeply tanned skin and deep-set brown eyes were reminiscent of the men in the lobby. They might have been brothers.

"Come here, I have a drawing for you. A beautiful drawing."

THE FLAVOR OF HEARTS

An unusual voice: high pitched but not unpleasant, like a flute.

The little man began walking to the right. Stunned Tim followed without a word and for the first time saw something more expected in a tattoo parlor. A shining stainless steel counter went the length of the side wall; a section held pristine glass bottles of inks in a rainbow of colors. They were flanked by large glass jars stuffed with new needles sealed in sterilized paper containers. In a hook welded to the lip of the metal workbench a large chrome tattoo gun hung poised for action.

A black leather chaise and matching leather upholstered table were placed at 45 degree angles in front of the metal counter. They looked comfortable and inviting. An adjustable stool with wheels, upholstered in the same overstuffed black leather sat between the chair and the table, clearly where the tattoo artist sat to apply his art. Everything was immaculate.

Itzi stopped at the far side of the counter before a huge leather book. Drawings, each about the size of a silver dollar, haphazardly covered the two open pages. The little man tore the top sheet from a white pad of paper next to the leather volume. He handed it to Tim.

A lion head stared back serenely from the sheet. Its mane, constructed of tiny golden lines in swirls seemed to glisten. Tim continued to be astonished by the artistic quality of everything he had seen at Buena Suerte.

The drawing reminded the assistant curator of the Venetian lions he had so admired during his internship in Europe. It was certainly his favorite animal; he was taken with the king of the jungle since he was a small boy. How many times had he pretended to be the noble beast; growling and crawling on all fours in his grandmother's garden? He had expected to look through the book and select a tattoo, but he couldn't imagine anything in there being more perfect for him. How did the artist know?

"Wow, it's beautiful. I love it. You're a wonderful artist."

Tim looked closer at the little drawing, now trying to decipher its medium.

"Is this ink?" he asked.

Itzi nodded and gestured toward a neat line of small ink bottles on a shelf above the workbench. There were pens there as well with various nibs also neatly arranged in glass jars. Beside the pens at least a dozen leather books were lined up, companions of the huge volume open on the counter.

Amazing. Tim had never seen an ink drawing like this; it was shiny, slightly metallic. More questions flooded his brain.

As if he sensed a barrage of interrogation, Itzi spoke, diverting Tim once again to the matter at hand.

"If the lion is to your liking, we will get started. Where would you like the tattoo?"

Before he saw the drawing Tim had planned to put the Wildwood souvenir on his leg; now he wanted it in a far more prominent place. He was glad he had never given into the temptation before and got a tattoo. He was a clean slate. The young man pointed toward his left upper arm, high up near the shoulder.

"Do you think it would look good here?" Tim asked.

The artist gestured toward the leather chaise and replied, "By all means, an excellent spot, if you could roll up your sleeve."

His accent was definitely Latin American, Tim thought, but there was a hint of British pronunciation especially in the words "excellent spot". Perhaps he learned to speak English in Britain.

As Tim settled into the leather chaise he noticed the wall opposite him. Another outstanding fresco, this time he recognized the subject: the impressive pyramid "El Castillo" from the ancient Mayan City, Chichen Itza. A night scene, the famous step pyramid gleamed in the skillfully rendered moonlight.

He turned his head to look at the wall above the workbench. As half expected, another huge fresco decorated the third wall. As with the first one, Tim did not immediately recognize the subject matter. It nagged at him though; he thought he should know the name of that place; the squat pyramid, the square temple on top and the forest of carved columns surrounding the base. Once he walked among those columns, what was that place?

Tim was always proud of his powers of observation and his ability to recall facts. He was annoyed at himself. It was late, he'd like to blame his memory lapse on fatigue, but despite the early morning hour, he actually felt pretty peppy. Maybe it was too much tequila. He sighed. Maybe it was sensory overload. Buena Suerte was certainly a place rich in things to see.

Tim's eyes traveled down from the fresco to the little man making preparations at the counter. A loosely woven shirt hung down to his thighs, matching white pants flowed over brown leather sandals. He was less than five feet tall Tim guessed, slightly built but well put together. His skin was so dark it was easy to see muscular arms through the white linen shirt. Straight jet black hair framed his skull; cropped so short it stuck up straight on top. His ears jutted out from his head, from the back he looked like a car with both front doors open.

The tiny gentleman turned around. Embarrassed to be caught staring, Tim immediately pointed to the fresco above the workbench.

"What is that place?" he asked as the little man approached him.

As Itzi put a stencil on Tim's deltoid and rubbed it to place the impression he replied, "The Temple of the Warrior."

"That's it! I've been sitting here trying to remember the name. I was there once. It's in Chichen Itza, right?"

Itzi examined the stencil's transfer. Satisfied with the result he looked at the blond man's face. With one eyebrow raised he responded,

"You have been to Chichen Itza?"

There was an element of surprise in his voice.

"I have," Tim answered. "During college I took a trip to Mexico. The Mayan sites were unbelievable, very moving."

Tim pointed to the wall opposite the two men.

"El Castillo, right?

Itzi nodded like a teacher would when pleased by a student. He seemed happy that his customer recognized the famous landmark.

"Yes, yes, also at Chichen Itza," the little man replied.

"That one," Tim pointed to the fresco opposite the entrance and admitted, "I'm afraid I don't recognize that one."

"El Adivino," Itzi furrowed his brow, trying to think in English for the American seated before him. The words came out in a rush, "The magician...The Pyramid of the Magician...that is it in your language."

Tim looked closer; the pyramid's smooth rounded sides made it look very different from the South American step pyramids he had seen. Funny, he didn't recognize its name either.

"Where is it?" Tim asked.

"Uxmal."

Now Tim's curiosity was really getting the better of him. Taking closer notice of the artist's prominent nose, broad oval face and large brown eyes he blurted out,

"Are you Mayan?"

Itzi again raised his bushy eyebrow and nodded. He answered with a slight smile,

"I am from the Yucatan."

He answered with the tone you give a child who asks too many questions while work needs to be done; friendly but finished with conversation.

Standing Itzi made his way back to the counter and selected a needle from the jar. He also chose three bottles from the line of tattoo inks, the first deep brown, the next orange and the third a rich gold.

Returning to the stool beside Tim, he laid the supplies on the counter and removed the chrome tattoo gun from its hook. Cradling the machine in his forearm he picked up the brown bottle of ink, shook it vigorously and removed the stopper. With a built in dropper he carefully filled the gun's reservoir and placed it back on the hook. After resealing the ink he opened a drawer set into the bottom of the bench. He extracted a paper envelope, and ripped it open to reveal a pair of sterile rubber gloves.

Tim was looking down admiring the stencil; the majestic lion head looked awesome even upside down. The sound of paper tearing got his attention. Looking up he saw the man donning the second glove and realized the artist was ready to begin.

Practicality came in like high tide.

Tim realized he never inquired about the price.

"Wait a second, how much is it, the tattoo, how much will it cost?"

"Forty five dollars, you will pay forty five dollars at the end, when you are satisfied."

"Oh...oh, OK."

This sounded extremely reasonable to Tim. For a minute he feared the price would be far more extravagant in such unusual surroundings.

"Sounds great."

The young man leaned back in the leather chair as the artist aimed the tattoo gun toward his shoulder. A buzzing sound accompanied the first prick of the needle. Not too bad, the assistant curator thought. Itzi carefully made his way around the stencil's outline.

First it felt warm but now a burning sensation was taking over, intensifying by the second. Man, thought Tim, I don't wanna act like a baby but this hurts. As if the man wielding the gun heard his thoughts, he spoke, still continuing his work.

"Don't worry; I am almost done the outlines. That is always the most painful part. Try to relax."

16

Tim closed his eyes and tilted his head back, leaning it on the padded chair. He tried to imagine he was anywhere else. Finally the buzzing of the gun stopped and Tim felt a soft cloth wiping his shoulder. His eyes popped open.

Momentarily he forgot the pain, the artist, the lion head and everything else.

The whole ceiling was covered with cut glass and crystals. The night sky was meticulously portrayed above, every constellation in its proper place, a mosaic far more intricate than anything Tim had ever seen. The crystal stars twinkled like real stars. Deep purple, indigo and black glass fragments gave the huge surrounding sky amazing depth. It was like sitting inside a giant geode. A display like that had to take months, even years to complete. Flabbergasted Tim could barely speak.

"Wow. That's the most beautiful thing I have ever seen." His professional curiosity returned. "Who did that? How long did it take?"

Still checking his outlines for quality, Itzi followed Tim's gaze and looked up at the ceiling.

"Yes," he replied, "I too think it beautiful."

The little man stood up; returning to the counter to remove the first color from his tattoo gun's reservoir.

"Who did that? Did the same artist do the calendar in the lobby too? The workmanship is incredible!"

Tim finally looked away from the overhead vista, facing the little artist as he returned to the stool beside him. By the look on his leathery face Tim feared his questions upset the tattoo artist.

"I don't mean to pry," he stammered. "I'm the assistant curator at the Philadelphia Museum of Art. The work here is truly amazing, all of it. I don't mean to sound conceited, but I know great art when I see it. This is great art."

The little man was barely audible,

"My sisters created these things. The paintings as well were done by my sisters."

"Really? Could I get their names?"

The artist stared blankly so Tim repeated his question.

"Their work is exceptional, do they work professionally? Could I get their names?"

The tiny man appeared hesitant but answered.

"Anita and Aneela Cenotes," his voice sounded strained.

Tim could barely contain his excitement. He more than expected to hear familiar names were responsible for such masterpieces. Could it be he had discovered unknown artists of this magnitude? It was like finding sunken treasure or a Picasso at a flea market. The assistant curator went on,

"I would love to contact them and possibly set up a showing at the museum. I could give you my card," reaching for this wallet the excited young man raced on; "perhaps you could give me their numbers or a way to reach them."

"No, no, I'm afraid you can not," Itzi stopped the assistant curator dead in his tracks. As he filled the tattoo gun's reservoir with the second color the little man explained.

"They are no longer with us; they were older than me. I miss them every day I have lived without them. Yes, very much I miss them."

The little man's voice dripped with sadness; he barely choked out the last phrase.

Tim felt awful; now definitely he had upset the tiny fellow.

"I am so sorry. Really, I'm sorry that I brought up something painful. I apologize. Please, I apologize."

Itzi looked up. His broad face was calm, his deep brown eyes slightly shiny.

"No need. They are better off I hope."

Taking a deep breath, Itzi stared at the American. Raising the tattoo gun he brought it toward Tim's shoulder.

"Let us now finish."

As promised the second two colors were not quite as painful as the first.

Tim looked down; watching transfixed as the little man shaded the lion, with orange and then highlights of gold. The swirling lines creating the lion's mane were just as fine as the paper example. In less than ten minutes the artist placed the tattoo gun back on its hook.

Taking an oversized hand mirror from the bench, the little man held it opposite Tim, so his client could see the work right side up and in all its finished glory.

The lines were finer than any he had ever seen on a tattoo. The lion's mane glistened, almost like it was infused with real gold. It sparkled. As redundant as it was beginning to feel, Tim was amazed. He had never seen a tattoo that shone, but then again, he had never seen one freshly applied.

"Thank you, it's spectacular. Stunning work."

Tim had never meant a compliment more.

"Very good, I am happy with the look as well," Itzi replied.

Opening another drawer under the bench he ripped a sterile bandage from its wrapper and applied a white ointment to one side. Gently he placed the gauze over the new tattoo, explaining that it contained an antibacterial agent. As he secured the bandage to Tim's arm with white adhesive tape Itzi gave additional directions:

"Do not remove the covering for at least two hours. Gently put oil on the new tattoo three or four times a day for the next two days: a light coating of babies oil, flax oil, corn oil, even olive oil will do. For the next week keep the tattoo out of direct sunlight and do not soak the tattoo in water for the same period of time. Do not rub the tattoo vigorously for the first two weeks. All these things will allow the color to stay vivid."

The little man removed the rubber gloves. Depositing them in a waste can he stood and walked back to the end of the steel counter. Tim followed. Itzi pulled out a cash drawer nestled under the bench near the large leather book.

"That will be forty five dollars, Mr. 'Oyle."

Surprised to be called by name, or the Mexican's version of his name, Tim was further shocked to see the diminutive man holding the brown card he filled out earlier in the lobby.

Wild! Was it in that drawer? How did it get there? Man, Tim thought handing over two twenties and a five; this place might really be magic.

Itzi placed the cash in the drawer and slid it shut. He wrote "45" on the card and dropped it through a slot neatly cut into the workbench.

Now, the little man walked his customer back to the arched passageway and motioned for him to exit. Tim thanked the tiny man again and shook his hand. Stepping into the stone hallway he heard Itzi say goodbye.

"Buena Suerte, Mr. 'Oyle, Buena Suerte."

Tim re-entered the tiny lobby. It felt even smaller than before but its beauty was no less impressive. Whoosh. Fonso slid the door open.

Glancing to his right Tim saw Lou's wife bent over at the counter.

"Yo, Dana!" he called to her shapely posterior.

"Tim," she exclaimed turning, "Did it hurt?"

She looked so excited he lied, "Noooo, piece of cake."

"Sir," interrupted Ildefonso.

His deep voice rang out like a church bell. Tim turned to face him. The huge man was wearing a toothy smile and pointing toward the open door.

"Thank you for coming."

Sensing the bum's rush Tim stepped into the humid night. Behind he heard the Bartolomeo's sing song voice, "Please, Miss, you will now fill in the card."

17

"Tim," Emily's voice was breathless, "Did you do it?"

"It's beautiful, Em, a lion head."

"Where?" his spouse asked wide eyed.

Once again the young man was distracted by beauty; his wife's blue eyes sparkled like gems, her light brown hair shone with the moon's reflected light. Man, she's something, Tim thought.

"Where?" she demanded.

Impatiently Emily moved closer, attempting to tear off his shirt right there in the street!

"Hold on, hold on." Tim was laughing out loud.

He rolled up his sleeve, revealing the small bandage.

"Let's see it."

He stopped her hand as she reached for the gauze.

"The guy said to leave it covered for two hours. He put an anti-bacterial on there."

"Ohhhh." Emily dragged out the word.

She sounded disappointed, like kids do finding out you're not stopping for ice cream.

Lou slapped him on the other shoulder.

"Way to go, Timmie Boy."

He nodded toward his pal's wife.

"Talk to your girl, Bud, she's chickening out."

Dana Torroni glanced up at the giant doorman as she moved toward the arched walkway. God, she thought, that guy is as big as my Lou. She eyed the glyphs over the arch. It was a Mayan date she was almost positive.

The ancient sun cultures always fascinated Dana; through the years she'd taken many Mayan history classes. Recently she attended a lecture at the University of Pennsylvania, "The Mayan Calendar and the End of Our World". It was amazing to find that many educated people actually believed the world would end in 2012 along with the end of the written Mayan long count calendar.

The air in the arched walkway was cool, Dana smelled something sweet as she reached its end. Honeysuckle or roses, maybe even orchids she thought.

"Oh my God," she said aloud as she stepped into the main room at Buena Suerte.

For a second Dana too thought she was outside. Her mouth was agape at the huge paintings that covered the three walls around her. The Mayan structures looked real, glistening in the painted moonlight. She was surrounded by an amazing array of flowering cacti and succulents.

The attractive woman looked up. Wow, she thought, as she admired the simulated night sky. The stars on the ceiling twinkled like real stars. How did they do that? Was it electric? This place had Disney World beat!

She lowered her head to take a closer look at the plants around her.

"Oh!" she gasped, startled.

A little man dressed in white was suddenly in front of her; she didn't hear him approach.

"I am sorry," he apologized, "I did not mean to frighten you."

His voice was musical and soothing.

"No, no. I'm OK," Dana assured the man.

He smiled and motioned for her to follow him.

"This place is beautiful," she told the dark little fellow, "it doesn't look like much from the outside…"

Her voice trailed off as they reached the gleaming stainless steel work bench. Dana saw the huge leather book, line drawings dancing across the open facing pages. Itzi tore a sheet from the drawing pad next to the oversized volume and handed it to her.

"Wow," she said out loud.

The drawing looked like something from a custom jewelry store. Dana stared at the amethyst heart, its cut facets drawn with varied shades of purple surrounded by the most delicate gold filigree imaginable.

Dana was astonished. She was thinking of a heart when she walked in there; a little heart with her and Lou's initials in there. Amethyst was her birthstone…was this little guy psychic?

"This could be a tattoo?" she asked incredulously.

The lines were so thin and sharp. It looked metallic.

"Oh yes," the tiny man nodded.

His jet black hair moved in a little wave with the movement of his head.

Dana gestured toward the leather book.

"Is that where the rest of the designs are?"

When Itzi nodded yes Dana took a closer look at the open pages. Numerous drawings were visible; various flowers, a beautiful prancing horse, a rainbow with a pot of gold. All the artwork shimmered. Dana's eyes rested on a tiny drawing of an open book with a long stemmed rose lying across the open pages. Her love of reading made her consider it as a possibility.

Dana turned the page of the huge leather volume. The paper felt old and thick like parchment. Finely drawn snakes slithered across the next two pages. A cobra face with golden eyes stared back.

"Oooh," she said laughing, "kind of scary."

She turned back to the pages that were originally open. She compared the design of the little book with the rose to the drawing on the paper still in her hand. Both were exceptional but she realized there was no comparison.

The amethyst heart was so perfect for her. The jewel's simulated gold setting was stunning. Dana held up the paper and voiced her decision.

"Excellent," the little man seemed pleased that she chose the first artwork.

Dana furrowed her brow. Holding up the paper she asked, "Is there any way you could put a "D" and an "L" on there? Maybe near the gold part?"

Itzi nodded and retrieved the sample from Dana's hand. After a minute at the work bench he returned the paper to her. He extended the filigree on each side of the amethyst heart artfully working the letters into the mock gold setting.

"Beautiful," Dana gushed, "you're very talented."

He smiled at the compliment and asked the dark haired woman, "Where would you like your tattoo?"

"Could you put it here?" she wondered putting her hand on the small of her back.

"Yes, yes, no problem."

When Dana asked the price Itzi was slightly surprised. Most beautiful women lacked practicality, but not this one. Dana was glad to hear the price was not exorbitant.

Itzi motioned toward the leather upholstered table. He instructed Dana to lie on her stomach and lower the waistband of her skirt just a little.

His accent was hard to place, Dana was reminded of some army brats she knew; they had lived so many places and assimilated so many different speech patterns now their origin was indiscernible.

"Where are you from?" she asked curiously.

Itzi answered as he made her stencil and prepared his tattoo gun at the workbench, "Yucatan."

Dana leaned up on her elbows and watched the preparations. He was built pretty well for a little guy she thought; kind of cute with those ears sticking out. Knowing the concentration of Mayan ruins on the Yucatan peninsula she now understood Buena Suerte's splendid décor. Taking the tiny gentleman's ancestry for granted she asked,

"Do you think the world will end in 2012 when the Mayan Long Count ends?"

Itzamna turned to face his beautiful customer. This girl was full of surprises, nothing like the vapid American beauties that usually frequented the tattoo studio. His huge brown eyes were wide with amazement at such a question.

"No," he answered her honestly. "I do not believe our world will ever end."

"Doesn't everything have to end eventually?" the dark haired beauty countered.

He approached Dana's back with the stencil as he answered,

"No, some things are eternal. More is eternal than we imagine."

She nodded thoughtfully, assimilating his opinion.

"Oooh, it's cold," she giggled as he applied the stencil.

The buzzing of the tattoo gun took Dana by surprise. Cold sensations went quickly from warm to hot.

"Wow, that burns!" she exclaimed, tears springing to her eyes.

Itzi assured his client that the outlines would soon be done and promised the rest of the application would be less painful.

Dana buried her head in her arms and gritted her teeth. A part of her wanted to run out the door with the tattoo half finished. Relief flooded over her when the buzzing stopped.

As Itzi filled the gun's reservoir with purple ink he apologized for any discomfort Dana experienced. Some people deserved the pain, he thought, but not this lady. He added an additional sterile needle to the chrome tattoo gun for the shading.

Dana took a deep breath as the little man resumed his work. It was less painful; but still it hurt like the devil. Dana was thrilled when the buzzing stopped.

"I would like to apply one more color to give your tattoo a nice depth. Are you all right?"

Itzi was sincerely concerned about the comfort of this customer.

"I'm OK. Do what you think is best."

Her voice was slightly breathless. The little man knew she was still feeling the burn; he admired her stamina. That design had a lot of fine lines done with a single needle, the most painful type of all tattoo application and she never complained.

He loaded the chrome gun's reservoir with the last ink, a rich brown a shade a little darker than Dana's olive skin. The little man felt Dana tense up when the gun began to buzz; he promised the brave lady that he would be done very shortly.

Working very carefully Itzi shaded under the gleaming filigree of the mock gold setting; giving the tattoo a three dimensional look.

"Yes," he said aloud satisfied with his work.

He spoke as he cut the gun's electric power. "There is a mirror to our left," the little man gestured toward the wall near the room's entrance.

The lady's gaze followed his outstretched arm. Wooden shelves lined the wall on the right side of the door. Between two potted palms in front of the bookcase Dana saw a full length oval mirror on a brass stand.

Dana hopped off the table and headed toward the looking glass, excited to see the faux jewel on her body. Itzi placed the tattoo gun on its hook and joined the young woman at the back of the room with the large hand mirror. He held the portable mirror so his customer could clearly see her back in the second reflection.

The purple faceted heart had all the depth of a real gem. It sparkled. The faux setting looked metallic and shone like genuine gold. Dana was speechless. It actually looked like an amethyst brooch pinned to her lower back.

Dana averted her gaze from the reflected tattoo and looked at the little man. His broad face wore a worried expression. She realized he misread her silence. With all sincerity she assured the artist,

"That is the most beautiful thing I have ever seen."

THE FLAVOR OF HEARTS

His leathery face lit up with a huge smile.

Dana went on, "You're an amazing artist, truly amazing!"

Itzi thanked his satisfied customer and asked her to return to the table; explaining the need for a bandage and the antibacterial cream.

Dana's eyes traveled to the bookcase behind the mirror. The shelves held an impressive collection of South American art: stone statues of all sizes, tightly woven baskets and various ceramics. The oddest thing was perched on top: a ball, maybe twenty inches in diameter, deep black mottled with lighter gray in random spots.

Her eyes traveled up to a framed painting above the bookcase: two slanted stone walls each with a large carved stone ring hanging parallel to the ground...a Mayan Ball Court.

The ever curious Dana knew of the Mayan Ball Game: a legendary mix of ritual and sport. Using only feet, legs, hips and elbows players had to bounce a large rubber ball off the slanted walls and through the stone ring. Supposedly games went on for days. Some histories claimed the two teams played to the death; others said the captain of the losing team was beheaded as a sacrifice.

Her gaze shifted back down to the strange ball...the flutelike voice interrupted her reverie.

"Miss, please, the bandage now?"

Reluctantly she returned to the upholstered table and motioned toward the bookcase.

"Is that a real Ball Game ball?"

The little man looked confused.

"Real?" he questioned.

Dana tried to explain.

"Yes, authentic?"

Itzi looked even more confused.

"Genuine? Ahh...the real thing?" she searched for words.

"I am very sorry," he apologized, "I am not understanding."

"No matter," Dana assured him lying on the table.

The last thing she wanted to do was upset the talented little fellow.

He applied the bandage and the antibacterial cream, repeating the same instructions for the care of the new tattoo.

Dana flipped over and sat on the edge of the table with her feet dangling down. She retrieved her purse from the floor near the table's leg and dug into the contents for her wallet.

"That will be $45, Ms. Torroni."

Itzi pronounced her name perfectly; rolling the R's with his tongue. He sounded just like Lou's great uncle from Sicily.

Dana's head jerked up with surprise, "How did you know my name?" her voice trailed off when he held up her brown card from the lobby.

She laughed as she slid off the table and approached him with her wallet.

"For a second I thought you really were a mind reader."

She went on as she offered him a bill from her wallet, "Have you been to Sicily? Your pronunciation of my name was perfect."

She was surprised to hear that he had spent time in the land of her ancestors.

"Yes, I have lived there. The Mediterranean, so beautiful..."

Itzi finished wistfully, "And the food, such wonderful food!"

He accepted the fifty dollar bill and gave Dana a five for change. She watched him write the price on her card and drop it into the slot on the workbench. He was so cute, she thought, so small and muscular.

They walked together to the arched passageway; Dana stopped before she exited.

"Thank you so much," she told the man beside her, "It's more beautiful than I could've ever imagined."

The Sicilian leaned down and hugged the tiny artist.

Itzi blushed. His high pitched voice echoed as Dana stepped into the stone passageway.

"Buena Suerte, Ms. Torroni, Buena Suerte."

THE FLAVOR OF HEARTS

18

Tim was right, Emily thought as she stood before the counter. The mosaics in the tiny lobby were stunning; the relief carving was exceptional as well.

Tim and Lou had used every argument to convince Emily to enter the little store. Tim was insistent; he gushed over the unbelievable artwork inside and the amazing talent of Buena Suerte's tattoo artist.

When the door slid open Tim practically begged his wife to go in; he called it the chance of a lifetime.

Emily's hand was shaking as she started to ink her name on the brown card at the counter. God, how did I let them talk me into this? A tattoo, she thought, I must be going crazy.

Trying to relax her professional side took over. She looked closer at the card the counterman had given her; high rag content, an expensive card stock she mused, taking note of the quality of the paper itself. Light blue Mayan glyphs were crisply printed along the borders. The former ad exec wondered what they meant. The date was printed along the top as part of the design too.

Strange, Emily thought, they print these up for each day? It seemed a crazy way to order printing.

"Em!"

Dana's voice was full of excitement as she entered the tiny lobby.

As Emily turned to face her friend Fonso slid the door open.

"Dane, did you do it?" Emily asked her pal incredulously, "Did you get a tattoo?"

"It's so amazing, Em! It's an amethyst heart with a gold setting; I can't wait for you to see it, it looks like jewelry!"

Emily could clearly see her friend's satisfaction; Dana was ecstatic. Still Emily could not shake the nervous feeling in the pit of her stomach.

"I'm scared, Dane," she confessed to her pal.

"Ohhh, Emmm, don't be afraid! It's awesome in there! You'll be fine," the dark haired woman went on in a more conspiratorial tone,

"The artist is really nice; he's cute too!"

"Ah-hem!"

Fonso cleared his throat commanding the attention of both chattering girls.

"Thank you for coming," he said to Dana and motioned toward the door.

The pretty accountant laughed. They were all business at Buena Suerte; but it was easy to see why. The quality of the work was astounding; she could imagine the line outside snaking around the corner at times.

"Don't worry, Em," Dana said as she walked back into the night.

She called over her shoulder,

"It'll be over before you know it."

Emily summoned all her courage and stepped under the stone archway. This place better be everything Tim promised, she thought as she walked to the end of the passageway, or he's gonna owe me for life.

Emily stopped dead in her tracks just beyond the entrance to Buena Suerte's main room; everything Tim said was true, far beyond true actually. Remarkable, Emily thought, the ceiling had to be two stories high; the mosaic night sky was more than stunning. Emily knew the night sky: every constellation above was portrayed accurately.

The frescoes were unbelievable; the ancient Mayan architecture looked so convincing and the realistic outdoor backgrounds made the room feet positively huge.

As equally impressive: the room's abundant tropical plants: cacti, ferns and palms were artistically placed along the walls and in groups all over the room's interior. The sweet smell of the flowering specimens was intoxicating.

Eying the long stainless steel table and work area to her left, Emily noticed the tiny man dressed in bright white linen. His back faced her; he was bent over at the workbench engrossed in something in front of him.

She approached and spoke when she got close to announce her presence.

"Hello."

Itzi turned and faced her.

"I'm almost finished a drawing for you," he said smiling.

Turning back toward the workbench he continued speaking,

"I'll be done in a minute or so."

The lighting in the large room was most unusual, Emily mused, taking a closer look around. It had the look of a bright moonlit night, subdued and diffused yet she couldn't identify a single light source. There were no bulbs on the ceiling or any visible lamps or fixtures.

Emily wondered how the lush plants lived. There were no windows; the only opening in the room seemed to be the stone archway she had just come through.

Itzi turned and offered a paper to Emily.

"Thank you for your patience."

The voice was high pitched and melodic; a slight accent colored his words.

Any questions the lanky Philadelphian had about her surroundings flew out the window when she saw the drawing.

The sailboat was skillfully rendered. A gleaming sun behind the vessel sparkled with rays of metallic gold. Gracefully curved blue and gold lines under the hull shimmered, like real water showing the sun's reflections.

Emily realized she was not breathing. This was impossible. The little drawing was an exact depiction of her father's oldest sloop, the Raven. She stared at the artwork, her mouth agape. The custom sloop's black hull was shaped perfectly, its gold details accurately portrayed. The spruce mast was exactly the right height; three of the Raven's four sails were raised. There were even two silhouetted figures aboard, one big and one small: little Emily and her dad!

"Did my husband tell you to draw this?" she stammered.

Itzi shook his head, confusion clouded his pleasant expression.

"Your husband?" he asked.

"Yes," Emily's words came out in a rush, "my husband Tim was in here before the last lady. Did he tell you to draw this?"

"No," the little man shook his head again, "nobody tells me what to draw."

Emily held the paper up.

"This is my father's custom sloop. There is no way you could have randomly drawn this boat. How did you know what to draw?"

The lady seemed perturbed, even on the verge of irate. Her voice rose in pitch and volume as she went on,

"Somebody had to tell you. Did he tell you that I liked to sail?"

Itzi was taken aback. He didn't know what to say to calm the lady; he had never seen anyone so disturbed by his artwork.

"I am drawing what I feel," he tried to explain. "I see in my head what I think you will like, and my hand makes the picture."

Emily felt his words washing over her, he was trying to soothe her; she realized she was scaring the little artist.

"I'm sorry," she apologized, "I didn't mean to yell at you. It's just so surprising."

She held the paper at arms length, trying to get a better look at it. She cursed her mild farsightedness; wishing for the second time that night that she'd remembered her reading glasses. Realizing the lady was having some difficulty seeing the drawing up close Itzi fetched a magnifying glass from the workbench and offered it to her.

She looked down at the paper through the lens and addressed the little man,

"My father taught me to sail on this boat, this exact boat. It was custom made and you have every detail correct, down to the color."

She looked up at him, trying to figure out how this could be; it was more than an amazing coincidence. The man looked as puzzled as she felt.

"I am sorry to make you unhappy. I am drawing for you what I feel..."

Itzi's voice trailed off, he was ready to tell her he would draw something else.

"No, no...I'm not unhappy."

Emily took a deep breath and tried her best to calm down.

"I think I'm just nervous about the tattoo," she tried to explain, "I never even considered getting a tattoo until tonight..."

When her voice trailed off he answered,

"Perhaps you would like to come back a different time, after more thought?"

Emily looked down at the incredible drawing. Suddenly she realized how much she would like to see that image everyday; yes, even for the rest of her life!

"No, no. I want it; I want you to put the Raven on me."

Emily smiled at the artist; he seemed relieved that she was less agitated.

"Will it look like this? Like real gold?" she asked, holding up the paper.

The drawing was unlike any tattoo Emily had ever seen. The little man pointed toward the array of ink bottles on the counter near the chrome tattoo gun.

"Yes, yes," he assured his client, "very good ink."

"Okay, let's do it."

Emily remembered Dana's advice and decided to put the tattoo in a private spot. At the artist's instruction she laid on her back on the leather upholstered table. She raised her sundress and lowered the left side of her bikini underwear to reveal her lower abdomen.

The dark haired gentleman appeared at her side with a lightweight blanket. It was meticulously woven in a multitude of colors. Gently he placed it over her legs and lower body, modestly covering her exposed panties.

Itzi returned to the workbench, preparing the stencil and selecting ink bottles. Emily tried to relax; the night sky so skillfully rendered on the ceiling above had just the right effect, tension drained from her body.

The little man reappeared beside her. As he carefully placed the stencil on her abdomen Emily took a closer look at him. Dana was right, he was kind of cute. His short thick hair stood straight up like a jet black brush. With his broad tanned face and huge nose, he looked like something out of a South American history book.

When he returned with the tattoo gun Emily fought the urge to jump off the table and run. She closed her eyes when he moved the chrome tool toward her body; a buzzing sound accompanied the first prick of the needle.

At first it felt warm, but in a minute it was burning like a hot poker.

"Wow, that hurts," she said to the top of his head.

Itzi kept working but assured Emily he would be done the outlines on the sailboat very shortly. Tears began to fall from the corners of the lanky ad exec's eyes, she wasn't exactly crying, but the intense stinging on her lower stomach made her eyes run.

The buzzing of the tattoo gun stopped and Itzi looked up. Seeing his client's tears he retrieved a box of tissues from the workbench and offered it to her. He apologized for her discomfort and explained that the rest of the process would be less painful.

Emily blushed with embarrassment and assured the little man that she was fine. God, she thought as she dried her eyes, he must think I'm the biggest baby.

Itzi filled the gleaming tattoo gun with the second color and resumed his work. Emily closed her eyes. As she tried to separate herself from the pain, pictures from the past surfaced: weekends sailing on the Raven with her dad, dropping the anchor in the inky blackness of the Atlantic off Montauk, the stunning sun rises out at sea. Emily could see her father's face; how proud he looked the first time she brought the Raven into berth unassisted.

The droning buzz of the tattoo gun stopped. As she opened her eyes Emily saw the artist already back at the workbench.

I have one more color to do," he told her over his shoulder, "we will be done very shortly."

Emily looked down at her partially finished tattoo. The Raven was about two inches high, portrayed in amazing detail. The black hull and blue water looked stunning on her creamy skin. The artist approached the table.

Emily spoke candidly, looking directly into the man's large brown eyes.

"I never thought much of tattoos; I really never thought they looked good on people but that," she pointed toward her abdomen, "that is striking."

The diminutive gentleman looked pleased and assured her she would be very happy when he was finished. Emily closed her eyes when the buzzing gun touched her skin. The burning was almost unbearable; Emily fought the urge to really cry.

Itzi expertly shaped the golden rays of the sun behind the boat's full sails. He added swirling gold lines to the blue under the hull rendering the sun's reflections on the water.

Cutting the power to the chrome gun he pronounced the tattoo finished and held the hand mirror so Emily could see the final image. True to his earlier promise, the gold sun shone like metal; looking more like jewelry than a tattoo. The skillfully shaded sails looked full of wind; the Raven looked magnificent. For a second the young woman wished she'd let the man apply the body art to a less hidden spot.

He applied the bandage and gave Emily instructions for the tattoo's initial care. Following him back to the workbench she watched him open the cash drawer. Her jaw dropped. The card she filled out in the lobby was there next to the cash partitions.

"How did that get in there?" amazement was in her voice.

"Magic." he whispered.

Emily's eyebrows shot up: her pale blue eyes were wide as saucers.

"My brother puts it there," Itzi said amused by the pretty lady's reaction to his little joke.

Looking down at the card he read her name,

"That will be $45, Mrs. 'Oyle."

Emily reached for her wallet in her purse. She never heard anyone else enter the room; it was possible she missed the sounds, after all her eyes were closed and the tattoo gun was pretty loud. Shaking her head she handed forty five dollars in cash to the little fellow.

As she watched the artist notate the price and drop the card through the slot in the workbench, she remembered the counter man pushing the card through a slot in the wall. She turned her head and eyed the wall at the back of the room. There was no evidence of an opening; the wall was lined with shelves and artifacts.

This is a wild place for sure, she thought, a wild place in Wildwood.

Itzi accompanied his customer to the stone archway. Emily shook his hand and thanked him for the fine tattoo; she also expressed her gratitude for his patience with her nervousness.

"It is my pleasure to make you even more beautiful, Mrs. 'Oyle," he replied.

As Emily made her way through the passageway, she too heard Itzamna wish her good fortune,

"Buena Suerte, Mrs. 'Oyle, Buena Suerte."

19

When Lou Torroni entered the tattoo parlor he expected the lobby to be small, but Tim's and Dana's descriptions were barely adequate. Maybe his large size made the place seem even smaller.

He signed the brown information card with a flourish and turned to face the huge doorman; Lou was ready to inquire if the two men in the lobby were related; other than a disparity in size, they looked exactly alike.

A noise under the stone archway distracted the attorney. When Emily appeared in the passageway Lou suddenly felt protective; she looked pale and she was walking slowly.

"Emily, are you all right?"

Lou took the lady by the elbow as she re-entered the lobby. He was relieved when she looked up and her smile lit up the tiny room.

"You were right, Lou. I'm glad I went in to check it out."

"Did you do it? Did you get one?"

Lou knew the transplanted New Yorker had guts; they were just hard to see sometimes under her veil of refinement.

"I did," she replied, proud of herself.

Lou hugged Emily as he congratulated her,

"Way to go, Em. That's our brave Philly girl!"

She was laughing when he released her from the bear hug. Lou knew Tim would be thrilled his wife took the plunge.

Ildefonso suddenly commanded their attention,

"Thank you for coming," he said to Emily, motioning toward the open door.

Lou watched his friend exit before stepping through the stone archway; he wished he could've been out there when Emily told Tim she was tattooed.

The door whooshed open. Tim was poised to re-enter Buena Suerte, he knew Emily was really nervous when she went in and it worried him that she had to go in alone. Relief flooded over him like a wave when she appeared in the doorway.

"Tim!"

Emily spoke loudly, like a little girl after her first pony ride.

"I did it, Tim! I got a tattoo!"

The people in line applauded. Tim took his wife in his arms and kissed her passionately. The people waiting hooted and hollered at the public display of affection.

Emily, Dana and Tim moved to the opposite side of the door to wait for Lou. Emily recounted her experience inside Buena Suerte. When she told her companions of the artist's perfect rendition of her father's custom sailboat it was easy to see their surprise.

"I was shocked that he knew I wanted a heart," Dana offered.

"Maybe he has ESP," Tim wondered out loud.

"Hey," Dana lowered her voice, "maybe this place really is magic."

The Hoyles looked askance at their dark haired companion.

All three burst out laughing.

Lou strode through the passageway; it was barely three steps for his long legs.

"Woo," he whistled as he entered the main room.

He was ready for the Mayan splendor; Tim's and Dana's descriptions were right on the money, still Lou was awed. He remembered their advice not to miss the ceiling.

Holy Mackerel, he thought when he looked up.

The sparkling faux night sky above was expected but no less extraordinary. As a reflex, after Lou looked up he looked down. Now it was his turn to be astonished.

The floor was polished black stone, maybe granite or marble. Oddly, there were no signs of seams.

"What the heck?" he said aloud, dropping down on one knee to take a closer look.

No way it's one piece, the former construction worker thought. He rubbed his hand in a semi-circle around himself; in at least four feet of the stone floor, no seams could be felt. Lou noticed a gold line snaking through the black stone; it got wider a few feet ahead. The big man slid on all fours along the smooth floor to take a closer look.

The stone floor felt cool to the touch, but the gold part felt warm; against all logic Lou guessed it was a solid obsidian floor with a vein of real gold. As a boy Lou accompanied his father on a million tile jobs, he had seen a multitude of stone floors, but never in his life had he seen one like this.

"Hello."

The flute like voice now shocked Lou back to reality. The little man's tone was full of surprise; he had never found a sober client on the floor.

Lou lifted his hands and swung his body to face the gentleman; on his knees Lou was still taller than the tiny man standing beside him.

Suddenly Lou was embarrassed, what the little guy must think finding him crawling on the floor. Itzi's neck cocked back as he watched Lou Torroni stand to his full height; both men were taken aback at the other's stature.

It was rare Itzi saw a man as big as his brother in the lobby; the attorney wondered if the tiny man in the linen suit was a midget.

The little man gestured toward the stainless steel workbench.

"I have some drawings for you."

Lou's curiosity got the better of him as he followed the little fellow toward the work area.

"Is the floor a solid piece of stone? I couldn't see any seams."

Itzamna was surprised for the second time that night by a question. No one had ever asked about the floor.

"I don't know," the little man replied honestly.

Itzi tried not to think, so far it had been a most disturbing night. He offered the giant American a paper from the drawing pad.

In a way Lou was ready to be amazed; Dana and Tim both said the same thing: the little artist had mystically drawn something personalized without seeing them or asking any questions. The handsome attorney shook his head; it was one thing to hear such a story but another thing entirely to experience it.

Lou stared at the bald eagle in flight, the national symbol held the American flag in his talons. The stars and stripes billowed majestically in the air. Metallic gold highlighted the bird's feathers and trimmed the flag. It was a stunning image in every way.

Wilder yet was the second drawing on the page: a gleaming golden key; not an old fashioned key, a modern one. The hole at the top of the key wasn't round; it was shaped like a heart. Looking closer Lou was taken aback; the letter "D" was artfully perched in the hollow heart shaped hole.

Earlier Lou had two ideas as he waited outside for his turn in the tattoo parlor: something patriotic, or a tattoo that declared his love for Dana.

He felt woozy looking at the paper; both his ideas stared back at him.

THE FLAVOR OF HEARTS

"I'm shocked," Lou looked away from the paper and down at the artist, "my friends told me you were an amazing guy...how did you know what I wanted?"

"I draw what I feel when I wait for you."

The tiny man shrugged his well developed shoulders, as if to say he had no idea how he anticipated the client's desires.

Lou noticed the huge leather volume open on the workbench; incredibly, many of the drawings visible on the two open pages seemed to illustrate parts of his personality. The Scales of Justice in gleaming metallic gold took his breath away; he saw the little gold bear and almost fell back on the floor.

"Wow," he pointed to the little animal drawn so perfectly in the book, "that was my nickname on my college wrestling team, 'The Golden Bear'!"

When he looked back at the dark haired artist Lou saw a look of astonishment on the little man's face as well.

"You have some gift," the attorney said eyeing the gentleman beside him.

"Hey," Lou said as an afterthought, "can you see lottery numbers or winning horses?"

Itzi looked up at his customer's smiling face and laughed.

"No, I only see pictures." he replied.

"That you do," Lou agreed, looking back at the paper.

Now the attorney pointed toward the little drawing of the heart key.

"This looks metallic, the tattoo can't look like this?"

It was a statement but the former wrestler asked it like a question.

"Yes, yes it will," Itzi bobbed his head up and down. His close cropped hair undulated, like ebony wheat in the wind.

"No way," Lou countered, "like metal?"

Lou had never seen a metallic tattoo in his life. The big man started looking around the room, there had to be some photos of previous customers. This was definitely one strange tattoo parlor.

"Do you have any photos of work you've done?" Lou asked, still suspicious of a metallic tattoo.

"Yes, yes, of course," the little man moved toward the end of the work bench and returned with a leather covered binder.

He placed the book on the stainless steel surface in front of Lou and opened it. A plastic cover sheet housed the first photograph: a man's arm clearly showed a gleaming gold Corvette tattooed on the bicep. It was perfectly detailed, down to the black racing tires. The car actually looked like it had a metal flake paint job!

The next page showed a man's leg; a lighthouse was tattooed on his calf. Metallic gold rays of light emanated from the summit. It glistened, even in the photograph.

Lou Torroni was astounded.

The next photo was a woman's shapely lower back. An angel with shining golden wings and a sparkling golden halo hovered on her skin.

Lou could barely believe his eyes, but he knew one thing for certain: he wanted a tattoo like this! He held up the paper the artist had given him earlier and pointed toward the golden key with the heart shaped hole.

"I want this," he said.

Then the big man put his hand on his chest over his left pectoral muscle,

"I want it right here."

Dana was the key to his heart; he didn't know how the midget knew, or how the little guy made golden tattoos, but Lou was more than excited about the possibility.

"Excellent," Itzi said gesturing toward the leather chaise.

He asked Lou to sit down and remove his shirt. After making preparations at the workbench the little man applied the stencil to Lou's massive chest. Itzi was relieved this client was acting more normally. Earlier, finding the giant American crawling along the floor the little man had feared the worst. On the rare occasions Fonso had to eject someone from Buena Suerte, size was usually in his favor. This customer was easily as tall as Ildefonso and maybe more muscular.

THE FLAVOR OF HEARTS

Lou watched the little man don the sterile rubber gloves and take the chrome tattoo gun from its hook. The gleaming instrument looked huge. Lou had never seen a tattoo gun that big. He wondered if it was an optical illusion, the artist was so small; maybe the gun looked extra large.

Itzi began tattooing the outlines of the golden key. The burning was intense; after a minute it felt like Lou was hit with a branding iron. The handsome attorney had been tattooed three times previously; none of them hurt like this. Once he'd suffered a third degree burn from a steam pipe, Lou swore that pain was less intense.

"Damn," he said out loud, "that stings."

Pausing Itzi looked up. He promised the giant American the shading would be less painful than the outlines.

By the time the last color was applied Lou's whole chest felt like it was on fire. The attorney was more than relieved when the tiny man shut the buzzing gun and declared the tattoo finished. Like a woman who sees her newborn baby for the first time, Lou forgot all the previous pain when he saw the finished body art reflected in the artist's hand mirror.

The key looked like a medal on his chest; true to the artist's word, it looked like real gold. The shading was perfect; the tattoo shone like golden chrome. The artist had expertly shadowed the open heart in the key's head; the gold "D" inside it was easily readable.

It was a rare occasion; the successful litigator was at a loss for words.

"You're amazing. "I've never seen such a thing. Unbelievable."

Itzi thanked his customer for the compliments as he applied the bandage and antibacterial ointment. He repeated the instructions for the care of the new tattoo and deposited the rubber gloves in the nearby trash can.

Lou buttoned his shirt as he watched the diminutive gentleman approach the workbench and open the cash drawer. Itzi produced Lou's info card and nodded when he read the name. Now the little man understood the "D" he felt so strongly to draw in the key. The beautiful lady earlier: "D" and "L" near the amethyst heart; this giant man was the "L". Well, Itzi mused, Lou Torroni was already a lucky man.

"That will be $45, Mr. Torroni."

Lou approached with the money and wondered how the little dude got a hold of that card. He wanted to barrage the small man with all kinds of questions but thought the better of it. Instead he thanked the artist and repeated his earlier compliments.

The mismatched pair walked toward the exit. Lou shook Itzi's hand and ducked into the archway, the handsome attorney couldn't wait to show Dana his tribute.

Lou heard the musical voice echo behind him,

"Buena Suerte, Mr. Torroni. Buena Suerte."

20

Lou re-entered the lobby and stepped through the front door as soon as Fonso opened it. He hugged Dana as he joined the trio waiting to his left.

"Wait till you see what I got, Dane!" he exclaimed.

"What?" his wife's voice dripped with curiosity.

"A key, a golden key, right here.

The big man was clearly excited as he placed his hand over his heart.

"A key?" Dana was stunned; of all the cool things that were probably in that huge book her husband picked a key!

The Hoyles were surprised as well.

"Didn't the artist draw something for you?" Tim asked.

"Yeah, he drew two things," the big man answered.

"It was wild, like you said," Lou went on, "I was thinking of something patriotic or something for you, Dane. When I got in there, he already drew an eagle with a flag and the key."

Dana interrupted. "The key was for me?"

"Yeah, Dane, you're the key to my heart. Wait till you see it."

Dana laughed. Her husband could be romantic in the craziest ways.

The four friends headed back up the street to the boardwalk. They walked toward Lincoln Avenue in the cool late night air.

"Do you think we really have to leave the bandages on for two hours?" Emily asked her companions as they strolled.

"Let's take them off now," Dana suggested.

She was anxious to see the gold brooch on her back again and she was more than curious about the key on Lou's chest.

"No, no." Lou spoke from experience.

As the only one previously tattooed, he gave the others the benefit of his knowledge,

"You gotta follow the tattoo artist's advice. It could get infected or it could scab up too much and the colors would fade."

"Scab up?"

"It's gonna get scabs?"

The ladies spoke simultaneously; both faces showed the same slightly disgusted expression. Lou laughed as he explained

"New tattoos get scabs, like a scrape or a burn; the needle broke the skin, it's kind of like a wound."

"Ooooooo."

Dana sounded like she smelled something bad.

Lou looked at his watch. He was shocked to see it was almost four in the morning. Other than a ravenous hunger, he felt pretty fresh.

"I'll tell you what," Lou suggested to the others, "why don't we go back to one room and we'll count down two hours for each of us, then we can take off the bandages, what d'ya say? Unless you guys are too tired."

His companions agreed to the plan. They were all surprised how alert they felt after such a long night.

"Probably the endorphins kicking in after all that pain," Tim commented.

The others concurred; the burning sensation at Buena Suerte was extraordinary.

THE FLAVOR OF HEARTS

Outside the Blue Palms the big man made another suggestion, "Why don't you girls go up and we'll go and get some food." Lou motioned toward Tim as he spoke.

The assistant curator readily agreed to the food run, he was starving.

Lou drove the Cadillac down New Jersey Avenue to Mr. D's. Many club hoppers were standing in groups around the famous sandwich shop; it was the place to go in Wildwood to kill late night hunger.

The men returned to the Blue Palms with two large bags stuffed with local delicacies and joined their wives in the Hoyle's room. Dana leapt off the bed and dove for the food bag in Lou's hand.

The girls had changed their clothes and washed off their evening makeup. Tim eyed his wife still sitting cross legged on the bed. Clad in her shorts and tank top, with her hair in a pony tail and her fresh scrubbed face, she looked like a milk commercial. He fought the urge to jump on top of her.

A commotion drew the Hoyle's attention.

Lou was playing keep away with the brown bag. Dana faked right and slipped left; she grabbed the paper sack and without missing a beat she announced,

"Let's eat."

21

Most work nights went quickly; but this night oozed and plodded like cold feet through unrelenting mud. It was a relief for Itzi to watch the 20th customer leave through the arch.

The little man sighed. Tonight he had done what he vowed never to do; he did what he had forbidden the family to do: he uttered the names of his two older sisters out loud.

Itzi stretched out on the customer chaise and took in the splendor of the studio's mosaic night sky; the sandy haired American had been more than impressed.

No wonder, the little man thought, the ceiling mosaic took his older sisters almost two hundred years to complete! Itzamna turned his head and eyed the fresco of his pyramid. He could still see the girls happily painting with the Italian Maestro DaVinci overseeing their progress.

Again Itzi focused on the mosaic above. He centered his gaze on the stunning portrayal of the White Boned Serpent; the Milky Way glowed impressively in his sisters' perfect artwork.

Itzi silently berated himself; that damned curator had made him say their names. Suddenly the little man's caged memories were running free.

What was it Anita had called herself? A long English word, the former High Priest struggled to remember it…anachronism!

Itzi had looked the word up later and found it meant a chronological mistake, something stuck in the wrong time. It had broken his heart that his sister looked at herself that way.

Anita had run crying that day from this very room; Aneela had followed, as she always did. They were constantly together; you never saw one sister without the other. That was the last time he had seen either of them.

The morning of First Father, the winter solstice…how many years ago Itzi suddenly wondered? The Mayan Calendar whirred in his head; wheels inside wheels…he translated the calculation: 52 years!

Itzi fought tears. The little man could count on one hand the times he had ever cried. He realized he was no longer angry; he was unbelievably sad, and more than a little worried. Itzi wondered what had really happened to his older sisters.

Chac had given many instructions for their new lives; the god was very specific. There were also warnings; some of these were not as easy to decipher. First the god had spoken on the move from place to place:

"Carve four stones, each the size of your palm from the base of this pyramid," the god had instructed on his second visit to the House of the Magician in Uxmal, "take one from each direction precisely. Paint the one from the north white, the one from the south yellow, the east stone red and the west stone black."

"On the day of First Father," the god continued, "find a place on solid, elevated ground with a clear view of the sky. Place the stones in a square in their proper alignment; make sure they are exactly North, South, East and West. That evening, right after the sun has fully set; all people and objects inside the square of my sacred stones will be Moved. On the first day of each following year: place the stones in the proper alignment inside the bottom of the house that I provide for you."

The god's first cryptic warning followed,

"Any member of your household not inside the house for the Move that evening will perish. They will not find the road to the Underworld as you know it; they will be caught between dimensions, a fate worse than any torture you can imagine."

Caught between dimensions. The words had made no sense to the tiny High Priest in ancient Uxmal; but by 1955 Itzi had read the pioneering theories of time running simultaneously in parallel. Itzi's mind flew back to the night the family lost Anita and Aneela.

"Every thing our god promised has come true," Itzi had practically begged his oldest sister, "Please, Anita, do not to stay out tonight! Chac has told of unimaginable torture in the space between dimensions. Please! Don't make me worry of you trapped in some tortuous place!"

Itzi was chilled remembering her reply.

"I am already trapped in a torturous place, Itzamna…this place."

Itzi lost his temper and screamed back at her. He ordered her to stay in the house and threatened to have Fonso tie her to a chair.

"You may have Fonso restrain me," she warned, "but I will walk out the door at the first opportunity and never return."

"Unimaginable torture! Listen to the words of our lord," the little man entreated more calmly, "please, Anita!"

"Torture? I have buried six husbands and twenty three children, Itzamna! I have already suffered unimaginable torture living on and on with each of their memories. I'm an old hag in a young woman's body," she sneered, "the great Chac has tortured me enough."

"Do not blaspheme our patron god, Anita," Itzamna warned quietly.

"Or what? Or what, Itzamna?" She spit the words at the tiny High Priest.

"I'm an anachronism, Itzi," she had shrieked "and I cannot stand another minute of being such a thing! I cannot stand another second!"

With that Anita was gone, and Aneela too; a chronological mistake.

Itzi hoped the agony was lessened for her, but he could hear the voice of the great Chac as if it was yesterday:

"They will be caught between dimensions, a fate worse any torture you can imagine."

Itzi heard laughter coming from the archway at the room's entrance. The little man rose from the chair to greet his two brothers.

"Itzi," Bartolomeo called jovially, "did you see the size of that guy tonight? He was bigger than Fonso!"

"He wasn't bigger than me," the family giant sounded slightly annoyed.

"Wasn't he, Itzi?" Tolo's eyes were twinkling.

It was a rare occasion that Fonso could be teased about a physical situation. At six foot five he was huge by ancient standards; even in the modern world most people looked up to him.

Itzi answered with grin, "He was pretty big, Fonso."

"I could take him," Ildefonso grumbled, now more annoyed by the good natured ribbing.

The big man had been a highly respected warrior in Uxmal, many stories were repeated extolling his cunning, stamina and strength. Through his extended life Fonso had studied and mastered many fighting arts.

"I'm sure you could've," Itzi assuaged his massive brother, "I was afraid you might've had to…I found him crawling around on the floor over there."

"What?" Fonso was shocked, "Why didn't you call for me?"

Though he was the youngest son, Ildefonso was clearly the family's protector.

"He got up and acted more normally," Itzi explained, "he asked what the floor was made of."

"What the floor was made of?" Fonso repeated shaking his head, "the people in this town are crazy."

Itzi nodded; it had been a disturbing night it many ways. Immediately the tiny man's mind wandered back to the curator…back to Anita and Aneela suffering between dimensions.

"Itzi, are you all right?" Ildefonso was suddenly concerned.

The color had drained from his older brother's face; the High Priest actually looked sick.

"Would you like to sit down, Itzi?" Bartolomeo wheeled the leather stool toward their older brother and shot a worried glance at Fonso; Itzamna had never looked so strange.

With a wave of his diminutive hand Itzi put them off.

"I'm fine. I'm fine," the little gentleman assured his younger siblings, "Fonso, let's take a ride in your boat. We still have some good hours left."

Itzamna pointed toward the small gold clock nestled among the ink bottles; it was just past four a.m. Itzi's favorite place to view the stars was out on the open sea; free of the light pollution of the modern cities.

Fonso nodded in agreement. The sea air would do them all good.

"First, I need my pik hu'un," the little man said.

Immediately Bartolomeo offered to fetch Itzi's ancient Mayan book and the brothers agreed to meet at Fonso's car.

22

Tolo took the stairs two at a time to Itzi's room on the third floor. The ancient volume was on the table beside his older brother's recliner. Bartolomeo carefully scooped up the folding manuscript and headed back toward the first floor.

A Mayan book is a wonder of ancient technology. The Maya peeled the pliable inner bark of a local fig tree and then whitened the sheets with lime. They called this paper hu'un; it was stronger than the papyrus created in Egypt at about the same time.

They created a book, a pik hu'un, by accordion folding a long bark paper and binding it between two wood or stone covers. A sophisticated society, the Maya produced manuscripts on almost every subject; from agriculture to advanced astronomy.

Unfortunately very few Mayan books exist in the modern world; after the invasion of the Spaniards, Catholic priests destroyed the volumes, mistakenly calling the intricate writing the work of the devil.

Bartolomeo had seen the four surviving examples housed in modern museums. One was barely a fragment. Tolo mourned the loss of his people's many books; a talented scribe in ancient Uxmal the young man still revered the written language of his ancestors.

He was grinning as he entered the garage section of their family's building.

What a collector would give to get his hands on Itzi's pik hu'un! It looked as fresh as the day it was made and it was thicker and more ornate than any known example.

Ildefonso rolled down the window of his Jaguar.

"Hurry up, Tolo, let's go." he cajoled.

The big man piloted the black luxury car under the hidden automatic garage door. He gunned the car's powerful engine down 21st Avenue. Ildefonso loved all modern modes of transportation; the faster the better.

"Go slower, Fonso," Itzi requested closing his eyes and leaning his tiny head back on the leather seat.

As always, Ildefonso obeyed his older brother and drove more leisurely toward the marina. The big man looked forward to driving the boat. For some reason Itzi had no objections to high speed on the open water; his tiny older brother seemed to enjoy the wind through his hair and the waves in their wake.

"Do you want coffee or anything, Itzi? I'll stop on the way," Fonso offered.

When Itzamna studied the stars from the boat, it was not unusual for the little man to consume a quart of cappuccino and a box of his favorite Ring Dings!

"Do you have beer out there, Fonso?" the High Priest asked.

Ildefonso's eyebrows shot up in surprise as he answered affirmatively. Itzi never drank alcohol when he studied the stars. The big man glanced through the rear view mirror and saw Bartolomeo's surprise as well.

There was a lot of activity at the marina; deep sea fishing trips were getting underway in Wildwood's early morning darkness. The harbormaster waved at the three brothers as they passed; the local man wished he had a dozen customers like Fonso Cenotes.

THE FLAVOR OF HEARTS

The big man rented one of the harbor's biggest slips; he had a multimillion dollar vessel, more a yacht than a boat. He kept the ship impeccably, never threw wild parties or did anything suspicious. A month before, when a local fisherman died suddenly, Fonso had donated enough cash to the charitable collection to pay off the widow's house!

Yes, the harbormaster thought as he watched the brothers cast off; he wouldn't mind a dozen like Fonso Cenotes.

Ildefonso steered the boat slowly through harbor then gunned the engine as he reached open sea. Bartolomeo brought two six packs of Heineken from the refrigerator in the galley below.

Putting three bottles aside he put the rest on ice in a cooler on deck. He brought a beer to Itzi standing at the railing on the boat's prow and joined Fonso on the bridge. He handed his younger brother the second bottle and kept the third for himself.

"Good," the big man commented after the first sip.

Tolo nodded in agreement. The brothers had developed taste for Heineken when they lived in the Netherlands.

Tolo motioned toward Itzi standing below at the boat's head. The wind blew their brother's cropped black hair straight backwards; the little man held on to the railing with one hand and sipped the beer he held with the other.

"What do you make of that?" Bartolomeo asked, still surprised at their older brother's request for alcohol before he studied the sky.

"Hard to say," Fonso shrugged. "He seems in a weird mood."

The GPS system beeped, signaling Fonso's preset coordinates. The big man stopped the boat and dropped anchor.

"Let's fish, Tolo" he suggested. "Maybe we'll get a tuna and Mama will make putun."

Itzi left the boat's prow when the anchor dropped. He found his younger brothers on the fantail preparing bait and checking their fishing lines. The little man threw his empty beer bottle in the waste can. Tucking the Mayan book under his arm, the former High Priest opened two more Heinekens from the cooler and wordlessly headed up the stairs toward his observation area.

Tolo shot another worried glance at Fonso. The big man shrugged again.

23

Itzi had a second powerful telescope on the top deck of Ildefonso's boat; it rested on a gyroscopic base that negated the movement of the sea. As on the roof of their house the little man also had a plush weather proof recliner to comfortably study the sky with his naked eyes. He appreciated the great details visible in the darkness of the open ocean.

Itzi placed the pik hu'un on a side table along with the second bottle of beer.

He stretched out in the chair and focused above on the constellation Cygnus. The ancient astronomer eyed the star Deneb; he loved knowing the star was a white super giant two hundred times larger than our sun. He pictured Cygnus X1, the suspected massive black hole in the constellation. Itzi was still amazed by the variety of celestial bodies and the depth of the universe.

That night he found it hard to concentrate. I should do some real work he chided himself glancing at the pik hu'un on the table beside him. Itzi had placed many modern calculations in the ancient book; recently he had been listing the magnitude and type of the visible stars. The former High Priest smiled wanly; he surely had the most up to date pik hu'un imaginable.

The little man sipped the beer and rubbed his eyes with his free hand. He silently cursed the American curator; Itzi could only think of his two older sisters.

He was positive they were suffering; everything the great god said on his second visit was spot on. Again Itzamna smiled wanly, some of Chac's statements in Uxmal were most mysterious until the moment the situation unfolded.

"When you arrive, local people will believe that you have always been there." Chac said, "Nothing will seem out of the ordinary by your sudden presence. When you leave, the memory of you will fade like the mist."

"People will speak differently, their words will be indecipherable at first," the god instructed, "listen closely to them, focus on the strange sounds and in ten breaths I will grant understanding. Allow your mouth to form the strange sounds, you will speak their words and they will understand you."

Itzi nodded his head still amazed, it had happened exactly that way. He and his family had spoken a multitude of languages through the years!

"People will dress and adorn themselves differently. Everything will be provided for you and your family to adhere to local customs."

Itzi smiled, he clearly remembered their fright seeing their modified appearances on the night of the first Move.

"You will find two stone chests marked with my image," the god had said, "in the first you will find objects of great value to barter in the local markets. This chest will never be empty. Take what you want and replace the lid, the contents will be replenished. The second chest will contain other things you will need in each new place."

There was a firm warning attached to Chac's stone boxes:

"Only you may open my sacred chests, Itzamna," the great god cautioned, "Only you! You must remove the objects first, then they will be safe for other men to touch."

Itzi fondly remembered giving each family member a well deserved gift from the lord's treasure that first night on Chac's journey: beautiful necklaces for his mother and four sisters and ornate gold wristbands for his two brothers.

Itzi eyed the ring he wore on his right middle finger. When the little man first saw its design he was positive that the god intended this object for his High Priest. Itzamna had worn the gift ever since as a daily reminder of the first night he met the great Chac in the flesh.

The little man sighed; the darkness of night was giving way to the grayness of morning. He started on the second beer, it wasn't cold, but it tasted good and the alcohol was soothing.

Itzamna closed his eyes recalling the god's instructions on the new way to claim the hearts for offerings. Chac had pointed to the Tzolkin, part of the Mayan calendar in Itzi's house atop the Pyramid of the Magician; it revolved in a twenty day cycle.

"Make the sacrifices to me for fifteen nights in a row, and then rest for five. I will send twenty humans each sacrificial night; no more, no less."

"Itzamna," Chac spoke slowly, like a teacher, "You will no longer remove the hearts from the bodies, mark the humans for me with a ritual tattoo. I have supplied a container of sacred ink in the second chest for this purpose; it will never run dry. Make the mark in any shape you like, it needn't be large, the size of a newborn's palm will do."

Itzi was familiar with the art of tattooing; Mayan people regularly marked their bodies and faces with ink and scarred designs at many stages in their lives. A clear warning followed,

"Never mark anyone else with the ritual ink, only the humans I send on the sacrificial nights," the god spoke sternly, as you would when you wanted a child to remember your words, "Never use this ink on yourself or any member of your household."

"No man will find your house unless I send him, or you invite him," the great god promised in a less severe voice.

The last thing Chac said that evening sounded like an afterthought, but it turned out to be the stickiest part of the new life in his service.

"You may take a wife, Itzamna, you may father children if you wish. I will move them all with your household, however, keep in mind one thing: I can grant the Gift of Time to only those who stand on the solid earth and make the first Move."

Chac's last and least cryptic warning came as he faded from Itzamna's view, "Remember, if any of you take a spouse and make a family, you will outlive them. Though it may take many years you will surely see them die."

Itzi had warned his family with Chac's last words and they had come on the journey of their free will; though the little man realized that the choice of staying behind and waiting for the fall of Uxmal was hardly a viable option. Anita's words echoed again in Itzi's head,

"I have buried six husbands and twenty three children..."

Itzi opened his eyes. The sun was in full view. He drained the last of the Heineken. For the very first time the High Priest felt sympathy for his sister's predicament; a woman must feel a special pain when she buries her offspring.

Itzi picked up the pik hu'un and the two empty bottles; he headed down the stairs to find his brothers.

24

"Check it out, Itzi!" Fonso said brightly as his tiny brother approached.

The big man opened a cooler and removed a fifteen pound tuna.

"Putun!" he announced.

Fonso loved the Mayan meal; fresh fish marinated in axiote paste and sour orange then grilled on banana leaves.

Itzi raised an eyebrow; his gigantic brother could probably eat that whole tuna himself.

"That little fish may be enough for you, Fonso," he teased "but what about the rest of us?"

"Awww," the big man groaned, "it's not that small!"

Bartolomeo laughed and pointed to the lines still in the water.

"Maybe I'll catch one for the rest of us, Itzi!" he offered.

Ildefonso opened the second cooler and handed each of his brothers a cold beer. The three sat in contented silence, enjoying the sea breeze, the sunshine and each other's company.

Out of the blue Itzi broke the peace with a bombshell of a question.

"Tolo, Fonso, do you know it is over fifty years since we lost Anita and Aneela?"

The brothers stared in shock. Itzi had made very few rules for the family in their amazing journey together but he had been more than clear when their older sisters missed the Move.

"I never want to hear of them again! Never!" Itzi had been furious, "They have blasphemed our god and deserted us."

He looked each remaining family member in the eye as he laid down his law,

"Any of you that dares speak their names out loud, I will banish you from this place and on the next night of First Father you can join them in their unimaginable torture."

Fonso stole a glance at Bartolomeo; Tolo was re-living the exact same memory and was clearly afraid to answer the question.

"Yes, Saku'un, I remember the year," Ildefonso replied softly.

Itzi could see their astonishment and he felt the wave of their unexpressed curiosity.

"One of the customers last night," the High Priest explained slowly, "The skinny blond haired man, he wanted to put their work in a museum. He said he was the curator of the Philadelphia Museum of Art."

Damn, Fonso berated himself silently; he knew something else had happened that night besides some giant jackass crawling around on the floor.

"Their work is certainly fine enough," Ildefonso agreed still choosing his words carefully.

"Tolo, when we get home tell Mama she may put the photos of Anita and Aneela back in the dining room. I was wrong to forbid speaking of them," Itzi finished, "we are all still family."

"As you wish, Saku'un." Bartolomeo's voice was barely audible.

Hzzzzzzzzzzzzzzzzz...Tolo's fishing line took off! The brothers leapt to their feet. Bartolomeo jumped into the fighting chair and grabbed the pole, the line was really moving.

"Get him, Tolo," Ildefonso was right at his brother's side.

Bartolomeo reared back with the pole in his left hand and reeled frantically with right; for three or four minutes Tolo gave the fish line and tenaciously reeled him in. After ten minutes the rod was bent nearly in half. Covered with sweat Bartolomeo breathlessly asked his larger brother to take over.

"Fight him in, Tolo, you can do it!" Fonso encouraged.

The big man supported his brother's arm rearing back on the pole and eyed the amount of line on the reel.

"He's close, Tolo! Keep reeling! Keep reeling!"

"Fight him in, Tolo!" Itzi yelled his encouragement.

Fonso donned gloves and ran to the side of the boat; leaning over he pulled on the line hand over hand.

"I see him, Tolo he's big!" he bellowed, "Keep reeling! Keep reeling!"

"Keep reeling!" Itzi echoed.

"Ahhhgggggg!" Bartolomeo grunted rearing back with the pole; his arms felt ready to fall off.

Itzi moved to Fonso's side with a gaff.

"Keep reeling, Tolo!" they yelled at their brother in unison.

"Here he is, Itzi!" Ildefonso hollered, yanking the line toward the boat.

Expertly Itzi hooked the head and smoothly handed the pole to Fonso. The big man hauled the yellowfin into the boat.

"It's at least eighty pounds, Tolo!" Fonso said excitedly.

Bartolomeo fought to regain his breath but he was smiling from ear to ear. It was the biggest fish he ever caught.

Itzi slapped his younger brother on the shoulder, "Good fight, Tolo, good fight!"

"Now that's enough for everybody, hey Itzi?" Ildefonso was grinning from ear to ear as well.

The little man nodded his head in agreement; he laughed a musical laugh when he replied, "That fish is bigger than me!"

25

"Cheese steaks are good," Emily declared.

The other three seated at the round dinette table nodded silently as they savored the early morning snack.

The couples sampled a delectable array of local comfort food: steak sandwiches on crisp Italian bread with warm melted cheese and fried onions, crisp salty French Fries, battered onion rings fried to perfection. They finished off the feast with Tastykakes.

"Krimpets are good." Dana declared, waving the company's signature gold snack cake.

"Blueberry pies are good," Lou chimed in, holding up Tastykake's gooey blue treat.

"All Tastykakes are good," Tim added, laughing.

Emily waved a small notepad in the air; earlier the girls had calculated each person's time to safely remove their tattoo's sterile covering.

"I'll tell you what's good, Tim, you can take off your bandage."

All six eyes turned to the blond man as he raised his shirt over his head. It was the first time Tim removed his shirt in front of Emily and she didn't take note of his perfect chest.

She focused keenly on the white gauze on his shoulder, watching him slowly pulling the bandage back.

The lion's head on Tim's deltoid looked three dimensional. It was expertly shaded with yellow, orange and brown. Delicate metallic gold lines in graceful arcs made up the animal's mane; the tattoo shimmered like polished gold.

The couples were stunned into silence; they stared for a good long minute.

Emily broke the hush, "Wow, I'm floored. It's incredible!"

"It's beautiful, really." Dana was breathless.

Tim broke into a grin and headed toward the hotel room's mirror. "It's even cooler than I remembered," he said eying his reflection.

Lou approached his buddy for a closer look. He was clearly still astounded by the tattoo's metallic properties, "I have never seen a tattoo like that in my life." He put his head closer to Tim's shoulder, "It looks like metal. How could it?"

"Maybe there's gold in the ink," Tim offered, "like a synthetic gold."

Lou's voice was reverent; he couldn't tear his eyes from the lion, "It's unbelievable."

"What time is it, Em?" Dana's voice sounded clipped and impatient, "I can hardly wait to see mine."

Emily picked up the notepad from the table. She checked her watch then read out loud.

"You're good at 5:40; it's actually 5:30 now. We were a little late with Tim; he was actually ready to go at 5:20 but we were eating. I'm good at six," Emily turned to Lou and went on, "And Lou, two hours for you is about twenty after."

Dana was relieved her time was almost up; she felt fidgety. Crossing the room she looked out the window down Pacific Avenue; the blackness of night was giving way to the dawn. Turning back to her companions she laughed, "I thought ten minutes was only a long time on the treadmill!"

The others nodded in agreement; it was funny how minutes elongated at the worst times.

Dana's patience wore thin at 5:35. When she announced she was removing the bandage immediately, her husband playfully pulled her on his lap and enveloped her in a bear hug.

"No, you're not; give the antibacterial the full two hours."

He snuggled with his lovely spouse to distract her.

Emily's voice rang out at exactly 5:40; Dana jumped off Lou's lap and headed toward the mirror. She lowered her pink shorts and exposed the small of her back. Slowly she removed the gauze and showed the gleaming body art.

Lou, Tim and Emily joined her at the looking glass, gazing at the faux jewel's reflection.

"Wow," Lou was almost speechless.

Dana's tattoo was even more stunning than Tim's. The gold filigree was so detailed; it shone like diamond cut gold. The amethyst heart looked like a real gem; the purple facets sparkled with an inner light.

"It's amazing how he shadowed that," Tim commented, "it looks like a real pin."

Emily agreed, "It looks like a brooch attached to your skin, Dane. It's crazy!"

Lou kissed his wife and he told her how much he loved their initials in the design.

"I am so glad we went in there," Dana spoke still staring in the mirror.

The others nodded; suddenly Emily felt impatience growing. She tried to busy herself; digging into her makeup bag she produced a small bottle of baby oil.

"You guys should put the oil on, like the guy said."

Lou tore his eyes from the small of Dana's back and agreed, "Definitely, Dane put the oil on; it would be a shame if that thing faded."

After the light coating of oil both tattoos shone even more.

"I still can't believe how they look," Lou was clearly stupefied as he went on, "You would think you'd have seen this advertised, or in the news, metallic tattoos. I never saw or heard of such a thing."

"That was a wild place, for sure," Emily offered.

"Yeah, I couldn't believe that place," Tim replied, thinking out loud, "The mosaics were unreal and the frescoes…who'd have thought that little place would have those enormous frescoes, I mean who paints frescoes these days? It's rare!"

"It looked like a dump from the outside." Lou declared.

"Oh, I don't know," Dana looked away from the mirror to pitch in her opinion, "The painting on the front window was really nice, the one of the sea."

"Yeah, it was," Lou consented, "I just mean the store seemed so small and then the room in the back was so big."

"I guess they made the lobby so small to make room for the back," Emily mused aloud.

"How about that ceiling?" Dana asked.

All three murmured agreement.

"I'd love to have a ceiling like that in our bedroom, Lou."

The big man laughed when he answered, "How much do you think the midget would charge to come home and do that? A lot more than $45 I would imagine!"

Dana gave her husband a sour look, "Little person, Lou." Dana supplied the more politically correct term.

"Sorry, honey."

"He said his sisters did the mosaics," Tim informed his friends.

All three turned to face the assistant curator as he explained further, "He said they did the paintings too. I asked him about contacting them, I'd have loved to show their work at the museum, but he said they passed on."

"Oh, that's a shame." Dana said softly.

The quartet fell into silence, almost like a moment of reverence for the enigmatic artist's loss.

Emily eyed her watch; excitement colored her voice, "Oooh, five minutes for me."

"It's a sailboat, right?" Lou asked.

Emily nodded and described the image to the best of her ability. She expressed her amazement again that the artist somehow drew her father's custom sloop in perfect detail.

"Yeah," Lou responded, "You could'a knocked me down when I saw my drawings. How do you think he knew about us? That big book on the bench had a bunch of stuff geared for me too, like the scales of justice, the midg…I mean the little person knew I was a lawyer! Know what else? There was a golden bear drawn there too."

Dana's eyebrows shot up; she knew Lou's former nickname.

Lou explained to the Hoyle's.

"In college, on the wrestling team, my nickname was The Golden Bear…they said I was as strong as a bear and I always came home with the gold."

"It's eerie. How did he know that?" Dana wondered.

"Maybe he's some kind of magician," Tim suggested, "one of the frescoes was the Temple of the Magician."

"Yeah," Dana agreed, suddenly remembering the painting on Buena Suerte's back wall, "they call that place the Temple of the Dwarf too! Supposedly the High Priest there was a dwarf with mystical powers. Wow…" she finished wide eyed.

Again the couples sat in silence; Buena Suerte was a weird place in so many ways.

Suddenly Emily looked at her watch. She jumped up and headed toward the mirror. The other three stood behind her as she untied the drawstring on her fleece shorts.

Tim admired his wife's toned abdomen as she lowered the pants on one side. He gasped when she unveiled the tattoo; the Hoyle's spent many weekends on the Raven when they were first married and every detail was perfect.

Emily spoke almost matter-of-factly, but she was clearly thrilled, "God, if I'd have known you could get a tattoo that looked like this, I'd have gotten one years ago."

"The sun looks awesome," Dana commented on the design, "it's shining, like real sunlight."

THE FLAVOR OF HEARTS

"Look at the water," Lou said incredulously, "it looks like real water."

"It's fantastic where he brought in the gold," Tim noted.

The metallic sun and its reflections were so expertly rendered, once again the four Philadelphians stared in silence.

This time Dana spoke first, "Louie, you're next. Twenty minutes, that's murder!"

The others laughed. Dana sounded like a kid waiting to see the Christmas presents.

"How do you think he knew what the Raven looked like?" Emily asked, still staring at the tattoo in the mirror.

"He told me he draws what he feels," Lou offered.

"Yeah, he told me that too," Emily reflected, still wondering.

Dana turned to Tim, "Did you see the glyphs above the doorway? I think it was the year, from the Mayan calendar."

Tim agreed. He definitely thought it looked like a date above the stone arch.

Suddenly Dana remembered the ball and her words came out in a rush, "Hey, did you see the ball on top of the bookshelf in the back of the room? Do you think he had a real Ball Game ball?"

"What?" Tim was flabbergasted, his eyes opened wide, "A Mayan Ball Game ball? Really? Where in there?"

Emily looked away from her tattoo for the first time; she could hear the excitement in Tim's voice.

"There were shelves," Dana explained, "like a big bookcase along the back wall, next to the archway where you came in. There were all kinds of statues and stuff there. The ball was up on top."

Tim was more than astounded. He didn't remember the shelves. Shaking his head he told Dana, "I didn't see it. I wish I did…it couldn't be. How big was it?"

Lou and Emily watched the exchange between their spouses with interest; it was easy to see that news of this ball shocked Tim more than anything else so far.

Dana made a rounded motion with her hands, describing a sphere of about twenty inches. "It was dull black," she tried to remember every detail for the assistant curator; "there were little spots where it was kind of gray...like it dried out. It looked old."

The size was right according to the historical descriptions of the legendary rubber ball. Tim was speechless. If that was an authentic ball from the Mayan Ball Game it would be a valuable historic artifact.

"It was probably just a ball, a regular ball," Tim finally spoke.

Dana shook her head. "Right above it there was a framed painting on the wall; it was definitely a ball court. I asked him, I asked him if the ball was real."

Tim's was suddenly consumed with curiosity, "What did he say? Did he say it was real?"

"He didn't seem to understand what I meant," Dana admitted sheepishly. Now she wished she'd pressed the artist a little harder.

Tim addressed all three of his companions, "If that ball is authentic, it's an historic find. I don't think any Mayan ones exist in the modern world."

"Really?" Emily was surprised.

She had seen the bookcase but didn't take any notice of the ball; she remembered the shelves held statues and baskets.

"Wow," Emily replied, "do you think it's real?"

Tim shrugged. If a Mayan ball existed from the ancient ball game, he wouldn't be too surprised that it sat on a shelf in the ultra strange Buena Suerte.

"I'm gonna speak to Ed when I get back," Tim said referring to his boss at the museum, "I'm gonna bring him down here to have a look at that place and we'll see."

The others nodded.

Dana looked over Emily's shoulder and eyed her friend's watch, "OK, Louie," she said to her husband, "let's see the key."

Lou removed his shirt and peeled the little bandage from his chest.

"Aww, Louie," Dana exclaimed when she saw the heart shaped hole and her initial, "that is so cool."

"Did he draw it for you just like that," Tim asked curiously, "with the 'D' in there?"

Lou assured them it appeared exactly on his chest as it did on the artist's paper.

"He's a psychic," Emily declared, "He's got to be."

"Maybe he remembered that I asked for a 'D' and an 'L'," Dana suggested.

"I don't think so," the handsome attorney reasoned, "I don't think he knew my name until I paid, when he pulled my card out of that drawer."

"Yeah," Tim said excitedly, "that's another thing…I was shocked when he pulled my card out of there. How do you think the card gets in that drawer?"

"He told me that his brother puts it in there," Emily's voice trailed off, she realized the explanation still didn't make a load of sense.

"Maybe he looked at your name before you got in there," Dana tried to force sense into the situation.

"Well," Lou acknowledged, "he could've done that, but that still leaves a lot of stuff unexplained: like the patriotic drawing and the golden bear."

"And the Raven," Emily chimed in, "he had every detail."

Again the two couples stared in silence.

"Well, no matter how he knew, it looks great, Louie Boy," Tim grinned at his pal.

The tattoo did look stunning. Like all the others the body art looked three dimensional; the highly polished key gleamed perched on Lou's massive pectoral muscle.

Emily carefully washed a tiny plastic container with a lid from the take out meal and filled it with baby oil.

"Take this so you have some for tomorrow morning." she told her girl friend.

The couples said their good nights and separated; the Torroni's quietly headed for their room down the stairs.

In the short time that Emily shut the door and turned around, her husband was in his underwear lying on the bed. She joined him and snuggled up against his side.

"I'm surprised I'm not more tired," he admitted.

"Good," she answered with a sly smile as she pushed her hand into his underpants.

Tim was shocked as his wife moved; sliding her head down between his legs. Emily had never initiated sex in the six years of their marriage!

Tim's head rocked back in ecstasy; if Wildwood was making his wife this wild, he was gonna look for property down here right away.

26

The Hoyle's joined Dana and Lou in the hotel lobby. Surprisingly they easily made it on time for the 11:00 a.m. checkout; it had been a short night of sleep for both couples. The girls decided to take a quick run to a boardwalk souvenir shop, leaving their husbands to settle the hotel bill.

The sun was bright but the late morning air was still a little cool, the humidity was down. A beautiful day was unfolding: a steady breeze rolled off the ocean, people were staking out spots on the huge beach and the boardwalk water parks were starting to kick into gear. Emily pointed toward the people waiting to ride in oversized inner tubes down the man-made streams at one of Wildwood's popular swimming attractions,

"I would love to come back here again." Emily commented as the girls walked. "I'd like to try the water rides sometime."

Dana was happy for her friend; it was rare that Emily seemed so contented.

"Definitely," she answered, "we have the whole month of August. Lou loves the water parks, I bet Tim would too. We'll come back."

Out of the corner of her eye Dana saw movement. A panhandler was approaching them on Emily's side, holding out a paper cup. Dana wondered if somehow these people could sense that Emily was an easy touch; beggars rarely approached when Dana was alone and never when Lou was by her side.

"Please, Miss, some spare change?"

He made his request from slightly behind Emily. The former ad exec glanced over her shoulder and kept walking. Dana's eyebrows shot up; the attractive Sicilian took advantage of her friend's unusual reluctance to stop for a handout and picked up the pace. The girls walked a little quicker so the man gave up and chose another mark.

Well what do ya know, Dana thought as they entered the souvenir shop; she had to wonder if Emily just didn't hear the hobo.

"Look, Dane!"

Emily already had a pink t-shirt in her hand. A silhouetted sailboat was nestled under the words "Wildwood by the Sea".

The girls easily selected a bagful of mementos and headed back down the boardwalk to find their husbands.

"Watch the tram car, please. Watch the tram car."

New Jersey's most famous electronic voice rang out in the morning air.

The ladies watched Wildwood's legendary public transportation pass by. The blue and yellow motorized train ferried passengers up and down the two mile boardwalk.

Dana leaned closer to Emily and laughed.

"When we were kids we would say 'Watch the damn car, please. Watch the damn car!'."

Emily laughed at the old joke too; yes, she definitely looked forward to coming back to Wildwood.

The men took the luggage to the Cadillac and stowed it in the ample trunk.

"I could spend a month here." Tim took a big breath of the crisp sea air.

"Yeah, I love Wildwood." Lou agreed.

"You ever think of a place down here?" Tim asked his friend, "What does real estate go for, do ya know?"

Lou was glad Tim liked Wildwood so much; it was also great to see how much Emily liked the legendary shore town.

"It's funny," the big man answered candidly, "now that I could probably afford it, I never thought of it."

The men agreed to look into the prospect.

"I'd like to go back to that tattoo parlor," Tim mentioned as they waited for the girls near the car.

Lou laughed out loud, "You already want another one?"

"No, no...well maybe," now Tim laughed.

The assistant curator had heard many times how easily people get addicted to being tattooed; frankly, now he could understand why!

"No, no," the blond man explained, "I would like to get a look at that ball."

Lou admired his buddy's eye for art and his expertise in his field; if Tim was so interested in a rubber ball it must really be something.

"We could take a ride over there," the tall man offered, "I don't think the girls will care."

Tim was more than tempted but declined; he didn't want business to intrude on the more than pleasant weekend.

"No, I'll get my boss to come down here," Tim finished slyly as the girls approached, "maybe I'll get another tattoo then!"

It was a twenty minute ride to Cape May down the Ocean Drive; traffic was fairly light and it was a smooth ride in Lou's luxury car.

Emily and Tim found the Victorian town enchanting; they were captivated by the restored gingerbread architecture in the nation's oldest seaside resort. Lou suggested lunch and parked the car on Washington Street. The couples walked to the

Washington Street Mall and entered The Ugly Mug: a long established pub popular with tourists and locals alike.

Seated comfortably in a large booth the Philadelphians were intrigued by the army of beer mugs hanging from the ceiling. The waitress said that the glasses belonged to the Ugly Mug Club. Members owned their own drinking vessels and when not in use their mugs were washed and suspended overhead. She pointed to a few that hung facing the ocean; in a more reverent tone she explained that when a member passed away they turned his or her mug to face the sea. The friendly server advised the couples to come back in the evening for a wild time; she guaranteed them that nobody partied as hearty as the Ugly Mug Club.

The couples selected appetizers and drinks; even Lou succumbed to the festive atmosphere and ordered a frosted mug of Heineken. Over delicious stuffed hot peppers and mini-tacos the four friends decided on the same entrée: The Ugly Mug's popular Ocean Burger. They all thoroughly enjoyed the huge patty of quality ground beef topped with shrimp and cheddar cheese.

Too stuffed for dessert the couples left the popular eatery. Walking down Decatur Street the friends made their way onto Beach Avenue, Cape May's main boulevard opposite the ocean. They browsed the numerous art galleries, gift stores, boutiques and antique shops.

Crossing the street the couples rested on a bench on the concrete promenade overlooking the beach. The sand was gleaming white and the navy blue Atlantic looked clean and inviting; people covered the tiny beach, frolicking in the waves and sunbathing.

"It's puny compared to Wildwood," Emily commented.

The others laughed but it was true. Cape May's beach was every bit as pristine as its neighbor's up the coast but it was easily one eighth the size.

Dana extracted a small bottle of baby oil from her purse, one of her earlier purchases from the store on the Wildwood boardwalk.

"We should put the oil on our tattoos," she suggested and passed the plastic container down the bench to Emily.

The light haired woman took the bottle and popped off its little cap. She dabbed a small drop on her index finger and modestly reached her hand down her shorts to apply a coating to her beloved sailboat.

Beside her Tim lifted his shirt sleeve and she applied a light coating to the king of beasts on his shoulder.

Returning the bottle to Dana Emily remarked, "I can't wait until it's safe to let the sun hit these tattoos, they must shine like nobody's business in the sunlight!"

Her companions agreed.

Dana slid up toward the front of the seat and turned her back toward her husband. Lou gently lowered Dana's waistband and dabbed the oil over the faux brooch. He raised his t-shirt and lightly coated the golden key.

"You know what else is weird about these tattoos?" Lou asked the others.

From their quizzical faces he knew they hadn't noticed anything. He answered his own question, "There's no swelling, no puffiness."

The others remained perplexed so the big man tried to explain.

"Every fresh tattoo I have ever seen was puffy, all three of my other ones puffed up at the very beginning." Lou looked down at the tattoo on his upper left arm.

He pointed at Taz, the Tasmanian Devil cartoon and tried to illustrate his point,

"Like here," he rubbed his finger over the image, "the shape stood up higher...about an eighth of an inch, it raised up everywhere they put the ink. It was like that for a couple of days, then it got a scab. When it healed the scab fell off and then it looked flat, like it does now."

Emily raised her waistband and peered in at her fresh tattoo. It was flat like her other skin; it looked exactly as it did the night the little artist bandaged it.

Tim checked the lion on his shoulder, it was smooth as well. Dana felt the small of her back; it felt like it always did.

"Maybe it's something new," Emily guessed.

"Yeah, Lou," Dana reasoned, "you haven't got a tattoo in years."

"Hey, I don't doubt it's something new," her husband answered, "I've never seen a metallic tattoo on anybody else, have you?"

The others admitted that they had not.

Their silence was filled by the sound of the ocean.

Lou finally spoke, "Maybe they just don't swell, or maybe it'll swell up later."

The big man spoke authoritatively but Dana could tell her mate's curiosity was not appeased.

The couples walked up Perry Street, heading back toward the Washington Mall. Dana took her girlfriend into one of Cape May's coolest stores, The Whale's Tale. Emily was impressed with the diverse inventory; the shop was stuffed to the rafters with the most unusual gifts, toys, clothes and house wares.

Emily purchased a set of cordial glasses embedded with sea shells and a small lamp shaped like a light house. Dana bought some holographic greeting cards, a dolphin pen and a new pair of sunglasses. They joined their husbands waiting outside.

Lou pointed toward the Dairy Queen.

"I could dig some ice cream, but if we're going to the Lobster House..."

Dana looked at her watch; it was close to 4:30.

"I'm actually still pretty full from lunch," Dana declared.

Emily nodded; she certainly wasn't ready for a meal. The couples decided to head toward home. They agreed to eat dinner later, closer to their neck of the woods.

The girls chose to forego the frosty treat, and this time they waited for their spouses outside. Emily wandered over to the front of the shop next door. The front window at Andrew's displayed a mix of new and old jewelry and a variety of collectibles.

"Dane," her pal called, "look at this."

Dana joined her friend and eyed the necklace that piqued Emily's interest. It was probably an antique, an array of multicolored gems were inlaid to form realistically shaped flowers. Rich green stones cut like leaves were delicately placed in between the colorful blooms.

Emily looked toward the Dairy Queen; their husbands were still inside waiting in line.

"I'm gonna go in and check it out," she told her dark haired friend.

The girls entered the tiny shop and asked the man inside about the necklace. Taking it from the window the salesman offered it to Emily. She was surprised by the weight of the piece. The choker fit perfectly at the base of her neck, not too tight and not too loose; the colorful flowers looked stunning against Emily's light skin.

The man described the necklace. It was an estate piece, circa 1950: precious and semi-precious stones in a platinum setting. The leaves were emeralds. The flowers consisted of white and colored diamonds, rubies, citrines, pearls, amethysts, sapphires and opals.

The salesman retrieved a paper from a drawer behind the counter; laying the document in front of the girls he showed them the exact carat weight of the gems and the estate's appraised value of eighty five hundred dollars. He told them the store's price was sixty five hundred plus tax.

"I'll take it." Emily's words hung in the air.

Dana's knees buckled; she rarely saw Emily even wear jewelry! Her friend usually wore her wedding and engagement rings, a watch and on occasions a simple gold necklace or gold bracelet.

"Em," she gasped, "are you sure?"

The salesman paused, halting in his preparations to finalize the sale.

He smiled when the lady replied in the affirmative,

"I'm positive, Dane, I want it."

Emily produced her American Express card and paid; she declined the man's offer to place the purchase back in its antique box, opting instead to wear the stunning choker.

The girls left the store; the necklace glittered in the sunlight. Pleased, Emily eyed her reflection in the glass window. Dana had to admit that her friend looked gorgeous in the colorful bauble; however she was still weak in the knees, it wasn't everyday you watched somebody spend almost seven thousand dollars on the spur of the moment.

The men joined their wives in front of the jewelry store. They were munching on huge ice cream cones.

Emily turned to her husband and pointed toward her neck, "I bought a necklace."

"Wow," Tim replied, "it's beautiful, you look beautiful, Em."

The couples made their way up the mall.

Lou looked down at his wife as they followed behind the Hoyle's. She looked strange.

"Dane, you all right?"

She pulled her husband's head down close to hers and whispered in his ear, "It cost seven thousand dollars!"

The attorney stood up to his full height; he almost dropped his half eaten ice cream cone. Even though he didn't exactly show it, Dana could tell he was shocked as well.

He shrugged at his astounded wife, it may have been a little out of character for Emily to spend so much so capriciously but he suspected that she could easily afford the purchase.

The couples crossed Jackson Street, then Decatur. As the very end of the open air mall Dana halted the little group.

She pointed at the window of a boutique called the Klothes Kove,"Em, look at that blouse, its metallic, like out tattoos!"

The others followed her gaze; the sleeveless tan shirt had an empire waist and was covered with gold metallic polka dots. As the girls entered the store the men retreated to a bench outside.

Emily helped Dana find the blouse her size. Her pal slipped the Liz Claiborne tunic over her tank top. Satisfied with the fit

Dana removed it and hung it over her arm as she shuffled through the rest of the tops on the rack.

Surprisingly she selected two more: both by Sigrid Olsen. The first: a wrap top with a floral print and plunging neckline and the second, a tape yarn v-necked sweater knitted in an open shell like pattern. She tried them both on the same way, right on the spot over her tank top.

As she signed the credit card receipt Dana turned to her gal pal and laughed, "Look, Em, I'm buying clothes!"

Emily shook her head in disbelief and joined in the laughter. She caught her own reflection in a mirror behind the counter and fingered the stunning floral necklace.

Well, if I got the urge to buy jewelry, she thought, Dana could certainly give in to the urge to buy clothes!

27

Lou steered the Cadillac onto the Garden State Parkway. He was glad they decided to eat dinner closer to home. Leaving the shore a little earlier they would avoid a ton of traffic.

After about forty minutes Lou exited the Parkway and followed a line of cars onto the Atlantic City Expressway. He leaned back a little and relaxed; now it was about an hour in mostly a straight line back to Philadelphia.

"This is a great car, Lou," Tim said from the back seat.

The thick leather upholstery and smooth ride made the Cadillac extremely comfortable for a road trip.

"It feels like you're riding down the street in your living room!" Tim joked.

"Yeah," the handsome attorney agreed, "I wouldn't trade my Caddie for anything."

Tim thought he would seriously consider a Cadillac the next time he shopped for a car.

In almost no time the couples passed the sign that thanked drivers for choosing the Atlantic City Expressway. They merged into the heavier traffic on Route 42. Emily knew from their trips to Atlantic City that this little stretch of highway led almost right to the bridge.

She reached down on the floor and opened her bag from the Wildwood souvenir shop. Extracting a colorful box and breaking its cellophane seal she asked her companions, "Anybody want some salt water taffy?"

All three expressed interest, not only because the gooey treats were delicious, but pre-dinner hunger was starting to develop in the travelers.

Emily removed the lid and held the box out to her husband beside her; suddenly the back seat was filled with white wrapped candies flying through the air.

Boom! It sounded like an explosion in the lane beside them.

As Emily turned her head toward the noise she saw two cars colliding. One of the vehicles ricocheted to within inches of the Cadillac. Emily felt her body shift hard and uncontrollably.

Boom! Boom! The sound of crashing metal and breaking glass was deafening; it was all around them like a mine field in a war movie.

Boom!

A loud piercing noise now filled the car; Dana was screaming.

Though her seat belt kept her in place, Emily felt her weight shift violently in the opposite direction; she heard squealing tires right next to her window.

Boom!

She closed her eyes and began screaming herself. Her body was pulled like a rag doll left and right again. She could feel Tim beside her, being tossed around in the same way.

As quickly as the commotion started, it suddenly stopped; the Cadillac was again moving smoothly in a straight line. All three passengers whipped their heads around to look through the back window; cars were strewn haphazardly over all three lanes and ominous black smoke was rising in plumes.

The scene of automotive carnage got smaller as they continued forward.

After the deafening cacophony the silence in the car was eerie.

"Jesus!" Tim exclaimed looking down; it was surreal, he was covered in salt water taffy.

Even though the whole episode took less than a minute Lou felt like he hadn't taken a breath in an hour. His hands felt like stone; he couldn't release the death grip he had on the leather steering wheel.

Hearing a choking sound the big man glanced to his right; Dana was crying.

He heard Tim comforting his wife from the back seat, she was sobbing as well.

A little way ahead Lou saw an exit marked Deptford; he knew there was a giant mall there. The big man piloted the car up the exit ramp and headed for the shopping center; he needed to stop for a minute and catch his breath.

Passing chain stores of almost every variety Lou brought the Caddie to a halt on the outskirts of the Sears parking lot and pried his fingers from the steering wheel. He released his seatbelt and took Dana in his arms.

"You OK, Dane?"

She nodded, pressing her head into his chest.

"You guys OK?" Lou turned his head toward the back seat.

The Hoyles assured him they were unhurt.

They could hear sirens far in the distance, probably the police and rescue vehicles attempting to reach the accident site.

"That was some piece of driving, Lou." Tim complimented his friend.

"It felt like a video game," the big man admitted. "I just kept steering out of the way of cars coming at us."

The couples sat in silence for a few minutes allowing the tension to dissipate.

As Emily picked up the salt water taffy and placed the little sweets back in the box, Dana took some tissues from her handbag and wiped her husband's brow.

"Poor Louie, you're all sweated up," she cooed.

Inside he wondered how they avoided being hit.

THE FLAVOR OF HEARTS

"We were pretty lucky," Lou commented. Thank God, he was starting to feel normal again.

Dana felt giddy; she was also recovering from the traumatic experience. "Maybe it was our tattoos," she said slyly, "we're supposed to have good luck forever."

The others stared at her blankly at first, then smiles broke out on their faces. Their smiles gave way to laughter and the laughter did them all a lot of good.

"What do you say we look around here for somewhere to eat?" Lou suggested.

His companions readily agreed,

"Funny how a near death experience can leave you starving," Tim joked.

"Yeah," Emily joked back, "I hate when that happens!"

Lou started the engine and drove along the road surrounding the Deptford Mall; just about every national restaurant chain was present. He asked if anyone had a preference and they left to the choice to him.

Rounding the corner Lou's eyes were drawn to a place on the opposite side of the street; Greek columns and statues surrounded the large attractively landscaped building. The blue sign said Adelphia. Lou drove the Caddie to the next red light and got in the U-Turn lane. With a nod to his heritage he approached the restaurant and parked. There were a lot of cars in the lot, a good sign when you choose somewhere unfamiliar to eat.

Before they exited the vehicle Dana stopped her friends. She pulled the travel sized bottle of baby oil from her purse and suggested they coat the tattoos before dinner. They complied then joined the small line waiting to enter the restaurant.

Near the hostess's station they waited while she seated a group of four then the pair in front of them. Suddenly a bell rang and loud music began playing, the lights in the restaurant blinked on and off.

An announcement came over a loudspeaker: "Ladies and Gentlemen, Adelphia would like to welcome our ten millionth customer!"

A welcoming committee approached the four waiting Philadelphians; as the one nearest to the hostess's podium Emily was declared the winner. A handsome man in a black suit presented her with a handful of helium balloons and introduced himself as the owner. Another man threw confetti in the air, peppering the stunned couples.

A third man laid a humongous gift basket at Emily's feet. When the owner asked her name Emily could barely choke out an answer. He then asked where she lived, and again, she could barely speak.

The owner spoke into a hand held microphone, his voice echoing over the restaurant's PA system,

"Welcome, Emily Hoyle of Philadelphia, our ten millionth customer!"

A photographer appeared and the owner posed with Emily. Emily introduced Tim and the Torronis and the photographer took pictures of all of them with the owner as well.

A waiter held the balloons as the proprietor escorted the astonished friends to a table. The patrons in the restaurant applauded. A waiter was already pouring champagne to toast the honored ten millionth customer.

The couples posed seated at the table with their glasses raised as the proud owner stood behind them. The photographer took more photos. When the waiter handed out menus, the man told Emily the dinner was now part of the prize and they should all order as much as they wanted.

Immediately waiters began bringing plates of appetizers and the owner encouraged the quartet to try them. Lou and Tim sampled the platters right away and sincerely complimented the owner. He seemed very pleased.

The proprietor asked if Emily had ever visited Greece. When she replied in the negative he beamed. Then he revealed another part of the prize: an all expense paid luxury cruise in the Greek Islands! He explained that the gift basket included

THE FLAVOR OF HEARTS

many other prizes with a total value of twenty thousand dollars!

The couples were flabbergasted.

Finding her voice, the lanky ad exec thanked the owner profusely, he laughed when she told him she had never won anything in her life. The owner thanked them for coming and said that he would return after dessert to escort them to their car with the gift basket. The welcoming committee retreated allowing the couples to enjoy dinner.

The four Philadelphians stared at each other, still in shock.

Dana chomped on a fried mozzarella stick and dipped a second one in marinara sauce as she spoke, "What d'ya think? It's good luck forever?"

Emily looked at her girlfriend in disbelief. "Dane, you can't really believe a tattoo can bring you luck!"

"I don't know," the accountant shook her head, "you just won $20,000 worth of stuff and you said you never won anything before…"

"We did avoid all those cars…" Lou spoke tentatively.

Emily looked at her husband; he was nodding like he was buying into it.

"Tim," Emily spoke breathlessly, "you don't really believe the tattoo made these things happen, do you?"

"It is wild, Em," he shrugged, "if we hadn't stopped to coat the tattoos with oil, we would've been in the wrong place in line."

"You guys are all crazy," she admonished her companions playfully.

Lou held up his champagne glass and laughed,

"To Buena Suerte, as the Spanish say: good luck."

The others touched their glasses on his and repeated the words like a mantra,

"To Buena Suerte, good luck!"

28

Tim called Emily from the museum around ten in the morning.

"You out of bed?"

She laughed, "Barely."

His beautiful wife was dead asleep when Tim left for work two hours earlier. He couldn't help but smile thinking of the night before.

The Hoyles returned to their apartment at quarter to nine and had sex until quarter to one. It seemed Emily had taken the wild home from Wildwood. She stuck her hand down Tim's pants again and it made him crazy. He still felt crazy and he couldn't stop thinking about her.

"You should see all the stuff in this basket," Emily was amazed; "there's a wad of gift cards in here that would choke a horse!"

"Really? Is there a horse in there too? It was heavy enough."

"Maybe," Emily chuckled, "I haven't made a dent in it yet."

"Lou called, we're gonna go to the gym after work," Tim went on, "he said Mrs. Genardi will make us all dinner, OK?"

"Yum," Emily readily agreed, "I hope Mrs. G. makes Veal Scaloppini."

"Okay then," Tim said, as an afterthought he added, "Rest if you're tired."

Emily put on a sexy voice, "I'll rest for tonight."

Ooooo, Tim thought as he hung up the phone, it felt like a verbal hand down his pants.

As soon as Emily cradled the phone it rang again.

"Em, what d'ya say we do a little shopping today?"

Dana giggled as she went on, "Last night Lou threw me on the bed and my nightie was so old it ripped right down the back!"

"Sounds convenient," Emily retorted.

"Oooo, you're bad." Dana cooed.

Emily laughed; it sounded like it had been a wild night at the Torroni's too.

"Sure, sounds great. I'll bring some of these gift cards,"

She eyed the prizes spread all over the dining room table,

"We could shop for a year with the cards in this basket!"

It was unusual, Tim left his office at five on the dot; he was eager to meet Lou at the gym. He hadn't been working out regularly and he hoped to improve that situation. After pushing the down button on the elevator he waited. The steel doors opened and a gaggle of women poured out.

Mary Egress exited last; she was the museum's capable supervisor of volunteers.

"Dr. Hoyle, we were just coming to your office."

Tim smiled politely.

Mary always reminded him of Aunt Bea from the Andy Griffith show; not so much in the way she looked but the way she talked.

"Doctor, these are the new docents."

"Girls," Mary addressed the dozen young ladies accompanying her, "This is Dr. Tim Hoyle, he is the man in charge of the new annex so many of you will be working with him in the upcoming year."

Volunteers were such an invaluable asset to the museum. Tim shook each young woman's hand and welcomed her by name to the museum family.

When he finally stepped into the elevator he was practically dizzy.

"Nice to meet you, Dr. Hoyle."

"Nice to meet you, Dr. Hoyle."

"Nice to meet you, Dr. Hoyle."

Twelve times in a row…Dr. Hoyle, Dr. Hoyle, Dr. Hoyle.

That does have a nice ring to it; Tim thought as he approached his car in the museum's parking area. Funny, it was the first time since he earned his doctorate that he didn't cringe when he was called by his title.

Tim unlocked his BMW with the remote key and reached for the handle. He was distracted by movement near his back tire. Litter, he thought, moving to pick up the paper blowing toward his car. He hated litter near the museum.

At closer look the little paper looked like a dollar bill.

Hah, he thought as he bent down, I won't get fooled again; the last time he thought he'd found money in the street it was a porno ad printed to look like a twenty!

It is money, Tim thought with surprise as he stood up. Shock enveloped him; it was a hundred dollar bill! The assistant curator looked around; he was the only person in the employee parking area.

Wow, he thought climbing into the driver's seat; I never found more than a coin in the street. He couldn't wait to tell Emily that she wasn't the only lucky one.

Driving toward the gym, he fingered the hundred in his pocket and pondered his good fortune; he knew exactly what Dana would say:

"Buena Suerte!"

Lou hung his suit jacket in the gym locker and started unbuttoning his shirt. Tim was a little late. The big man hoped his friend remembered; their workout sessions had become a little sporadic as of late and both men hoped to get back on track.

Lou hung his shirt next to his suit jacket. He eyed the golden key peeking out over his undershirt. The tattoo looked every bit as shiny as the first night it was applied. It never swelled or itched and it showed no sign of scabbing.

Wild, the handsome attorney thought; the Buena Suerte body art was unusual in many ways. He smiled at his mother's reaction to the golden key:

"Tony, peel that crazy thing off and eat."

Lou had joined his mom at the nursing home early that morning for breakfast. With his weekend out of town, he missed his regular Sunday afternoon visit. Katerina Torroni still looked the picture of health. She ate her breakfast heartily and Lou couldn't have been more pleased.

"Yo, Louie Boy, sorry I'm late."

Tim threw his gym bag down on the bench and started to unlock the locker next to Lou's. The blond man went on excitedly as he opened the little metal door,

"You'll never guess what happened to me; I found a hundred dollar bill in the parking lot near work!"

Lou eyed the bill Tim held up as proof.

"Get out," Lou laughed, "I never found money in the street; once I found a five dollar chip in the parking lot in Atlantic City."

As Tim changed into his workout clothes Lou pointed toward the lion tattoo gleaming on his buddy's shoulder,

"Dana would say the lion sent you the money!"

"Yeah," the blond man snickered, "Buena Suerte!"

Lou was surprised at Tim's strength in the weight room.

"You been coming here without me?" he asked his lanky buddy.

Tim insisted that his last workout was a month ago, same as Lou's.

The former wrestler's strength was legendary but that day he felt a little weaker than usual. Blaming it on the lack of regular exercise Lou cut back the amount of weight he lifted. Tim on the other hand was every bit as strong as his last workout, he actually bench pressed ten pounds more than his personal record.

Spotting his friend on squats, Lou noticed that Tim's body looked more muscular: he was definitely filling out. Tim was a pretty skinny guy when they first met.

"You sure you're not working out without me?" Lou prodded.

Tim again replied negatively. Never much of an athlete, he was never into regular exercise until he met Lou Torroni the year before. The former wrestler had taught him a lot about weight lifting and working out in general. Lou was a great workout partner; Tim couldn't imagine the gym without Lou.

The men approached the pull up bar; they always ended their workouts there.

"Look who it is, it's Lou Torroni."

The voice came from behind them; Tim kept up his repetitions on the bar as Lou turned to see who recognized him.

"Hey, it's the Furey brothers, Frick and Frack!" the big man said jokingly.

When Tim released the pull up bar, Lou introduced him to the men standing there.

"Tim, this is Frankie and Freddie Furey, prominent tag team attorneys, as you can probably see they're twins. Boys, this is my good friend Tim Hoyle."

Tim shook hands with brothers. They were nearly as tall as Lou but beanpole thin. They were identical in everyway, down to the last freckle and strand of red hair.

"I used to kick their asses ON a court," Lou kidded, "and now I kick their asses IN a court!"

"The hell you did," Frank responded, "you never played ball better than us."

Tim smiled; the gangly brothers seemed to concede Lou's superiority in the court room.

"Hey," Lou rubbed an old wound with salt, "look up the stats, boys, who was on the championship team?"

"We couldn't carry the whole team, Torroni!" Fred Furey sounded exactly like his brother.

Lou explained to Tim that the three men had played high school basketball in the same league; their schools were long time rivals in the city. In their senior year, Lou's team had slaughtered the twin's team in the league championship.

"Now, occasionally, I run into these boys in court," the big man finished, "slam dunk, same deal!"

The twins wore identical sour expressions.

"You want to see some slam dunk, Torroni?" Frank Furey sputtered, "I bet you a grand me and my brother could take you and him two on two."

"Yeah," Fred backed up his brother, "we'll make it quick, half court two on two, first team to twenty wins."

Lou didn't immediately respond; it had been a while since he even shot baskets. Plus, it'd been a long day after a late night; he wasn't sure messing around with the Furey brothers was worth the effort.

"What's a matter, Torroni," Fred challenged.

"You afraid to lose a G?" Frank finished his brother's question.

"Boys, calm down," Lou spoke in a mock soothing voice, "I know where you work, you sure you have a thousand dollars between you?"

The twins were livid.

"You're scared, Torroni," they said in unison.

"You're on," Lou declared, "We'll meet you on the court in ten minutes."

Emily dragged the last shopping bag out of the back seat of the Mini-Cooper.

"Well if you haven't clothes shopped in a year," she said, "you made up for it today."

Dana had to agree; even she was shocked to realize she bought four bulging bags of outfits. She was grateful Emily was there to help carry it all; Dana decided to tease her friend on the way to their building's elevator,

"Yeah, and two of my giant bags equals your one tiny bag!"

Emily laughed, it was true. Earlier she couldn't resist the ring in the window at Leo Robbins. It was an uncanny match for her new necklace: precious stones in a spray of flowers. The ring didn't even have to be resized; it fit perfectly and looked stunning on her middle finger. Truthfully, what she spent probably equaled three of Dana's bags of clothes.

Emily shrugged, she quoted an old saying her father used to use,

"The heart wants what the heart wants."

Lugging the bags toward Dana's apartment Emily playfully jabbed back,

"My bag may be heavy on price, but yours are just plain heavy, my back is killing me!"

Tim and Lou approached the gym's indoor basketball court. Right before they walked through the door Lou looked down at his buddy; Tim looked rigid and his expression was grim.

"Relax, Timmie Boy. When we walk in there you gotta look like we're gonna win; that's half the fight right there."

Lou was imparting wisdom from his courtroom experience; a confident attitude could make the difference between a win and a loss.

Tim took a deep breath and smiled; he pushed his shoulders down into a more relaxed posture. After all, he really had nothing to lose but pride. Lou had already insisted

THE FLAVOR OF HEARTS

on covering Tim's half of the bet. The charismatic attorney had never asked about Tim's salary but the big man suspected he had his friend beat on payday.

As the pair entered the court they spotted the Furey brothers warming up on the far side. Tim straightened up to his full height and did his best to appear positive. Lou would've made a great gladiator, Tim thought; the big man sauntered toward their opponents like he smelled victory.

"OK, boys," Lou's voice rang out, "time to go down."

The red haired brothers approached Lou and Tim as a gray haired man came toward the two pairs from the bleachers on the sideline.

"Lou," the older gentleman spoke, "Frank and Fred asked me to referee this game. OK with you guys?"

Lou introduced the gray haired man to Tim; Jerry was part owner in the center city gym and regularly refereed the basketball games there. Tim and Lou nodded in agreement. The owner went on,

"It's totally against gym policy to gamble on the premises, so as far as I'm concerned this match is for bragging rights. I didn't hear anything about anything else, OK? I'll call this game right down the middle, any problems you have after the game, you take far away from here, understand?"

All four of the combatants nodded. Jerry flipped a coin for first possession of the ball; Lou liked the omen of winning the toss.

In the ten minutes Lou requested between the challenge and the game, the big man had questioned Tim about his experience on a basketball court. Tim wished he had more expertise to offer than playing on his junior high squad. The lanky blond told the truth: he was a pretty good dribbler and ball handler, but his shooting skills were far from great; he had a decent lay up, but he was not good enough to make his high school team.

Tim took the ball to the half court line and mentally went over the strategy Lou outlined earlier. He entered dribbling with his back to Frank Furey and immediately passed the ball to Lou. Tim ran toward the basket in time to receive the return pass and laid the ball up on the backboard. The shot rolled around the rim and the ball fell into Fred's waiting hand.

"Shit, Tim thought as he chased the red haired twin toward the half court line. As Lou ran past his partner to cover Frank he whispered into the blond man's ear,

"Don't worry, Tim, relax!"

The Furey brothers had the mental connection teammates develop, a link made even stronger by their bond as twins; Fred rocketed a pass behind his back to his brother. Fred leaped gracefully into the air sending an arcing jump shot through the hoop.

Two points ahead Frank handed the ball to Lou with a smirk,

"Two down, eighteen to go."

Lou sauntered to half court; Tim did have a good lay up, the last one should've gone in. The big man stepped in bounds and fired the ball to his waiting buddy; Tim faked Frank to the right and charged left toward the basket, this time Tim's perfect lay up went right through the hoop.

Cheers erupted from the sidelines; apparently word had spread around the gym about the thousand dollar game.

Frank Furey took the ball in from half court; Tim tried to block the taller man, but the twin easily shot the ball over the assistant curator's head. The ball bounced off the backboard through the hoop; putting the Fureys ahead again.

Tim stepped in bounds and faked a pass, fooling the twin guarding him. The lanky blond took advantage of the opening and drove toward the basket. Fred Furey slipped by Lou and aggressively moved toward the assistant curator. As he left the ground for his third lay up Tim felt himself flying sideways through the air; the lanky blond hit the ground hard to the sound of the referee's whistle.

"Foul!" the referee called.

He raised his hand halting the Furey brother's protests.

"Two shots!" he told the groaning twins; by his expression it was easy to see that Jerry was not going to allow this game to descend into a street brawl.

Tim took his place on the foul line. For once he was grateful for the hours he spent as a kid shooting baskets alone in the park near his house; Tim loved to shoot foul shots.

Swish. The first shot easily met its mark.

Cheers again erupted from the bleachers. Lou hoped Tim wouldn't be distracted by the unexpected audience. The amount of spectators had grown; from the intensity of the viewer's responses Lou was sure many of them were also ignoring the gym's rule prohibiting gambling.

Swish. The second foul shot followed the first through the net.

The score see-sawed back and forth; the two teams were never more than four points apart. All four men glistened with sweat. Lou was feeling the effects of the intense aerobic exercise but adrenaline also filled his body and now more than ever he wanted to pound the Fureys into the ground.

The score was 16-16. Lou took the ball to the half court line. Stepping into bounds he avoided Frank's defense; dribbling twice he faked a pass to Tim. Then, shocking everyone, Lou shot the ball from two feet shy of the half court mark. Every eye followed the arcing ball headed toward the backboard.

The long shot seemed like it was in the air for an hour.

Swish, nothing but net!

The spectators erupted; it was an amazing shot by any standards. The Fureys groaned in frustration. Tim ran toward his partner, slapping Lou on the back he grinned,

"Way to go, Louie! Way to go!"

Frank Furey approached the men near half court with the ball,

"Fucking luck, Torroni. You guys didn't win yet."

Lou stood in front of Frank as the twin dribbled the ball into bounds; the freckled man slammed a pass from half court to his brother. Tim anticipated the move and intercepted the ball. With his heart pounding he quickly dribbled toward the half court line. From the corner of his eye Tim saw Frank Furey headed his way; he could hear Fred pounding the floor from behind.

Tim fired the ball toward Lou. The big man was still standing near the half court line. By his shocked expression Tim knew his partner was surprised by the interception as well.

The Fureys followed the ball and raced toward Lou. Almost in slow motion Lou Torroni left the floor and gracefully arced a jump shot from half court.

Every head turned; every eye in the gym followed the ball floating toward the basket.

Swish!

The eruption was immediate; the impromptu audience cheered the incredible shot like the last score in an NBA championship. Tim leaped in the air with both hands raised; he never felt so exhilarated. He ran down the court and jumped on Lou. The big man was still riveted in the same spot; Lou T. was thrilled but he didn't have an ounce of energy left to show it.

He banged chest to chest with Tim, celebrating as athletes do and spectators poured from the bleachers to congratulate the two winners.

The Furey brothers came through the crowd.

Frank Furey held out a check for $1000.

"You're a lucky bastard, Torroni!"

Shock was etched identically on each twin's face.

Fred Furey echoed his brother's sentiments,

"They were the luckiest shots I ever saw."

"Hey," Tim interjected, defending his friend, "once is luck, twice is skill!"

The twins shook their red heads in unison as they headed toward the locker room.

Frank called over his shoulder, "Torroni, you are the luckiest man alive!"

29

Bartolomeo went to Ildefonso's room. The air conditioning was probably set on 60 degrees. Fonso was sprawled on his massive sectional sofa watching the movie "300" on his equally massive television: a one hundred and three inch Panasonic HD TV with full surround sound.

Every member of the family loved television, there were screens in almost every room hooked to satellite and every available form of cable TV. Fonso watched basketball, hockey, soccer, pro fighting and any movie with non-stop action; "300" portrayed the Spartans historic stand against the Persians at Thermopylae, a movie right up the big man's alley.

Ildefonso lowered the thundering audio when his brother entered.

Bartolomeo got right to the point. "Fonso, do you think Itzi is considering staying out?"

Staying out? At first Ildefonso misunderstood the question.

Itzi had joined the big man the previous evening night clubbing; the two brothers had spent their first night off in a high roller suite in Atlantic City with some stunning women. Females in droves were drawn to Itzamna; he was four feet tall but perfectly built and where it counted he was far more endowed than most men. Other than his stature it was exactly the same for Ildefonso; women practically threw themselves at him.

"I don't know. Itzi was pretty tired," Fonso said slyly, "but he'll be ready for round two by tomorrow night! You should come along, Tolo," the big man pointed toward his brother's laptop and the pile of books Bartolomeo had been carrying; "you should take your nose out of that stuff once in awhile."

"I don't mean stay out like that, Fonso," Bartolomeo answered quietly, "I mean on the night of First Father."

Ildefonso's handsome jaw dropped; he was stunned by the suggestion.

"You must be kidding, Tolo! Itzi? He would never! He's the Ah K'uhun!" Fonso used one of their brother's official Mayan titles, it literally meant "he of the holy books".

"What would make you say such a thing?" the big man was incredulous.

"He's been acting weird," Bartolomeo countered, "you said so yourself the other night."

"Hey," Ildefonso quickly defended his former words, "I said he was in a weird mood, I didn't say he was acting crazy!"

The brothers sat in silence, but Fonso could see Bartolomeo was clearly troubled.

"Tolo," the big man spoke more softly, "what makes you say this? Do you really think he's acting so differently?"

"He said he was wrong the other night, he's never said that in his life, Fonso!"

The big man glanced at the photos he had recently re-hung in his living area.

"He was wrong about Anita and Aneela. He realized it and he admitted it. It took him a while..." Ildefonso's voiced trailed off, then he added an honest observation, "Actually, Tolo, I can't think of another time Itzi has been wrong!"

Bartolomeo threw out another argument. "He thanked us at his birthday dinner, he thanked us for being with him, he's never done that."

"Bullshit, he's always acted grateful to us...especially that first night." Ildefonso clearly recalled the terrifying first Move,

"Tolo, he gave you that very bracelet, he thanked each of us personally!"

Bartolomeo shook his head slowly looking down at the gold band around his wrist; he desperately wanted to believe nothing was wrong with Itzamna.

"Maybe he's talked to the god again," Tolo began thinking out loud, "maybe he knows what's going to happen to us after the Union of First Father with First Mother...maybe that's why he's acting strange, maybe it isn't good!"

Ildefonso shrugged. Speculation of Itzamna's communion with the great Chac was certainly out of bounds. Fonso eyed the photos on the wall again as he answered,

"I don't think he's acting any differently," the big man insisted, "other than changing his mind about Anita and Aneela."

It definitely felt good to speak of their older sisters once more. In his mind's eye Ildefonso pictured Itzi the night before...the little man had been totally relaxed; he had thoroughly enjoyed the partying and the attention of the females.

"Itzi is fine. Believe me, he would never do anything against the will of his god, our god," Fonso immediately corrected himself.

Bartolomeo nodded. He had come to Ildefonso hoping to be convinced that everything was all right.

"You worry too much because you think too much, Tolo." Fonso pointed to his brother's books again and changed the subject, "What are you working on now?"

Bartolomeo was a genius in his own right; he devoured libraries in every place they had ever lived. His room was half library, half laboratory; his amazing mechanical devices were all over the house. It was Bartolomeo who had designed and built the satellite system that provided the family with television and broadband internet even in the most remote places.

Even Itzi had been impressed when Tolo put a tiny conveyor belt under the work bench in the tattoo parlor to send the customer's cards from the lobby to the cash drawer; Bartolomeo's invention preceded Henry Ford's by five hundred years!

"I'm magnetizing a microscopic slurry of saline and mercury, then flip flopping its polarity," Bartolomeo's voice took on a less troubled tone, "it gives off heat."

"That's one of the things I love most about you, Tolo," Ildefonso admitted, "Half the time I don't know what the hell you're talking about!"

"Hopefully it'll generate useable power," Tolo laughed, "like a battery."

Fonso nodded. He didn't totally understand but he certainly appreciated the fruits his brother's advanced ideas.

"You're coming out with us tomorrow night, Tolo," Ildefonso insisted with a twinkle in his eye, "you need a girl to suck the worries out of you!"

"Yeah, maybe," Bartolomeo grinned, "I'll take the leftovers."

Tolo always claimed he went unnoticed between the handsome giant Ildefonso and cute little Itzamna.

"Hey, remember what that beauty queen said!" Fonso reminded his sibling.

The three brothers had met the reigning Miss America at the Palms Hotel in Las Vegas a few years prior. When she went off with Bartolomeo she made her choice very clear: she said Fonso was too big, Itzi was too small and...

"I was just right!" Tolo said grinning from ear to ear.

"Yeah, and she was fine!" the big man said licking his lips.

Bartolomeo agreed. That was a night he would never forget. He scooped up his books and headed for the door.

"Don't forget, Tolo," Ildefonso called after him, "tomorrow night, you're going out with us!"

Bartolomeo waved as he left. He appreciated his younger brother's easy going attitude more each day; Fonso never seemed to worry. Bartolomeo resolved to try to do the same.

30

Ildefonso raised the movie's audio but he had lost all interest in the Spartans defense of the pass at Thermopylae.

Bartolomeo's words echoed in the big man's head: "maybe he knows what's going to happen to us after the Union of First Father with First Mother".

Chac had called their great odyssey a journey; clearly a journey has a beginning and an end. Ildefonso chided himself, Tolo thinks too much and I probably think too little. Fonso had never given a single consideration to the journey's end.

He clearly remembered the beginning; Fonso's thoughts flew back to ancient Uxmal. The big man easily recalled his amazement when he felt the metal blade on the axe Chac had given his tiny brother.

Fonso smiled wryly. That axe had changed everything; it had changed his heart. Before that night the big man was far from religious. Oh, he followed the rituals and said all the proper words; but in truth, when the priests looked to the sky and called on the great gods, Fonso was positive they spoke to empty air.

As a warrior in Uxmal's army Fonso accepted the blessings of the priests and fulfilled their supposedly god given demands;

he prayed for the god's protection with his soldiers but secretly he was sure that they could only rely on themselves.

Of course Ildefonso hid his real beliefs; he would not disgrace his family with such heresy. When Itzamna was named the High Priest Fonso buried his feelings even deeper; to this very day he had never told a single soul that he ever doubted the existence of their gods.

Again Fonso thought back to the night in Uxmal when Itzi had called them all to their mother's house. When the High Priest relayed the story of Chac's visit Fonso honestly thought his oldest brother had lost his mind. That is until the little man revealed the amazing weapon he had brought wrapped in a tapir skin.

Twenty days later Ildefonso personally stood guard at the pyramid temple; standing at the top of the first stairway the big man never took his eyes off Itzi's home on the peak. In the darkest part of the night Fonso saw a flash above in the House of the Magician; it looked like lightning had gone off indoors! The big man fought the urge to run up there; fitfully he stayed on the spot the where Itzamna had placed him.

About a half hour later the tiny High Priest had emerged and motioned for Ildefonso to approach; Fonso took the second stairs to the pyramid's summit two at a time. His older brother told him of the god's return and the instructions Chac had given.

At dawn from their high vantage point Itzi selected an elevation just outside the city. Later that day Ildefonso had taken five of his most trusted soldiers to that hill and cleared a square on top of all vegetation.

Fonso remembered the last day in Uxmal like it had just happened.

Early in the morning on the day of First Father he and Tolo had taken their mother's household belongings and carefully concealed them on the cleared hilltop. She had wrapped her best pots, bowls, baskets, knives and spice containers in a tightly tied blanket woven from bark.

THE FLAVOR OF HEARTS

That afternoon after the High Priest's holy rituals were complete, Ildefonso had accompanied Itzamna to the hilltop; carefully the little man made his calculations and placed the stones painted in Chac's sacred colors on the four cardinal directions.

Fonso left a soldier in his command to guard the hilltop and returned to the city with Itzi. The High Priest instructed his brother to bring their family with their personal belongings to the designated spot before sunset.

"Then come to the temple," Itzi had said "and I will leave Uxmal with you."

Fonso clearly remembered his brother's face; the little man was pale and his voice choked on the last of his words.

Ildefonso returned to his home at the House of the Warriors. The big man recalled perusing his quarters. What does one take on a journey into the unknown?

Fonso put aside his two best obsidian knives and put the rest on a deerskin. He laid his supply of obsidian spear tips there as well. He then added his spear thrower, a blowgun, a slingshot, a wooden mallet with a heavy stone head, all his spare arrows, darts and the tools he used to make and repair the weapons.

Lastly he included his personal valuables: his jade bowl and drinking cup, jade ornaments, jewelry and his ornate ceremonial breast plate, fashioned from jade, shells and intricately woven beads. The big man rolled the skin, tied it tightly with hide strips and lashed it to three of his heaviest spears.

As the sun began to wane Ildefonso donned his best armor: a chest plate and back piece made of squares of bone tightly stitched to a fitted tapir hide. He slipped his hands through matching forearm protectors and added a similar piece around his neck that protected his upper arms. Finally he sheathed the two obsidian knives on his belt and slung a full quiver of arrows over one shoulder.

The big man decided to carry his helmet; he'd be far less conspicuous on the way to his mother's house with the plumed head gear under his arm. Placing his wooden bow over the other shoulder, he picked up the loaded deerskin and left the House of the Warriors for the last time.

Ildefonso noticed some curious looks on the way to his family home but he dodged anyone with the status to ask questions. He could tell his mother and sisters were terrified when he arrived. Bartolomeo was putting on a brave face, but Fonso could tell his brother was pertified as well.

The whole family had their belongings ready wrapped tightly in animal skins. They wore their finest jade jewelry and ceremonial clothes.

Keeping a close eye on the waning sun Fonso took his mother's bag and urged his family to go. Bravely they hefted their belongings and followed. Fonso almost laughed when he saw the plants his sisters held in watertight baskets under their arms.

Fearing further curiosity the big man chose a lightly traveled route from the city and they circled back to the designated hilltop.

The big man hid his companions from view and dismissed the soldier he had left on guard. When he was sure the man was out of earshot Ildefonso ushered his family into the clearing.

Fonso sat his mother on a large stump he had put aside when they cleared the hilltop. The big man motioned for his sisters to comfort her; though her eyes were glistening when she left the city, now the spirit woman was openly weeping.

Bartolomeo unsheathed his own obsidian knife when Fonso told him to watch over the family.

"Don't be nervous, Tolo," the big man assured his brother, "I'll be right back with Itzi."

31

Fonso planned to escort Itzamna down the temple's rear stairway, away from the prying eyes in the buildings near the front.

As the big man trotted through Uxmal's ceremonial quadrangle he realized the High Priest had plans of his own. Itzi was already standing at the foot of the pyramid's front stairs. He was wearing his best traveling clothes; a gleaming jaguar pelt was draped over his well formed shoulders and at his feet laid two large bags exquisitely made from jaguar skins and other exotic hides.

Nervously Ildefonso eyed a line of priests atop the pyramid's first level; clearly they were watching their leader and wondering what was going on.

"Ah K'uhun," Fonso bowed his head as he greeted his brother, "I would've come up for you."

"No need," the little man made a move toward picking up his bags.

Fonso immediately grabbed the High Priest's belongings and followed as his tiny brother strode down the center of the main causeway at the pyramid's front. The big man felt a thousand eyes on them as the pair made their way past the city's school, the army barracks and the ball court; people stared but no man had the nerve to question them.

Itzi never looked back until just before they left the city limits; the little man took one backward glance at Uxmal then plunged into the rainforest.

For the first time Ildefonso took the lead and safely led his tiny brother through the thick foliage. As they made their way up the designated hill Fonso broke the palpable tension.

"Itzi," the big man grinned and spoke over his shoulder, "what's in these bags? They're heavier than I am soaking wet!"

"My ceremonial breast pieces and headdress, my figures and bowls, pik hu'un, cocoa beans...." Itzi's voice trailed off.

Fonso expected the contents to be heavy, as the High Priest Itzamna possessed pounds and pounds of jade: the Yucatan's most valuable commodity. He imagined his tiny brother took half the library and all the stored cocoa if books and beans were responsible for the rest of the weight.

"I took the ball." Itzamna suddenly sounded like a young boy.

Fonso still remembered his surprise, that night the big man almost stopped dead in his tracks.

"The Sacred Game Ball?" Ildefonso was shocked.

"I wanted it." Itzi stated flatly, "Let them make another."

Now he sounded totally like the High Priest again. Fonso almost laughed. As the pair reached the hill's summit the big man held back the tree branches and allowed Itzi to enter the clearing first.

The family's relief was apparent; they crowded around the High Priest as he hugged their mother. Fonso was relieved to see she was no longer crying.

"Thank you all," Itzi looked around the circle of faces surrounding him, "my thanks to each of you for coming on the lord's journey."

"We are a family," the spirit woman answered for all of them, "and we will stay a family."

Fonso brought the second stump he had saved for a chair. He seated Itzi on one and his mother on the other. The rest

THE FLAVOR OF HEARTS

sat on the cleared earth surrounding them as they waited for total darkness. Ever vigilant Ildefonso stayed on his feet at Itzi's side.

The air was cool but the potential was there for a frigid night. The sky was clear; now stars twinkled through the opening in the dense foliage.

Itzi eyed the constellations visible above; suddenly he rose. The sky was cloudless, but he was sure he felt a rain drop. When the High Priest suddenly stood the others immediately did the same.

It was an unmistakable sound; raindrops were slowly starting to fall through the surrounding trees. The family felt the rain as it fell harder. Surely it was the great Chac's message...they were in the midst of the dry season!

As they all craned their necks toward the sky surprise gave way to amazement; there wasn't a cloud above, the stars shone brightly through the falling water.

The rain progressed from a sprinkling, to a downpour, to torrential sheets; Fonso herded the family into a tight group. The ground below was softening; rivulets of mud and water were swirling at their feet.

Fonso felt himself sinking into the muck. After freeing his own legs the big man lifted Itzamna by the shoulders and pulled him from the muddy ground. The rain was so heavy they could barely see through it.

Thunder rumbled in the distance. Again Ildefonso freed his feet from the mud. Bartolomeo kept both hands on their mother's shoulders; it was becoming difficult to stay standing on the eroding ground.

A crack of thunder cancelled the sound of the driving rain; it was so sharp it hurt their ears. Lightning followed; its brightness was blinding.

Soaked they all fought for balance as the cleared ground washed away. Ildefonso grabbed Itzi and again freed the little man from the mud that was halfway up his miniature shins. This time Fonso did not release his grip; he held his tiny brother tightly lest the rushing water carry High Priest off.

Although it hardly seemed possible the thunder grew louder. Each eruption pounded their ears, the pressure became extremely painful. Bartolomeo fought hard to support their mother; he was sure the spirit woman was on the verge of collapse.

As huge lightning bolt cracked in the clearing the girls began screaming. Suddenly Fonso feared for all of their lives. Another enormous bolt of lightning pierced the air, Ildefonso blinked; he could feel the rain but he was totally blind; a burning acrid smell filled his nose.

32

    The sudden quiet was deafening. Fonso could feel that he was no longer wet; the big man was sure he was dead. He blinked his eyes repeatedly, his vision was returning but everything was fuzzy.
    Fonso realized he was still clutching Itzi; the big man released his iron grip and focused on his tiny brother. Itzamna was wide eyed.
    "Ah K'uhun, are you all right?" Ildefonso realized he was talking very loud.
    Itzi nodded affirmatively, but he looked shaken.
    With his eyesight fully restored the big man now stared in shock at the High Priest; all the decorative jade imbedded in Itzi's teeth was gone along with the ceremonial tattoos that previously circled the little man's forehead and cheeks. Itzamna's face was as bare as the day he was born!
    Suddenly Ildefonso realized Itzi was staring back at him the same way. The big man raised a hand and felt his own forehead. It felt smooth; the intricate scarred pattern near his hairline was gone! By Itzi's expression the big man assumed his own facial tattoos had disappeared as well.
    As he heard the gasps around him the big man realized his hearing had fully returned. When he heard laughter Fonso

almost exploded in a rage. What could anyone find funny in this situation?

Following the sounds he focused on his youngest sisters; they were pointing at him and roaring with amusement. A rebuke stuck in his throat when he took a closer look at them; a strange material was draped on their bodies, it was belted under their breasts and billowed around them hanging almost to their ankles. Their feet were obscured with pale green coverings; Fonso had never seen such footgear.

It made the big man look down at his own feet; he was floored by the well tooled red leather sandals he was wearing. Fonso realized he too was dressed in weird attire; he ran his hands over the white linen; he had never felt anything like it; it was as soft as bird feathers.

It was two pieces: a long undergarment and a second piece draped over his shoulder wrapped around and fastened over his opposite arm. He could feel a soft loincloth wrapped around his private parts and tied on the side; Ildefonso was dumbfounded. Eying the rest of the family it was clear they were all equally as puzzled by their sudden odd clothing.

For the first time Fonso examined their surroundings. He berated himself, as a military man he should've immediately thought of securing their location.

It was a rectangular room, all stone; the far end looked like it led further into the building. Ildefonso was astonished by the polished marble floor; he could almost see his reflection. Colorful paintings covered the side walls: ornate geometric patterns and human figures. A large square was hollowed out of the middle of the floor; it appeared to be full of water!

When Itzi moved toward the room's center Ildefonso followed at his tiny brother's side. Dropping to one knee Itzi placed a finger in the pool and touched his lips; it was fresh water.

"A sign from our lord Chac," Itzi spoke reverently of the Mayan god of rain and thunder.

Looking up Fonso spotted a hole in the ceiling directly above the indoor pool; he tapped the High Priest on the shoulder and pointed to the stars visible through the opening. Amazingly rainwater was funneled through the hole and collected in the hollowed out square below.

Noting the night sky Fonso suddenly realized the room was well lighted; looking around he saw two flaming braziers in opposite corners of the room. Bartolomeo was already examining one of the strange light fixtures with their mother.

Three narrow legs supported a bowl filled with oil, fire burned brightly from a wick inserted in the middle. The strange light was made from a material they didn't recognize; it resembled the blade of Chac's axe, but didn't gleam as brightly. Four small closed vessels made of the same material hung from hooks attached to the bowl.

A rumbling noise distracted Fonso; it grew louder as the big man pinpointed its location. He strode back toward a narrow doorway at the room's near end and ducked through the opening seeking the sound's source. Ildefonso found himself in a small passageway; his eyes adjusted to the unlit space, the unidentifiable noise was coming from a narrower exit at the opposite end.

By the rush of fresh air Fonso guessed it was the way out. The sound reverberated; it wasn't thunder but it rumbled; a mysterious clanging sound accompanied the roar; the big man stepped outside into the waning darkness just as a carriage flew by.

Ildefonso gaped, he had never seen anything but a jaguar move that fast on land. The vehicle's iron covered wheels made an unworldly racket on the cobblestone street. Frozen the big man watched the strange contraption disappear from sight.

Turning his head in the opposite direction Fonso could make out stone buildings lining the street. Stepping into the road the big man eyed the building he had just exited: it was two stories high; three narrow openings faced the front. Strange interlocking pieces covered the roof.

His gaze was drawn farther upwards, palatial stone structures lined the hillside above; some were enormous. Light glowed from tiny slits in their polished walls.

Fonso heard drumming to his right, when he turned two of the biggest animals he had ever seen were bearing down on him. Jumping back toward the building the big man flattened himself against the façade. He didn't breathe until the team of draft horses thundered by. At top speed they pulled a delivery wagon loaded with wine casks. The wagon bed slammed up and down and the iron horse shoes made a din like Ildefonso had never heard.

Let alone what he had heard; he couldn't believe his own eyes! What kind of vehicle was that? Fonso staggered back into the building. He didn't expect them all to be clustered around the entrance; they didn't expect him to look like he saw a ghost.

"What was that noise, Fonso?" at first Itzi sounded merely curious but he was becoming more concerned by his brother's expression.

"I...I don't know." it was rare that Ildefonso sounded bewildered.

The High Priest's eyebrows shot up in surprise.

It was difficult enough for Fonso to describe the draft horses but drawing a verbal picture of the wagon was nearly impossible. Though the three part Mayan calendar was based on a series of rotating wheels strangely the Maya had never harnessed the physical power of the wheel.

"It was like a square canoe perched on top of our calendar, two Tzolkien on each side spinning so fast a second would be a day! It flew by on the ground faster than anything I have ever seen. It moved ten times faster than any boat on the river during the rains or near the falls!" Ildefonso's words picked up speed and he finished breathlessly, "Two giant animals ran ahead of it as fast as jaguars, the drumming was their feet on the stone street!"

Curiosity immediately drove Bartolomeo and the girls toward the door but Fonso blocked the way. The big man appealed to Itzi as their leader.

"Ah K'uhun, there are a multitude of buildings on a hill above us, some as big as any I have ever seen. It is dark, but I think we are in a large and strange city. I am unarmed," Fonso gestured toward his new garments, "it may be unwise to leave this place until I find a means to protect us if the need arises."

All eyes turned to Itzamna. Though the little man was more than curious to see the oddities Fonso described he could appreciate the wise advice of his warrior brother.

"Ildefonso is right; we will at least wait for daylight to study our surroundings. For now I think we should examine this place." Itzi instructed the group, "Our great lord promised everything we would need; now it is our duty to find it."

The family turned from the entrance and headed somewhat reluctantly toward the building's interior.

The High Priest could feel his brother's distress at the loss of his weapons and his precious armor.

"Fonso, stay with me." Itzi instructed. "The great Chac promised to move our belongings; your things are here someplace but first we need to find our lord's sacred stones,"

"Fonso," Bartolomeo interrupted from the room's far corner.

He was holding one of the strange vessels that hung by a hook on the flaming lamp stand. Tolo had discerned its use; lighting the wick that protruded from the lid he held the portable lantern out toward his warrior brother.

Fonso crossed the room and took hold of the bronze oil lamp; the big man was amazed. The little vessel was hardly bigger than his hand but it furnished as much light as a burning torch.

"I think it's full of that...stuff," Bartolomeo pointed toward the olive oil filling the brazier's bowl.

Both brothers shook their head in appreciation of the invention; the thick liquid smoked and had a weird smell but it was astounding the amount of light it provided.

Looking back Fonso almost laughed out loud remembering how shocked they had all been to find that local people also cooked with the lamp oil and regularly ate it on greens and vegetables. Yet olive oil was only one of the marvelous things they saw that first night and day.

Fonso took the light toward Itzi and offered it to the High Priest; the little man examined the bronze lamp and was equally amazed. Handing it back Itzamna motioned toward the opening to the outside,

"We have to search the inside perimeter of this building, Fonso. The lord's stones are here and they will show us the cardinal directions."

Before the little man strode through the door Fonso put a hand on his brother's shoulder.

"Please, Ah K'uhun, allow me to take the lead," the big man requested. Itzi nodded; in actuality he was more than grateful for his gigantic younger brother's protective nature and his military prowess.

Entering the entrance hall they heard rumbling again from outside. Fonso knew the High Priest would not allow his own curiosity to go unsatisfied.

"Stay close to the door, Ah K'uhun," Fonso spoke forcefully over his shoulder as he exited the building for the second time.

He would take the chance of speaking disrespectfully to the High Priest if it kept tiny Itzi out of the way of those gigantic animals. A vehicle was just passing as the pair stepped through the structure's entry way.

Itzamna was astonished when he saw the wagon. It was moving at a far slower pace than the one Ildefonso had seen initially; this time the big man got a better look at the animals.

That first close sighting in the waning darkness sparked Ildefonso's life long appreciation of the horse; starting that year and in the many years following Fonso had become a skilled rider and unparalleled judge of equine quality.

Itzi was shocked by the wheels; he was slack jawed seeing them rotate and propel the cart. As much as he wanted to stay outside and see another of those amazing contraptions Itzi knew he shouldn't be deterred from his original plan, they needed to gather Chac's sacred stones and store them safely. The little man looked up toward the sky, stars were no longer visible; sunrise seemed to be approaching.

After motioning toward the building's entrance Itzamna followed as Ildefonso re-entered.

33

Little rooms and alcoves surrounded the large room with the fresh water pool; they found the first of the stones in one of these.

There were very few furnishings in the stone building; however, this room contained three long couches surrounding a low highly polished wooden table. The padded material covering the settees was softer than the robes they wore. Fonso aimed the lamp and pointed to the room's front left corner; Chac's red stone was on the floor.

"East," Itzi said aloud as he retrieved the sacred rock.

Immediately the little man looked diagonally toward his right. Quickly exiting the furnished room Itzi bee lined through another room and further into the home's interior. When the little man stopped dead in his tracks, Ildefonso almost knocked him over.

They were outside again! The light predawn sky was clearly visible above; the air was crisp and cool. Trees and bushes were arranged tastefully in the square enclosure.

"It's an indoor garden," their mother informed them. It was easy to hear she was still surprised by such a thing. Their youngest sisters were carefully examining the local foliage.

Bartolomeo pointed to the entrance behind Ildefonso.

"That's the only way in or out." he informed his brothers.

Marble columns surrounded the area; doorways lined the right and back walls. Itzi ducked into the first room and emerged with Chac's black stone.

"West," he said motioning toward the room he had just exited.

"Fonso!" Anita's voice rang out from above.

The family looked toward the sound of her voice; she and Aneela were on a second floor balcony that circled the indoor garden above. She pointed to a doorway barely visible under the colonnade's roof.

"We found your armor and your weapons!"

Immediately Ildefonso's eyes darted around the garden searching for the way up.

"There," Anita and Aneela said in unison pointing toward a stairway to the left of the courtyard's entrance.

Fonso fought the urge to run up; instead the big man looked toward Itzi. The High Priest requested help finding the sacred stones and Ildefonso's military discipline would not allow him to abandon his given task. Smiling Itzi motioned toward the stairs knowing Fonso would be much happier once he was armed again.

With a slight bow of his head the big man ran to his left and took the stairs three at a time. The girls let him enter the room first. His rolled deerskin and armor were placed neatly on the bed along with his bow and full quiver of arrows. His plumed bone helmet was on a chair in the corner along with his belt, loincloth and two best obsidian knives.

Immediately Fonso tied the belt around his waist under the top layer of the odd clothing he wore. When he slipped the largest of the knives in its hide sheath at his back he sighed with relief.

"Is that the beast you saw outside?" Anita asked quizzically.

The two girls had entered behind him. They were pointing toward an ornate painting of a charioteer on the bedroom's wall. Four horses were reared up on their back legs, the vehicle was different but that was certainly the animals!

Fonso nodded, impressed by the perfect rendition.

"But there were only two, and that was different...."

The big man's voice trailed off; he had no idea what to call the first vehicle he had seen that day let alone this one. Though Fonso wanted to examine the weird image more closely he was sure Itzi would be impatient to continue his search.

Fonso immediately returned to the balcony and perused the garden below; Itzamna was already gone! The big man ran down the steps at full speed; Bartolomeo eased his larger brother's rising concern and pointed toward a doorway at the garden's rear. By the time Fonso reached its entrance the High Priest was emerging holding the yellow stone.

"South." the little man stated gesturing behind with his head.

Bartolomeo suddenly called out from the garden's center.

"Ah K'uhun, the mark of our lord!"

He was pointing toward two stone chests nestled in the greenery beside another central pool of water. The glyph of the Mayan god of rain was expertly carved on both lids; Itzamna immediately recognized the boxes Chac spoke of the second night on the pyramid.

"Tolo, don't touch those," the little man warned, "don't let anybody else touch them either."

"Fonso," he continued, "north has got to be toward the front of this place, but I don't remember seeing see the white stone up there."

Slight tension had creeped into Itzi's voice.

"We will find it," the big man picked up the oil lamp he had previously laid on the stone floor and turned toward the garden's entrance.

Striding past the indoor water pool Fonso aimed the light toward the front room's left corner; surprisingly the stone was not there.

"That has to be north," Itzi sounded clearly annoyed.

Ildefonso pointed toward the home's narrow front entranceway.

"There is more of this place than we think, Ah K'uhun." Fonso was through the opening before he finished the sentence; he suddenly remembered the three entrances on the building's façade.

On his third trip outside the oil lamp was unnecessary; daylight was coming into full bloom. The street was now crowded with people walking and vehicles of all varieties. Servants carried curtain clad litters with well dressed men perched inside.

Fonso stared slack jawed at a man on horseback; it had never occurred to the big man that people would stride the great beasts and ride. Ildefonso looked down at Itzi; his little face was lit up with sheer amazement. The noise was almost deafening to the two men fresh from the Yucatan.

Looking back toward the traffic Ildefonso deduced that he and his brother were dressed as well as any of the city's upper class residents. It was easy to see someone's station by the differing qualities of the garments they wore; especially the coarse brown materials in the clothing of the servants or possibly slaves.

Eventually Fonso realized the strange people found Itzi just as curious a sight; some stared openly at the tiny gentleman, especially the children going by.

"Ah K'uhun," Ildefonso pointed toward the opening to the left of the building's main entrance.

Walking through the door the little man sighed with relief when he picked up the white sacred stone in the room's front corner. There were two chairs in the square space with a table next to one of them. Both men gaped at the table's contents; the High Priest's tattoo kit was there.

Itzi picked up the small rolled animal skin decorated with jade and looked around the square stone room. It only had the one entrance to the street; the rest of the house was inaccessible from there.

"Well," the little man reasoned, "I guess this is where our great lord will send the offerings."

Fonso felt slightly weak kneed; the whole situation was becoming overwhelming. A strange aroma unexpectedly reached the big man's nose. Fonso couldn't identify the smell but it made his stomach growl; he realized it wasn't his courage waning it was his stamina, he was starving!

"What is that, Fonso? It smells good!" Itzi proclaimed, heading back toward the street.

The smell was even stronger outside; it permeated the air but the big man could not pinpoint its original direction.

Fonso grinned; over a thousand years had passed and he still loved the smell of fresh baked bread. He stretched his muscles and rested back on his plush sofa. Eyeing the thick gold band around his own wrist he ran his fingers over the bracelet's tooled squares; yes, there were many things about that night he would never forget.

34

Back outside Itzamna was now oblivious to the street traffic; he was taking deep breaths of the new intoxicating smell.

"I'm hungry, Fonso." the little man declared.

His appetite for food was legendary; suddenly Ildefonso feared the High Priest would take off down the street in search of the aroma's source but thankfully Itzi had a more reasonable plan.

"Let's store the stones and figure out what we're going to eat."

They found the rest of the family in the indoor garden; the girls had spread their woven bark blanket under a tree and thankfully they were already covering the surface with food.

Mama had found her household belongings in a large room next to the indoor courtyard. It was clearly the kitchen; there was a stone fireplace with an iron spit along with some far more puzzling pieces of equipment.

Fresh food lined a stone work surface; the greens and vegetables were totally unfamiliar. They found a huge ceramic container of the thick liquid they saw in the lamps; a large cask of wine mystified them; the girls ran their fingers curiously over the barrel's smooth wooden surface.

What most initially impressed the ladies were the iron cooking pots; their mother was seated on the grass next to the blanket still holding one of the smaller ones.

"Look at this Itzamna!" Mama was awestruck, "what do you think this is made of? It would outlast our children's children!"

The spirit woman turned to Fonso; by her voice it was apparent she knew her youngest son was about to be awed.

"Ildefonso, look at this," Mama reached on the ground behind her back and produced an iron meat cleaver; she grinned at her son's face as she handed him the butchering tool.

The iron blade was honed to a razor's sharpness; the hardwood handle was perfectly balanced; Ildefonso was floored.

"Fonso, it was in the kitchen," Bartolomeo was exhilarated by all the metal objects they had found, "can you imagine the weapons here, if that thing was in the kitchen?"

Ildefonso nodded; as an experienced warrior he jumped a grim step ahead of his older brother; what sort of devastating weaponry could be used against them in this new place?

"Fonso, taste this!" Aneela held up a cluster of grapes.

She broke off one of the little purple orbs and handed it to her brother. Fonso's hunger far outweighed his trepidation; he popped the soft little sphere in his mouth. When he bit down a sweet liquid burst in his mouth; his handsome face lit up with pleasure. Aneela immediately handed him the rest of the cluster.

"Watch out," she warned, "there's tiny seeds inside each little ball, don't bite down on them, they're bitter."

Fonso ate more grapes, maybe it was his hunger but nothing had ever tasted more delicious. The big man handed some to Itzi; the little man was pleased as well by the strange fruit.

The High Priest placed Chac's sacred stones on top of the chests marked with the god's glyph then joined his family now seated around the blanket under the tree. The little man's eyes

THE FLAVOR OF HEARTS

bulged out when he saw the fire roasted turkey on banana leaves in the center of the makeshift feast. Totally surprised he pointed toward his favorite food.

"Mama, where did that come from?"

"I brought it with me in my bag. I didn't know what we might find to eat..." the spirit woman's voice trailed off.

She had felt a little silly when she saw the bounty provided by the great Chac in the home's kitchen. They had found foods of all kinds there: grains, flour, vegetables, fruits; there was even a butchered animal ready to roast. All the girls had eyed the lamb quizzically, though it was about the size of a tapir it was certainly no animal they had never seen.

"I love you, Mama!" Itzi sounded like a boy again.

The little man tore off a leg and had it in his mouth before he finished the sentence. When she saw her eldest son's obvious happiness the spirit woman felt less foolish.

The family savored the turkey and vegetables Mama had brought from Uxmal. They ate their fill of the grapes and olives they found. Impressed they wondered what kind of plants grew these things.

"Maybe it's one of these trees," Itzi's youngest sister suggested.

"There's a painting in that room over there," Anita offered, pointing to doorway along the courtyard's back wall, "it shows a tree like we're sitting under with yellow balls all over it."

All eyes looked up at the lemon tree; it was bare except for green leaves.

"Maybe it blooms later in the season," Tolo wondered out loud.

"I hope they taste like these," Ildefonso held up a grape, "I could eat a mountain of these."

"You could eat a mountain of anything," Anita kidded the family giant, "you can be the food taster, Fonso, there's a lot of weird stuff in that kitchen."

"Really?" the big man's hunger was satisfied but he was curious.

The girls described the strange butchered animal and the wine cask.

Bartolomeo was still floored by the home's apparent running water.

"Itzi, see that thing over there," he pointed to a marble basin carved into the wall with a bronze spigot above it. "When you turn the top part water comes out, and it just keeps coming!" Tolo still sounded like he couldn't believe it.

Both Fonso and Itzi raised their eyebrows in surprise.

"There's a wooden box in the kitchen with a hole in it, it covers a hole in the floor," Bartolomeo went on almost breathlessly, "there's water running below it like a little river, it must wash away anything you throw in there."

"It smells like shit in that hole!" Anita said slyly.

"Anita! We are eating!" the spirit woman was surprised to hear her daughter speak this way at a meal

Itzamna shook his head laughing.

"There are many strange things here," the little man admitted.

"Most of all us." Anita retorted.

Fonso turned and tickled her belly with his huge hand,

"Speak for yourself, girl!" the big man bellowed in mock offense.

He was ready to tickle her until she cried for mercy. The whole family roared with laughter as he forced her to say he was the most normal man in the world. When the hilarity died down they sat in silence.

"We look weird," Itzi's youngest sister Waykan suddenly spoke. "I miss my birthday marks, I look like a baby."

She was pointing toward her face. Mayans adorned themselves with ritual body art; when a person sported many elaborate designs it was a sign of bravery and maturity; many scarred and tattooed designs were done as worship to the gods.

"Ah K'uhun, your teeth, your beautiful teeth..." Waykan's voice trailed off.

The Maya filed their teeth to sharp points; some say in homage to Ba'laam, their sacred animal the jaguar. Wealthy

THE FLAVOR OF HEARTS

Mayans imbedded jade stones in their filed teeth; a green smile of the precious material was considered the highest of status.

Itzi had looked just this way until that morning, as High Priest of Uxmal he had more jade in his mouth than many Maya owned. Fonso unconsciously put his hand toward the side of his own head; the thick jade ornaments that went through his pierced and stretched earlobes were gone, his ears looked the way they did the day he was born.

"I know things have changed in the way we look, Waykan," Itzi spoke softly and patiently to his youngest sister, "our god has altered our appearances to fit in easier in this new place."

She nodded but still appeared distressed. Itzi tried to further placate her.

"When you go out later today, you may become more comfortable with the way you look now."

She appeared to perk up, suddenly considering exploring the outside world.

"While I have you all here," Itzi went on, now addressing the whole family, "I want to tell you a few things."

35

Itzi stood and walked a few feet to his left. He pointed to the stone chests carved with Chac's symbol.

"These are gifts from our great lord," the High Priest began, "it is very important that you never open or remove anything from these boxes. The great Chac was very specific; he said the objects inside would not be safe to handle unless I remove them. Never remove anything from the lord's chests; do you all understand?"

One by one Itzi looked squarely at each family member and got an affirmative nod or reply. When he removed the lid from the smaller chest everyone gathered around in amazement.

Gold chains, bowls, goblets and jewelry almost overflowed the box's confines. Mixed with the gold were tooled silver and jade objects. They gawked at the gemstones inside. Itzi immediately removed a ruby; the little man had never seen anything as beautiful; a smooth oval rock the deepest color of the most sacred blood.

Itzi passed the stone to his mother; her face was full of wonder. He removed an assortment of gems and passed them around.

THE FLAVOR OF HEARTS

Anita held a brilliant green emerald up to the light; she had a diamond in her other hand.

"What are they, some kind of rocks?" she asked Bartolomeo.

He shrugged. They all agreed on the beauty of the strange stones.

Itzi removed eight gold bowls and handed them to his mother. The High Priest noticed their youngest sister had not stopped staring at the chest.

"What has caught your eye so completely, Waykan?" Itzamna smiled; she was transfixed.

Shyly the young girl pointed toward a jade necklace sticking up among the silver cups and plates. When Itzi pulled it out even he was surprised by its weight; in Uxmal only a queen would've had such adornment. He turned and handed it to his sister.

"For you, Waykan. Thank you for coming with me on our lord's journey. May this gift always remind you that you are beautiful, no matter how you may change on the outside."

She hugged her tiny older brother. Tears fell from her eyes but she was beaming as Mama helped her put the jade around her neck.

Itzi decided since he started with the youngest in the family he would go right up the line. The little man dug through the valuables; he pulled a necklace of gold braided from three separate strands, one of the clear gemstones hung like a gleaming drop of water from the chain's center.

"Ixkeem," he handed it to the older of his two youngest sisters; "this is for you. Thank you for coming with me on our lord's journey. You always see things clearly," Itzi pointed to the diamond "this makes me think me of you."

Next Itzi selected two heavy gold wristbands both woven in a criss crossing lattice pattern; it reminded the little man of the decorative carving on his former home atop Uxmal's temple pyramid.

"Fonso, my warrior brother," the little man smiled as he placed the first gold band on his gigantic brother's wrist. "I never feel safer than when you are at my side. Thank you for coming with me on our lord's journey."

"And you, Tolo," the little man grinned broadly as he placed the second on Bartolomeo, "I have yet to find a man with a mind as quick as yours. Thank you for coming on our great lord's journey."

Itzi did the same for his two older sisters and their mother; he thanked them for their loyalty and bestowed a gift he thought suited them. The women looked beautiful in their new finery. The box was about a quarter empty when Itzamna replaced the top. Quickly he removed the lid to reveal the treasure was again overflowing.

The gasps were deafening; even the unflappable Ildefonso had sucked in air and not let it out!

"How? How could it be full again?" Tolo stammered.

"Praise to our lord Chac." Itzi said, "He promised it would always be replenished."

The family exchanged shocked glances. The repercussion of a never ending box of treasure was starting to sink in; they were suddenly wealthier than even the most legendary rulers of the Mayan Empire.

They all smiled when Itzi removed a ring and put it on his own middle finger. The gold human skull dwarfed his little hand; delicate gold lightning bolts bisected shining yellow stones filling the boney eye sockets. Instantly they recalled Itzi's story of the lightning in the great god's eyes that first night on the pyramid temple.

"Praise to our great lord Chac." Bartolomeo said aloud.

The family repeated the words.

Itzi replaced the lid and opened the second chest and extracted a round stone container. Chac's glyph was delicately inlaid on the top and sides with tiny pieces of jade and gems. The High Priest gently shook the jar; he could hear the liquid inside but couldn't see how the vessel opened.

"Tolo," the little man offered the container to his brother, "the lord's sacred ink is in here. How do you think it opens?"

Curiously Bartolomeo examined the object. It was easy to see that it was in two pieces, a cylinder shaped bottom and a form fit lid. The top did not lift off, it was stuck tight. At first the young man was stymied; suddenly an idea struck him.

Tolo held the bottom of the jar with his left hand and the top of the jar with his right; he turned the two parts in opposite directions. When it moved he carefully unscrewed the top. Tiny spiraling grooves were carved into lid; matching shapes protruded on the vessel's rim. There was a pointed groove carved down the jar's inner side to facilitate the pouring of the ink

Bartolomeo was astonished by the mechanics of Chac's stone container. The rest of the family was more impressed with the ink inside: it looked like liquid gold.

"Praise to our lord Chac." Mama said reverently.

"Can you put my marks back with that, Itzi?" Waykan was again mesmerized.

Itzamna refused and recounted Chac's warnings concerning the sacred ink. Tolo carefully rescrewed the lid and handed the vessel back to the High Priest; the indescribable engineering had suddenly taken on a more ominous connotation.

After replacing the jar in the chest Itzi removed a stack of square Mayan bark papers. Reading the top five glyphs on the first sheet he could easily see it was the day's date in the Mayan Long Count calendar. Below that Itzi's own name and birthday was written; oddly a new symbol followed his first name: the glyph for dzonot, a Mayan word for a natural fresh water well or a water filled grotto. Additional lines of undecipherable lettering lined the bottom of the page.

Thumbing through the sheets he could see there was one for each of them and the new glyph had been added to everyone's name. He handed his family their personalized hu'un.

"The great lord has inscribed these for us?" Anita was thunderstruck.

Bartolomeo was astonished as well; the quality of the Mayan writing was more than perfect; as a trained scribe he had never seen such fine work. He found his voice when he noticed the new glyph.

"Dzonot...Bartolomeo Dzonot? What could this mean, Ah K'uhun?"

"Perhaps our great lord has given us a new family name," the little man guessed.

"Why would we have a new family name?" Mama asked perplexed.

Dzonot; they all let it sink in. The great lord had renamed them after a deep hole full of water. Bartolomeo laughed first.

"I believe the great Chac is showing us his sense of humor." Itzi said wryly, a dzonot was also one of the sacred ways to the Underworld.

Fonso held up his paper and pointed toward the odd writing at the bottom.

"Tolo," the big man asked, "What do you think this means?"

"Hard to say," Bartolomeo answered still looking at the strange shapes at the bottom of his own hu'un. He ventured a guess. "Maybe it's our names in the language they speak here. This could be a date, I would think."

As usual Bartolomeo was right on his first guess: their new surname was translated phonetically at the bottom in Greek, Latin and Old English as Cenotes. The odd writing ended with the day's date in the Julian calendar: December 22, 950CE.

Lastly Itzi retrieved a pile of clothing from the second chest; there was a cloak for each of them; the material was heavier than the robes they wore, clearly a covering for the colder climate. The girls immediately wrapped the material around themselves.

"I hope it doesn't get chillier than this," Mama said, pulling the covering around her shoulders.

The others nodded; though it was almost 50 degrees it was far colder than they were used to. Itzi placed Chac's four sacred stones safely in the second chest and reiterated the warning.

"Remember what I said about these boxes," Itzi said as he closed the lid, "never, ever remove anything yourself, I will retrieve anything you need or want."

The family again murmured their agreement.

Itzi went back to the first box and removed a handful of gems. He dropped them in the leather bag that he had found earlier tied to his belt.

"Fonso, maybe you and Tolo could carry these boxes to whatever room will be mine." the little man requested, "then you and I will go out and see if we can figure out where we are."

The High Priest turned to the rest of the family.

"I'm sure you are all curious. You can go out by the front of this building, but don't go any farther until Fonso and I return."

36

Before he left with Itzi Ildefonso made sure Bartolomeo was inconspicuously armed. Each of them had found their belongings in rooms around the second floor balcony.

"These puffy clothes are good to hide a weapon, eh Fonso," Tolo grinned as he strapped his own obsidian knife to his back.

"Remember that when you're out there later," the big man warned his scholarly brother, "anybody could have anything."

The High Priest appeared at the bedroom's entrance. Fonso was on his feet before the little man drew breath to ask.

"Tolo, watch for the girls and Mama." Itzi knew his sisters personalities, with a slight laugh he went on, "If Anita and Waykan run off just stay here with Mama alright?"

The men found the girls at the front of the house clustered around the first of the two doorways to the outside.

"Mama won't go outside until Tolo comes," Anita sounded slightly exasperated.

"Good," Fonso did his best to sound forceful, "remember what Ah K'uhun has said 'stay by the front of the building'. Don't run off till we see what we're up against around here. Got it, Anita, Waykan?"

They were giving him a look he didn't like; Ildefonso lowered the boom with his worst fears.

"Suppose we're smack dab in the middle of our worst enemy's stronghold and they're all armed with those kitchen axes."

All the family except Itzi now wore frightened expressions.

Feeling guilty Fonso softened his warning, "Don't be afraid; we are unknown here, we have no rivals."

Sensing their relief he put some starch back in the situation, "but we cannot allow our curiosity to make us act stupidly; we wouldn't want to wander unarmed into someone else's battle."

"Fonso is right. Stay by the house until we come back for you." Itzi looked at his youngest and oldest sisters, "I mean it. Waykan? Anita?"

"Why do you single us out?" Anita was perturbed.

Itzi didn't have to answer; the rest of the family's outburst of laughter was enough of a reply.

The street was congested with vehicles and foot traffic when they stepped out; the noise was now deafening to Ildefonso. Looking over his shoulder he could tell Itzi was stunned by the increased volume as well.

The family filed out; one by one Fonso watched their faces; he grinned broadly at the memory. Traffic was moving slowly enough for a great look at the draft horses and all sorts of carts, carriages and wagons; the use of the sacred calendar wheel to convey oneself was a stunning revelation to the rest of the family too. Bartolomeo figured out the axle system immediately, again Fonso grinned at the memory. Looking back it was definitely sensory overload; they stood awake in a dream world.

Personally Ildefonso was most affected by the men on horse back; that morning he vowed to be on top of one of those beasts as soon as possible.

Itzi motioned toward their left as he spoke to his warrior brother, "They go that way empty handed, and come back with their bundles."

Fonso had noticed the same thing. Leaving the family to their amazed observations Itzi and Fonso joined the crowd moving to their left; the High Priest was sure it was northwest. They were both amazed by the carved columns and immense stone buildings along the way.

Most of the people took a right over a causeway so the brothers followed; eventually they could see a huge marketplace in the distance down the hill. The raucous din was audible half mile away.

With a population of 25,000 Uxmal had a thriving marketplace; it was large and lively, especially during harvest times. This market was easily double the size of any they had ever seen; it even rivaled the market place at the Yucatan's larger city Chichen Itza.

The foot traffic bottlenecked at the end of the causeway. The local people spoke loudly and their language sounded hard and guttural to the Mayan brothers.

Itzi focused on the conversation of the two men directly ahead of him; they appeared to be servants. Taking Chac's advice the little man concentrated on the strange words; five or six sentences were exchanged and it sounded more and more like grunts and gibberish. Fonso too was paying close attention to the language.

Suddenly two women slid in between the brothers and the servants ahead. The older of the ladies began firing sentences directly at Itzi; he stared back blankly. She spoke even louder reeling off another barrage of words.

Miraculously, as the great Chac had promised, both brothers suddenly understood the last of her tirade.

"Are you both deaf? Or just stupid? Look here," she said to her companion, "we have big stupid and little stupid!"

Itzi stared at the youngest of the pair as he finally answered, "Forgive my rudeness; I was transfixed by your beauty."

The young redhead giggled. Fonso almost laughed out loud as well; not only did the words sound odd coming out of Itzi's head, his tiny brother was already charming the ladies with the new language. The dark haired woman turned toward Ildefonso.

"You're a tall one, and handsome too," she pressed a small square of parchment paper into his hand, "come by later, we'll give you both a discount."

The big man shook his head in amazement when he easily read the strange squiggles. It was an address along the Clivus Capitolinus for the Capo Villa Brothel. Fonso showed the paper to Itzi.

The little man understood the writing as well; he could read the words and see it was an address of a business; but he was as confused as Fonso as to what a brothel was. There is no translation in Mayan for a whorehouse; such a thing did not exist in their world.

"What will happen here?" Fonso tried his hand at the strange language; it felt more than weird rolling off his tongue. Even Itzi smiled at the odd sounds coming from his brother's mouth.

"What will happen?" the madam exploded in a throaty laugh and rubbed provocatively against him, "You bring your purse, big fellow, and I'll ride you like I'd ride a bucking horse, that's what will happen, rest assured."

The young red head had not taken her eyes off Itzamna; clearly she was just as intrigued with him as he was with her.

"Bring your little friend, my lord," she told Fonso batting her clear blue eyes, "I'll make him just as happy."

The ladies suddenly turned toward two other men approaching.

"Wait," Itzi stopped their departure, "my good lady, what is the name of this place?"

With a quizzical look the older one answered, "Why, the Forum, my lord." she gestured to the marketplace ahead of them.

"No," Fonso took up Itzi's line of questioning, "this city. What is the name of this city?"

Clearly startled by the question, she now took a long hard look at the Mayan brothers.

"Rome," she answered slowly, "this is Rome."

For a second Fonso thought she was going to call them stupid again; ever the businesswoman the madam thought better of it. This time when she took her leave they let her.

"I knew this had to be a place we've never heard of." Fonso turned to Itzi, "Ah K'uhun where do you think we are?"

The little man looked up; the comparative calculations of the sun's place in the sky had been moving in his head since dawn.

"I want to see the stars tonight before I'm positive in what direction we have gone. For now," Itzi nodded his head, "it doesn't matter where…it matters what. We need to see what kind of a place this is."

37

They were astounded by the amount of unrecognizable goods in the Forum. Though Rome was in her very worst stages of decline politically and economically, the goods from all over the Mediterranean were impressive to the men from the Yucatan.

"These people talk so loud!" Ildefonso had to lean down and practically yell in his tiny brother's ear to be heard.

Itzi nodded. Even in friendly conversation the people practically screamed at each other. The brothers quizzically eyed the sheep, bulls and calves; they greatly admired the horses.

Ildefonso mulled over the woman's offer to ride him like a bucking horse; the big man grinned at the thought, with their powerful looking hind quarters he guessed these animals must be a sight when they mated.

As they walked Fonso noticed that he and Itzi were the only well dressed people shopping alone; most had at least servant or two in tow as well as what appeared to be armed body guards. There were also a few levels of servitude Fonso discerned; slavery was definitely in vogue in this place.

The brothers were familiar with such practices; the Maya regularly enslaved their captives from battles, especially the women. Much of the economy of a prosperous Mayan city state was fueled by the free labor of slaves.

Itzi too had noticed the plethora of servants and the presence of slaves; the little man was already considering the acquisition of household help. Someone knowledgeable in the local customs would certainly help them blend into this strange society.

Eventually the brothers reached a section where the goods took a pricy turn; heavily armed men protected the doors of the ornate marble enclosures. Fine mosaics were laid on the floor at many of the entrances that depicted the goods on sale inside.

When they came upon a stall loaded with steel swords and knives Ildefonso's eyes bulged; he was entranced by the broadswords and battle axes. The knives were something neither brother had ever imagined. The big man sounded like a young boy when he first spotted chain link armor.

"I want that," Fonso pointed toward the gleaming shirt of interlocking steel rings.

"Than puny thing won't fit you, Fonso," Itzi laughed, "we'll need to have them make one for you."

Fine porcelain pitchers and bowls were on display in another enclosure. Itzi smiled at his younger brother and pointed toward bolts of colorful silk cloth and intricate Persian rugs.

"The girls will go crazy here," the little man predicted.

Fonso nodded in agreement and gestured toward a sign up ahead: it was gilded with gold leaf and shimmered even in the shaded colonnade. A gold crown encrusted with jewels was carved in relief. Three heavily armed guards the size of Ildefonso protected the front of the shop.

Itzi showed the first guard at the doorway one of the green stones from Chac's treasure. Immediately the brothers were granted access to the first room. The man who approached them took one look at the emerald and politely asked the brothers to wait; he returned in a minute with a man clearly in charge.

THE FLAVOR OF HEARTS

"My lord," the fat merchant said to Itzi with a slight bow, "I'm told you have something for sale?"

Itzi offered the emerald to the goldsmith; it was easy to see the man was impressed though he tried to hide his excitement. He immediately ushered the brothers to a more private room and offered them seats. He weighed the stone and offered a price.

Though neither of the Mayan brothers knew the emerald's value or even the exact worth of the mountain of bronze coins the merchant put on the table before them, they knew enough to reject the first offer given.

Ever the trader Itzi rejected the second offer as well; finally when the mountain of coins had nearly doubled the High Priest nodded in agreement. Fonso caught the man stealing glances at the gold ring Itzi wore. Now the merchant tried to recoup some of his money; he showed the brothers some finely made rings and brooches.

The fat vendor seemed disappointed when Itzamna declined to purchase additional jewelry; but he perked up when the little man requested a look around the shop.

Itzi immediately picked up a polished bronze hand mirror; he was shocked to see his reflection so clearly in the metal object. Pearls encircled the rounded back and lined the handle. The merchant was thrilled when Itzi asked the price; he was even more thrilled when Itzi made a bid on all five of the hand mirrors on display.

Itzi did not drive nearly as hard of a bargain on his purchase as he did on the previous sale of Chac's stone; he wanted the vendor to be comfortable making further transactions. When they agreed on a price Itzi took a handful of coins from the bulging leather purse on his belt and offered them back to the merchant.

The goldsmith stared quizzically when he got the impression the little fellow had no idea how many coins made the total. Taking the appropriate amount the owner had a clerk wrap the bronze mirrors in a bundle.

As he walked the brothers back to the street the goldsmith urged them to come back; he promised the best deals and the finest precious goods in the city. The vendor seemed pleased when Itzi said they would certainly return.

All five of the mirrors barely made a dent in the coins in Itzi's leather bag. They stopped back at the stall selling weaponry. Fonso selected a gleaming steel short sword and matching leather scabbard; they bought one for Bartolomeo as well. Itzi picked a double edged knife with a ten inch blade for himself; this time after agreeing on a price the brothers made an attempt to count out the coinage.

When the young apprentice handed two of the coins back Itzi noted the different values for the future. Even after the second purchases Itzi's coin purse was still bulging.

"The lord Chac's colored stones are really valuable, Ah K'uhun," Fonso was awed.

Itzi agreed as they walked back in the direction they came from; amazingly he hadn't even offered the goldsmith the biggest emerald.

"Let's get the others and bring them back here. What do you think Fonso?"

The big man nodded affirmatively. The market was big and loud but it did not appear overtly dangerous. Though he had noticed a few less than savory characters Fonso was sure he could offer any protection the family might need, especially with the new weapon safely strapped below his obsidian knife.

Fonso pointed toward a vendor just before they left the Forum; Itzi grinned recognizing the tantalizing smell from earlier that morning. They brought two fresh baked rolls each; nothing had ever tasted better to either of them.

"Now I could eat a mountain of these," Itzi laughed in delight between bites.

Ah, Ildefonso savored the memory of that first taste; fresh baked Italian bread was still one of the big man's favorite foods. He stretched again on his comfortable couch; his stomach was starting to rumble thinking about the

THE FLAVOR OF HEARTS

Mediterranean food they had all learned to love. Fonsos's mouth watered thinking of the meals Dorcas made.

Dorcas...talk about a blast from the past; Fonso hadn't thought of Dorcas in ages. It was right after they ate the rolls that they found her.

38

Just outside the market Fonso paused with Itzi on the side of the roadway to finish the last of the bread. A man passed, clearly a noble by his dress and adornment. He was accompanied by a burly lightly armored bodyguard and an old woman. She was loaded with packages. Bundles were tied to her back as well as hanging from both her shoulders and piled in her arms; neither man carried anything.

The giant guard was pushing the woman with the hilt of his broadsword. Each time he poked her she stumbled and valiantly fought to retain her hold on the parcels. Loudly he berated her for clumsiness and sluggishness.

It seemed a sad and dishonorable sight to the Mayan brothers; slave or not, the lady was older than their mother and she was clearly overburdened. Suddenly the noble felt their eyes on him.

"What have we here?" he spoke loudly almost like an actor on a stage, "do you have some interest in me, little man?"

Itzi replied politely in the negative.

"Then what rudeness would allow you to stare my way with such a look?"

THE FLAVOR OF HEARTS

"Perhaps I am not accustomed to seeing such interaction between people." Itzi replied, putting an emphasis on the word people.

The noble's eyebrow shot up in surprise; he was clearly surprised by the veiled criticism.

"How I treat a lazy slave is certainly my business," the noble's voice turned more threatening, "do not make it your business."

Hearing his employer's mounting agitation the bodyguard moved toward Itzi but stopped in his tracks when Fonso stepped in front of his tiny brother.

"We have no interest in your business," Ildefonso spoke calmly but forcefully, "we will keep it that way." Fonso put the emphasis on 'keep it that way'.

The noble held out a hand toward his guard; it seemed a gesture to stand down. The gentleman curiously assessed the Mayan brothers; they were dressed impeccably in the finest clothes available and though they spoke the perfect Greek of the Roman upper class there was an exotic air about them.

"I am Antonio, third son of the house of Frangipani; and what house do you hail from?"

"I am Itzamna Cenotes." Itzi answered, "I am head of my house."

As High Priest of Uxmal Itzi was venerated as a god and when he wanted to he could affect the pure arrogance of such an earthbound deity.

"Cenotes?" the noble said with a slight bow of his head, "I regret I am unfamiliar with the name. Who are your allies, Lord Cenotes?"

"We have no allies...nor enemies." Itzi spoke in an almost offhand way.

"Hah." the young lord seemed amused by the answer, "perhaps an enviable position in this city."

Suddenly it seemed the noble remembered bigger things on his schedule. "Good day, Lord Cenotes," he said the last part almost over his shoulder.

"Lord Frangipani," Itzi called, "perhaps you would like to relieve your great house of that old woman?"

The lord turned his head but not his body; now he seemed totally amused and more than surprised. "Are you making an offer?" he asked.

When Itzi answered affirmatively the lord took two steps back to face the little gentleman. The bodyguard suddenly looked extremely uncomfortable, for a second Fonso thought the man might drag young Antonio Frangipani off down the street.

"What price do you deem fair, Lord?" Itzi asked almost innocently.

On one hand the High Priest wished he'd checked the value of slaves in Rome; on the other hand he frankly didn't care about the cost.

Still, Itzi cut Lord Frangipani's first demand in a quarter and predictably the lord pretended to take offense. Itzi brought the price up to a third of the original number.

"After all," Itzi said slyly "you said yourself she is lazy."

"Ah, so I did." the young lord laughed out loud, "I find you very refreshing Lord Cenotes. Sold!"

"Lord Antonio, we are in the public street," the bodyguard sounded ready to choke.

Fonso got the impression the slave was not exactly this young man's property to sell.

"Shut up, Rodolfo." the noble hissed to his protector, "I have last night's debts to pay. Nobody will miss this old hag."

Smiling he took the coins Itzi counted out; with another slight bow of his head the young Frangipani laughed.

"A pleasure, Lord Cenotes. A most fortuitous encounter." he turned toward his bodyguard, "Rodolfo, get the packages."

Fonso wished he could laugh out loud; if the bodyguard was annoyed previously, now he was positively steaming. Veins were popping out on his neck by the time he sheathed his sword and took the last of the parcels.

The old lady stared at the departing pair; she tried to steal a glance at her new owner but respectfully averted her eyes.

"Look here," Itzi spoke kindly, "take a good look at us."

Almost shyly she looked at both men squarely. She had an attractive but weathered face; her deep set brown eyes twinkled when she got a good look at the brothers: the family resemblance was unmistakable and the size disparity was startling!

"As you probably heard," Itzi said, "I am Itzamna Cenotes. This is my brother Ildefonso Cenotes. What is your name?"

She introduced herself as Dorcas. On the way back to the house they found she was a native Roman and oddly she was not born a slave.

39

Ten years prior, after the death of her husband, Dorcas had gone to live in the household of her daughter's husband. When that daughter died in childbirth, the head of that house offered Dorcas a position as a servant, or the option to be sold to the larger and more prosperous house of Frangipani.

For reasons she didn't discuss Dorcas decided on the latter; for eight years she was the personal maid to the oldest sister of the lord of that house. Recently the aged Mistress Frangipani had passed away, leaving Dorcas again with an uncertain future.

As the woman articulately explained her background Itzi was sure he had done the right thing in his impetuous purchase.

"Well, Dorcas, welcome to the house of Cenotes," Itzi said warmly as they turned left off the causeway on to the Via Nova.

"My family is new to Rome." the High Priest warned the unsuspecting woman as he pointed to the ladies and Bartolomeo up ahead. "Hopefully you will help us all to learn the customs of this place."

THE FLAVOR OF HEARTS

Dorcas assured Itzi that she would do anything required of her; later they would learn of her relief to be free of the uncertainty in the house of Frangipani.

Fonso eyed the family as soon as the house became visible in the distance; Waykan was the first to spot her brothers approaching. That was no surprise to the family warrior; if his youngest sister had been a male she'd have been a more than welcome addition to Uxmal's army.

Fonso smiled watching Waykan pointing out their approach to the others; though they eyed Dorcas curiously at first the family took to the old woman like she was born to them.

They all appreciated her help in their return visit to the marketplace. If Dorcas was curious observing their severe culture shock she never showed it; she politely ignored the girls' private conversations in their native Mayan and patiently explained even the most common European goods. She directed Bartolomeo to the city's library later that afternoon.

That first night at sunset Dorcas prepared a traditional dinner; she called it the coena. The family was totally surprised to find the room with the couches was the Roman dining room; they were also shocked to hear the upper crust locals reclined as they ate, a custom the Mayans never got used to.

They started the evening meal with olives, lettuce and red peppers drizzled with spiced olive oil. The family was clearly delighted by the taste of the watered wine common at every Roman meal. Dorcas had expertly roasted the butchered lamb and served it as a main course along with a steaming bowl of oysters in garlic and olive oil. The meal ended with third course of fruit, nuts and sweet honey cakes. Dorcas never batted an eye when she had to instruct the Mayan family in the proper way to peel and eat the oranges she served.

They all stuffed themselves almost to the point of discomfort. The girls and their mother immediately retreated to their bedrooms. Excitement had allowed all of them to stay awake well over twenty four hours; fatigue had set in heavily after the meal and Itzi apologized to his warrior brother.

"The lord will probably send the first of the offerings tonight, Fonso. I think we should go to that room up front and wait." The High Priest rubbed his own tired eyes, "I'm sorry, we should've rested in the afternoon."

Ildefonso immediately waved off his brother's apology.

"I am by your side, Ah K'uhun, as always," the big man promised.

"Me too," Bartolomeo insisted, "I will help you both in any way I can with the lord's work."

Itzi nodded; he was grateful for the company and the loyalty of his brothers.

The little man went up to his bedroom and took the sacred ink from Chac's chest. He opened his tattoo kit and filled the tiny jade ink bowl then joined his brothers waiting at the bottom of the stairs.

Bartolomeo held up two leather bound books and some writing materials.

"I bought these at the market today, Ah K'uhun." he showed Itzi the blank pages of bound parchment; "perhaps you would like to draw the mark first before you lay it on the skin."

"A very good idea," Itzi agreed, the god had said any mark would do and the High Priest realized he hadn't given any thought the shapes of the designs.

"I could keep track of the numbers in this book, if you like," Bartolomeo offered, holding up the second volume, "that way we'll know when we hit twenty."

Itzi grinned; he appreciated Tolo's logic and Ildefonso's courage more and more in this strange place and he told them so.

"I thank our god for giving me a brother as smart as you, Tolo," Itzamna said sincerely, "and I thank the great Chac for a brother as brave and formidable as you, Fonso."

Itzi laughed out loud as his brothers both blushed. They took a bronze oil lamp to the room at the front of the building; it was pleasantly quiet that late in the night. Itzi sat down in the chair next to the table and laid out his tattoo kit. Tolo put down a container of ink and a stylus, along with the blank parchment book for Itzi.

The three brothers stared at one another; it seemed odd to just assume people would show up, but every other strange thing had happened exactly the way Chac described.

The High Priest yawned. Ildefonso leaned on the wall near the doorway to the outside; the street was pretty much deserted.

Bartolomeo sat down in the extra chair and offered to tell his brothers what he had learned that afternoon at Rome's impressive library. Gratefully they agreed; anything to help them stay awake.

"They use a different calendar here than we're used to," Tolo started, "It only has one part and most closely resembles the Haab."

One third of the three part Mayan Calendar was a civil section called the Haab. Based on a 365 day cycle the Haab was a wheel broken into 18 sections of 20 days each, followed by 5 extra days. The Maya called these five days Uayeb: an unlucky time of year set aside for prayer and mourning.

Tolo looked down at notes he had written in the leather bound volume he had kept for himself.

"It's called the Julian Calendar," he explained, "they call a kin a day, so it's 365 days, divided into 12 parts they call months. Some of these months have 30 days and some have 31, I think one month had 28...they call a full 365 day cycle a year."

This calendar sounded strange and arbitrary to Itzi; as the numbers turned in the little man's head he suspected inaccuracies in this Julian calendar over time.

"What of Uayeb?" the High Priest asked curiously, "they have no time of mourning?"

"No, they don't appear to." Bartolomeo answered. "They also count the day from midnight of the night before, not from sunrise like we do."

Both Itzi and Fonso shook their heads; it seemed crazy to start a day in the dark.

"The history of this city seems to go back way over a century, that's one thousand years or full cycles of the Haab." Tolo went on, "It was part of a huge empire divided into two halves; this city was the capital of the Western part. They say it was really something till about five hundred years ago; supposedly today it's is a shadow of its former glory."

That was a surprise to all three of the Mayan brothers; to them Rome seemed an amazingly vibrant and bustling place. Bartolomeo continued.

"At first it seems to be ruled by a succession of emperors, that's what they call a king here. Like I said about five hundred years ago it changed; then they were ruled by two men: an emperor and a High Priest they call a Pope. That happened when they all became Christians; they gave up all their gods to worship one god called Christ. This is him," Bartolomeo pulled a small gold crucifix he had stuck in the leather book he still held. He offered the artifact to Itzi, "supposedly they put metal spikes through his body and attached him to that post until he was dead, but in three days Christ came back alive."

Fonso left his spot near the door and looked over Itzi's shoulder at the Roman god.

"They worship this man and no other god?" Fonso was surprised. "What of Chac? What of Kulkulkan?"

Tolo shrugged wide eyed, "I found nothing of our gods in their library."

Itzi nodded his head as he examined the gold rendition of Christ on the cross, "Surely a man must be a god if he returns from Xibalba."

Itzi spoke of the Mayan underworld; it was a treacherous place in nine levels where gods tricked and tortured the deceased. In Mayan legend only two men had ever defeated the lords of Xibalba: the hero twins Hun Ahaw and Yax Balam. The Maya believed after many trials the twins avenged the death of their father by defeating the underworld gods in a sacred ball game. The hero twins were then transformed into the sun and the moon.

"They celebrate a festival for their god Christ in a few days, they call it Christmas. Supposedly they used to have a wild week long festival around this time for one of their other gods," Bartolomeo looked at his notes again, "a god called Saturn, they called it the Festival of Saturnalia. Apparently it was wild and crazy and a lot of people miss it; some of them still celebrate it but kind of secretly."

Tolo went on, "About a hundred and fifty years ago their last great ruler died; a king called..." the former scribe referred to his notes again, "Charlemagne. Then somehow all the power shifted to the north and to the eastern half of this empire. This city has no allegiance to any kingdom from what I can gather; it's supposedly ripe for the taking. The last real war was with men from the south, men they call Saracens; they invaded and looted about fifty years ago."

"Right now the governor here is named Alberic; he's brought peace to the streets for the last twenty years or so, but nobody expects it to last past him. Every big house has a private army, that's all those guards we saw in the market. Everybody's always fighting; from what I heard this place is really ruled by two noble families: the Frangipani and the Pierleone."

Fonso and Itzi both nodded; they were slightly acquainted with the House of Frangipani. They were also more than familiar with nobles fighting for control of a city; their father had died in just such a war in the Yucatan.

Bartolomeo pulled a folded parchment sheet from the back of the leather volume and smoothed it out it on the table.

"This is a copy of a map drawn by a man called Ptolemy about eight hundred years ago...they say it is accurate." Tolo pointed to a tiny boot shaped landmass jutting into inked blue water on the upper left corner of the rectangular sheet, "this is where we are."

Nothing on the map seemed in any way familiar. The great Chac is all knowing, Itzi thought; I am totally ignorant of the world we stand upon.

"Do you think one of these places is Uxmal, Itzi?" Fonso asked pointing toward the lower end of the parchment, "maybe this Ptolemy calls it something else?"

"I looked at the stars," Itzi spoke slowly staring at the map, "Everything is as I have always seen it except shifted slightly to the south; even the moon is sitting farther to the south. The sun rose here shortly after we arrived; it wouldn't have risen in Uxmal for at least another five hours. I believe we have moved far to the east of Uxmal and slightly north."

Ildefonso suddenly turned his head; he moved back to the door in three large steps. In a second a barrel bodied man appeared at the opening, he was dressed in leather tunic and matching britches. His voice was deep but he spoke almost breathlessly,

"Is this where I buy the Mark of Good Fortune?"

40

Fonso stared dumbfounded.

"The mark of what?" the big man thought.

Itzi's voice startled both his brothers.

"Yes, this is the place," the High Priest answered.

When the man looked toward the voice an amazed look appeared on his face.

"Yes, yes..." his voice was even more breathless, "a tiny lord with immense power, that's exactly what she said!"

Bartolomeo rose from the chair as the man approached their brother; the stranger bowed deeply to the High Priest.

"I have come for the Mark of Good Fortune, great lord, if I am worthy to receive it." the man spoke reverently, "I have brought tribute for you."

He held out a valuable coin; it was worth more than they paid for Dorcas!

Itzi motioned toward the chair his brother had vacated. Now the man took notice of the tattoo supplies on the table. An indecisive expression clouded his features.

"It is a tattoo, great lord? The Mark of Good Fortune is a tattoo?" the man sounded like he couldn't believe it.

When Itzi nodded affirmatively the man appeared torn; he was definitely mulling over some ramifications the brothers were unaware of. Later they were to find that throughout history only slaves were tattooed in Roman society; in fact about one hundred fifty years prior Pope Hadrian I had outlawed the practice altogether.

The man closely eyed the tiny jade vessel holding Chac's sacred ink.

"That is the coloration?" he asked, the amazement was back in his voice, "you will tattoo the mark with gold?"

When Itzi replied affirmatively the man suddenly appeared to make up his mind.

"To hell with the Church, it has never done a thing for me," his broad face lit up with a manic smile as he placed the coin on the table in front of Itzi, "I will be tattooed with your golden mark, great lord, if you find me worthy."

When Itzi assured the man of his suitability he seemed pleased, but again nervousness colored his voice when he inquired about the size and location of the tattoo. The leather clad man sighed with obvious relief when Itzamna offered to put the small mark anywhere the man desired.

Removing his leather tunic he raised his undergarment to reveal the whitest skin the Mayan brothers had ever seen up close. They were totally surprised by the thick covering of dark hair on the man's muscular chest and arms.

"Could it be here?" the man gestured toward a spot on the lower part of his pale protruding belly, "What will it look like?"

As the man was so relieved to pick the location of Chac's mark Itzi decided to leave the shape of the design up to the man as well.

"Could it be an anvil? I am a blacksmith. Forgive me, lord, I never introduced myself." He bowed his head as he gave his name, "I am Emilio Martorano, master blacksmith for the house of Pierleone."

"I am pleased to make your acquaintance, Master Martorano." Itzi replied as he began drawing the outline of an anvil in the book Tolo supplied.

Thankfully the High Priest and Ildefonso had watched a blacksmith at the Forum that day; Dorcas had explained the

THE FLAVOR OF HEARTS

use of the anvil, the hammer and the tongs as they watched the craftsman deftly make horseshoes.

Itzamna smiled as he shaded the illustration. He liked to draw since he was a young boy though his former position as High Priest of Uxmal did not allow him the time or opportunity for such pursuits.

When Itzi showed the design to the blacksmith the burly man excitedly nodded his approval. He winced many times as the High Priest pricked the skin repeatedly with the obsidian tool and dripped the sacred ink in the wounds.

"I wish I had real one like that!" Master Martorano beamed when he saw the finished golden anvil, "Perhaps soon I will afford such a thing!"

He thanked Itzi repeatedly as he donned his tunic and prepared to leave. Itzi wished him good luck as he exited. After watching Master Martorano mount a horse tied outside and ride off down the Via Nova; Fonso turned toward his brothers and laughed,

"Perhaps his mother was Ek Ba'laam!"

They grinned at the big man's joke; he suggested the hairy man was born of a black jaguar. Bartolomeo opened the front of the leather book and wrote the blacksmith's name under the date he had inscribed earlier.

"What do you think he meant by the Mark of Good Fortune, Itzi?" Tolo asked.

The High Priest shrugged; he was also puzzled by the things the blacksmith said. There was no opportunity to discuss the situation as a second man appeared in the doorway. Strangely he too asked for the Mark of Good Fortune.

Bartolomeo learned from the fifth man to arrive that a local psychic of great renown was telling of a tiny lord with gigantic power on the Via Nova. She told her customers to seek him out in the darkest part of the night and she swore that once they wore the tiny lord's mark they would experience good fortune for the rest of their lifetime.

When nine men had come and gone Bartolomeo told his brothers about the fortune teller as they waited for the tenth. Fonso's jaw dropped when he heard the story.

"How could she say such a thing, Ah K'uhun?" he was astonished.

"The Lord Chac said he would send the offerings," Itzi shrugged. "how he gets them here is his business."

By the time Tolo's list was twelve men long, there was another lull in the action.

"Eight more, Itzi." Bartolomeo tried to sound encouraging.

They were all dead tired. Hearing a footstep Fonso turned numbly toward the doorway. All three brothers were shocked to see Dorcas enter. She was holding a tray with three cups and small container of honey.

"Lord Cenotes," she bowed her head toward Itzi, "I realized you are all working into the night and thought you might need refreshment."

She placed the tray on the table and explained that the brown liquid was a stimulant. Offering each of the brothers a cup she told them it was a tea made of yohimbe, the bark of an African tree. She suggested adding a little honey to improve the taste and promised the drink would ease their tiredness.

Eagerly the brothers downed the hot liquid; it had just the result Dorcas predicted. With renewed energy the last eight tattoos went quickly.

41

Dorcas. Fonso sat up on his couch. He suddenly wished he could go down to the kitchen and find her chattering away with his mother. So many things they learned from dear Dorcas, and not just customs and the way around Rome.

She taught the family the most important lesson they needed to learn on Chac's great journey; the down side to the great god's amazing Gift of Time.

The Roman lady stayed with the family for almost twenty years; Fonso admired her bravery in choosing to come on Chac's journey. Dorcas had been wide eyed when they explained what would happen on the evening of the Winter Solstice; she had been even more wide eyed after living through it.

Ildefonso recalled the pain of watching Dorcas grew older; somehow the sadness of her death still felt fresh. They buried her in Vienna in a tomb befitting royalty; it had been the most heartrending day the family had experienced as a whole since leaving Uxmal.

The big man eyed the photographs lining the wall above his massive TV screen. In the first he was posed with a tiny baby in his arms; in the next he stood beside a withered old man.

Ildefonso looked exactly the same in both shots yet both were pictures of Fonso with his only son Josef.

The big man had many photos in between, photos of many happier moments of fatherhood, but he purposely displayed these two as a reminder. They forced him to remember the lesson he first learned from Dorcas; that time would ravage anyone he chose to love and his heart would be ravaged right along with them.

Ildefonso looked farther down the line of photos to the one of Anita. He wondered how his sister had done it; she must've buried twenty kids.

Fonso took a deep breath. Focus on the good, focus on the amazing parts of the lord's journey; that was Itzi's sage advice. Fonso bowed his head and thanked the great Chac for the life he was given and for the love of his family.

Thank you, great lord for my boat and my Jaguar, for my Lear jet and helicopter, my stereo, my TV, my wave runner and my motorcycles.

Fonso's mood lightened as he continued the almost ridiculous litany: thank you for the girls that climb all over me, my horses, jiu-jitsu training and hockey, thank you for hockey. He almost laughed out loud as his mind raced on: thank you for crabs and spaghetti, lasagna and Italian bread; thank you for pizza and fried shrimp and ice cream.

The big man turned and checked the time, it was almost five o'clock. He picked up his cell phone and dialed Itzi's number; the little man answered from his bedroom above.

"Are you awake?" the big man asked.

"Barely."

Fonso grinned. Itzi had shared a bed with three women the night before; there was nothing tiny about Itzamna's sex life.

"I'm starving, let's go to Alfred's and eat," the big man suggested.

Itzi readily agreed; Italian food was irresistible to the High Priest and he loved Wildwood's Italian restaurants.

"I'm gonna take a shower and then I'll come up and get you," Fonso promised.

He threw the phone on the couch and headed toward his well appointed bathroom.

Turning on the water in his oversized marble shower the big man grinned as he watched the steam rise. He remembered their first visit to the Roman bath; they had all easily learned to love that place.

As Fonso stepped below the steaming water and lathered himself up he began to laugh. He remembered their horror when Dorcas explained the mysterious wooden box with the hole in the kitchen; Anita had been right on the money when she said the hole smelled like shit. He still found it hilarious that the Romans kept the toilet in the kitchen. Ildefonso burst out laughing; Dorcas had looked equally horrified that day when he said he'd rather shit in the indoor garden and bury it.

42

Wednesday morning the girls drove toward the yoga studio in Dana's Mini Cooper. Emily turned to her friend in the driver's seat.

"Do you know a store around here where they sell John Deere lawnmowers?"

"Not off hand," Dana answered honestly, "why, you gonna plant a lawn on the terrace?"

Emily laughed at the thought.

"No," she explained, "I got a Fed-Ex this morning. I'm supposed to work on an ad campaign. I'd like to see one of these tractors up close."

"I think there's a Home Depot over on Oregon Avenue," her dark haired pal suggested, "I would imagine they would have something like that, we could go over there and check it out if you want."

Emily agreed as they parked the little car; she could write a campaign from the pictures and the DVD John Deere had provided, but seeing and touching the actual product always made it easier.

Yoga was invigorating. Emily was glad after every session that she listened to Dana and tried it out. She glanced at her friend's posterior as they bent over for the last stretch of the cool down.

"Uh oh," the ad exec thought.

Surreptitiously Emily moved up toward her girlfriend and whispered in her ear. The two girls left the class and ducked into the locker room.

"Oh brother," Dana grimaced as she eyed the small red stain on the back of her white cotton pants. "I haven't gotten a period in months, probably a year, and I have to get it here!"

The shapely Sicilian grabbed her gym bag, accepted the tampon Emily offered and headed into the bathroom. In a fresh pair of underwear she rejoined her long legged friend near their lockers.

"Where's my luck now? I ruined my new silk panties!"

Dana practically spit the last sentence out; she had such a sour look on her face Emily found it comical.

"Hey," the former ad exec laughed, "it could be worse."

Dana knew her friend was right; it wasn't like she had fallen down and broken a leg.

Still, the dark haired beauty thought taking her jeans and shirt from the locker, how embarrassing. "Now I gotta call the gynecologist," she grumbled.

"Hey," a voice came from behind the girls, "what's that?"

Dana looked over her shoulder; it was the girl with the spike in her nose.

"Excuse me?" Dana asked, surprised that Spike In Her Nose was making conversation. Usually the heavily pierced and tattooed yoga practitioners eyed the other girls like straight old fogies.

"That," Spike In Her Nose was pointing toward the tattoo on the small of Dana's back. "Is that stuck on?"

"No, it's a tattoo," Dana answered.

"No it's not."

Spike In Her Nose moved a little closer, her eyes were riveted on Dana's back.

"It is too," Dana responded.

Emily watched the exchange of words and took the opportunity to take a closer look at their yoga classmate. She had tattoos covering both of her arms; the colors were vivid against her pale skin. That spike in her nose was even wilder up close.

"No way. I work at The Body Shop, it's a tattoo place," Spike sounded adamant, "that's no tattoo."

"I got it at a tattoo parlor," Dana stated.

"Where?" the pale girl finally looked Dana in the face.

"Wildwood," the accountant answered.

"Wildwood? At Oxygen?"

Dana shook her head, before she could reply with words the pierced girl interrupted,

"At 24th Street Tattoos?" Spike In Her Nose sounded unbelieving.

Dana shook her head, "No, I got it at Buena Suerte."

"Buena Suerte? Where's that?" the pale girl was wide eyed with curiosity.

"Wildwood," Dana said again.

"So you said," Spike used the tone of voice you use with your grandmother when she forgot her own phone number, "where in Wildwood?"

"I don't know the exact address," Dana turned to Emily, "do you remember the street's name?"

For the first time the pierced girl noticed Emily. Dana spoke again,

"She got one too."

Spike In Her Nose's eyebrows shot up. Emily noticed that Spike's eyebrow was pierced too, as well as her upper and lower lip.

"It was on a side street, up toward the end of the boardwalk..." Emily's voice trailed off. Emily suddenly realized they didn't have a business card from Buena Suerte. Strange, they didn't have any paperwork to speak of, not even a receipt.

"Show her yours, Em," Dana suggested.

THE FLAVOR OF HEARTS

Emily untied the drawstring on her yoga pants and lowered the waist band, revealing the sailboat and gleaming sun.

"Wow," the pale girl bent over for a closer look.

Dana and Emily shot puzzled looks at each other.

Spike In Her Nose's voice was full of wonder, "I've never seen a tattoo like that in my life."

She stood up and eyed Dana and Emily with a new respect, "Could you guys come down to The Body Shop and show those to my boss? It's on South Street."

Dana turned toward Emily and shrugged. When Emily nodded in agreement Dana replied, "Sure, I don't see why not."

"I can't go today," Emily informed the other two. "I have to work this afternoon; I gotta get started on that campaign."

Dana turned toward Spike In Her Nose, "How about next Wednesday? We'll follow you over there after yoga."

"Great," the pale girl smiled. "I appreciate it."

Dana was surprised how Spike looked when she smiled; under all the metal in her face, she was a pretty girl.

"I'm sorry," Spike In Her Nose suddenly realized she hadn't been very polite, "I'm Sarah."

One at a time Dana and Emily shook her hand and introduced themselves.

"Thanks again for coming down to work," Sarah said as she turned to walk away, "I'll see you next week."

"Hey, Sarah," Dana called to the girl as she retreated.

"Did it hurt to put that thing in your nose?"

The pale girl smiled broadly, "It hurt like a bitch!"

On the way home Dana and Emily made a stop at the CVS on Market Street.

"I don't believe you asked her about that thing in her nose!" Emily grinned as they headed down the aisle marked Feminine Products.

"I don't believe how that thing looked close up. What about her name? Sarah? Can you believe that?" Dana said with amazement as she selected a box from the multitude of sanitary products.

"Yeah," Emily agreed, "I was expecting something far less traditional."

"Like Pulsar or Wolverina?" Dana suggested the girls headed toward the front of the store.

"Well, I don't know if I expected anything that wild," the slender adwoman answered laughing, "but she certainly didn't look like a Sarah."

"Yeah," Dana paused in front of a display of magazines and books, "do you get the feeling there's a lady in a nice dress some where wondering why her beautiful little Sarah punched massive holes in her face and filled them with metal?"

Emily nodded. She wasn't surprised when Dana paused before the reading materials; her pal was like a moth to a flame when it came to books. However, she was as puzzled as Sarah's fictional mother when Dana picked up a cookbook.

"What are you gonna do with that?" Emily asked wide eyed.

"Oh, I don't know," Dana replied as she put the cookbook under her arm, "I was watching a cooking program the other day and I thought maybe I'd read up on it a little."

Emily was still in disbelief as they went through the checkout and left the store. That's why she loved Dana so much: she was always full of surprises!

"Please, do you ladies have any spare change?"

Emily eyed the young man in the tattered jeans and dirty t-shirt.

"Why don't you go and get a job?" she replied sweetly.

He scowled and moved on to the next group exiting the drug store.

"Way to go, Em!"

Now it was Dana's turn to be surprised.

THE FLAVOR OF HEARTS

Emily spent the rest of the afternoon poring over the package of information from John Deere. The lawnmowers were impressive. She was surprised to see in the statistics included the large percentage of machines owned and operated by women.

She watched the DVD provided by John Deere. The lawnmower looked like fun to drive; Emily looked forward to going to the Home Depot to see one of the green and yellow tractors in person.

Rubbing her eyes she looked at the clock; it was quarter to five. The afternoon had flown by; it was so nice to work again. Maybe it was Dana's influence, Emily decided to cook dinner.

Heading toward the kitchen the slim brunette tried to remember when she cooked last. So many excellent restaurants in the area delivered gourmet meals; she and Tim had easily fallen into the habit of ordering in.

Opening the freezer Emily spied a package of raviolis. Tim loved the little pillows of cheese stuffed pasta. She went to the cupboard and took out a can of crushed tomatoes and a can of tomato paste. As she selected jars from the spice rack she silently thanked Mrs. Genardi. Dana's cook had answered a multitude of questions about Italian cooking.

Emily started the gravy simmering and planned the rest of the meal.

Tim opened the door at seven thirty. For a minute he thought he'd made a mistake and arrived at the Torroni's! The apartment was filled with the delectable aroma of tomato sauce.

Approaching the kitchen he saw his wife in front of the stove. She was lightly sweating standing above a boiling pot of water; she looked gorgeous.

"Em, what's going on? It smells great!" he spoke from the doorway, not wanting to startle her.

She turned and smiled, now she looked even more striking.

"I'm making dinner: raviolis, garlic bread and tomato salad with sharp provolone cheese!"

"Wow, let me kiss the cook!"

The assistant curator took his stunning wife in his arms.

Emily's meal was delicious. Tim pushed his chair back from the dining room table and declared himself stuffed. He patted his stomach and complimented his wife,

"Maybe it's Buena Suerte," he said slyly, "I have a beautiful wife, and she can cook! I might be the luckiest man on earth. Whew!"

Emily left her seat and headed toward her husband. Tim thought she was going to take the empty plate; instead she straddled him in his chair.

"Maybe it's Buena Suerte," Emily repeated coyly, "I have a handsome husband and he's a stud!"

She reached down and undid his fly. Craziness enveloped Tim before she put her hand down his pants; he stood up, carrying Emily still straddling him. Walking to the opposite side of the dining room table he placed her on the end.

The Hoyle's had sex right there. Tim felt like a wild beast; he never had sex like that with Emily before; he banged his wife hard. At one point he lightened up, the table was swaying like it might break; she egged him on,

"Don't stop! Fuck me, fuck me like an animal!" she gasped the sentence in his ear.

Emily had never been one for dirty talk; it pushed Tim from crazy to the point of insanity. He was electrified, he thrusted into her like a piston in a race car engine; he wanted to break the dining room table! He'd buy a new one and break that too!

Emily moaned like a tigress; they finished together and collapsed still sandwiched together on the table.

43

Early Thursday morning Emily spread the photos of the John Deere lawnmowers across her desk. She started listing possible slogans on a legal pad.

Leaning back in her office chair she thought of her husband. He was so shocked that morning when she joined him in the shower. She remembered the warm water raining down over her back as she pleasured Tim with her mouth. She massaged his firm wet butt with her hands as she worked her lips up and down his penis.

Emily laughed recalling the minute her husband exploded and his knees buckled.

It's funny, she always loved sex with Tim; but lately she couldn't get enough. Well, she mused, after six years of marriage I ought to consider myself lucky that my husband still gets me going.

Lucky! She knew what Dana would say: Buena Suerte!

Emily shook her head and looked back at the photos. Picking up the John Deere catalogue she caught an insert as it dropped from between the pages: a list of authorized dealers arranged by state. Emily scanned the section of dealerships for Pennsylvania and decided to show the addresses to Dana when she saw her friend later. Putting the insert aside she picked up a business card, it listed the contact info for the local district sales manager for John Deere.

Good, the adwoman mused looking at the phone number and email; if I don't find a lawnmower at the Home Depot tomorrow I'll call this guy and ask the closest place to see one...

Suddenly Emily froze; she stared at the business card in her hand with its tiny writing. She could see it. She could see the tiny text without her glasses! Impossible. She slid open the desk's bottom drawer and pulled out a phone book; she always needed her glasses to read the phone book listings.

Opening the white pages at random she read Gordon, Gordy, Gorham. Paul Gori, 34 Mulberry Lane. Holy smokes. She fell back into the chair dropping the phonebook into her lap. How could it be? Could a person's eyesight improve?

Emily couldn't remember the last time she even saw her glasses. Scanning the desk top she didn't see the case, she rose and headed for the living room; from across the room she could see her glasses weren't at the counter where she always read the morning newspaper.

A memory popped up: a little dark man in bright white linen shirt; he was handing her a magnifying glass. Buena Suerte. She couldn't see up close in Buene Suerte. He gave her a magnifying glass to see the drawing clearly!

For some reason Emily held her breath as she strode down the hallway and into her bedroom. She threw open the door to the walk in closet and practically ran for the straw beach bag on the shelf.

Emily still held her breath as she rifled threw the contents: sunscreen, hairbrush, handiwipes, crosswords…Emily froze.

Her glasses.

There's no way I haven't needed my glasses for almost a week!

No way, she thought as she removed the glasses case from the beach bag.

THE FLAVOR OF HEARTS

Reflex made her open it: the reading glasses stared back nestled safely inside. Emily snapped the lid shut and stared down at the case.

She could see the faux alligator pattern clearly; every tiny line and fake scale. There was no doubt about it; she could see up close without her glasses!

She staggered back into the bedroom and sat down on the end of the bed.

She held her hand in front of her face and saw every line in her palm clearly. Unreal. A chill went up her spine. How could it be? Could a person's eyesight suddenly improve?

Taking a deep breath she pondered the reality of the situation.

She couldn't think of a down side; for whatever reason, it was great to realize she no longer needed glasses.

The phone rang. Emily leaned over to the night stand and picked up the bedroom extension.

"Em, Lou just called." Dana sounded all excited, "his firm is part of a big charity wing ding down in Atlantic City tomorrow night. I know it's short notice but he just found out that we can bring two guests. What d'ya say, are you and Tim busy?"

"No...no, it sounds great."

"You OK?" Dana asked suddenly concerned, her girlfriend sounded strange.

"It's the weirdest thing..."

Emily filled Dana in on the turn of events with her eyesight.

"Wow," Dana was clearly amazed, "how long have you needed the reading glasses?"

Emily explained that she was diagnosed as farsighted back in junior high. Admittedly it was a mild case, she could usually see fine enough for everyday life, but she needed her glasses to read small text or examine things closely, that is until some time about a week ago!

"Damn, it's a miracle."

Dana rarely cussed and the swear word in the context of the sentence made Emily laugh.

"So what's this thing tomorrow?" Emily brought the phone call back its original purpose.

"Oh, yeah. It's for breast cancer." Dana went on with the explanation, "Lou's boss, Joe Carbine, his wife died from it about 10 years ago so the firm always gives mega money. It's one of those things where you buy tables for a big donation and there's dinner and dancing. They're sending a limo for us and all!"

"Sounds awesome," Emily was catching her girlfriend's enthusiasm.

Dana was glad to hear the Hoyle's were free to go along and she went on excitedly,

"I got a new outfit to wear. I got this new bra too, wait'll you see me in it, in makes my boobs look two sizes bigger! Lou's gonna love it!"

Emily laughed again. She wrote down the time Dana said to meet Friday at their apartment below.

Suddenly Dana's voice took on a less jovial tone, "I gotta go, I gotta get ready to go to the gynecologist. I'm sorry now I made the appointment; the red river already dried up!"

Emily grinned, Dana described things the funniest ways; she told Emily when they first met that everybody from South Philly had that ability!

"Go and make sure everything is OK," Emily encouraged her friend.

"You know," now Dana sounded serious, "maybe you ought to go to an eye doctor; make sure everything's OK with you."

"Why? My eyes are better, not worse."

"Well," Dana answered, "changes in vision can be a sign of different things…"

The perky Sicilian hesitated to say the word tumor.

Emily had never considered that there might be something wrong.

"Yeah," she agreed, "it's probably a good idea. My regular eye doctor is in Manhattan, I'll try to see him when I go up there next week to make my John Deere presentation."

44

Tim took the stone steps into the museum's annex two at a time. He eyed the traffic behind him on the Ben Franklin Parkway; it was early Friday afternoon and the cars were already plentiful.

Once he approved the sample display case that was just delivered he would head straight home to get ready to go to Atlantic City with the Torronis. He was looking forward to the evening.

Tim paused just inside the entrance. The main room at the annex was completely restored and it looked amazing. Emily's face popped into his mind.

The curator shook his blond head. Talk about restored. He was floored the night before when his wife read the phone book without her glasses. He too wondered how it could be. All evening she read aloud any tiny text she could get her hands on: ingredients on packages, directions on pill bottles, miniscule disclaimers in newspaper ads.

Tim was as thrilled as Emily at the strange turn of events, but he was relieved when she said she'd visit the eye doctor for an explanation.

"Tim," Marv Healy waved his arms in semi circles as he approached, "what d'ya think?"

The foreman was grinning from ear to ear. It was easy to see his pride in the restoration. Tim assured the man he felt the same way as the pair walked to the holding area for deliveries.

The display case was everything Tim had hoped for; the heavy seamless glass was unbreakable, even bulletproof, but crystal clear. He signed his name with a flourish on the approval form and now looked forward with great anticipation to the delivery of the rest of the cases. They were getting there now; the opening of the annex seemed closer and closer.

"Tim," Marv asked, "Did you ever make up your mind about the anteroom?"

There was a small room off the annex's main room. The original plans for the restoration called for the side room to be sealed off. A year ago when the project started Tim had looked differently at the space. When it was deemed structurally sound, the young curator considered using the little room for changeable presentations; the museum had so many beautiful things in storage, additional display room would be welcome.

Tim knew he had to make a decision. He left the store room with Marv and they re-entered the annex's cavernous main room.

"Where are you going with that?" Marv yelled, running toward the front entrance. A worker was beginning to drive a forklift off across the newly marbled floor.

Tim walked to his left and entered the anteroom. He strode to the little room's center. A small area, Tim thought turning a full 360 degrees, but still a lot could be done in here.

Bang! Unbearably loud, the sound hurt, Tim covered his ears instantaneously. The thunderous roar echoed; Tim started choking. He was gagging, suddenly enveloped in a cloud of white smoke.

"Holy shit!"

Tim heard the voice through the din; he felt himself being lifted off his feet.

Suddenly he was gulping fresh air like he had come up from too long under water.

"Tim, are you all right?"

Tim turned toward the sound of the voice. He was surrounded by faces that moved in and out of focus. What the heck, Tim thought, his eyes felt so scratchy.

"Doc, are you all right?"

The young curator realized he was sitting in the floor; he recognized the marble in the annex's main room. Construction workers surrounded him.

"What happened?" Tim's voice cracked.

He looked down; his suit was covered in a fine white powder. His hands were covered too!

"Give him room, back up, give him room!"

Tim recognized Marv Healy's voice. "Tim, are you all right?

Tim nodded and gratefully drank from the water bottle one of the men offered him.

Now he remembered, he had been in the anteroom; but he wasn't now. The curator tried to stand up.

"No, no, no…"

He heard a crescendo of voices urging him to stay seated. He got his bearings and looked toward the entrance to the little side room; smoke was still billowing out the door.

"What happened?" Tim asked Marv; the foreman was pale and kneeling down beside him.

"The ceiling came down."

Tim was astounded. He assured the concerned workers still clustered around him that he was unhurt. This time when he tried to stand up, the union guys helped the long legged blond to his feet. They cheered when he reached his full height. When he started to brush the plaster dust off his suit, twenty hands gently joined in and dusted him off.

Tim walked on shaky legs toward the anterooms entrance and joined the gaggle of construction workers peering through the door.

Chunks of plaster, three inches thick, some as big as six feet long littered the floor; the only space not covered in debris was the very center. Two footprints were still visible there; every other spot was covered in plaster and dust.

Tim looked up at the little room's ceiling; nothing was left up there, just the metal form the plaster had previously clung to.

It's a wonder I wasn't killed, the curator thought grimly. By the looks on the men's faces around him he knew they thought the very same thing.

"Seal it up." Tim said turning away from the door toward Marv.

"You got it." Marvin Healy grinned; relief was all over his face.

Marv offered to have somebody drive Tim home, but the young curator declined and headed for the main entrance. Every worker within arms reach patted him on the back. The last guy rubbed Tim's blond head, as plaster dust made another little cloud the union guy laughed.

"I just bought a lottery ticket at lunch time," he joked, "and I wanna rub the head of the luckiest man alive."

Emily knew it was probably a closer call than her husband admitted. As he headed for the shower she thanked her lucky stars that Tim was standing in the right place at the right time.

She pondered their good luck as of late as she put on her makeup and cocktail dress. She remembered those cars on the highway, another close call. She didn't want to even face the fact that she suspected that her eyesight was improved since visiting Buena Suerte. Maybe Dana was right, maybe it was the tattoos. Emily couldn't even entertain the idea; her practical nature wouldn't allow it.

Lou Torroni threw open the door before the bell stopped ringing. He looked extremely handsome in his tuxedo.

"Come over here, we have something to celebrate!"

The big man led the Hoyle's toward the living room. There were four champagne flutes on the oversized coffee table flanked by two ice buckets.

Emily joined her girlfriend on the couch; Dana was smiling like she might burst at the seams. Lou took a bottle of Dom Perignon from the first bucket and filled three of the flutes. From the second ice bucket he pulled a green bottle of Peregrino sparkling water and filled the last glass.

He handed Tim a flute of champagne and gave another to Emily.

Tim wondered if Lou had been offered a partnership at the law firm.

The big man picked up the two glasses left. He handed the sparkling water to Dana, holding the last glass of champagne in the air he announced,

"We're having a baby!"

"Oh my God," Emily quickly put her glass on the coffee table and embraced Dana, "I'm so happy for you!"

Tim jumped to his feet and pumped Lou's hand in a congratulatory handshake. The men drained their champagne glasses. The former wrestler refilled the flutes and the couples drank an official toast,

"To Louie Junior," the attorney laughed as he held up his glass.

"Or Lou Ann!" Dana waggled her finger at her husband with mock seriousness.

On the limo ride to Caesars in Atlantic City Dana explained that the gynecologist said everything was normal and he estimated her pregnancy at about the sixth week. He reminded her that her eggs were totally viable, it was just that her body produced very little of them.

"And like he said it only takes one!" she said beaming.

"Oh, Dane, it's so awesome."

Emily was thrilled for the Torronis, she was sure they would make wonderful parents.

A nagging thought flew through Emily's mind; this was the pinnacle of good luck.

It was as if Dana read her thoughts, "Buena Suerte! Right, Em?"

The adwoman shook her head, it was hard to ignore the evidence. It seemed since their trip to the strange tattoo parlor all their fortunes had taken a turn for the better.

"Yeah," Tim agreed, "Buena Suerte!"

He went on to tell the Torronis his experience at the annex. This time he told the story closer to the way it happened. Emily listened, growing more and more wide eyed. When her husband described the scene in the demolished anteroom Emily shuddered.

"I swear," Tim said "the chunks closest to my footprints, none of them weighed less than three hundred pounds, they missed me by inches. The only clear spot was the place I was standing!"

"Wow, thank God," Dana said.

Lou agreed.

"Who certified that place as sound?" he asked, "it seems to me somebody is liable."

"I wasn't hurt though, Buena Suerte, right?" Tim responded.

Dana nodded her head vigorously, she now totally believed in the power of the golden tattoo. After all, they had told her she had a better chance of winning the lottery than having a baby.

Emily tried to cling to her last shred of rationality. The evidence was hard to refute, so much had happened.

"Either way, Buena Suerte, a gift from God, whatever," Lou stated. He pulled the complimentary bottle of champagne from the limousine's built in ice bucket, "I'll take good luck any way I can get it."

Emily nodded; it was hard not to agree with that.

The charity dinner was enjoyable for both couples. The banquet room was decorated exquisitely and the food was wonderful. Many toasts were made at the table to the Torroni's good fortune. Lou's colleagues were thrilled to hear that the big man would soon be a father.

Tim slow danced with Emily; she smelled so good; he buried his head in the nape of her neck. "I love you, Em," he whispered in her ear.

She held her husband close, picturing the roof falling in around him.

"I love you, Tim," she answered fervently. She stayed in his arms even after the song ended; she didn't want to let him go.

"Ladies and Gentleman," the Emcee announced from the bandstand, "if you would care to return to your seats, we will now award the door prizes." The dance floor emptied as the master of ceremonies went on,

"Courtesy of Steven Singer Jewelers, a set of His and Hers Presidential Rolexes."

Everyone applauded. A girl brought a giant glass bowl filled with slips of paper to the Emcee on the stage.

"Tonight when you signed in, your names were placed in this bowl," he put his hand in the container and began rustling the papers around.

"The winner of a set of Presidential Rolexes, valued at forty-five thousand dollars, courtesy of our good friends at Steven Singer Jewelers is…."

The emcee extracted one white square and read the name,

"Lou Torroni of Philadelphia!"

Their table erupted in cheers. Lou walked up to claim his prize with his hands over his head like a champion boxer. Tim could tell his friend was feeling no pain.

"Hey, what the hell," the curator thought, "Lou deserved to party."

The big man brought the box back to the table and placed it ceremoniously in front of Dana. The whole room applauded.

THE FLAVOR OF HEARTS

45

The Torronis entered Portofino and spotted the Hoyles seated at the bar.

"Sorry we're a little late," Lou said as he pulled out a barstool for Dana. "Traffic is nuts out there...even for a Saturday night."

Tim assured them that he and Emily also got stuck in traffic and they hadn't been waiting long.

"I put my name in already for a table," the long legged blond stated.

"How did it go?" Emily asked her girlfriend.

Lou and Dana had gone to visit Dana's aunt in South Philly where they announced Dana's pregnancy to the Correlli family.

"It was packed," Dana laughed, "every cousin came from miles around! As you can imagine, everybody's thrilled."

The couples sipped their drinks.

Dana pointed toward her iced tea. "This is the only down side to being pregnant. I never realized I was such a wino until I'm not supposed to drink!" she lamented.

The others laughed. It was funny how human nature always made you want what you couldn't have.

"Table for Dr. Hoyle," the hostess came to the bar entrance, "Dr. Hoyle?"

Dana, Lou and Emily stared as Tim waved toward the hostess.

"Dr. Hoyle?" Dana laughed as they rose from the bar.

She had never heard Tim called by his official title.

"Dr. Hoyle, calling Dr. Hoyle," Lou teased as they followed the hostess toward a table.

Emily was also surprised to hear her husband paged like that.

Tim blushed at the good natured kidding as the couples sat down.

"I figured it would get us table faster," he explained, "I'm starving!"

Early Sunday morning Lou drove the Cadillac out to St. Michael's. He wished his mother could have a small moment of lucidity; just long enough to hear and understand about the baby. Before the Altzheimers befuddled her, Katerina would have been elated to hear the news of a grandchild on the way.

Lou wound his way through the nursing home. He picked up the pace as he got to her hallway; they were wheeling a gurney into his mother's room!

"Tony," Katerina said as Lou appeared in the doorway, "they want to take me to the doctors!"

The nurses tried to put Lou at ease immediately, "Don't get worried, Mr. Torroni, we just want to bring your Mom for an x-ray."

The second nurse took the big man into the hallway and explained. "Your mom got a touch of a cold, we're afraid it might have developed into a mild case of bronchitis so we're gonna bring her to the hospital section overnight just to keep an eye on her."

They assured Lou there was nothing to worry about; relief spread over his handsome face. The nurses gave the big man a room number in the medical unit. They suggested he wait there and they would bring Katerina over right after her chest x-ray.

Lou made his way through the doors to the hospital part of the nursing home; he was glad the medical facilities were so readily available and grateful that his mother rarely needed them.

He entered room 46. The hospital rooms were double occupancy. There was a lady in the bed by the window. A slight woman with curly red hair sat in the chair at the foot of that bed; she appeared to be crying.

She looked over toward the door when Lou entered and moved her hand across her cheek to push away her tears.

"I'm sorry," the big man apologized, "they told me to wait in here for my mother to come back from her x-ray."

Looking more closely, Lou thought he recognized her. "Do I know you? My name is Lou Torroni."

Recognition flashed across her pale face. "I thought I knew you too; I'm Margie Dunkirk. We sat together at the Christmas party here last year. Your mother was friends with my mother."

She gestured listlessly toward the bed in front of her.

For the first time Lou took a closer look at the lady lying there.

Poor Mrs. Dunkirk was skin and bones. Lou could see why Margie was crying; her mother's complexion was almost gray.

Lou's heart sank. He remembered the party; Mrs. Dunkirk was a vibrant old Irishwoman, full of jokes and stories. She and Katerina had been good friends; they enjoyed watching the soap operas together and shared the hobby of tatting lace.

"Oh, I'm so sorry," Lou said softly, "what happened?"

"Cancer," Margie answered almost in a monotone. "It started in her intestines and now its spread. It's in her brain, it's all over her now."

Tears welled up in the little woman's eyes. Lou moved closer. He leaned down and put his arm around her shoulders. Standing up she buried her head on Lou's chest and sobbed. The big man fought the urge to cry along with her.

THE FLAVOR OF HEARTS

In about a minute she dislodged herself. "Oh, God," she said wiping her cheek again, "I'm so sorry."

Lou assured her that she had nothing to apologize for, "I wish there was something I could do for you," the big man felt helpless.

"There's nothing anybody can do at this point. They took her off life support four days ago; they thought she would drift off..." Margie took a deep breath, "She's in a coma. She moans when the morphine wears off, the hardest thing is watching her hurting..." She lowered her head and sobbed.

Lou took the poor lady in his arms again. He patted her back and watched the auburn curls move up and down with her jagged breaths. This was his biggest fear with his own mother.

Lou looked over Margie's head at Mrs. Dunkirk; she was certainly a shadow of her former self. Jesus, the big man thought, they'd put a dog out of its misery. What would he do if Katerina was in that position? He hated to admit what he might do.

Margie dislodged herself again from the attorney's embrace.

"Thank you, Lou." She dried her eyes with the back of her hand. Smiling wanly she went on, "I'm all alone in this. I got divorced last year, my sister doesn't want anything to do with mom...they never got along. The last two weeks have been horrible, but the last four days...I'm not sure how much longer I can take it. I can't leave her..."

She sat back in the chair and Lou pulled another seat up beside her. He patted her hand. It was easy to see that Margie Dunkirk appreciated the big man's support.

"There's nothing they can do to help her along?" Lou asked; he was trying to put it the nicest way he could.

"No, you know how doctors are," Margie spoke in a monotone, "I don't think they expected her to last this long after they removed the ventilator."

Lou and Margie both turned toward the noise at the door; they were bringing Katerina toward the other bed. Her olive face lit up when she saw her son stand up.

"Tony," she said brightly, "I'm home!"

Lou approached his mother and watched the nurses quickly make her comfortable in the bed by the door.

Margie came up behind the attorney, "Thanks for being there for me, Lou." she smiled as she walked toward the door, "I'll have some coffee and leave you alone to visit with your mom."

Lou nodded and watched her leave. He had never felt such pity for another human being. Margie Dunkirk was holding up a lot better than he would in her situation.

"Tony, where's my lace? I wanna work on my lace but I can't find it."

Katerina seemed puzzled by her new surroundings. Maybe her needle work would make her more comfortable.

"I'll get it for you, Mama."

Lou kissed her forehead and headed out the door toward her room in the assisted living section. He easily found the lace work and headed back.

When he re-entered the hospital unit a doctor stopped him near the nurse's station. "Mr. Torroni, I have the results of your mother's x-ray. As we suspected she has a slight case of bronchitis. We gave her some medication and she should be back in her regular room by tomorrow."

Lou was relieved. He thanked the man for taking such good care of Katerina. As the attorney turned toward room 46 the physician warned Lou that the medicine may leave his mother a little drowsy.

When Lou entered the hospital room Katerina was sleeping peacefully; her olive face looked angelic. The big man quietly put the lace work on the nightstand beside her. He sat in the chair and watched her slumber. Despite her bronchitis Katerina's breathing was even and slow, a stark contrast to the poor woman in the bed by the window.

Lou looked over at Mrs. Dunkirk; her breaths were short and raspy. Lou eyed the chair Margie Dunkirk vacated; he pictured the pale face under the auburn curls. I'm all alone in this. Her sad words echoed in his head. I'm all alone in this.

THE FLAVOR OF HEARTS

The big man stood up. Quietly he approached the bed by the window. He picked up a spare pillow propped up on the bedside chair. Swiftly he placed the pillow squarely over the lady's gray face; his big hand easily covering her head.

Her raspy breaths got shorter and closer together. Lou held the pillow down tightly, he could feel her delicate face through the padding. Thirty seconds felt like thirty years; a small convulsion went through Mrs. Dunkirk's emaciated body as she gave up the ghost. She went to her reward without a whimper.

Lou lifted the pillow and dropped it back on the bedside chair like it was on fire.

The room was now eerily quiet.

In a daze he walked toward the door. He glanced back over his shoulder at his own mother; Katerina was sound asleep.

The next thing he knew he was sitting in the Cadillac; the big man didn't remember navigating the hallways. Like a robot he had smiled and waved at the nurses as he left like he always did.

Lou leaned his head on the padded headrest and closed his eyes. He could hear the nun who taught religion back in grade school; thou shall not kill. His mind stuttered over the word. Kill.

He'd gotten more of a stomach ache killing a spider; why was that? The big man answered his own question. It was different killing something that clung to life. He didn't feel life squishing out of Mrs. Dunkirk; he felt relief for her and for Margie.

He was like an archangel he reasoned. The archangels killed; they killed in God's service. He brought peace to the Dunkirks; that couldn't be wrong. It couldn't be.

Lou decided. He would take the memory of the last half hour, wrap it up in an imaginary box and close the lid. He would bury the box deep in his head and never think of this morning again.

46

"Yes, this is Dr. Tim Hoyle; I'm returning your call."

Early Monday morning Tim listened to the man from Allied Display.

"No, that is not acceptable," the blond man responded, "you promised the display cases by September 30th and I expect you to deliver them when you promised."

Again Tim listened to a litany of reasons why the cases would take an additional month. He interrupted the sales representative in mid sentence,

"No, I will not consider a partial delivery. This order is pre-paid. I don't care where you get the glass; take it from somebody else's order. I will expect my display cases on September 30th or you will hear from our attorneys."

Tim cradled the phone and tried to calm down.

The assistant curator decided to work in the basement vaults; being surrounded by the museum's vast holdings always made him feel better. He grabbed the manifests of inventory and his laptop and headed for the cellar.

Tim entered the holding area that housed the art intended for the new annex. One by one Tim inspected the pallets loaded with crates; carefully checking off each item on the

THE FLAVOR OF HEARTS

master list on his computer. Everything seemed in order for the move.

Tim looked at his watch; it was almost two o'clock.

Hah, the lanky blond thought, time does fly when you're having fun. He closed his laptop and started collecting the individual manifests he had placed on each pallet. As he turned to leave the holding area he noticed a small wooden crate off by itself near the back wall. Fearing something misplaced Tim headed to the corner.

As he got closer he read the label: Northeast Pediment-Jennewein Miniature. Ah, he remembered the box. It contained a scale model of one of the museum's most stunning exterior displays. Up under the peaked roof of the museum's north wing freestanding terracotta statues depicted ten Greek gods and goddesses. The figures were brilliantly colored with gold and ceramic glazes, some standing as high as twelve feet tall. Sadly it was a detail many people missed entering the building, but Tim was mesmerized by the colorful display from his first day at the Philadelphia museum.

He suggested the annex display the miniature; thinking it would be a nice way to tie the annex to the main museum. The art selection committee did not agree; Tim could somewhat understand their trepidation; the tiny Greek statues didn't exactly fit any of the themes in the new display areas.

He picked up the crate and took it to the makeshift workbench in the holding area. Using a pry bar the assistant curator removed the wooden top from the crate. Straw cushioned the cloth wrapped object inside. It smelled old. Tim was fairly certain that this box was untouched since it was sealed in the 1930's.

The young curator donned a pair of cotton gloves. He pulled the tiny mock up from the straw; carefully unwrapping the cloth protecting it. The gods and goddesses fit the triangular shape perfectly, standing full height in the center, kneeling and sitting down toward each side. Colored statues were common in antiquity but much more of a rarity in the modern world. Glazing the terracotta with ceramics made the color even more stunning than the ancient method of painting. Tim carefully re-wrapped the scale model. He would not argue the point with the committee for the opening but he decided to eventually find a spot for the colorful miniature at the annex. The young man tried to place the scale model back in the protective crate. Something kept the wrapped carving from touching the bottom. Carefully Tim laid the model down on the table and groped through the straw lining the wooden box.

He was surprised when he felt another object. He extracted a cloth wrapped piece about as big as his hand. Unwrapping the material he was surprised when a tiny griffon stared back. The mythical animal, half lion and half dragon, was ceramic gold, its wings and dragon head brilliantly colored with ceramic silver, white and blue.

No signature, Tim thought examining the little statue more closely. It had to be done by Paul Jennewein, the assistant curator mused. It looked a lot like the Greek gods under the northeastern roof; in style and construction it greatly resembled the scale model he had just examined.

Tim put the little figure down next to his laptop. He searched the museum's database on his laptop for a Jennewein griffon. Surprisingly he found no listing. He typed griffon into the database. The museum had a lot of these; the mythical creature was the Philadelphia museum's unofficial mascot. A flock of them stood on the roof of the building, facing in almost every direction.

Tim scrolled through the multiple listings; no ceramic glazed griffon was mentioned. Many bronze, stone and even wooden griffons were catalogued, but nothing of this description.

Highly unusual, thought the assistant curator. He wrapped the little statue back in its protective cloth. Placing the scale model of the Greek gods back in the crate he tapped the nails in place and resealed the wooden top.

He examined the crate's inventory label more closely. It listed the artist as Paul Jenewein and the title of the work as

THE FLAVOR OF HEARTS

"Western Civilization (Miniature Scale Model of the Northeastern Pediment).

No other art was listed in the box's contents. The little griffon was even more of a mystery. Tim made a mental note to have the crate brought back to its original vault for storage. He scooped up his laptop, the shipping manifests and the misplaced griffon then made his way back to his office.

He spent the rest of the afternoon trying to locate the little statue's rightful place in the storage vaults. Suspecting a key puncher had inadvertently missed a listing when the database was made Tim went down to the archives and examined the written logs that preceded the digital lists of the museum's holdings. To his complete surprise the colorful griffon was not mentioned.

On his way back to his office the curious blond veered off and walked outside through the museum's east door. Tim always enjoyed the view of Philadelphia from the art museum's front entrance but this afternoon he didn't take even a minute to imagine Rocky running up the famous steps. He strode to his left toward the outside of the north wing. Looking up atop the six Greek columns he eyed the full sized version of the miniature he had examined earlier.

The colorful Greek gods stood majestically nestled under the peaked roof. An owl stood in the leftmost corner, but no ceramic coated griffon was part of the Jenewein sculpture. Tim's gaze shifted to the corner of the building above the edge of the stone peaked roof. A bronze griffon stood sideways facing the museum's front courtyard.

The ceramic colored griffon looked like him, Tim mused. The left paw was raised and the pointed wings looked the same. The many bronze griffons on the roof were all listed in the museum's database.

Shaking his head Tim went back to his office. Unwrapping the griffon from its protective cloth he sat facing the mythical figure on his desk. It had to be made by Paul Jennewein, the assistant curator reasoned. He returned to the museum's archives and examined the complete written records for that artist. No mention was made of a terracotta griffon with a ceramic glaze.

Seeing it was close to five o'clock the assistant curator decided to call it a day; Lou would be waiting at the gym. Tim made his way back to his office; he closed his laptop and shut the monitor on his desktop computer. Putting on his suit jacket he eyed the little griffon still perched on his desk. The golden glaze and muscular lion body reminded Tim of his new tattoo.

It's a shame I can't find out where you belong he thought, picking up the statue. He cradled the mythical figure in his palm. The dragon face stared back; the colorful little statue was endearing. Nobody knows anything about you, he thought, addressing the little figure like a pet. Nobody knows.

Tim slipped the little griffon in his jacket pocket and left the museum.

47

Lou was glad to see his training partner. Tim had been a quick study over the last year and it was great to have somebody to work out with regularly.

The men changed from their suits to sweats and hit the weight room. Lou felt as strong as an ox that day, but he was clearly amazed by Tim's strength. His fair haired partner added ten extra pounds to each of his lifts and hefted the weight easily.

As they finished their workout on the chin up bar Lou watched his buddy complete his set, for the first time noticing the changes in Tim's body. It appeared that his pal had packed on twenty pounds of muscle.

Tim's upper arms looked three inches larger around, his chest and calves had grown noticeably in size as well. Lou was somewhat amazed; the changes seemed to have happened overnight.

As the men approached their lockers Lou pondered his buddy's sudden strength and improved physique. Could it be I just never noticed Lou wondered? He hoped Tim wasn't doing anything crazy.

Simultaneously the men opened their adjacent lockers.

Tim eyed his suit jacket on the hook inside; it was hanging way lower on one side than when he hung it up earlier.

The griffon in the pocket weighed it down.

Jesus, Tim thought, what did I do?

The realization hit the assistant curator like a punch in the stomach. He had taken artwork from the museum. An acid taste filled Tim's mouth; he had stolen something.

What the heck was I thinking, he grilled himself silently.

"Tim," Lou broke his friend's screaming reverie, "are you taking anything?"

The blond haired man's head whipped around to face the taller attorney.

"What?" Tim replied incredulously; how had Lou discovered his thievery?

The big man repeated his question,

"Are you taking anything?"

Lou was accustomed to reading body language and facial expressions; it was an invaluable skill in cross examination. The guilty look on Tim's face scared the attorney; now his buddy's sudden strength was really worrisome.

"Tim, are you taking steroids?" Lou's tone was colored with concern.

The blond man burst out laughing. "Are you kidding?" he answered with a noticeable sigh of relief.

"Tim," the former wrestler countered, "you were stronger today than I have ever seen you, not by a little, by a lot. Look at you; nobody would call you Stringbean now."

Tim's eyebrows shot up; for a second he forgot that he confessed his childhood nickname to Lou. All his life Tim had been painfully thin; he secretly hated being so slender and the names the kids called him.

The curator turned to look in the wall of mirrors opposite the lockers; he eyed his body like he was seeing it for the first time.

Wow, Tim mused, Lou was right; he looked downright muscular.

"It's funny," he said out loud, "I noticed my shirts seemed a little tight."

Tim turned back to Lou and laughed; flexing his chest and arms like a wrestler.

"Yee-ah," he said in a gravely voice, "look at me, I'm the Macho Man!"

The big man didn't seem amused by his buddy's imitation of the famous wrestling star.

"It seems sudden, Tim." The attorney went on, "You're not taking anything? Supplements? Protein drinks?"

"No," the blond man sounded surprised by Lou's continued concern, "I swear, just the vitamin I always take: Centrum."

Lou shook his head; he pointed toward the scale in the locker room's corner, "Weigh yourself."

Tim was surprised to find he had gained eighteen pounds; he didn't think he was eating more. Amazement set in. The blond man shrugged his now well developed shoulders, "I don't know, Lou, maybe the workouts are finally paying off."

Lou believed his friend but decided to warn him again anyway. "Steroids are no good, Timmie Boy. Don't get tempted. Remember, they'll build your muscles but shrink your wiener!"

Tim really laughed as they headed for the showers. "No problem there, Louie Boy!"

Tim laughed even harder inside; considering his latest antics with Emily, definitely no problem there.

Lou was shocked to find Dana beside Mrs. Genardi at the stove.

"What's going on here?" he bellowed as he entered the kitchen.

Dana turned to face her husband and announced triumphantly, "I cooked dinner, Louie!"

Mrs. Genardi looked proud as a peacock. She showed Lou the lasagna bubbling in the oven and the tray of garlic bread waiting to take its place. She pointed toward the antipasto on the counter.

"Dana made all this by herself," the little old lady smiled at her new pupil, "I told you that you could do it."

Lou kissed Dana and told her how surprised he was. Maybe the baby inside his beautiful wife made her want to do more homemaker type things.

Dana set the table for three and Mrs. Genardi protested. "No, no, no. The first meal you cooked, you will eat alone with your husband."

Now Dana protested; repeatedly asking their valued housekeeper to stay for dinner as she usually did. The dark skinned lady winked, "No. Two's company. I will definitely stay to eat the second meal you make."

Mrs. Genardi took off her apron, picked up her purse and headed for the door. Lou followed her down to the building's lobby; he always felt better to see her directly into a taxi.

"Thanks, Mrs. G, you're the best!" Lou said as he opened the cab's back door.

The little lady looked up the handsome attorney; her brow slightly furrowed as she responded. "Dana will become a good cook, and then you won't need me any more."

Now it was Lou's turn to protest and he did so vigorously. "Oh, no, no, no, Mrs. G! You're not getting away from us that easy! What would we do without you, especially with the baby coming? You're stuck with us! That's it, we couldn't live without you!"

"Hah!" the little lady replied as Lou closed the car door.

By the smile on her face the former wrestler knew she was glad to hear the comforting words.

Lou practically ran down the hallway when the elevator door opened; he realized he was famished on the ride up to the twenty second floor. Dana was putting the lasagna on the dining room table when he re-entered the apartment; she never looked more beautiful.

THE FLAVOR OF HEARTS

Lou complimented Dana's antipasto and the garlic bread; and then he raved about her lasagna. He ate heartily and Dana did too. She seemed pleased as punch.

"I didn't make any dessert," Dana apologized, "Mrs. G said one thing at a time. I have some spumoni in the freezer. You want some spumoni, Louie?"

"No, I couldn't eat another bite." The big man grinned, "I do want dessert though, I want some Torroni."

Dana eyed her husband quizzically, "Some what?"

Lou stood up from the table and scooped his wife up in his arms, "I want some Torroni. Some Dana Torroni."

Dana giggled as Lou carried her toward their bedroom like a newlywed on the honeymoon night.

"What about the dishes?" she asked coyly.

"We'll do them together after dessert," he replied, laying her gently on their king sized bed.

The Torronis made love. Their sex life was always great, but this night for some reason the sex was even more special. Maybe a man makes love more passionately with a belly full of delicious food prepared lovingly by his wife.

Dana laid her head on Lou's ample chest; she was tired from the cooking and the active "dessert", but she never felt more contented.

She looked up at her husband's handsome face. His eyes were closed and he wore a blissful smile. She knew he felt as happy as she did; it was a magical night. She should have tried cooking sooner!

Dana eyed the golden key tattooed on Lou's massive pectoral muscle. It made her even warmer inside; remembering the night in Wildwood when Lou called her the key to his heart. She looked up and ran her hand through his curly black hair.

"I love you, Louie. I love you so much."

His brown eyes opened and he eyed her beautiful face.

"I love you too, Dane. I love you more than words can say!"

"Lou!"

Dana's voice took on a tone of total surprise.

"Did you dye your hair?"

She leaned up on her elbow moving her head closer to Lou's as she continued to run her hand through his hair. The two gray patches near Lou's temples were gone; his hair was solid black again.

"No, I didn't do anything to my hair," the big man sounded surprised.

"Yes, you did," Dana countered.

She almost climbed on top of him to check out the other side of his head,"Your little gray patches are gone!"

"What?" Lou sounded incredulous.

The big man sat up and eyed his reflection in the mirror on the bed's headboard.

"Damn," he was astounded.

Dana was right. His hair looked like it did when he was in his twenties; the small patches of gray were completely gone. How could it be Lou wondered? He ran his hands through his own hair. Not even a small sign of gray was visible.

"I swear, Dane. I never did anything to my hair!"

Lou sounded so astonished Dana knew he was telling the truth.

The couple sat wide eyed, peering at Lou's reflection.

"It's Buena Suerte!" Dana said suddenly. She went on in a rush of words,"Emily got her eyesight and I'm having the baby! You're getting younger! It's Buena Suerte!"

Lou shook his head in disbelief. Still, it was hard to refute their good luck as of late. Lou told Dana about Tim's strength at the gym and the changes in their friend's physique.

"He told me the first time we went to the gym that he always wished for muscles, but his body never bulked up, no matter what he tried."

"See, it is! It's Buena Suerte! Tim got his wish too!"

Maybe she's right, Lou reasoned. It made no sense at all, but he would be the last one to ignore the plain facts; they had all been uncommonly lucky since their trip to Wildwood.

When Tim came home from the gym he found Emily hard at work on her John Deere campaign. "How's it going, Em?" he asked from the doorway.

"Good." she answered, "It's good to be working again but I feel a little rusty."

Storyboards for TV ads were leaning against the wall; mock ups of three different print ads were tacked to the bulletin board.

"Looks like you got a lot done," Tim commented.

"Yeah," the adwoman replied, "I got some good stuff, I think."

Tim left Emily to continue her work and ducked into their bedroom to change his clothes. He removed the little griffon from his jacket pocket. Tim stood in the bedroom and again cradled the mythical animal in his palm.

He had berated himself in the car all the way home from the gym. He fully intended to bring the stolen statue back to the museum the following day. Standing in his bedroom his resolve was weakening. The little guy was so cute; Tim really liked the colorful griffon. Weirdly, the statue looked like it was smiling; the dragon face looked happier here than in the museum.

You want to stay here with me and Em don't you, little buddy? Once again Tim silently addressed the statue like a real pet.

Tim knew it was wrong, with every fiber of his being he knew it was wrong to keep the griffon. He looked at himself in the dresser mirror. He had never stolen anything in his life. Well, Tim thought, I guess there's a first time for everything.

Ignoring any sane and honest thoughts, Tim put the statue on the dresser.

He eyed the little fellow the whole time he put on jeans and sneakers. The assistant curator was amazed how little guilt he felt. Tim slipped his Wildwood souvenir tank top over his head. He admired his pumped arms in the dresser mirror and the gleaming lion head on his deltoid. For the first time in his life he was thrilled with his reflection.

Tim walked across the hall to Emily's home office.

"I'm almost done for today," she said not looking up from the computer screen.

"Take your time, Em" he replied.

Tim walked over to the bulletin board and took a closer look at the new John Deere print ads.

An attractive lady, dressed in form fitting overalls eyed a handsome, well built man in jeans, a white t-shirt and a cowboy hat. She had her hands folded up near her chest and had a wistful look on her face. The headline read, "The heart wants what the heart wants."

The lady had tiny green and yellow hearts floating above her head. At closer look Tim realized the lady was eyeing the John Deere tractor behind the cowboy, she wasn't in love with the man, she was in love with the lawnmower! The next two ads had basically the same theme with different tractors, models and outdoor backdrops.

"Wow, Em," Tim said excitedly, "these ads are really great."

Emily turned and faced her husband. "You think so?" she asked.

Using her father's favorite saying as slogan seemed almost like a cop out, but she too thought it made a perfect basis for the new ad campaign.

"Yeah, I do, they're great." he assured his wife.

Emily rose from her chair and joined Tim at the bulletin board.

"I'll tell you what else looks great," she said slyly, encircling his waist from behind with her arms, "You!"

Tim turned and embraced his wife. Emily always loved her husband's lean physique, but today he looked like one of the models in her ads! She rubbed her hands over his well developed arms and shoulders. Her eye paused on the gleaming lion head. The tattoo looked even more striking on Tim's newly bulging, well defined deltoid muscle.

"Those workouts with Lou are really paying off," she commented.

Emily rubbed her hands on Tim's rock hard chest. She slid her hand down his six pack abs and made a move toward unbuttoning his jeans.

Tim didn't waste a second; he had his pants down in a flash and made love to Emily right there on the office floor. Tim performed like a man who had just been released from prison; Emily egged him on, entreating him to pound harder and harder.

Tim was sure they were shaking the floor but he hardly cared; their passion was all encompassing. The Hoyles finished in a heap, drenched with sweat and gasping for air.

Emily thought of the Torroni's in the apartment below.

"I hope Lou and Dana aren't in their bedroom," she giggled, "they might think we're having an earthquake!"

48

"Lou came home from the ballgame last night sloshed!" Dana sounded like she hardly believed her own words. Emily was surprised as well.

"He was so funny. He was singing Beatle songs to me," Dana laughed as the girls entered the yoga studio, "I didn't know he knew so many Beatle songs...it was crazy!"

"Tim and I, we've been going crazy too," Emily confessed on the way into the dressing room.

As the girls approached their lockers Emily went on. "We're having sex all over the apartment. The other night we did it on the floor in my office!"

Dana laughed as she changed into her yoga pants and top. "Sounds good to me!"

"Hey, I'm not complaining!" Emily responded. "It's weird, though," the adwoman lowered her voice to almost a whisper, "I've never been so horny in my life. It's like I can't get enough. I didn't think I was into rough stuff, but now..."

When Emily's voice trailed off, Dana's curiosity escalated.

"Rough stuff? What do you mean? You're hitting each other?"

"No, no!" Emily laughed out loud at the thought. She tried to put her feelings into words, "I want him to do it harder and

THE FLAVOR OF HEARTS

harder. Harder than I ever did, look at this," Emily pointed as she took off her jeans to change her clothes. She showed Dana two bruises, one on each of the insides of her upper thighs.

Dana's eyes widened with surprise as Emily explained. "I kept telling him to go harder and harder. It felt great, really great, but when the bruises came up the next day...I'm wondering if I'm going crazy!"

Dana was at a loss for words. She had never seen anyone bruised from sex! Once she had taken a rape awareness class, they described the bruises on a woman used as evidence, but bruises from sex with your husband?

"Well," the pretty accountant searched for the right words. "If you both like it that way, what could be wrong with it?"

"Hi, Dana. Hi, Emily."

The girls turned to the voice behind them.

Sarah Spike in Her Nose was smiling as she went on, "Is today a good day to come down and show those tattoos to my boss?"

"Sure," Dana responded nodding, "we'll follow you over there after the class."

"Great, I totally appreciate it," the tattooed girl went across the room to her own locker.

Dana and Emily eyed each other. They read each other's minds; both hoped Sarah hadn't heard their earlier conversation. Who looks like the wild one now, Emily thought?

The girls followed Sarah's Volkswagon Jetta down Broad Street. A sticker on the rear bumper said NIN.

"What do you think that is? NIN?" Emily asked Dana.

The second N was printed backwards.

"It means Nine Inch Nails." Dana informed her pal.

"Where? Through her nose?" Emily sounded puzzled.

"No," Dana laughed out loud, "It's a band. Nine Inch Nails is a band. Lou listens to them sometimes on his iPod when he runs."

"Oh," Emily suddenly felt out of touch. "I never heard of them."

"I think they're broken up now," Dana ventured, "but they're still popular, I guess. It's pretty hard stuff, kind of dark sounding. The lead singer is real cute though, I forget his name."

Dana followed Sarah's car, steering the Mini Cooper on to South Street.

"We should have tried to find out the address of Buena Suerte." Emily said changing the subject, "I felt like a real idiot last week when she asked where it was and I didn't even know."

"Got ya covered," Dana said laughing again, "I felt like a moron myself. Lou said he thought it was on 21st or 22nd Avenue. He said he didn't think we walked more than six or seven blocks from the end of the boardwalk when we saw it."

Dana eased the tiny British car into a little space on South Street.

"Know what's weird?" Dana went on as the girls exited the vehicle and headed toward Sarah waiting down the block, "I called information and they said there was no listing for Buena Suerte in Wildwood."

"Maybe it was too new to make the phone book." Emily offered.

The girls joined Sarah and followed her into The Body Shop.

Looking around the popular Philadelphia tattoo emporium, both Emily and Dana were struck with the same thought. Buena Suerte had little in common with this place.

Framed art for possible tattoos covered the walls. Huge sections of photos were hung showing customers and their newly applied body art. Looking closer at the pictures Emily realized what Lou meant that day about the puffiness of new tattoos. Tattoo stations lined one wall; three artists gave tattoos simultaneously. No wonder the big man had called Buena Suerte the weirdest tattoo parlor he had ever seen.

THE FLAVOR OF HEARTS

Sarah ushered the girls into an office off to one side of the lobby. A man covered in tattoos stood up from the desk and introduced himself as the owner; he smiled broadly and thanked the girls sincerely for coming down.

"I'm really excited to see your ink," he said to Dana and Emily, "Sarah couldn't say enough about it."

Dana raised her shirt and turned around. The tattoo was visible above the ultra low waistband of her Frankie B. jeans.

Emily was floored by the shocked expression on the owner's face. He practically jumped across the desk to get a closer look at Dana's faux broach.

"Jesus," he exclaimed. "Do you mind if I touch it?"

The owner bent down for a closer look and with Dana's permission he gently rubbed his index finger across the small of her back. He was obviously more than amazed.

"I've never seen such a thing; it seems like some kind of metallic ink."

"What did I tell you?" Sarah said.

It was clear from her tone of voice that the owner doubted her previous descriptions.

"You got this in Wildwood? Sarah said the place had a Spanish name?"

"Buena Suerte," all three girls said the name in unison.

The owner stood up to his full height; he looked weak in the knees. He turned toward Emily and she lowered the waistband of her jersey skirt to reveal the sailboat.

"Oh my God," the owner exclaimed, "that's incredible!" He sat on the edge of the desk looking stunned. Finally he shook his head and spoke, "I go to every major trade show," he pointed toward a bookshelf lined with magazines, "I read every industry publication. I've never seen or heard anything about metallic tattoos."

He walked toward a shelf on the wall and held up his personal tattoo gun, "Did they use a gun like this?"

"It was bigger, right Em?" Dana responded.

Emily nodded and answered, "Yes, it looked like that but bigger and it was chrome; it was very shiny."

The girls described Buena Suerte. Sarah and her boss seemed surprised by the "one at a time" policy at the Wildwood tattoo parlor. When Emily recounted the story of the artist's uncanny drawing of her father's custom sloop the pair looked positively flabbergasted.

"Sarah said you didn't remember the address of the place?" the owner asked.

Sheepishly Dana admitted that they still didn't know the exact location, "My husband said he thought it was either 21st or 22nd Avenue. He said he didn't think it was more than six or seven blocks from the north end of the boardwalk."

"Looking from the boardwalk it was on the left side of the street," Emily offered.

"I called information to get the address," Dana shrugged, "but there was no listing."

Both girls were surprised to hear that Sarah and her boss had also tried to locate Buena Suerte with no success.

"There's no listing on Yahoo or Google either," Sarah said with a puzzled look.

"Well," the tattooed man addressed his employee, "we're gonna have to take a ride to the shore and check this place out."

The owner thanked the girls profusely for coming to show him their unusual body art. When he walked them to the door he offered a discount on a future piercing or tattoo.

As Dana and Emily climbed into the Mini Cooper the pretty accountant turned to her pal and laughed, "Well what do you think, should we go back next week and get rings through our noses?"

Emily grinned and answered with mock sincerity, "No, I want a spike like Sarah's."

Both girls laughed as they headed home. The conversation took a more serious tone when they discussed the owner's reaction to the Buena Suerte tattoos. It was odd that he had never seen or heard of metallic tattoo ink, he appeared to be a man on top of his business.

"What do you think he would've said if we told him the good luck forever part?" Dana wondered out loud as the girls boarded the elevator in their building.

"I think he would have thought we were insane." Emily said wryly.

Dana turned back as she exited the elevator on the twenty-first floor.

"Hey, come down for dinner tonight, come around seven. I'm gonna cook!"

Emily agreed. The adwoman shook her head as the steel doors shut. She wasn't sure which was harder to believe, good luck was coming from the tattoos, or Dana Torroni was cooking dinner.

Dana's lasagna was delicious.

"Pretty good for her second one, huh?" Lou asked beaming with pride.

The Hoyle's agreed. Over dessert and coffee the girls recounted their experience at the South Street tattoo parlor.

"Did you tell him that the tattoos never swelled up?" Lou asked after hearing of the owner's downright amazement.

"No, I didn't. I meant to," Emily replied first, "I saw some photos in there. I saw what you meant about the swelling. I meant to mention that. Did you tell him that, Dane?"

The accountant shook her head, "No, I never thought to tell him that."

"We left the good luck forever part out too!" she added.

Lou shook his head. He wasn't sure himself about the luck of the tattoos; that was certainly a hard thing to wrap your head around. However, he was positive that the lack of swelling was a very weird aspect of the Buena Suerte body art.

"He probably wouldn't have believed either of those things," Lou ventured.

49

Emily sat down early Thursday to organize her John Deere presentation. As she turned on her computer monitor she decided to first satisfy a nagging curiosity. She clicked the desktop icon and opened the Internet Explorer.

Navigating to Yahoo she typed Buena Suerte into the search box. One and a half million hits appeared; many sites contained the Spanish words for good luck. Refining the search Emily typed "Buena Suerte Tattoos" in quote marks.

More like it she thought, eyeing the five results.

Clicking the first link she was taken to a gallery of tattoos. Thumbnail images represented each entry. About a third of the way down the page a familiar golden glow was evident, the caption below read: "Buena Suerte, Waikiki Beach".

Waikiki? She clicked the thumbnail to see the full sized image. Two gleaming gold rings were interlocked. They sat on a puffy white cloud with a blue sky and a tiny rainbow behind it. A golden date was drawn underneath: 2/8/05.

It looks like a wedding commemorative she reasoned. It was plain to see the similarities in this tattoo and hers: the golden sheen was unmistakable, the fine lines were remarkable.

Emily backspaced and navigated to the web site's homepage. It was dedicated to the art of tattooing; visitors

THE FLAVOR OF HEARTS

were encouraged to send photos of their own body art for inclusion in the many galleries. The adwoman made a bookmark to the page and saved it in a folder called Buena Suerte.

Navigating back to the original search Emily clicked on the second link.

The image took her breath away. This tattoo occupied a man's whole shoulder blade. A surfer was shown "in the pipe" crouched down on his board with a golden wave washing over him. As with her tattoo: white, deep blue and metallic gold gave the water the realistic shine of the sun on the surface. It was stunning.

The caption below the photo read, "Thanks Buena Suerte Tattoos, Waikiki Beach. Definitely the coolest tattoo place in the world."

Again Emily navigated to the site's homepage. The website was posted by a surfing enthusiast; he had photos of himself in many exotic locales. The lanky brunette assumed that the tattoo was his. As with the first site she visited that morning, Emily made a bookmark and saved the surfer's site in the Buena Suerte folder.

Again she retuned to the original Yahoo search results. The third entry seemed to be a blog site...

The phone rang and interrupted her research.

"Em," Dana was breathless, "turn on channel six, hurry up, hurry up, channel six!"

Immediately the adwoman picked up the remote on her desk and powered up the small flat screen TV on the office's side wall.

The local morning show was airing. Lottery officials were presenting a giant check to a jackpot winner.

What the heck, thought Emily?

The anchorman spoke over the film, "Yes, there's one winner, folks. The winner of three hundred and fifty million dollars in last night's Mega Million..."

"It's her, right? From the line, from the line!" Dana sounded incredulous.

Emily paid closer attention to the girl holding the check.

Lettering on the bottom of the screen said: Tina Conway of Millville New Jersey Sole Mega Million Winner.

When the camera zoomed in for a close-up Emily's jaw dropped. It was definitely drunken Tina from the Buena Suerte line. Emily could still hear the girl's slightly slurred words, "Buena Suerte, get a tattoo here and have good luck forever."

Jesus, suddenly Emily felt dizzy. The camera pulled back to include Tina's companion in the shot.

"It's him!" both girls spoke in unison on the phone.

"The boyfriend!" Dana's voice was a pitch higher than usual.

The anchorman finished the segment saying, "Ms. Tina Conway and Mr. James Billings, both employed at the Wheaton Glass Company, have announced that they will not return to their jobs and will now consider the many options open to them."

The girls sat on the phone in silence for a few seconds.

"Unbelievable." Emily was still too stunned to say much more.

"It was definitely her, right?" Dana asked.

"For sure. Definitely," Emily assured her friend.

"That's big time Buena Suerte," the accountant exclaimed.

Emily could hardly find words to argue the point, "Dane, do you really believe it's the tattoo?"

Dana was unshakeable,"Winning the lottery? Three hundred and fifty million? I don't think you get luckier than that; that's textbook lucky! Hey, you know we've been pretty lucky too."

That fact was extremely hard to refute.

"It's weird," Emily spoke softly and she sounded worried, "it kind of scares me to think it's magic."

"Forget about it," Dana felt a twinge of guilt. Emily really sounded frightened. "Conway, right? Maybe Tipsy Tina had the luck of the Irish long before she ever saw Buena Suerte. Forget about it."

As only Dana could, she turned the conversation on a dime and cheered Emily up.

"Hey, I'm making you a pie. This afternoon Mrs. Genardi is teaching me to make pie crust and I'm making one for you and Tim!"

"What? You're making what?" Emily was stunned again; Dana Torroni was baking a pie?

"Oh, yes," Dana laughed and put on a sappy Julia Child voice, "I'm going to bake a blueberry pie and I'll bring it up later unless it looks like a manhole cover."

She went on in her normal voice, "Lou went to the Bar Outing today; he's playing golf up in West Chester someplace. The lawyers have a big dinner too, so Mrs. G. says it's a good time to try baking something."

Emily shook her head in disbelief as she hung up the phone. Dana was turning into quite the homemaker. Maybe it's the baby on the way, Emily mused.

Turning back to her computer monitor the adwoman eyed the Buena Suerte search results. She decided to save them with a bookmark for later and move on to her real work.

50

It was a beautiful day for golf, warm and sunny with very low humidity. Lou and his foursome squared all their side bets as they left the 18th green. The big man was pleasantly surprised; he won every wager. Looking at his scorecard Lou realized he had never played better.

Hard to believe the handsome attorney thought as he entered the club house's locker room; lately he had very little time to work on his golf game.

The Bar Association dinner was always interesting. It was good to hear all the news and gossip in the local legal community. Many attorneys made it a point to congratulate Lou on his upcoming fatherhood. He drank more than a few shots celebrating the baby's future arrival.

Making his way to the bathroom the big man vowed to curtail any additional drinking. He could feel the whiskey he had already imbibed and knew his limits.

Stepping out of the men's room door, Lou suddenly stopped dead in his tracks. Still he smacked hard into a young woman in a waitress's uniform. It took both arms for the big man to steady the petite lady; he almost knocked her to the floor.

"God, I'm sorry," Lou stammered, "are you OK?"

She appeared shaken but told the big man otherwise, "I'm fine, I'm fine," she assured Lou, "I shouldn't have stopped so close to the door."

Glad she was unhurt the olive skinned attorney turned toward the dining room.

"Hey," the young lady called to his broad shoulders.

Lou turned back toward her voice. She was now standing in front of a service door next to the rest rooms. She crooked a finger toward the big man as she pushed the door open, "Come with me, come on," she invited.

Lou followed her into a long hallway. At the end they stepped into a storage area attached to the country club's kitchen. The pretty waitress opened a heavy steel door and entered a huge walk in refrigerator.

Lou followed like a robot. The cold air felt refreshing.

"Are you all right?" Lou asked suddenly aware of the weird situation.

"Oh, I'm all right," she answered turning toward him and encircling her arms around his waist, "and you're more than all right. You're the hottest guy in this place."

In a split second she had his pants undone and his penis in her mouth!

Lou responded as most men would.

It was surreal; the cold air, her warm mouth.

The big man was stunned; it was like an out of body experience. She finished him off like a professional. When she rose from her knees she laughed out loud at his shocked expression; then pressed a slip of paper into his hand.

"Call me, OK?" she said over her shoulder as she exited the refrigerator.

Lou stood alone in the cold air. What the fuck have I done he thought.

The big man practically exploded out of the steel door and ran down the service hallway. He eyed his Rolex as he re-entered the dining room; less than ten minutes had passed since he left his table to go to the rest room.

He had never in his life even considered cheating on Dana! More than dreamlike, it was hard to believe what had just happened. The slip of paper still clutched in his hand was the only proof that the whole scenario had really taken place.

Lou strode toward the bar and quickly downed a shot of Jack Daniels. He crumpled the paper into a tiny ball and left it on the bar in the empty shot glass.

Seated with his colleagues he pretended to listen to their jokes and stories. The big man realized the waitress was not standing in his path by accident. He felt like an idiot; an unfaithful idiot.

Lou vowed to do something really special for his treasured wife. He decided to call the Hotel Hershey and book the most expensive suite for the weekend. He would treat Dana like a queen in the world famous chocolate town. For the first time Lou Torroni felt that his wife deserved a better husband.

51

Early Monday morning Emily selected a business suit from the closet and a tailored blue dress. She placed them both on the bed and then decided to wear the suit to New York for the John Deere presentation. By her attire she hoped to remind the executives at Satchi and Satchi that she used to work there.

On second thought the charcoal gray suit was a little plain. Emily caught a glimpse of the floral choker she bought in Cape May laying on the dresser. That will definitely spark up the outfit she thought; she decided to wear the matching gem studded ring as well.

The phone on the nightstand rang,

"Hi, Em. How was your weekend?" Dana was slightly out of breath.

Emily smiled; her pal must've eaten a ton of chocolate in Hershey, PA to be on the treadmill this early!

"Great," she answered, "Tim must've felt guilty so we spent Saturday night up in New Hope ourselves!"

"Wow, no way. Did you shop?" Dana asked.

New Hope, PA was a town renowned for antiquing.

"I bought a bracelet. Natural pearls. Victorian era," Emily told her friend, "What about you? How was Hershey?"

Dana recounted an amazing time at the luxurious hotel spa in the world famous chocolate town.

"They did a treatment on me where they covered my body in liquid chocolate. It sounds weird but my skin feels really soft."

"If I covered myself in chocolate, Tim would want to lick it off!" Emily said slyly.

"Funny you should say that. Louie found a bottle in a gift shop. Chocolate Love Syrup. It said "make your loved one an edible delight." Dana giggled when she said the next part, "He bought a bottle for you and Tim too!"

Emily burst out laughing, "Did he make you into an edible delight?"

"More than once!" Dana answered laughing again.

In a jovial but more serious tone Dana went on, "We brought you a killer box of chocolates too. What are you doing later? Want to go to The Gallery? There's a serious shoe sale going on."

"Ah, I can't," Emily declined, "I gotta go to New York today and give my John Deere presentation."

"Oh, that's right, I forgot. You're gonna do great there, Em. I think the ads are perfect. The guys are hot!"

"I'll call you as soon as I get back." Emily promised.

Cradling the phone the adwoman smiled. She was glad Dana liked the ads; after all the campaign was geared toward women. Hopefully the executives from John Deere would feel the same.

Emily entered her closet to select the rest of her outfit. Perusing her shoe collection Emily wished she could've made it to The Gallery with Dana. Funny, the adwoman thought, they'd been doing a lot of shopping lately. She couldn't remember the last class or lecture that Dana attended.

Once again the lanky brunette wondered if Dana's pregnancy was responsible for her culinary activities and the onslaught of purchases. Emily smiled. There was a name for that, when a pregnant woman goes overboard cleaning and

THE FLAVOR OF HEARTS

buying stuff. What was it? Nesting, that's it! Emily smiled broadly as she finished dressing; Dana was feathering her nest!

Emily felt right at home back at Satchi and Satchi. Though she was nervous at first her presentation went off without a hitch. The John Deere executives were more than enthusiastic over the new campaign.

At the in-house meeting after the presentation Bob Satchi called the campaign another home run. He congratulated Emily warmly and thanked her for continuing her work with the company. She was surprised to hear that she was nominated for another Clio; her Dunkin Donuts campaign was highly successful and it was thrilling to hear she might receive her first advertising award as a freelancer.

Emily visited with her friend Joan DeMeter before she left the agency. Seated comfortably in the executive's plush corner office she filled her old pal in on the latest news. Joan was shocked to hear that her straitlaced friend was now tattooed; but she was highly impressed with the Buena Suerte body art.

Before leaving Emily suggested that Joan come and spend a weekend in Philly. Later in the elevator Emily laughed out loud at the thought. As hard as it was to believe, she really had learned to appreciate the city and wanted to share it with her old friend. She knew Joan would love Dana; they were a lot alike in many ways. Emily grinned at the thought of the three of them tearing up Philadelphia.

For the first time the adwoman exited the tunnel without tears in her eyes. She sang with every song on the radio all the way back to Philly. After Emily parked her car next to Tim's in the basement garage she practically ran to the elevator. She was excited to tell him how great things went and of her latest Clio nomination.

Letting herself into the apartment Emily tossed her portfolio on the couch and headed into the bedroom. It was odd, Tim wasn't there. She made her way back toward the kitchen and saw a paper propped up on the counter.

Tim's note said to come down to the Torroni's when she got home. She grabbed her purse and headed for the door. She guessed that Dana was making another dinner; good thing, Emily thought, I'm starving!

Tim answered the Torrini's door and hugged Emily tightly as she stepped through the doorway. Over his shoulder Emily saw Lou sitting on the couch with his head in his hands. She heard a voice and noticed a man in a suit over near the kitchen talking on a cell phone.

"Em, it's bad," Tim whispered in her ear, "Dana was killed this afternoon."

Emily's knees buckled. Tim caught his wife before she hit the floor.

When the adwoman regained consciousness she was laying on the love seat in the living room. Faces came into focus above her; Lou and Tim looked distraught. Emily sat up, still feeling a little dizzy. Remembering Tim's words she fell backwards on the little couch and began crying.

Lou ran toward the bathroom. They could hear him sobbing behind the closed door. Slowly Emily sat up. Tim joined her on the love seat and put his arms around her.

"What happened?" she barely choked out the words.

"She was hit by a taxi cab. She died at Jefferson's emergency room."

Tim's voice cracked on the last sentence. A tear rolled down his cheek as he hugged his wife even tighter. Emily buried her face in his chest and wept uncontrollably. She heard a voice and turned toward it.

"Here, drink a little," the strange man in the suit put a goblet of wine on the coffee table as he introduced himself, "I'm Gary Forrest. I'm a friend of Lou's from work."

THE FLAVOR OF HEARTS

Sitting down in the armchair next to the Hoyle's he picked up the glass and again offered the wine to Emily. She accepted it and gratefully gulped the red liquid.

Gary explained that he was a private investigator attached to Lou's law firm. He told Tim and Emily in a hushed voice that he just got off the phone with the Philadelphia police.

"I spoke to a friend of mine over there," he recounted, "he was off duty and actually saw the whole thing. Dana crossed Market Street. She got to the curb and then turned around and ran back into the intersection. My buddy said it looked like she might've forgotten something. She turned quick and didn't notice the light changed. A taxi pinned her against a bus pulling away from the curb. My buddy called for the ambulance, it came right away but she was hit pretty hard..."

Gary's voice trailed off as he saw the tears streaming down Emily's face.

The private investigator returned to the Torroni's bar and returned with two more glasses and the open bottle of merlot. He refilled all three glasses and the trio sipped the calming wine in silence.

Lou re-entered the room and Emily rose from the couch and embraced him. By his uneven breaths Emily could tell he was choking back tears. She led him to the couch and sat down beside him.

When Gary offered Lou a goblet of wine, the big man asked for Jack Daniels. The distraught attorney ignored the shot glass his colleague provided and drank the bourbon straight from the bottle.

The quartet drank in stunned silence until Lou passed out on the couch. Gary assured the Hoyles that he would spend the night with Lou and watch over him. Numbly Emily and Tim returned to their apartment.

52

The week went by like a whirlwind. Lou's brother came in from California. Joseph Torroni took a leave of absence from his job to stay a few weeks and help his younger brother over the rough spots.

If it weren't such a sad situation, Emily would have laughed to see the Torroni brothers together. The men looked like bookends. It was actually hard at first glance to tell the two apart.

Lou asked Emily to look through Dana's things to find an outfit to bring to the funeral home. The adwoman was surprised to find her girlfriend's closet bursting at the seams. Many of the new clothes still had the tags attached.

Joe Torroni and one of Dana's cousins helped Lou through the rest of the funeral arrangements. Mrs. Genardi moved into the condo's guestroom and took loving care of both the Torroni brothers.

Saturday morning the Hoyles dressed in silence for the funeral service in South Philadelphia. Emily almost burst into tears in the apartment building's garage at the sight of the Dana's Mini Cooper nestled in its parking space.

The church was packed to the rafters; the huge Corelli family was out in full force. Their grief was palpable; Lou sat in the first row with his brother. He looked shell shocked and pale.

Emily clung tightly to Tim's arm as they found seats for the service. The Catholic funeral mass was a little mystifying to the Hoyles but they followed the cues of the crowd and stood and sat at the right moments.

It was clear from the heartfelt eulogies that Dana was deeply loved in the community; people openly wept at the kind words and deeds recounted from Dana's shortened life.

A long line of people stood in line to receive the Catholic Sacrament of Communion. Emily sat back in the padded pew and closed her eyes. She remembered clearly the first time she ever laid eyes on Dana Torroni:

Emily walked two blocks from her apartment to try a different dry cleaner. A petite woman with shining black hair was already at the counter. She was holding a huge man's suit on a hanger; it looked absolutely humongous in her tiny hand.

"Please, I know I'm twenty minutes too late for the same day service," the dark haired woman was asking, "but I really need this suit cleaned. Couldn't you ask if I could possibly have it by tonight? I could pay extra..."

The young counter girl looked unmoved as she answered, "I don't think so; they don't like when I take same day stuff late..."

It sounded to Emily like the young employee didn't want to buck the store's policy.

"I'm always in here, come on, it's twenty minutes," the dark haired woman tried to be convincing. Eyeing a class ring on the counter girl's hand the desperate customer went on, "You go to Goretti?"

St. Maria Goretti was a Catholic girl's high school in Philadelphia.

"Maybe you know my cousins," the petite woman with the suit went on, "the Corellis: Marie, Antonia and Carla? They all go to Goretti."

"Toni Corelli is your cousin?" the counter girl suddenly smiled, "she's on the soccer team with me." The counter girl paused a second then took the suit from the lady's hand, "Okay, give it to me, I'll go in the back and ask."

The tiny olive skinned woman turned to Emily waiting behind her in line, "I'm sorry to make you wait longer," she apologized. "My husband thinks his lucky suit is clean." She laughed as she said the last part. Her laugh was infectious.

"No problem," Emily answered smiling, "I wish I had your power of persuasion."

"What do you mean?" Dana asked. Her insatiable curiosity was piqued.

For the first time in her life Emily confided a personal situation to a total stranger. She showed the friendly woman with the laughing eyes her engagement ring.

"The stone is really loose and I took it to a jewelry store on Eighth Street, they want me to leave it there. I wanted them to fix it while I waited but they wouldn't."

Dana eyed the stone, it was probably at least four carats.

"I don't blame you," the stranger said, "I wouldn't let that rock out of my sight either."

The counter girl returned and told the olive skinned woman that the suit would be ready at five. The petite lady thanked her profusely and took the claim ticket.

When Emily finished at the counter and exited the little shop, the dark haired stranger was standing outside by the door.

"Hey," she said to the lanky New Yorker, "my cousin works on jeweler's row. I bet he would fix your ring while you watch."

Pointing to a gleaming silver Mini Cooper at the curb the friendly lady went on, "You could follow me if you want, this is my car."

Emily explained that she had walked to the dry cleaners from her apartment nearby.

"Hop in then," Dana offered, "I'll take you down there."

Emily paused a second, considering the generous offer of help. She had often heard tales of the kindness of strangers but had little first hand experience with such phenomenon. Dana sensed her reticence.

"I'm not a serial killer or anything," the dark haired beauty giggled. She held up her hand. A huge diamond engagement ring and diamond studded wedding band dominated her tiny left ring finger, "I have my own," she laughed, "I promise I won't steal yours!"

For the second time that afternoon Emily did something highly out of character, she climbed into a car with a total stranger.

On the ride through the Old City section Emily mentioned her recent move from New York. Dana explained that she was a native Philadelphian and offered to suggest the city's best places. She immediately began pointing out shops and restaurants of interest along the way

After parking Mini Cooper the girls approached a storefront on Walnut Street. The sign in the window said Levy's. Dana rang the bell and they were buzzed in to enter. A dark haired man with the same laughing eyes hurried around the counter and embraced the petite Sicilian.

"Dane, how are you? What a surprise! What brings you down here?"

Dana motioned toward her lanky companion, "My friend, ah..."

"Emily," the transplanted New Yorker supplied her own name.

As easy as the conversation had been on the ride down there, Emily was surprised to realize that the two women had never really introduced themselves.

"Emily's stone is really loose," Dana spoke as if they had known each other for years, "could you tighten it up while we watch?"

After he examined the ring Eddie Corelli took the two girls into the back work room. Expertly he tightened the setting and returned the engagement ring. When Emily produced her wallet and tried to pay he waved her off.

"No, no, it's on the house; anything for a friend of Dana's."

Emily protested but he insisted. She thanked him repeatedly and he smiled as he escorted the girls to the front door,

"Dane, I guess I'll see you at dinner on Sunday."

She assured him that he would and the girls headed back to the Mini Cooper.

Emily turned toward her new friend and made it official, "I'm Emily Hoyle."

She stuck out her hand and Dana shook it firmly as she replied, "I'm Dana Torroni."

Both girls laughed at their previous lack of formality. Climbing into the little silver car Emily commented on Dana's apparent plethora of cousins.

"My father had nine brothers and sisters. That does make for a lot of relatives!"

Dana headed up Ninth Street and offered to take Emily directly home. The girls were shocked to find they lived in the same building, a new high rise of luxury riverfront condos not far from the store where they originally met.

Dana parked her car in the underground garage and the pair headed for the elevator.

The new friends were further astonished to find they lived a floor apart on the same end of the building: the Torroni's in 2102 and the Hoyle's in 2202. The girls exchanged phone numbers. The next day Dana called and invited her neighbor to yoga class. Emily had never made such a good friend so easily.

Tears steamed down Emily's pale face. The somber organ music made the happy memory even more painful. Tim put his arm protectively around his wife. He fought hard to keep from openly sobbing himself.

53

Sunday afternoon the Hoyles went down to check on Lou. They found the big man on the couch cradling a bottle of bourbon. Mrs. Genardi cajoled the distraught attorney to eat; she used the Hoyle's as bait.

"Come to the table, Mr. Lou. Eat with your friends."

Reluctantly he joined Emily, Tim and his brother Joe in the dining room. Mrs. Genardi served delicious meatball parmesan sandwiches with steaming bowls of Italian Wedding soup. Lou brought the bottle and drank more than he ate, but at least the poor man managed a few bites.

After lunch Joe Torroni suggested they sit out on the balcony. Secretly he hoped the fresh air would slow Lou's whiskey consumption. He could certainly understand why, but he had never seen his little brother drink so heavily.

It was comfortable on the terrace, the sun had already passed over the building and a slight breeze made the balmy August day very pleasant. The grieving quartet made small talk. The friendly conversation helped Lou sip the Jack Daniels rather than gulp the powerful liquor.

Suddenly he shocked his companions with a statement out of the blue, "It's my fault," Lou spoke almost on a monotone, "it's my fault that God took my Dana from me."

"It is not," Emily immediately argued the point.

"No, Lou, "Joe Torroni spoke softly but forcefully. It was obvious that Lou had expressed this crazy thought to his brother earlier.

"It was an accident," Tim offered.

"God is punishing me," Lou argued.

"He is not, Louie," Joe wished he could convince his sibling.

"Oh yes He is." Lou was unflappable, "God punished me and took my Dana."

Emily was clearly stunned that Lou felt Dana's death was his fault.

"Why? Why would God do that?" she asked trying to sound rational.

The big man gulped bourbon and explained as tears rolled down his handsome face.

"I've been bad lately. Really, really bad. God saw everything. I was forgetting what I've done but God never forgets. He took my Dana because I've been so bad." Lou put his head down and sobbed.

"Lou, don't think like that," Tim looked perplexed, "it was an accident. You're a good man."

Lou looked up wide-eyed. The big man wore a crazed expression. Suddenly Lou upended the Jack Daniels and drained the last quarter of the bottle in one swig.

"I killed somebody," he began ranting, "I'm not good, I'm evil. I killed somebody and then that girl, she made it worse, but it was my fault that I let her do it."

Lou put his head back on the padded chair and closed his eyes, "It is my fault," the big man murmured, "I killed somebody and God took my Dana."

The Hoyles looked at Joe Torroni. He shrugged helplessly. It was probably the whiskey causing this crazy talk.

Shortly Lou's breaths became deeper and more even. The massive intake of bourbon sedated the big man; he was sound asleep. Joe Torroni saw the Hoyles to the door and thanked them for being such good friends to Lou. They promised to return and headed for the elevator.

"What do you make of that?" Tim asked his wife on the way to their apartment.

"Poor Lou," Emily said, "it's hard to believe that he blames himself."

"He killed someone?" Tim was astounded.

"Oh, he was loaded, that's nonsense," Emily opined. She went on, "He has been drinking a lot lately though."

"Oh, Em," Tim sounded pained, "you can't blame him, he's devastated!"

"No, no, I don't mean this last week," she tried to explain, "I mean over the last month or so."

Tim had noticed that lately Lou joined them more often in the occasional beer or glass of wine. "You could hardly call him a lush," he offered, defending his friend.

"I wouldn't," Emily explained, "I'm just saying that it's a little weird, he never drank at all and then in the last couple of months he starts drinking, and now he's saying all this weird stuff…"

Tim's eyebrows shot up, "You believe he's evil and he killed somebody?" the blond man was incredulous.

Emily shot her husband a sour look. "Sure," she said wryly, "he probably pretends to be lawyer and works as an assassin for the CIA."

The Hoyles settled down on their living room couch. Emily snuggled up to Tim. The couple sat in silence staring at the television; each more buried in their own thoughts than the programs playing.

Tim had noticed subtle changes in Lou; and in Dana too. Everybody changes a bit along the way, he reasoned, you live and evolve. Suddenly he feared he was making excuses for some of the recent changes he felt in himself.

Sadly Emily considered the irony; Dana believed so strongly in the Buena Suerte: the luck of the magic tattoo. At the moment she couldn't feel unluckier and she was positive

Lou felt the same. Getting killed, that was textbook unlucky; using Dana's own words made the situation even more grim.

Tears filled Emily's eyes. She silently berated herself, I gotta stop this crying; it's selfish too. Finally she allowed her most self centered thought full bloom; how would she face the days without Dana?

Tim felt his wife shudder. He encircled her with his arms and hugged her close. She felt tiny. Wow, he noticed, my arms are really a lot bigger; and my shoulders too. Tim was amazed to see in himself the muscular physique he had long envied in others. Lou was right the assistant curator thought; it does seem as if my body changed overnight. Dana would have said it was Buena Suerte. He almost smiled at the thought. Eerily as if she read his mind Emily spoke out loud.

"I guess Dana's Buena Suerte ran out."

Tim spoke almost breathlessly, "I was just thinking that, how much she believed in the Buena Suerte!"

"She had me going," Emily admitted, "I was starting to believe it."

Emily expected Tim to scoff at her gullibility; surprisingly he did the opposite.

"Me too," his words came out in a rush, "after that girl in line won the lottery, it was really hard to argue the fact. And jeez, how about the run of luck we've had?"

"Up 'til now," Emily corrected him.

"Yeah, up 'til now." Tim couldn't agree more, "I'm sure Lou isn't feeling too lucky."

Emily placed her hand over her lower left abdomen. Strangely she did it almost protectively; she loved the golden tattoo of the Raven more everyday. This time Emily allowed her most crazy thought full bloom and she spoke it out loud.

"Tim, do you think you've changed in any way since you got the tattoo?"

Tim was taken aback. Clearly Emily was reading his mind. The last part of her question finally hit him.

"Since I got the tattoo?" he couldn't make the connection.

THE FLAVOR OF HEARTS

"Forget it. I'm sounding as crazy as Lou," she sounded embarrassed.

The blond man furrowed his brow; he had never kept secrets from his beloved wife.

"I think I've changed lately in some ways," he said slowly, "my body, some things I think and some things I've done..." his voice trailed off.

Emily lifted her head from his shoulder and looked him directly in the eyes, "What things you've done?"

Tim spoke the truth, as his soul mate she deserved no less. The assistant curator admitted the theft of the griffon from the museum. He recounted finding the unlisted sculpture and taking it; but he found no words to explain his ongoing desire to keep it. Emily was wide eyed. She had noticed the little statue on the dresser and assumed it was a gift shop item for the annex opening. Emily was surprised she didn't feel compelled to make Tim return the griffon.

"I think I've changed too. Lately I think things I've never thought," Emily's blue eyes grew wider, "Dana changed and Lou too!"

"I'll admit I see some changes, but I can't imagine it has anything to do with the tattoos. God, Em, that sounds positively crazy." Tim was slightly exasperated.

"I know. I felt crazy enough believing the tattoos brought us luck. It scares me, Tim."

Emily sounded worried and Tim searched for words to comfort her.

"I know I said I believed in the Buena Suerte," he stated, "but I really think the same things would've happened whether we got tattoos or not. Maybe we got luckier because we believed we were luckier."

Emily nodded. She wanted to believe Tim was right; he sounded so logical. Yes, she would grasp at that straw and cling to it.

54

Monday morning Tim sat at his desk in the main museum. After answering a few in-house emails he prepared to go to the annex.

He sat back in the padded leather chair. Since the day before Emily's strange hypothesis had nagged at him. Following a timeline in his mind Tim tried to pinpoint the most obvious changes in all of them.

Emily initiated sex far more often than she ever had; that was a huge difference. He grinned, that was certainly Buena Suerte in his opinion. When was the first time she shoved her hand down his pants? It was in Wildwood he realized, and it was the morning they revealed their tattoos!

He recalled Emily saying that she could trace the improvement in her eyesight back to Wildwood. Tim recalled donning his new bathing suit at the shore; he definitely didn't remember looking particularly muscular that day at the beach.

Emily was right Tim mused, Lou had a beer with them in Cape May and he drank some champagne when Emily won the gift basket. Wow, what about Dana cooking and baking? Heck that was almost a transformation! As hard as it was to admit, Emily's timeline was on the money; it did seem like some definite changes since their return from the shore town.

THE FLAVOR OF HEARTS

Tim turned to his computer and navigated to Yahoo. Unbeknownst to him, he retraced his wife's steps in an internet search for Buena Suerte Tattoos.

"Hmm, no company webpage; curious," the blond man thought.

He perused the five search results and visited the first two. He could easily see similarities in his tattoo and the first two examples. The gold wedding bands and the surfer's tattoo definitely had the familiar metallic look. Tim was also very surprised to see Buena Suerte's location listed as Waikiki Beach.

The assistant curator clicked the third of the search results. It was the blog section of a personal website. A tingle went up Tim's spine as he read the online log entry of July 17, 2006:

"My vacation was great. I got the most splendid tattoo at a most amazing place: Buena Suerte Tattoos. It's a stunning shop in every way and the artist there is extremely talented. I highly recommend it. Click the link below to see my new tattoo."

Tim held his breath as the sample image downloaded; a clown face smiled back. Metallic gold makeup gleamed around the clown's eyes and mouth; metallic gold lines and gold polka dots sparkled on the figure's colorful clothes.

Tim navigated to the website's homepage. The owner was listed as Mackenzie Cromwell. It seemed to be a site devoted to his life and his ongoing business as a clown. The assistant curator clicked a button that said Contact Me.

Outlook Express, Tim's internet mail program opened automatically. The message was pre-addressed. Tim typed a note in the appropriate spot. He told the blogger that he was impressed with the tattoo of the clown. He mentioned his own tattoo and asked Mr. Cromwell if there was any way they could talk about Buena Suerte. Tim supplied his email address and his cell phone number.

Tim navigated back to his original search. The last two results were postings on two different tattoo forums. The first extolled the beauty and unusual metallic nature of the tattoo from Buena Suerte. There was no photo or email address on the posting, just a screen name and a date in June 2003.

Oddly, the second forum was totally in Italian: Arte Dei Tatuaggi. Tim scanned the posting without much understanding although the last phrase was easy to discern: Buena Suerte Tattoos e magnifico! The foreign entry was dated: 11 Luglio 2004.

Hmm, the assistant curator thought, he had expected to find more current results or at least one listing talking specifically about the Wildwood tattoo parlor. Tim shook his head; he knew less than now than when he started his search.

He headed for the annex. At first it was hard to concentrate on the work at hand but the day went quickly and Tim was growing more excited about the upcoming opening.

About 4:30 the assistant curator returned to the main museum. He stopped in the head curator's office and gave his boss a report on the latest progress. Before he left for the day Tim recalled his email to the blogger. Hoping for a reply the assistant curator sat at his desk and opened his email program.

Four messages downloaded, Tim held his breath as he clicked on the last one. Mackenzie Cromwell's reply was short but promising. He told Tim that he would be glad to talk about Buena Suerte. Mentioning that he spent time at an online chat site the man provided a link and told Tim to look him up under the screen name Macro7.

The assistant curator clicked the link to www.paltalk.com. and logged on as a guest. Tim found the blogger easier than expected and the assistant curator introduced himself. Mackenzie told Tim how to navigate to a private area for chat. Tim began to feel nervous about the online meeting; the blond man hoped he wouldn't seem like a maniac.

MACRO7: Hi, nice to meet you. What can I do for you?
GUEST: I hope you don't think I'm crazy. Did you ever hear anything strange about the tattoos at Buena Suerte?
MACRO7: I know the tattoo is very unusual, with the metallic look. What do you mean by strange?

GUEST: My friends and I heard a rumor from a girl in the line. She said that if you got a tattoo there, you would have good luck forever.

MACRO7: Well, never heard that. Did you have good luck?

GUEST: I have to admit that we've had some really good luck.

MACRO7: Cheers, good for you.

GUEST: Thinking back since you got yours, have you noticed good luck or any changes in yourself?

MACRO7: Funny, now that you mention it, I won a car at the Autumn Fair. I won a raffle at work as well, free airline tickets! Did you win things??

GUEST: My wife also got a tattoo at Buena Suerte, she won a gift basket at a restaurant worth a ton of money. I've been finding money in the street.

MACRO7: Wow. I hope it is true, I wouldn't mind good luck forever!

GUEST: Once again, please don't think I'm crazy. My wife says she thinks we've changed since we got the tattoos. Have you noticed any changes in your personality since you got your tattoo?

MACRO7: That's a weird question.

GUEST: I know.

MACRO7: Thinking about it, I'm not as shy as I used to be. My business as a clown has grown a lot since last year. In fact it's going so splendidly I might resign my daytime position in data entry. I'm definitely a better clown, but really, I don't know if I can say it was the tattoo. I'd like to think it was my hard work, mate!

GUEST: I can certainly understand that.

MACRO7: I really do love the tattoo though, I was thinking of going back for another one.

GUEST: If you do go back to Wildwood, give me a call maybe we could get together for dinner and compare tattoos in person. My treat.

MACRO7: Wildwood? What's that?

GUEST: Wildwood, the town.
MACRO7: Never heard of it. I got my tattoo in Brighton.
GUEST: Brighton? Where's that?
MACRO7: England. Where R U?
GUEST: Philadelphia-USA.
MACRO7: Wow. I'm in London. You got your tattoo in the US?
GUEST: Yes, in Wildwood, New Jersey
MACRO7: That explains your odd looking phone number ;-)
GUEST: Your Buena Suerte, was it decorated with Mayan motifs, with big frescoes inside of the South American step pyramids?
MACRO7: Yes! Stunning night scenes. There was a mosaic ceiling of the night sky that I still think about. Yours?
GUEST: The same. Did it have a tiny lobby with carved Mayan reliefs?
MACRO7: Yes, really tiny, rather claustrophobic!
GUEST: Was the artist a small Mayan man from Mexico?
MACRO7: Yes, he was a dwarf I think! That was something strange...he drew the clown on a paper for me before I got in there. I wondered how he knew I was a clown!!! Did he draw a picture for you this way??
GUEST: Yes he did! He drew a custom sailboat for my wife that her father actually owns, he had every detail correct!
MACRO7: Damn. You say you got your tattoo a month ago?
GUEST: Yes.
MACRO7: I'm sorry to hear they have moved to America. I would have liked another tattoo.

Tim was too shocked to think of anything else. How could mosaics of that magnitude be moved? He decided to end the chat session and go home. He thanked Mackenzie for the meeting and his honest answers. The man known as Macro7 signed off, telling Tim to return to the same chat site if he wanted to converse again.

THE FLAVOR OF HEARTS

Tim shut the computer. He leaned back in his chair and took a deep breath. Once again he wondered how huge mosaics and frescoes nearly two stories high could be relocated. It seemed impossible. If they did manage to move that artwork from Europe the cost would've been staggering. Oddly, Tim did remember a slight British accent in some of the tattoo artist's words.

When he returned to the apartment Tim told his wife of his computer search and the online chat with the man in England. Wide eyed Emily recounted her Buena Suerte search. The Hoyle's discussed with amazement the various locales they had seen for the tattoo parlor.

"Two mentioned Waikiki, Hawaii," Emily was breathless.

"There was a forum in Italian," Tim offered, "I couldn't understand the post but it mentioned Buena Suerte."

"Maybe we could put that post in an online translator," Emily suggested.

The couple decided to do just that. They logged on to the internet in Emily's office and pulled up her previous search. Emily located the Italian forum easily and copied the post onto the computer's clipboard. She pasted the words into a free online translator. Eagerly the Hoyle's read the post in English:

"This summer during my vacation in Sicily I got the most fabulous tattoo in Mondello. I am a harp player and the artist skillfully rendered my harp with golden strings and tiny golden music notes above it. It shines like gold jewelry. The work at Buena Suerte Tattoos is magnificent!"

The translated date read July 11, 2004.

"Sicily in 2004?" Tim looked at Emily with disbelief. "Waikiki in 2005, England in 2006 and Wildwood in 2007?"

"Could it be multiple locations?" Emily wondered out loud.

"Maybe, but the English guy described the same mosaic ceiling and the Mayan frescoes," Tim was incredulous.

"Maybe they all look the same, like Disney parks or theme restaurants," Emily spoke as if she hardly believed her own theory.

"I don't know." Tim shook his head, "He said the artist in Brighton was a dwarf. Remember the little guy's voice? He sounded a little British. Plus, Macro7 said the artist drew his tattoo before he got in there, he had the clown ready, like when we went in!"

The Hoyles looked at each other in shock. The décor in Buena Suerte might be hard to repeat but not totally impossible. The little artist with his uncanny ESP; now that was another story entirely; it had to be the same man.

Emily suggested leaving a message on the first tattoo forum. The Hoyles logged onto the site and registered. They started a new thread called Buena Suerte. They asked if anyone who had visited the unusual tattoo parlor could say where and when. They also asked if anyone else had heard the rumor that the tattoo would bring good luck.

"We'll probably get a bunch of nuts out of the woodwork," the lanky brunette said wryly.

Tim nodded. He felt like a nut himself.

55

Tim left work early Thursday afternoon. Even if he had to use physical force he was going to drag Lou out to the gym. The big man was despondent; it was understandable, but Tim was positive that a good workout would do his grieving friend a world of good.

It took some arguing but eventually Lou succumbed and joined Tim. As the pair entered the lobby of the center city gym they passed the owner.

"Hey, look who's here!" the proprietor bellowed, "You been slacking off, Torroni! What are ya? Waitin' to turn to Jello?"

"Yeah, I'm a lazy bastard these days," Lou smiled wanly and headed straight for the locker room.

Tim lagged behind. He leaned over the front desk and told the gym owner about Dana's passing.

"Oh my God," the man looked distraught, "I didn't know, Tim, I'd a never said that shit. Jeez, if there's anything I can do for Louie would ya let me know?"

"Sure," Tim replied, "I think it's just gonna take some time."

The big man was glad in the long run that Tim had forced him out of the house. It felt good to pump the iron; Lou felt tension draining from his body with every lift. Once again, it was amazing to see the strength in Tim.

"Swear to me you're not on the juice, Timmie Boy." Lou said, "You benched two forty five today. That's twenty five pounds more than last time!"

"I swear, Louie," Tim answered with all sincerity, "I'm kind of shocked myself."

Tim went on in a more conspiratorial tone, "Emily thinks it's the Buena Suerte tattoo. She says it changed me," the blond man shrugged, "maybe it did. Maybe it made me bigger and stronger."

Lou's eyebrows shot up with surprise, "Get outa here, the tattoo made you stronger? That's some crazy shit, Tim."

"I know," Tim agreed, "I know it sounds crazy, but I swear, I'm not doing anything differently than I've done in the last year, yet I'm bigger all over and I'm way stronger."

The men approached the chin up bar. Lou watched his buddy easily pull his weight, Tim's arm and shoulder muscles were literally bulging.

"Maybe it's your age," Lou offered, "you're over thirty now. People have metabolic changes. It's natural to put on some weight and with the workouts you put on muscle."

It sounded reasonable.

"I'd rather believe it's the workouts," Tim said watching the big man complete his chin ups, "but it seems like I got ripped overnight. I know it sounds crazy to say the tattoo made me stronger."

"I'd like to go down to Wildwood and get another one." Lou said as they headed for the locker room, "As a matter of fact I was thinking of taking a ride down there on Sunday."

Lou's plan took Tim off guard and for some reason the blond man felt a sense of foreboding.

"You're gonna get another Buena Suerte tattoo? Why don't you just go to that place down on South Street?"

"Nah," the big man shook his head, "I wanna get an angel and Dana's name all shiny and gold. Wanna go? Take a ride down with me."

"Don't get another tattoo there, Lou. Emily's been saying the tattoo changed us. I know its nuts but some of what she's been saying makes sense."

Lou turned from his locker to face his friend, "Like how? How've we changed?"

Tim mentioned the changes in his body again and the improvement in Emily's eyesight.

"Plus Em and I have been going crazy in bed since we went to Wildwood," he confided to his friend, "she starts it and she never did that!"

"None of this sounds bad to me, Timmie Boy," Lou laughed.

Tim didn't want mention the subtle differences in the Torronis; talking about Dana would only add to Lou's grief. Yet for some reason Tim really had a bad feeling about going back to Buena Suerte. The blond man decided to speak candidly, "There's more," Tim explained, "I'm not too proud of some of the changes in myself."

Lou stared at his friend. Jesus, the big man thought, how often he'd thought the same thing about himself the last few weeks. Misinterpreting Lou's silence for tact Tim explained before his buddy had to ask.

"I stole something from the museum," Tim admitted looking at the floor, "I still don't believe I did it, but the wildest thing is I don't feel any guilt."

Lou started laughing. Tim's head jerked up; laughter was not the response he expected.

"What d'ya take, Timmie Boy, some paper clips?" amusement dripped from the big man's voice.

"A statue."

The assistant curator recounted the shameful story for the second time that week. Lou definitely looked surprised; this was certainly way out of character for Tim.

"Maybe the devil made you do it." Lou said sarcastically.

"Maybe," Tim sounded frustrated.

"Timmie Boy, people have all kinds of excuses for what they do: they eat too many Twinkies, ADHD, they drink too much; bottom line is we do what we do."

The blond man looked so crestfallen the big man tried to feather the truth, "Tim, I've done things too, worse things. Live and learn; that's what you do. Don't go on a crime spree, OK?" Lou grinned, "the tattoo defense; it's a weak one."

Tim had to laugh; Lou had brought him crashing back to earth.

The men hit the showers.

As the warm water washed over Tim he tried to forget every crazy thought. Out of the brain, let it wash down the drain. He stared at the golden lion head on his bulging deltoid; it gleamed when it was wet. How could I think ill of you Tim asked the king of beasts? He loved the lion tattoo more each time he saw it.

Lou eyed the key on his chest the whole time he showered. He washed it lovingly thinking of Dana. She totally believed the tattoo was lucky. The big man smiled. She was so wide eyed and cute when she'd say, "It's the Buena Suerte!"

On the way home Lou cajoled Tim to take a trip to Wildwood that Sunday.

"I'm taking my brother to the airport right after we visit our mother then I'm going down the shore. Come on, you don't have to get a tattoo; just come along for the ride."

The attorney was surprised that his pal seemed so against the idea; a month before Tim had seemed totally captivated by Wildwood.

The big man threw his trump card, "Don't ya wanna get a look at that rubber ball?"

Lou baited his friend remembering Tim's keen interest in the artifact Dana had spotted at Buena Suerte. The assistant curator mulled over the prospect of finding an actual ball from the Mayan Ball Game. That was an exciting possibility but still a weird feeling persisted.

By the time the men parted company in their building's elevator Tim had finally agreed to the trip. Despite his lingering unease about Buena Suerte Tim couldn't allow his good friend to pay tribute to his deceased wife alone.

56

The Hoyle's met Lou in the building's garage about 1:30 on Sunday. The sun was shining brightly as they made their way over the Ben Franklin Bridge; there wasn't a cloud in the sky.

Wildwood was packed; cars and pedestrians filled the streets. Lou navigated the Cadillac up New Jersey Avenue toward the northern part of town.

"I think that place was on 21st Avenue," the attorney said.

"I still can't believe I didn't pick up a business card or anything." Emily commented.

"I didn't even see any," Tim added.

The big man nodded, "I didn't even get a receipt. I paid cash and left. I guess I couldn't wait to tell Dana about the key."

"None of us got a receipt." Tim interjected.

The attorney mulled that over. That was definitely another Buena Suerte oddity.

"What kind of a business doesn't give you a receipt?" Lou asked quizzically.

"Well, I guess you can't return a tattoo," Emily stated.

Lou smiled. That's what Dana said when they discussed Buena Suerte's possible location and their lack of paper work.

The big man turned the Caddie onto 21st Avenue and drove all the way to the end. They saw no sign of the tattoo parlor. Lou made a u-turn and made his way down 22nd Avenue; no sign of Buena Suerte there either.

"Maybe it was closer toward the end of the boardwalk than I remembered," the big man thought out loud.

Lou threaded the Cadillac through the crowds and traffic and headed north again. He steered the car up and down every street from 20th to 17th to no avail.

"Do you think we missed it?" the attorney asked his companions.

"I don't see how," Tim responded.

"Maybe we should walk down the boardwalk like we did that night," Emily suggested.

"Good idea, Em," Lou agreed.

They parked the car on 16th Avenue and walked to the boardwalk. Lou glanced at the railing at the end of the famous wooden walkway. He remembered holding Dana in his arms right on that very spot; a stab went though his heart.

The trio walked south retracing the steps of their previous vacation carefully scanning each block along the way. Suddenly Lou stopped in his tracks and pointed toward a sign over a small boardwalk storefront: it said 24th Street Tattoos and Piercing.

"No, we've come too far," the big man sounded frustrated, "I remember this other tattoo parlor, it was closed that night when we walked by."

"I think it was definitely closer to the end of the boardwalk," Tim offered.

"Maybe we could ask somebody in there," Emily suggested pointing toward 24th Street Tattoos.

Lou expressed reluctance to enter a store and ask about a competitor.

"Yeah, why would they help us find their competition?" Tim agreed.

Emily shook her head; men were ridiculous in so many ways.

"I'm going in and ask," she said striding toward the entrance before the boys could protest.

Tim shrugged at Lou; Emily had a mind of her own.

"Dana always yelled at me when I wouldn't ask for directions," Lou laughed.

In a few minutes Emily returned; she looked utterly perplexed, "They said they never heard of it. They say there are only two tattoo parlors in Wildwood: theirs and place called Oxygen about eight blocks down the boardwalk."

Tim and Lou wore identical shocked expressions.

"They said there's a tourist center down there too," Emily went on, "at Schellenger Avenue; they said we could ask in there if we wanted to."

The former ad exec omitted the rest of the encounter; the people in there looked at her like she was absolutely crazy.

"What d'ya say?" Lou asked his friends. "Should we go to the tourist center?"

They agreed. The trio bought ice cream cones and strolled down the boardwalk enjoying the creamy frozen custard. Before they knew it they passed Oxygen, Wildwood's other tattoo parlor. A crowd of young customers stood outside. Lou pointed surreptitiously to a skinny young man with a purple Mohawk; the spikes on his head were eight inches high and he had more piercings than you could count. The memories of Buena Suerte's clientele made the Mayan tattoo parlor seem even stranger.

The trio reached Schellenger Avenue and entered the tourist center. The lady there was friendly enough but she had no information to give; as far as she knew Wildwood had no other tattoo parlors other than the two boardwalk establishments. She seemed extremely surprised to hear of Buena Suerte.

Offering Lou a brochure with the address and phone number of the Wildwood Chamber of Commerce she suggested inquiring there; although she warned the three friends that the office may not be open on Sunday.

"A tattoo parlor needs some pretty specific licenses with the Board of Health," she further informed the trio as they left, "maybe you could track it down through there."

Shell-shocked the three friends sat on a bench facing the ocean.

"How could it be?" Lou asked, "How could it be that nobody has heard of that place?"

Tim told the big man about the computer search and Buena Suerte's possible previous locations.

"Maybe it moved out of town," the blond man suggested.

"No," Emily spoke adamantly, "they said they never heard of it being here at all."

They sat in puzzled silence until Lou eventually suggested heading back toward the car.

"I want to try to find the exact spot on the boardwalk where we stood the night we watched the people coming and going," he stated, "what do you think?"

The Hoyle's declared it worth a try and the friends walked back toward North Wildwood. Approaching 21st Avenue Lou suddenly pointed to a white storefront. The sign outside said Seaport Village.

"Hey," he said excitedly, "I remember leaning on the railing there, near that store."

The big man practically ran toward the iron rail at the boardwalk's edge. The Hoyle's followed closely behind and stood beside their friend. The trio peered down the side street. It seemed very familiar other than the absence of Buena Suerte Tattoos.

Emily noticed a sign painted over a storefront down on 21st Avenue. A shudder went down her spine as she read the lettering: 21st Avenue Bicycle.

"This is the spot," her voice was a pitch higher than usual; "I remember that sign. I remember that arrow that points down and says 'Open 6am'." Her eyes were wide when she looked at her companions.

"Are you sure, Em?" Tim was stunned.

The assistant curator looked down 21st Avenue. There was no empty storefront to explain the missing tattoo parlor. In fact the building wasn't there at all; there was just a parking lot next to the bike rental store.

"I'm positive," Emily's voice was shaking, "I remember that night thinking that we might still be in line at six am!"

Lou nodded. He remembered the bike place; Buena Suerte had been right next door! Lou practically ran down the three wooden ramps to the street. The Hoyle's watched the big man enter the bike rental shop.

Shortly the handsome attorney returned to the boardwalk.

"Nobody ever heard of Buena Suerte," the big man sounded stunned, "the guy in there says he's worked on this street for over ten years and there's never been a tattoo parlor here. He says there's never been a building right next door, just the parking lot."

Lou was ghostly pale when he went on, "I know it's the right street. There's a hole in the sidewalk that I know I saw that night. When we were in the line I remember telling Dana to watch her step because the whole corner of the sidewalk was missing."

Emily nodded; she remembered avoiding the triangular section of broken sidewalk as well. Suddenly she felt weak. Tim saw his wife crumple and he grabbed her protectively around the waist.

"I'm okay, I'm okay," she assured the men, but inside she wanted to cry.

Tim glanced down 21st Avenue. He remembered the street too. Next door to the tattoo parlor a light blue hotel sat sideways in the lot. He definitely recalled the back of that building from standing outside waiting for the others: three stories of windows arranged in pairs. Tim also remembered thinking it odd that the back of the hotel faced the boardwalk. Tim furrowed his brow: this was definitely the street.

"Let's go," Lou said suddenly.

The big man practically ran down the boardwalk; the Hoyles followed barely keeping up. The trio was breathless by the time they reached the Cadillac. Lou started the car immediately and headed toward the Rio Grande Bridge. He didn't know what to think but he knew one thing; he wanted to leave this weirdness far behind.

The three friends rode in silence halfway back to Philadelphia.

Finally Lou spoke, "Is this the weirdest shit in the world or what?"

The Hoyle's readily agreed. Emily told the frustrated attorney of their posting on the tattoo forum online.

"Maybe somebody'll shed some light on the situation," she offered.

Both men wondered how anyone could explain the missing building. The trio stopped at a South Philadelphia restaurant for dinner. They barely picked at their meals but the red wine was comforting.

Lou turned toward his friends before he exited the elevator in their building, "Thanks for coming with me to the Twilight Zone," the big man smiled, "I hate to get the creeps alone!"

The Hoyles had to laugh at Lou's comical assessment of the strange situation; they promised to call.

Lou opened the door to his apartment. He expected emptiness. Joe was gone; Mrs. Genardi went to visit her daughter and would return on Monday.

The attorney threw his keys on the marble table by the door. Catching a glimpse of himself in the entry way mirror he stared at his reflection. He eyed his solid black hair; now that was another mystery.

Suddenly he wondered exactly when the gray patches had disappeared. The big man headed toward the desk where Dana kept her computer. Lou shuffled through a pile of photographs he found still lying next to the printer.

Extracting the ones from their Wildwood vacation, Lou looked closely at one Dana took of him on the beach. He was wearing his new bathing suit and smiling broadly. The gray patches at his temples were clearly visible highlighted by the sun.

He found a shot Dana took outside their hotel room right before they checked out. He was standing shirtless on the balcony; the new tattoo gleamed.

Lou's eyes opened wide. His hair was solid black. The big man's legs turned to jelly. For the first time in his life he felt weak. Falling into the desk chair he quickly rifled through the other photos.

It had to be trick of the light the big man reasoned. He found a photo Dana took in Cape May. Standing next to Tim he was holding the gigantic Dairy Queen ice cream cone. Lou was flabbergasted; for sure his hair was solid black.

The attorney threw the photos on the desk and jumped from the chair. Like a bullet from a gun Lou headed toward the bar in the living room. He cracked the seal on a bottle of Jack Daniels and collapsed on the couch.

Tim's words echoed in the big man's mind: she says the tattoo changed me. Gulping the bourbon Lou pictured the man on 21st Avenue, "there has never been a tattoo parlor here."

Jesus, what the hell is going on? Lou poured the Jack Daniels down his throat.

57

Early Monday afternoon Emily hailed a cab on Madison Avenue. The meetings at Satchi and Satchi had gone even better than expected. The selection of models was finalized for the John Deere ads and a tentative shooting schedule was complete for the TV commercials.

Emily was grateful for work to do; daily life in Philly was certainly empty without Dana. Emily paid the cabbie and entered the midtown building to see her eye doctor.

Dr. Pierce had been Emily's doctor since she was a teenager. He was happy to see her and more than surprised when her vision checked out at 20/20. He told her he saw nothing abnormal in his examination other than the improvement in her farsightedness.

The physician asked Emily if she had recently experienced headaches or blurred vision. When she responded negatively he seemed relieved. She was a little taken aback when he suggested a CAT scan. He assured her that it was an extremely remote possibility that changes in her brain had caused the differences in her eyesight.

As she prepared to leave the office Dr. Pierce told Emily he would do some research on improved hyperopia. Again he told her not to worry; so far she had tested normally and she showed no outward signs of anything more serious.

Emily stopped at the newsstand in the lobby and bought the New York Post and a candy bar. She stepped into the sunlight and hailed a cab. She tried to put the CAT scan out of her mind.

On the ride back to the parking lot where she left her car she tore open the Midnight Milky Way. Watching the pedestrians as the cab made its way through Manhattan she enjoyed the creamy dark chocolate and the caramel.

Glancing at the candy wrapper before crumpling it writing on the inside caught her eye. She carefully opened the packaging and read the message:

CONGRATULATIONS! YOU'RE AN INSTANT WINNER!

Emily's eyebrows shot up as she read further. She won a set of in-line skates as part of an X-Games promotion. It gave a phone number to call to redeem the prize.

An anxious feeling came over her and she berated herself. Why couldn't she just revel in the good luck as Dana had? Emily exited the cab and walked toward the parking lot.

A woman passed her holding the hand of a little boy; he appeared to be six or seven.

"Excuse me," Emily turned and spoke to her.

The lady stopped and eyed the lanky brunette with New York suspicion.

"Here," Emily held out the candy wrapper, "It's an instant winner for a pair of in-line skates. I don't want them. For the little boy..."

The child's face lit up, "Take it, Mom!" he implored the lady holding his hand.

She took the wrapper from Emily and examined it. Looking up smiling she handed the winning wrapper to the little boy.

"Thank the nice lady, Willie," she instructed her son.

The child thanked Emily profusely; he was so thrilled it warmed Emily's heart. She pictured his happy little face all the way home.

When she arrived back at her apartment Emily took off her suit and stepped into a hot shower. It revitalized her. As she towel dried she eyed the beautiful sailboat on her lower abdomen.

After donning fresh panties and a soft fleece sweat suit she decided to go online and see if anyone posted a reply to their Buena Suerte thread. Surprisingly there were three new posts; eagerly she read the first.

"My former boyfriend had a Buena Suerte tattoo. He got it in Hawaii in the summer of 2005. It was a beautiful tiger, very cool with shiny gold stripes. He was an extremely lucky guy. He won a progressive jackpot in Vegas for 3.2 million. He won so many raffles that people in our town used to joke not to buy a ticket if Lucky Jim bought one. He was killed in a bike accident last summer so I can't ask him if he thought the tattoo was lucky, although that sounds kind of crazy to me."

It was signed with the screen name BikerMaMa35.

Emily scrolled down to the second post.

"I visited Buena Suerte in Sydney Australia in January of 2003. I heard the good luck forever rumor from a surfing buddy of mine. I did and still do have lot of good luck since I got the tattoo. I've had some really bad luck too; recently I was diagnosed with inoperable brain cancer. It seems to me if the tattoo did anything for me it made my good luck really good and my bad luck really bad."

A chill went through Emily as she read the last part. She shuddered at the words inoperable brain cancer. The third post was brief and to the point.

"Good luck from a tattoo? What are you guys smoking? I want some."

58

That night Tim was sleeping fitfully; he was dreaming. It was a baseball field; he was standing in the outfield on bright green grass. He heard the crack of the bat. High above him he spotted the ball; it was dancing in and out of the bright sun. Aiming he held his glove up for the catch.

The ball looked bigger and bigger falling toward him from the sky. It was bigger and bigger; it blotted out the sky. The baseball was two feet in diameter! The giant ball hit him on the head and knocked him to the ground.

Tim jerked himself awake. He rubbed his eyes and almost laughed out loud. The giant baseball looked so bizarre! Softly he slipped from the bed trying not to waken Emily.

He went to the bathroom and relieved himself. Tim noticed red and white lights flashing faintly outside. He stopped at the window and looked down at the street below. It was hard to see directly in front of the building from his vantage point but he could see a lot of police cars and an ambulance parked directly across the street.

Tim shook his blond head and quietly slipped back into bed. People drove down Delaware Avenue like it was a race track; especially late at night. The enormous baseball crossed his mind again and he smiled as he fell back to sleep.

When the alarm went off Tim dove on it; he hated to see Emily disturbed. Hell, the blond man thought, I'd sleep in if I could! After his shower he found the bed empty when he returned from the bathroom.

He dressed and found Emily reading the paper at the kitchen counter, "Morning, Em," he said as he kissed her.

She poured him a steaming cup of coffee and he regaled her with the dream of the giant baseball. Emily laughed hysterically as Tim acted it out. Before he left for work he asked his wife her plans for the day.

"I might stop by this real estate agency," she said pointing toward an ad in the newspaper. "I'm thinking of renting office space and advertising for freelance business."

Tim was more than pleasantly surprised; he would love to see his wife's career really take off again.

"Why don't you stop by the museum around noon and we'll eat?"

Emily agreed; the Philadelphia Museum had an excellent gourmet restaurant and she and Tim always enjoyed it. The Hoyles kissed goodbye at the front door and Emily headed toward the bedroom to shower and dress. Again she imagined Tim catching the huge baseball.

She grinned as she removed her nightie. I know what I'm gonna do she thought. I'm gonna stop at that gift shop in The Gallery and buy one of those huge mylar baseball balloons. I'll hang it over the bed. She knew Tim would definitely laugh when he saw it.

The assistant curator stepped into the elevator. He was thrilled to hear Emily was considering officially opening a freelance business. He was also glad to know she was coming to museum for lunch; Tim knew Emily's days were still hard to fill without Dana.

It was a surprise when the elevator stopped at the floor below; he usually dropped directly to the basement garage when he left for work at his usual time. Half a dozen elderly ladies poured through the steel doors, the last was Mrs. Genardi.

"Mr. Tim," she said as soon as she spotted him towering over the others, "Mr. Tim. It's Mr. Lou. He went to Dana, Mr. Tim…" her voice cracked.

Went to Dana Tim thought?

"Last night," Mrs. Genardi barely choked out the words, "Mr. Lou fell from the balcony. He went with Dana." The little old lady's face was twisted with grief.

Tim fell against the back wall of the elevator; he was lucky it was there to support him.

With the stunning news and the downward motion, it was all Tim could do to keep the coffee in his stomach. He was ghostly white when the elevator stopped in the lobby. Stepping out with the others he tightly embraced Mrs. Genardi, then walked her to the cab her lady friends had waiting. He offered any assistance as he saw her into the back seat and closed the taxi door.

Tim stared up at the high rise. Louie, what did you do? Tim felt sadder than he had ever felt. The man had one thought on his mind as he re-entered the elevator, how was he going to tell Emily?

She was in the closet selecting shoes when she thought she heard the front door open and close. "Tim?" she called out.

Emily definitely heard steps in the living room.

"Tim, is that you?" she called as she moved into the bedroom.

She gasped as her husband appeared in the doorway; he was deathly pale.

"Tim, are you all right? What's wrong?" she sounded frantic.

He moved toward her and took her in his arms, "It's Lou," he blurted it out, "Lou died!"

Tim put his head down and buried his face in Emily's shiny brown hair. He held her so tight she could barely breathe.

"He fell off the balcony last night," Tim could hardly believe the words he spoke, "Mrs. Genardi just told me."

Emily burst into tears and sobbed uncontrollably into her husband's chest. Like zombies the Hoyles moved to the couch in the living room. Numbly they sat nestled in each other's arms.

"Do you think he jumped?" Emily's voice was thin and strained.

"I don't know." Tim wondered the same thing. Lou had never seemed like the type of guy to punch his own ticket.

The good was really good, but the bad got really bad. For the second time that morning Emily burst into tears.

59

The Hoyles moved through the week in a trancelike fog. On Friday morning they attended Lou's funeral. The coroner ruled Lou Torroni's death accidental; no witnesses saw the actual event. At six foot eight the theory could not be entirely ruled out that the big man fell backwards over the railing. Despite his recent tragedy Lou had not seemed suicidal. Many people at the service expressed the same intense feelings of grief and disbelief.

"Poor Joe," Emily said to her husband as they rode home from the funeral luncheon.

Tim nodded grimly. The Hoyles tried to no avail to convince Joe Torroni that he was not responsible for his younger brother's death. Many other friends and relatives tried as well; but Joe was convinced that if he had only stayed in Philadelphia a little longer Lou would still be alive.

"It's funny how Lou said he was responsible for Dana dying and now Joe thinks he's to blame for Lou," Tim stated matter-of-factly.

Emily agreed. Grief certainly made mincemeat of rational thought.

The Hoyles spent the weekend quietly in their apartment; neither had the heart to go out in public. The couple ate

THE FLAVOR OF HEARTS

delivered takeout and drank too many bottles of wine. They had sex in almost every corner of the apartment trying to find solace in each other. Tim offered to call in sick from work on Monday but Emily insisted that he go.

"We have to try to get back to normal life," Emily opined, "work will help both of us."

Emily contacted the realtor about prospective office space. That afternoon and most of Tuesday Emily inspected possible locations; a few were good but none were great.

On Wednesday morning after Tim left for work Emily eyed the clock. For over a year she had met Dana at this time for yoga class. The former ad exec had not been to the studio since Dana's passing.

Maybe it's time I really try to get back to life. Emily knew in her heart that Dana would have insisted on it. It felt odd to drive herself and to walk into the yoga studio alone. Emily almost turned back as she approached the door.

She chided herself; she could hear her pal's voice in her head, "What're you, a baby? A scared little baby?"

Emily stepped through the doorway and walked quickly to the locker room. She tried not to look at Dana's locker next to her own. A familiar voice from behind hijacked her attention.

"Hi, Emily! Where's Dana? I was hoping to see you guys today!" Sarah Spike in Her Nose was smiling broadly. Her pleasant look faded when she saw Emily's expression. Emily's voice cracked as she told her classmate that Dana had died.

"God, I'm so sorry," Sarah grabbed Emily in a spontaneous bear hug.

The adwoman fought the urge to cry. When Sarah released her hold they stood in silence by the lockers. Emily knew she couldn't speak of Lou's death without breaking down.

"If there's anything I can do for you," the tattooed girl offered with all sincerity, "I know what it's like to lose a close friend."

Emily thanked her and smiled weakly, "I think it's gonna just take some time."

"I wanted to show you guys this," Sarah held out her left forearm and pointed toward a spot on the underside.

A slender ice blue candle in an old fashioned brass holder was tattooed on her inner arm. Metallic gold rays emanated from the candle's bright orange flame; the brass candle holder gleamed like real metal. It was stunning against Sarah's pale skin.

Emily's jaw dropped, "Where did you get that?"

Both of Sarah's pierced eyebrows shot up in surprise. "Buena Suerte!" she answered clearly shocked at the question.

"Where was it?" Emily's voice went up in pitch.

"Where was it?" Sarah sounded positively flabbergasted, "Wildwood!"

The tattooed girl was looking at Emily in utter disbelief.

Emily desperately tried to explain her odd reaction, "I went down there with my husband and Dana's husband, we couldn't find the place. We asked around but nobody had even heard of it. We swore we were on the right street, it wasn't there!"

"It wasn't there..." Sarah's voice trailed off. Suddenly she had the feeling she was talking to a mental patient. Funny the tattooed girl thought, the straighter somebody looks, the more of a burnout they turn out to be.

"What street did you find it on?" Emily stammered.

"Twenty first. It was on the end of the block closest to the boardwalk, just like you said."

Emily sat down on the bench in front of the lockers. She had to sit before she fell.

"I don't know what to say," Sarah sounded perplexed. "It was exactly where you said and like you said. It was beautiful inside, the pyramids were incredible!"

Joining Emily on the bench Sarah Spike in Her Nose went on, "The little artist, he drew this candle before I got in there," she pointed to the gleaming tattoo and spoke glowingly of her experience, "He knew, just like he knew about your sailboat.

THE FLAVOR OF HEARTS

I've made candles all my life, it's my hobby, my mom taught me when I was little, he knew!"

The familiar story put a knot in Emily's stomach.

"When did you get it? When did you go to Wildwood?" the adwoman gasped out the words. Emily prayed it was more than two weeks ago.

"Friday night, last Friday night."

Emily shot to her feet.

"I gotta go," the adwoman grabbed her gym bag from the locker and rushed toward the door. Sarah watched with slack jawed amazement as Emily ran from the room.

Emily ran down South 24th Street like somebody was chasing her. Breathlessly she unlocked the Mercedes and climbed behind the wheel. She barely looked when she pulled into traffic.

Emily could only think of Tim as she wound her way to South 22nd Street. She pressed the gas pedal and flew down the straight line toward the Benjamin Franklin Parkway. Running every traffic light on yellow and a few on red she barely made it safely to the Philadelphia Museum of Art.

The lanky brunette careened up the circular driveway toward the museum's rear entrance. She left her car parked at the foot of the steps and ran toward the door.

"Miss," the guard tried to block her way, "you can't leave your car there…"

Emily pushed past him and yelled back over her shoulder, "I'm Mrs. Hoyle. Tim Hoyle's wife."

She sprinted through the museum dodging patrons and employees; she avoided every attempt to stop her and burst through the door of Tim's office. Ignoring the secretary's shocked protests Emily threw open Tim's door. "Tim!" the adwoman stopped dead in her tracks in the empty office.

"He's downstairs, Mrs. Hoyle," the secretary was wide eyed, "is everything OK?"

Almost simultaneously a security guard appeared with Tim closely on his heels.

"Em, what's wrong?" the assistant curator was breathless.

"Tim" Emily sounded panicked and her words came out in a rush, "Sarah got a Buena Suerte tattoo! She got it on Friday night, it was there last Friday!"

The security guard and the secretary looked askance at the adwoman; it appeared she was having a nervous breakdown.

"I'll take care of this," Tim addressed museum employees as he steered them toward his office door.

"The car, Dr. Hoyle…" the security guard didn't want to see Mrs. Hoyle's vehicle towed away.

Tim retrieved the keys Emily still had clutched in her hand. Tossing them to the guard the assistant curator asked the uniformed man for a favor, "Could you park it for me, Mannie?"

"Sure thing, Doctor Hoyle, right away," the guard scurried through the office door and closed it behind him. The security force would do anything for the assistant curator.

"Tim, I'm sorry." Emily was desperately trying to calm down; she realized she might have caused Tim some embarrassment at work.

"Em, what happened?" Tim could've cared less what his co-workers thought; he cared only for his wife's well being.

Slowly Emily told her husband of her yoga classmate's tattoo. Tim was clearly surprised to hear that Buena Suerte was there and open the previous Friday night.

"There has to be some explanation," he said out loud, but inside he couldn't imagine how it could be possible. Tim called his secretary through the office intercom and told her he would be leaving for the rest of the day.

"Let's take a ride down there," he suggested to Emily, "and we'll see for ourselves." The Hoyle's left the museum and took Emily's Mercedes from the visitor's parking area. Tim was sure that his car would be fine overnight in his reserved space.

They stopped at their apartment so Tim could change from his suit to something more comfortable. As they exited the building's underground garage Tim suggested first going to South Street to talk to Sarah.

"It's not that I doubt anything you've said," he assured his wife, "but I'd like to ask her a few questions myself."

Emily nodded. The whole situation seemed so surreal the adwoman was glad to have Tim see the tattoo for himself.

As soon as the Hoyles entered The Body Shop the owner recognized Emily. "Hey, did you see Sarah's tattoo? Sarah," he yelled toward the back, "your friend's here!"

Sarah Spike in Her Nose looked out from behind the half wall surrounding the piercing station. She didn't look entirely surprised to see Emily. The adwoman introduced her husband and Tim looked stunned when Sarah showed the gleaming candle on her forearm. The assistant curator complimented the heavily pierced girl's new body art.

"That's amazing," Tim said sincerely, "and it really looks beautiful. Emily said you got it done last Friday. Was it at late at night?"

"It was about 12:30." Sarah answered, "I don't think it's open during the day. We got there during the afternoon but it wasn't open."

The Hoyle's eyed each other. Tim asked Sarah a few more questions; all her answers seemed to indicate that she truly was in the same Buena Suerte in the same location.

"I told the artist where I work," Sarah added. "I asked him where we could buy some of that metallic ink. He said his brother took care of all the supplies," she smiled, "I don't think he wanted to tell me and I guess I can't blame him."

The Hoyles thanked Sarah for her time and candor; as they prepared to leave she stopped them, "Hey wait," she called, "Tim, can I see your golden tattoo?"

Tim lifted the sleeve of his t-shirt and revealed the gleaming lion head. The patrons and employees of The Body Shop were duly impressed. Many expressed future plans to visit the enigmatic Buena Suerte.

Tim steered Emily's car toward the Ben Franklin Bridge. The weather was overcast and small raindrops dotted the windshield as the Hoyles drove toward the New Jersey shore.

60

Late afternoon traffic was light into Wildwood. As the Hoyles crossed the Rio Grande Bridge Emily spotted Uries, the legendary harbor restaurant; a knot grew in her stomach as she recalled the wonderful dinner there with the Torronis.

Tim retraced the route Lou had taken a few weeks earlier; heading toward North Wildwood he turned onto 21st Avenue and drove toward the boardwalk. A shudder went through the blond man's body. The tattoo parlor was not there.

Emily gasped with the realization. Tim parked the car in the parking lot where Buena Suerte should have stood.

"Jesus how can it be?" Emily voice shook, "Tim, I'm scared."

Tim searched for words to comfort his wife, but couldn't come up with one logical reason that would explain the tattoo parlor's nonexistence. The couple sat in the car in silence and the blond man could feel the tension escalating.

"I'm hungry." he declared starting the car's engine.

Tim wasn't really in the mood to eat, but he desperately wanted to do something that felt normal. He drove the Mercedes back toward the harbor and parked at Uries. Seated before well loaded plates of crispy fried shrimp, golden French fries and creamy coleslaw the couple picked at the deliciously prepared food. They took some comfort in a carafe of white zinfandel.

Through the restaurant's huge wall of windows they eyed dark clouds rolling in over the harbor. The wind was gusting as they made their way to the Mercedes; raindrops were starting to accumulate on the windshield.

Tim piloted the car from the parking lot, instead of heading over the bridge he drove back into Wildwood. Fortified by the food and drink he needed to see the street one more time. Emily knew his intention without even asking and she didn't object to the plan.

Once again they traveled down New Jersey Avenue and took 21st toward the boardwalk and as before Buena Suerte was nowhere to be found. Tim made a u-turn and parked the Mercedes directly across the street from the missing tattoo parlor.

"How could she have been here last Friday?" he turned in the car's seat to face his wife.

Emily eyed the city block over her husband's shoulder as she answered, "I'm stymied myself," she admitted, "but we saw the tattoo. It was definitely a Buena Suerte tattoo."

Tim nodded in agreement. Thunder rumbled in the distance. Although it was dusk the rain clouds made it darker than normal for that hour of the day. The stormy weather made the situation even more eerie; it also explained the absence of people on the normally crowded street.

"Maybe it only appears on weekends," Emily suggested, still eying the parking lot occupying tattoo parlor's former location. Her voice dripped with sarcasm.

Heavy rain began falling; a huge clap of thunder shook the Mercedes. Strobe like lightning followed a second later and illuminated Emily's face. Tim saw her eyes open wide with terror.

"I saw it," she screamed the words, "I saw it in the lightning it was there, it was there!"

Emily was shaking as she pointed across the street. The color had totally drained from her face. Tim was sure the scary atmosphere had affected his wife.

He turned and faced the street behind him as another loud clap of thunder shook the vehicle. In the brilliant flash of lightning Tim suddenly saw the storefront; he easily read the orange letters on the sign. Emily screamed behind him, he knew she saw it too. Tim's eyes grew wide, now peering through the heavy rain the tattoo parlor was gone.

Tim immediately turned the key and threw the Mercedes into gear. With the tires screeching he flew up 21st Avenue. He rubbed his eyes and steered with the other hand. He knew what he saw; for a second Buena Suerte was there!

Tim turned on two wheels onto New Jersey Avenue. A white flash passed through the gray rain in front of the hood.

Emily's high pitched scream pierced the air, "Tim, it's a pedestrian!"

The man dove to get out of the way of the oncoming car and fell in the street. Really panicked Tim jammed on the brakes and stopped by the curb. He jumped from the car and ran back through the rain toward the pedestrian lying motionless in the street.

Tim feared the worst as he approached the downed walker. Thankfully the man stirred as Tim reached his side.

"You son of a bitch!" the guy screamed. "You sorry son of a bitch, I had the light. I had the fucking light!" The man was trying to get to his feet.

Tim helped him up and stammered an apology, "Jesus, I'm sorry! Are you all right?"

"I'm OK," the man was definitely shaken up if not injured.

The pedestrian looked down; his jeans were newly torn on both knees.

"You bastard, I just bought these pants! Oh man!" he pointed to a squashed bag in the gutter. A cheese steak and an order of French fries were lying ruined in the wet street. "You motherfucker. Look what you did to my food." He looked

Tim directly in the face, "Where the fuck did you learn to drive?"

Both men were now soaked from the rain.

"Please, come back to my car," Tim begged the man, "Let's get out of the rain and make sure you're really OK. I'll pay for your dinner and your pants."

The man followed Tim to the Mercedes. The pedestrian scowled at the Pennsylvania license plate, "You bastards come here from Philly and you act like a bunch of assholes."

The man opened the back door and slid into the rear seat. With a worried expression Emily turned and asked if he was all right. The man responded that he was OK. He became more of a gentleman in front of the lady and stopped swearing.

He refused Tim's offer of monetary compensation; but agreed to accept a ride home. They drove him to a little cottage about three blocks away. Tim tried again to give the pedestrian money, but now the man was calmer.

"Nah, I'm all right," he looked down at his torn jeans, "maybe it'll be a fashion statement."

Climbing from the car the pedestrian cautioned Tim, "Be careful. Try not to kill yourself or your pretty wife…or anyone else!" he said as he slammed the door.

Tim drove slowly to the Rio Grande Bridge and for the second time the Hoyles drove back to Philadelphia in silence. Numbly they entered their apartment and settled in on the couch.

"Tim, I'm scared," Emily said, "I feel like I'm going crazy."

"If you are then I'm right there with you," her husband commiserated.

"How could a building appear and then disappear before our eyes?" she wondered aloud.

Tim admitted he had no idea; it sounded like mass hysteria.

"I'm scared, Tim," Emily repeated. "I feel like we're living in a Stephen King novel. Do you think everybody who gets one of those tattoos dies?"

"Everybody dies eventually, Em," Tim spoke rationally but deep inside he wondered if the Buena Suerte tattoo was a form of curse.

"What are we going to do?" Emily's voice trembled.

Tim knew the question was inevitable and he hated facing the answer.

"What can we do? Call the police? The FBI?" the blond man sounded more than frustrated, "What do I say? I think a Mayan dwarf put a magic tattoo on me and I'm afraid I'm gonna jump off a balcony or get hit by a taxi cab?"

Emily burst into tears.

"Stop, stop, Em, I'm sorry," he hugged her tightly, "Please, don't cry. Nothing's going to happen to us. Nothing bad. It's stress, Em. This last year and half has been nothing but stress, especially lately…"

Emily looked up; her face was pale and her eyes were rimmed with red.

"Let's go home, Em," Tim suggested, "Let's go back to New York. Let's get out of here and forget all about it. Let's forget Buena Suerte and everything else."

Tim wasn't sure it was the right plan, but he could tell the words gave his wife hope.

"Life turned to shit for us way before the tattoos, the only thing that's been good for us here has been my work. Fuck work, Em, fuck work. Right after the annex opens next month I'll give my resignation and we'll go home."

That night the Hoyles slept peacefully in each other's arms; it felt like the first good night's sleep they'd had in months.

61

Friday morning Emily told the real estate agent about the change of plans. She explained that she no longer wanted to rent office space locally; and instead asked the lady to put the riverfront condo on the market.

Tim tightened up loose ends for the gala opening of the museum annex; they were ready ahead of schedule. The blond man sat as his desk and stewed. He told Emily to put the weird disappearance of Buena Suerte behind them; but for some reason he couldn't follow his own advice.

Tim had suddenly found empathy with UFO sighters; something incredibly bizarre had definitely happened and certainly nobody in their right mind would believe it. He put his head in his hands. Eventually he looked up and turned to his computer. He searched for a phone number for the Wildwood Chamber of Commerce.

Tim correctly predicted the outcome of the call. No one at the Chamber of Commerce had ever heard of Buena Suerte; according to them Wildwood had only two tattoo parlors, both on the boardwalk.

Tim looked at the clock and stood up. He needed to get to the bottom of this disappearing act. I will not go gentle into that good night Tim thought as he headed over the Ben

Franklin Bridge; he glanced over his shoulder at the high rise condos looming above Penns Landing.

The blond man knew he should tell his wife he was going back to the shore but Emily was so spooked when it came to Buena Suerte. If I find answers I'll tell her Tim thought, if not I'll keep this trip to myself.

On the way to Wildwood he made another prediction and guessed the elusive Buena Suerte would be absent from view. This time the blond man was wrong. As he rode down 21st Avenue he spotted the building as soon as he crossed Surf Avenue.

Buena Suerte was nestled between the bike shop and the back of the light blue hotel. The sign's orange lettering gleamed in the sunlight and the mural of the ocean and the cliff was just as Tim remembered it.

With his mouth agape he drove toward the tattoo parlor and parked right in front. Tim sprang from the car and ran his hands like a blind man over the painting spanning the building's front. It was solid; he could feel the roughness of the painted waves. He moved toward the wrought iron screen door. The ornate black frame was cold to the touch; the metallic mesh was smooth and flexible.

Tim was flabbergasted. He pounded on the door to no avail; as Sarah said Buena Suerte appeared to be closed during the day. That's when it's here, the curator thought grimly. He decided to walk around the tiny building; maybe it had a back door.

It was a narrow space between the tattoo parlor and the bike shop; Tim had to turn sideways toward the back of the walkway. No other windows or doors were visible; except for the front entrance the building appeared to be concrete all the way around.

Tim pounded on the entrance again when he reached the front; still no answer. He looked around the neighborhood; it was eerily quiet and oddly no other person was within sight. Tim was tempted to bang on doors at the hotel next to Buena Suerte.

"What would I say?" the blond man thought. "Hi, I'm a visiting maniac; do you see the building next door? Is it always there?"

Tim took his cell phone from his pocket and took a picture of the storefront. He walked out into the middle of 21st Avenue and shot another photo of Buena Suerte with the two buildings surrounding it. He stored both images in the phone's memory.

The blond man returned to his car and watched the building; he sat there for at least an hour. As crazy as it seemed the curator half expected to see the structure disappear before his very eyes. Tim stared at the mural on the storefront. The sea scene was so artfully painted, the pristine beach shone in the sunlight. The aqua water looked crystal clear, the breakers pure white.

Suddenly Tim did a double take. The painting's wave broke along the beach and another rolled in and did the same; the white pigment dissipating like frothy water. Tim shook his head hard; the mural was moving like a cartoon! He was in shock as he brought his hands up. He rubbed his eyes hard; he had to feel the sensation to be sure he was awake. Pushing his fists into his eye sockets he felt the orbs through his eyelids.

Lowering his hands, he took a second to refocus. No blue, no moving white…no Buena Suerte. Tim gasped and jumped from the car. Buena Suerte was gone! There was nothing but a parking lot in between the bike rental shop and the back of the light blue hotel.

For the second time Tim jammed his fists into his eyes. Again he looked and refocused; the building had disappeared. He knew he had touched the structure; a second ago that building was there!

He couldn't breathe; the air felt thick and heavy. Leaning his weight on his car Tim rubbed his eyes again until he saw red. His heart was pounding as he opened his eyelids again; the building was definitely gone.

The curator cocked his head back and hollered at the blue sky, "God, if you are up there you gotta help me. What is happening here? What is happening to me?"

Tim was petrified; he felt a pain pierce his chest. He closed his eyes and the sun turned his eyelids a bright orange.

62

Emily shut her computer about five thirty. She went into the living room with a long printout of possible condos and co-ops in Manhattan. Pouring a glass of wine she sat on the couch and perused the real estate listings; although the prices for Manhattan property had risen in the last few years she was certain they would easily find a new place to live. It was times like this Emily truly appreciated her trust fund.

The adwoman glanced at her watch. Tim was a little late; he was usually home by six. There were times in the last year and half that she would have been ecstatic contemplating a move back to New York. Granted she was happy but oddly she had come to like Philadelphia. However lately life had become so empty without the Torronis; the adwoman was positive a new start would do her and Tim a world of good.

Again Emily gazed at her watch; she was glad to hear the muffled sound of the elevator stopping on their floor. Expecting to hear Tim's key in the lock she was startled by the doorbell. Laughing she flung open the door expecting her husband.

"You locked your keys in-" she stopped mid-sentence.

Two Philadelphia policemen stood in the doorway; both held up badges with picture ID's. "Mrs. Timothy Hoyle?" one asked.

Emily nodded; her stomach was starting to churn.

"Mrs. Hoyle, could we step inside? I'm afraid we have some bad news for you."

Emily was shaking as she gestured for the officers to enter.

"Ma'am," the young officer looked like he wished he was anywhere else, "we received word from the Wildwood Police Department in New Jersey that your husband Timothy Hoyle was brought to Burdette Tomlin Hospital this afternoon. He died there in the emergency room."

Emily woke up on the couch with a weak feeling that was becoming all too familiar. Like deja-vu, faces above her came slowly into focus: two strange men, a strange young woman and Mrs. Genardi.

"Mrs. Genardi?" Emily spoke out loud.

"Oh, Emily, I am so very sorry," the old lady enveloped the adwoman in a hug.

The policemen looked relieved. Using the phone next to the couch they had called the first number on speed dial hoping to find a friend for the devastated woman. It rang below at the Torronis where Mrs. Genardi was cleaning out the apartment with Dana's cousin Brenda. Both ladies ran immediately to Emily's side.

The door bell rang. Emily nearly jumped out of her skin.

"I'm sorry, ma'am, that'll be the EMT's," one of the police officers apologized as he motioned for his partner to answer the door.

Emily sat up insisting that she was all right.

"What happened to my husband?" she asked still stunned.

"From the information we received we believe he suffered a stroke," the policeman handed Emily a card and went on, "this is the phone number of the Wildwood Police Department. This officer will help you get in touch with the Cape May County Coroner's Office; they'll have the details for you."

The emergency technicians surrounded Emily. They examined the shaken adwoman despite her numerous protests. Finding her vital signs normal the EMTs took their leave when Emily declined further medical treatment.

Mrs. Genardi promised the policemen that she would stay with Emily until a family member could be contacted. As they left one of the officers gave Emily his business card. He offered the Philadelphia Police Department's condolences and any help she might need in the future.

63

Emily's mother Diana arrived from New York City in a little over an hour. She insisted that her daughter pack a few bags and return to Manhattan that night. Emily offered no resistance.

Diana lived in a three bedroom condo in the East Village with her second husband; they assured Emily that she could stay with them as long as she liked.

The next two weeks went by in a blur. Emily floated just above real life doing the waltz of the living dead. Diana handled everything. She arranged the funeral, then emptied and sold the condo in Philadelphia. She had Emily's car brought to Manhattan and parked in a local garage.

Emily attended Tim's funeral in a trance. That day like every day since two Fridays before, she breathed, she talked, she even smiled but it wasn't her. It was an empty shell; like one of those Easter Eggs with the yolk blown out through a tiny hole. Emily was sure something blew her yolk out through a tiny hole.

She read the coroner's report. Tim died from a brain hemorrhage; caused from an aneurism they suspected he had since birth. She knew why he went to Wildwood; many long nights she wondered what he had seen or not seen. Mostly she ached when she wondered why he thought to go alone.

Emily walked down Avenue A toward Tompkins Square Park; she felt the sidewalk beneath her feet but nothing else. The corner playground was quieter now since the kids were in school; she entered by East 9th Street and looked for a bench.

It was a cloudy autumn day, breezy but not cold. The sun came in and out, in and out. Emily watched the shadows come and go; it was dark, it was light.

Recovery was unexpected; like a switch was off and suddenly flipped on.

Emily pulled her cell phone from her sweatshirt pocket and hit the first preset.

"Joanie, it's me, you were right. I'm gonna come back Monday, if it's OK."

"OK?" Joan DeMeter laughed from her corner office at Satchi and Satchi, "I had your name put on the door last Friday!"

Emily's first day back at work felt like she had never left. In a lot of ways it was like she went back in time instead of forward. She had worked at Satchi & Satchi before she met Tim. Lately it was easier to pretend that they had never met, never married, never loved. It was probably wrong to pretend, but it was easier.

That was one of the reasons Emily decided to move to TriBeCa. She was living in lower Manhattan before she met Tim. When she started looking for a place of her own Joan begged her to come back to the Upper West Side. They were close neighbors there before the Hoyles made the move to Philadelphia. Emily was sure the memories of Tim would be far too unbearable anywhere near Central Park.

Joan was unimpressed with anything below midtown but the she had to admit the condo Emily found on Vestry Street was amazing. It was a spacious triplex loft atop a nine story building with walls of windows and a gorgeous terrace. Everything was new and perfect; the building was barely a year old.

The girls had a grand time searching for furnishings. They traveled all over the city and beyond. Cutting in and out of cars down Houston Street Emily was suddenly reminded of the days zipping around in Dana's little car.

"Did you ever ride in a Mini-Cooper?" Emily asked Joan.

"No," the executive replied, "Too small, I prefer to sit above the street."

"Easy to park though, Dana used to put that car in the smallest spots; she'd find a parking space anywhere!"

"You should talk!" Joan exclaimed. "You are the luckiest person I have ever seen when it comes to parking!"

"What do you mean?" Emily glanced at her companion from the driver's seat.

"I have seen you find a parking space where I have never seen a space open the whole time I've lived in the city. Up near the Met, those lots are always full, not for you. I've seen you find a space in the Village!" Joan sounded unbelieving.

Emily mulled it over. It was funny, she used to hate to drive in the city before; she always told Tim it wasn't the driving she hated but the parking. Joan was right; lately anywhere she drove there was a space. Actually, Emily couldn't remember the last time she had to even circle a block to look for a space; there was always one there.

"It's the Buena Suerte." Emily spoke softly, still unwilling to utter the truth too loudly.

"Oh, Em," Joan hoped Emily had forgotten the crazy stuff about the tattoo.

"I know you don't believe me," Emily said matter-of-factly.

"It's not that I don't believe you," Joan argued "how could anything like that affect your life? Do you believe in lucky charms too? Let me ask you, if the tattoo was supposed to be so lucky, well how come...forget it."

"Tim died? How come Tim died?" Emily sounded so convinced, "It's not just good luck, the tattoo makes your good luck really good and your bad luck really bad."

"Oh really?" Joan almost sounded sarcastic, "and how has your luck been so all fired good lately?"

"Well," Emily thought over the last month, "my condo...a couple had it under contract and they lost financing. I was sixth on the list and I wound up getting it! I won a Toyota at my mother's church raffle last Sunday. I donated it back to the church. I won a gift basket from the East Village soccer league raffle. I won an iPod on a Coke bottletop. Oh and I won a jet ski: it was a door prize at my father's yacht club dinner a couple weeks ago."

Emily glanced over at her friend in the passenger's seat. Joan's eyes were wide with astonishment.

"I'll admit that's a lot of luck." she stammered, "but God, a magic tattoo? It seems like a wild story you'd tell at Halloween."

"I know." Emily eased the Mercedes into a parking space.

Looking directly at her buddy Emily laughed, "And don't forget I'm the luckiest person alive when it comes to parking! You said so yourself not five minutes ago!"

"Maybe you missed your calling," Joan grimaced, "you should have been a lawyer."

64

Itzi came down the stairs a little before midnight and found his two brothers waiting in the family's living room. As always the television was on; Tolo motioned toward the screen.

A documentary was airing; Itzi joined them on the couch for the ending. It showed aerial views of the ruins of the ancient Mayan city state Caracol. The narrator spoke of the long bloody wars with the neighboring city Tikal.

The program panned carved images depicting Mayan human sacrifices. They showed gory modern illustrations of the Sacrificial Rites followed by a painting of a mountain of decapitated bodies. The narrator called the Maya a ferocious society steeped in violence.

"They worshipped a bloodthirsty pantheon of strange gods," the host had finished his summation, "using their religious beliefs to take many human lives in bizarre rituals of torture and human sacrifice."

The brothers stared blankly at the screen.

"They make us sound pretty bad," Bartolomeo sounded crestfallen.

He was aware of the modern perception of their people but it hurt hearing it so bluntly stated on The Discovery Channel, his most beloved television station.

"People are killed everyday in this world for no reason at all," Ildefonso sneered, "Today they kill each other for a parking space or a pair of sneakers."

"I think people valued their lives more in Uxmal than in any other place we have ever been," Bartolomeo was disheartened.

Wars were fought constantly in their ancient world; fought for the same reasons wars are fought today: territory, sources of food or fresh water, mineral and natural resources, economics.

The High Priest tread a very fine line in his head. He would not accept the wondrous blessings of god as great as Chac and then dare question the lord's methods.

"Our god? Bloodthirsty? Then as now, what we need our god provides; what he asks of us, we offer. He needs what is most precious to us." Itzi went on, "Bloodthirsty? I have never enjoyed the taking of the Sacred Blood."

Itzamna shook his head. In ancient Uxmal he had given much of his own blood in ritual blood letting ceremonies. The Maya believed the blood of a king or High Priest was highly sacred; they would a pierce body part and bleed heavily onto bark paper. When the sheets were burned the blood rose up in the smoke as one of the most hallowed offerings to the gods.

"They call us a ferocious society," Fonso was irritated, "after what the Spaniards did to our people? We're steeped in violence? We didn't sail across the ocean to plunder their riches and destroy their way of life."

"We have lived through much history," Bartolomeo agreed, "and I have read accounts of many historical events; I don't think our ancient society was any more violent than others. The wars between the Greek city states were easily as violent as any in our records."

"It's the sacrifice," Itzi said quietly, "modern people can't comprehend the power of the Sacred Blood."

"They've all killed for their religions, their god, whatever they choose to call him," Fonso spit out the words.

"Many societies have made human offerings, Itzi," Bartolomeo was leaving despondency behind for anger, "Phoenicians, Carthaginians, Druids, they did it in ancient China and India too. We saw the Hawaiians sacrifice virgin girls to Pele; and what of all the people killed in retainer sacrifices during the burial rites of the Norsemen and the Egyptians? We saw those too! There were horrible atrocities during the Crusades and the Spanish Inquisition. They single us out like we're, like we're…"

"Like we're what, Tolo?" Itzi asked, surprised a television show had this effect on his brilliant brother.

"Like we're some kind of savages." Tolo was fuming.

Ildefonso burst out laughing.

"Tolo, who cares what the say about us on television?" Fonso roared with laughter; in a back handed way he considered it a compliment to be called a savage. Suddenly the big man spoke more seriously, "There's a certain irony in it, don't you think?"

"What do you mean?" Bartolomeo rarely sounded confused.

"Well…we're still doing it." Fonso said it so matter of factly; the words hung in the air.

"Well, we are…I mean, I guess we are…" Tolo's voice trailed off.

"You guess we are? You guess we are?" Ildefonso was astonished.

Itzi eyed the family giant, "Leave him alone, Fonso."

The big man shot a look skyward, but complied.

"I know what we're doing." Bartolomeo was barely audible, "I know, Fonso."

The brothers sat in silence.

"Itzi, what do think will happen after the 13th Baktun? A doomsday, like they're all saying?" Bartolomeo motioned toward the widescreen TV. The High Priest had deduced his brother was troubled by more than a television documentary.

65

"I remember our god's words exactly," Itzi repeated Chac's words verbatim, 'our universe will be reborn, not only ours, but worlds you cannot imagine' ".

"What the heck could that mean?" Bartolomeo's words came out in a rush.

"I know you are curious, Tolo," Itzi smiled wanly, "Your amazing inventions are a testament to your great mind; but do not presume to guess our god's intentions, it will imply that you believe you are on equal footing with him."

Bartolomeo nodded but it was easy to see he was still bothered.

"You never wonder at all what will happen, Itzi?" out of the blue Fonso spoke up.

Both of his brothers stared, Ildefonso rarely thought past the present moment; it was a total surprise to hear him ask about the future.

Again Itzi tread that fine line and chose his words carefully.

"I have watched the great scientific discoveries of the current ages with much amazement but I can't help but go back to the things we believed in Uxmal. After all it is the great Chac, our ancient god, who has blessed me with the longevity to appreciate modern knowledge."

Tolo nodded in agreement; Fonso too respected the power of their patron god.

"Our Long Count was never intended to mark the end of time, no matter what modern people believe." Itzi started, "Our elders always taught of time in cycles, when one ends another begins.

"Change was always expected at the end of a cycle, the bigger the cycle the bigger the change." Itzi continued, "We are in the end of the thirteenth baktun; the end of a Great Cycle. This occurs every 26,000 years. We call this the Time of No Time, the night before dawn. There were many teachings passed down pertaining to this time of transformation."

"The elders said at the end of this Great Cycle, when First Father aligns with First Mother, a spark from Hunab Ku, galactic center, would feed our sun causing it to burn brighter. This will change the earth: men would develop our ancestor's advanced abilities. It would be a Golden Age. Some elders even predicted the actual return of our people through Tz'Ab'Ek, the tail of the rattlesnake."

The Maya believed they were not indigenous to earth; stories have been passed down through generations of their arrival from a place in the night sky they called the rattlesnake's tail. Contemporary astronomers call this place the Pleiades, a star cluster near the constellation Taurus.

"Then why do the modern men predict this date as doomsday, Itzi? What would make them think such a thing?" Fonso was perplexed.

"Our people too thought bad things could happen at this Union of First Father with First Mother." Itzi explained, "Our elders warned that if the first sun of the New Year lacked power, it would fall into First Mother and be swallowed by the crocodile that lurks there. Ironically, modern men fear the same basic thing; they fear the alignment with the dormant black hole at the galaxy's center will affect the sun, and in turn cause damage to the earth."

"Do you think any of their fears are valid, Itzi?" Bartolomeo had been following the modern predictions too.

"Tsunamis, earthquakes, solar flares...these things could happen at any time." Itzamna shrugged, "The wilder predictions: the shift of the earth on its axis? The emptying of the Great Lakes into the Caribbean? Even with perfect alignment I think our sun is too far from galactic center for such drastic effects. Now the awakening of the black hole at the galaxy's core..."

The tiny High Priest had wondrous look on his face,

"That too could happen at any time! Nobody really knows why one black hole sucks in everything around it and others lie in wait until something big comes close. A NASA x-ray telescope picked up a dormant black hole swallowing a neighboring star about two years ago; amazing data. Once again I don't think our sun is close enough or big enough to have any effect on the black hole at our galaxy's center. But, the Milky Way is full of stars, most far more massive than our sun, if one of them wandered too close..."

"I should watch more on TV than hockey and cage fights," Ildefonso lamented, "I feel like an idiot."

"You have the right idea, Fonso," Bartolomeo was envious, "it's better not to think."

"Some things are inevitable; worry is a waste of energy better spent. As for us..." Itzi reminded his brothers, "it is the will of our god...not our own. We have always known the Sacred Blood fuels the sun; we have given the great Chac all he has asked for; First Father should rise with all the strength he needs."

"Itzi, what will happen to us?" Tolo summoned all his courage to ask, "What do you think will happen to us at the end of the 13th baktun?"

Ah, Itzamna thought, we have reached the root of Bartolomeo's anxiety.

66

The High Priest felt torn, an odd situation; Itzi usually made decisions very easily. He wore a strange expression that gave the impression that he'd rather not say. Eyeing his loyal brothers he knew they more than deserved his honesty. Itzi spoke his thoughts out loud for the first time.

"I believe we will be the final hearts taken, first each of yours and the last will be mine."

Bartolomeo's eyes grew wide and the color drained from his face, "We'll die, Itzi? We'll die at the end of the Great Cycle?"

"We owe the great Chac," the High Priest answered softly, "for all he has given."

"Wow, that isn't what I expected at all." Bartolomeo was pale and suddenly dejected.

"You expected to live forever, Tolo?" Fonso asked almost amused. Somehow the former warrior was not surprised by their older brother's words.

"I thought maybe we would live out our lives in the lord's Golden Age, you know normally, grow old and die at the ordinary rate. We've given all he has ever asked…" Tolo's voice trailed off.

"We would be rewarded if we are the last hearts taken," Fonso spoke up, "we will rest in Yaxche, right, Itzi?"

Certain types of death assured your immediate place in Mayan heaven; anyone sacrificed went directly to Yaxche; a place in the sky where they would live in peace under the heavenly Ceiba Tree, the source of all of life. Mothers who died in childbirth also avoided Xilbalba, the tortuous underworld, and went directly to peace in the sky.

The High Priest laughed, "So you do remember the lessons of your schooldays in Uxmal, Fonso!"

The big man blushed. As a boy he would pass by their school at any opportunity; he preferred to take cover and watch the soldiers train. Ildefonso was suddenly embarrassed quoting religious doctrine to the Maya's most legendary High Priest.

Itzi turned to his other brother.

"Tolo, try to put all this out of your mind; your guess is as good as mine regarding our future. Concentrate on what you know to be certain; in a week we will make The Move and we will serve the great Chac until he decides otherwise."

Itzamna placed his tiny hand over Barolomeo's stomach and grinned.

"The churning in your belly is the exact reason it doesn't pay to worry about the future, all you will get is a stomach ache!"

Tolo smiled weakly. His stomach was doing flip flops, Itzi never missed a trick. Warmth surged through the High Priest's hand into his brother's abdomen, up Tolo's spine, into his head and back: a warmth cycle. In a breath the flip flopping stopped; Bartolomeo felt...free.

His eyes opened wide; he stared at his older brother.

"A gift from our god," Itzi grinned, "released negativity."

"Do you boys want coffee before you work?"

All three heads turned to their mother's voice in the doorway to the kitchen. She was removing gloves and a winter coat.

"It is so cold out there," she went on, "how could the weather be so nice here five months ago and turn into this? Wildwood, New Jersey is too wild for me! I hope the great lord will send us someplace nice and warm."

Itzi was glad to see his mother speak so comfortably of The Move. They had all become quite old hands at Chac's yearly instantaneous delivery into the unknown. It had certainly been bumpy at first; Itzi grinned, the first Move had been downright terrifying. Successive relocations were less and less stressful; in the modern world, with the internet, Swiss bank accounts and private aircraft, they had parts of Chac's Move down to a science.

The brothers rose and joined their mother in the kitchen. They sat at the table as she expertly brewed espresso; a comforting ritual they'd witnessed thousands of times.

"Mama, have you heard from Waykan and Ixkeem?" Itzi asked after his two younger sisters.

"They're still in West Palm Beach," she answered, "they will fly up to Philadelphia on Tuesday and leave their jet in the hangar with Fonso's. They promise to be here sometime that evening."

As she placed the miniature cups on the table along with a box of Ring Dings she continued, "They're complaining it's too cold and boring here now...but they will be here. I'm sure they will."

"It's a week today," Itzi sounded annoyed.

Since the advent of modern travel the family freely roamed the world. Through the years they had acquired and kept much real estate. In many places they began to live separately; sharing the duties of running the tattoo business from the place they now called Chac's house and gathering there on the day of First Father for The Move in the evening.

Fonso stole a look at his older brother. He felt responsible for the stress Itzi now felt around the time of The Move; he also felt responsible for what the family called "The Rule of 1964".

67

The family had landed that year in Scotia, a rural lumber town nestled among the redwoods in Northern California. All the family loved California. It seemed Chac valued the hearts of Californians; they had done yearly stints all over Golden State in many different eras.

In the late 1800's the family had purchased a beautiful home with a vineyard in the Napa Valley. Ildefonso still kept fine stable of horses there. In December of 1964, on the day of the Winter Solstice, Fonso left Napa heading north to Scotia for The Move that evening.

It rained torrentially all the way up US 101; the time more than doubled on what should have been a three or four hour ride. Unexpectedly the weather became much worse when the big man reached Humbolt County. Pounding rains flooded the streets. When the Eel River overflowed its banks flood waters rose quickly to over twenty feet.

Caught in a sudden wave Fonso wound up on the roof of his floating Corvette. Logs from the mills rushed by, box cars from the railroads that serviced the lumber industry twisted and turned as they passed in the swollen waters.

Fonso had never been so terrified; the big man clung to the sports car's roof in the blinding rain. He dodged debris of every variety. As men usually do in a disaster Ildefonso called out to his god.

"Please, great lord Chac, Fonso begged, please let me get back to your house for The Move. I will never bitch in my mind about work again. Please, great lord, I swear I will never leave Itzi alone again on a night of your work."

A man in a power boat picked Fonso up just as the sun was setting; however he adamantly refused to steer the vessel back toward Scotia. Desperately Fonso offered to buy the boat. The old man eagerly snatched the soggy ten thousand dollars in cash Ildefonso had in his pocket for The Move; the craft was barely worth a thousand!

They sped down the floodwaters where the old man rendezvoused with another ride; as Fonso roared back toward Scotia he thanked Chac for the greed of men. The deepening darkness was more terrifying than dodging the floating trains and lumber.

Fonso had never been as thankful as the moment he spotted the top of Chac's house. Abandoning the boat he climbed onto the roof and broke the skylight over Itzi's room. Dropping through the hole relief washed over Ildefonso as he landed square on his older brother's bed.

He found the family huddled in the front bedroom eyeing the rising water through the second floor window. They all cried out in relief when they saw him. Fonso had never seen Itzi so pale.

Hence the High Priest's Rule of 1964: no matter where they roamed, they must all live in Chac's house for the week approaching the Night of First Father. He was immovable on this decree.

Mama looked sideways at her oldest son, "It's only a few days shy of a week, Itzamna."

"If this area becomes covered in ice or snow, then what?" Itzi insisted, "Waykan is impressive and tenacious, Mama, but I doubt she has the resourcefulness of Ildefonso."

Their mother nodded, she clearly remembered the night they feared the loss of the family giant.

"I will call them and tell them to come immediately," she made a move toward her cell phone on the table.

Itzi put his hand out and stopped her, "I will call Waykan later myself."

The High Priest turned toward Fonso.

The little man smiled and made a confession,"I thought I would never feel fear as great as the night Chac moved us from the hilltop in Uxmal, but I recovered. I still have a scar on my heart from my terror that night in Scotia; I was sure we had lost you."

"I don't think I ever felt real fear until that night of the first Move." Fonso admitted, "When we landed in the Roman atrium, I swore we were dead. That night in Scotia? I have never been so afraid," the big man lowered his eyes; he couldn't meet his family's gaze as he made his own confession, "I think our great lord was teaching me a lesson and I am still sorry that you all had to suffer in the process."

Itzi's eyebrows shot up in surprise; for the second time that evening Fonso's words were unexpected. Yes, they all had grown immensely on Chac's journey.

"I hope we go someplace warm next week," Mama reiterated as she stood and removed the espresso cups from the table.

"I wouldn't mind going back to California," Bartolomeo offered.

"Tolo," Itzi turned to his brother, "do you still keep a list of everywhere we have ever been?"

"Yes, I have the list and my diaries. Why do you ask?" Bartolomeo was suddenly curious; Itzi rarely seemed interested in the past.

"Do you think we have been to California more than any other place? I was thinking about it the other day, it seems we have been there most often through the years."

"It could be," Tolo shrugged. "I'd have to look the list over; I know we've spent a lot of time around the Mediterranean. I'll check, if you want."

Itzi nodded and rose from the table as he spoke, "We should get to work, the people are probably already frozen solid out there."

Fonso winked at his brothers as they headed for the doorway, "Mama," the big man said as they passed by their mother at the sink, "do you want us to roll up the rugs for next week?"

Itzi and Tolo burst out laughing.

Over a thousand years before, as they prepared for the first Move from inside the house in Rome, their mother had insisted that the boys roll up the Persian carpets she had purchased in the Roman marketplace. She was convinced that her rugs would be ruined when Chac made it rain inside the house!

Mama shot Fonso a sour look; unexpectedly she smacked him hard on the behind as he passed. All three men roared laughing; their mother hadn't done such a thing since their ages were in single digits!

68

"You look lovely tonight, Ms. Hoyle."

Emily thanked the doorman as she stepped outside her building and moved toward the waiting limousine. She pulled her sable jacket closed. She loved the Valentino gown but now she hoped the sheer fabric on the top would be warm enough. The night was mild for December but chilly.

"You look great, Em." Joan commented as soon as Emily entered the vehicle.

"For sure, you're a knockout," George agreed. He was Joan's on and off again boyfriend.

Emily thanked her companions. Her black silk gown was cut down to the waist in the back and crisscrossed over see through embroidered mesh in the front. It was form fit to the knees then flared out with a fishtail hem.

Without regular exercise she was sure she wouldn't have felt the confidence to wear such a revealing dress. Emily was glad she had found a yoga studio in the Village and took classes often.

"Are you nervous?" Joan asked smiling.

Emily admitted that she was. The trio was on the way to the Tavern on the Green. Satchi and Satchi always had a year end banquet there. It was a social affair mixed with a little business; yearly bonuses were handed out and promotions announced.

Emily was slated to take Joan's job as Creative Director; Joan was being promoted to Vice President of Operations. It was a big night for both women.

The trio started the evening near the bar. George went to fetch drinks for both ladies. Many gentlemen eyed Emily; she was stunning in the Valentino gown.

"That dress was worth every penny and you were smart to come stag," Joan whispered in her pal's ear, "I didn't realize there were so many hotties at Satchi and Satchi."

Emily blushed. It was times like these she missed Tim the most. She still couldn't imagine going out with another man and she really wished her husband could have been there to see her promoted.

"I love the dress too," Emily whispered back, "but I'm still not sure it's worth eight thousand dollars."

"It is," Joan laughed, "judging by the reaction around here, it is!"

The ladies took their seats at the table closest to the dais. Many bonuses were awarded; Satchi and Satchi experienced record profits that year. The promotions were announced from the bottom of the company to the top. The girls applauded politely until the last two.

Emily was shaking when they announced her new title; she took a deep breath as she approached Bob Satchi at the podium.

"I am pleased to introduce our new Creative Director: Emily Hoyle."

Emily posed for pictures with both Satchi brothers. She smiled broadly recalling Joan's advice when they were out shopping:

"Buy a nice dress to wear. Those promotion photos will haunt you for life otherwise!"

The dinner was delicious. Emily was sitting at the table during the dancing portion; she had declined all invitations. The thought of another man's arms around her made her slightly nauseous.

Maybe it's the wine the new creative director thought. She stared at the flute of Dom Perignon; this might be her seventh, she'd lost count.

"Can I have a dance before you're officially my boss?"

Emily looked up toward the voice; Lyle Hatch was smiling. He was first in line for the promotion to Creative Director until Emily's recent return to the company.

"I'm sorry, Lyle." she meant it sincerely.

"Sorry, you won't dance?" he asked as he slid into the chair next to her, "or sorry you're my boss?"

"Both." Emily replied honestly.

"Don't be. Ordinarily I'd say you got the promotion because you're beautiful and lucky, but you deserve it, Emily. I'm being honest," he added.

"Better watch that," Emily said jokingly, "we are in the advertising business!"

Lyle laughed out loud, "See that's what I mean, you're quick and you're brilliant!"

Lyle filled her glass with the champagne on ice at the table. He held up his glass and they drank to the success of the upcoming year; the pair drank to a few other things as well.

When Joan returned to the table she could tell her pal was two sheets to the wind if not three. When the new VP suggested leaving, she could tell Emily was relieved.

When they reached Emily's building in TriBeCa it was little after midnight.

"You gonna be all right, Em?" Joan asked, offering to walk her friend to her door; George chimed in and offered too.

Emily declined; she assured them she would make it upstairs easily and exited the limo. She did feel a little shaky walking in the Valentino shoes; the heel was higher than she normally wore. The doorman saw her safely into the elevator and told her to buzz him if she needed anything.

THE FLAVOR OF HEARTS

Emily kicked the high heels off as soon as she entered her living room. She reclined on the couch expecting to sleep but sleep didn't come. Standing she headed for the wine rack; making a selection she uncorked it.

Returning to the couch she sat cross legged in the Valentino gown and sipped from the bottle. They ought to take my picture now she thought and laughed out loud.

A box near the door caught the adwoman's eye. She abandoned the wine bottle on the coffee table and carried the carton to the couch.

It was the last of her boxes from U-Store. Diana was so efficient; she had immediately placed her daughter's belongings safely in a storage facility. It had taken some time for Emily to face the past squarely but this was the last of it. Slitting the packing tape with a letter opener she was surprised to see lingerie.

It's the rest of my stuff from the bedroom dresser Emily realized. She dug through the sexy underwear. A stab went through her heart when she pulled out the gold frame. Tim looked so handsome in the picture Emily had kept on the bureau.

He was standing on Penns Landing in jeans and a tank top; bathed in sunlight and grinning from ear to ear. Dana took the photo at the restaurant festival during the Hoyle's first summer in Philadelphia. Emily smiled as she stood the frame on the coffee table; Lou was shocked at the amount of food Tim ate that day!

Again she dug down to the bottom of the carton; she felt the carved wooden box she used to keep on the dresser's top. There was something beside it; it was soft on the outside but hard. Emily was surprised when she extracted a tube sock with something stuffed inside.

She peered into the footwear's opening, large white eyes peered back. The griffon! Emily freed the mythical beast from his knitted prison. The little statue was stunning; the ceramic coloring was exceptional. The dragon head and wings were rendered in remarkable detail, the golden lion body glistened; it was easy to see why Tim was so captivated by it.

"Welcome to New York, little fellow," Emily thought as she placed the small figure on the coffee table next to the framed photo.

She could picture her husband's face the night he admitted taking the griffon from the museum. For some reason she was glad to have the only object Tim had ever stolen; it felt like all she had left of him.

The adwoman retrieved the wine bottle from the table and finished it five long gulps. God she missed her husband. She had imbibed enough alcohol to knock her unconscious; why was she still awake and still feeling the massive hole in her heart?

Emily poked through the cardboard carton and removed the wooden box that used to be on the bureau. It was basically a catch all: safety pins, business cards, tiny vials of perfume samples. When she opened the lid she was surprised to see photos.

69

"Wildwood pictures," she thought taking them from the wooden box. The adwoman had forgotten these shots. Dana had brought them down only a few days before she died.

Emily sighed when she saw the shot of the Torronis on the boardwalk; she had taken that one herself. Dana had loved that photo; because her old pal usually functioned as the photographer Dana said there were very few photos of her with Lou.

The adwoman laid the picture on the coffee table in front of the griffon. The next photo showed the Hoyles taken in the exact same spot. Laying that print beside the Torronis Emily realized with a little Photoshop magic she could place both couples in one shot; definitely something she would frame for her new home.

Tears filled Emily's eyes as she eyed the next picture. Tim looked so cute on the beach in his new bathing suit; Emily felt like a knife pierced her heart. She yearned to kiss his smiling face and feel his arms around her.

Misery drove the lady back toward the condo's bar. She feared she was immune to wine; she should be comatose from all the champagne at the dinner and the bottle of merlot. What was the stuff Lou was drinking Emily wondered?

She perused the bottles on the fully stocked home bar. Easily she recognized the black label and broke the seal. She sniffed the liquor first then took a little mouthful.

Although it burned like liquid fire the Jack Daniels tasted good to the distraught woman. She took the bottle back to the couch and sipped the famous Tennessee bourbon as she looked through the rest of the photos. She laid each picture on the coffee table side by side, by the time she placed the last one in the line she was sobbing.

Tim looked so proud and handsome in the final one; it was taken in the hotel room right after he took the bandage from the lion tattoo. He looked so happy; he was shirtless facing sideways with his head turned. The golden body art looked awesome on his bulging deltoid.

Wait a minute, Emily thought. Her eyes traveled down the line to the photo taken the day before on the Wildwood beach. Her eyes grew wide with astonishment; Tim was far less muscular. She placed the Jack Daniels bottle on the coffee table before it fell to the floor. Picking up the two prints she compared them side by side; in one day his body looked like he spent a year at the gym.

Emily gasped. It was proof, proof of a physical change from a Buena Suerte tattoo! Suddenly she lost her breath. Dropping the photos she jumped to her feet; she desperately needed fresh air.

The adwoman staggered toward the terrace. The glass door was heavy and the brisk air felt solid as she stepped outside. Emily gulped the cold oxygen like a parched man drinking water at an oasis.

The sheer Valentino gown offered no protection from the winter night, but the liquor warmed her body from the inside.

The photographic proof scared her to death. It wasn't her imagination; the tattoo was definitely causing changes! Sweat rolled down Emily's back despite the December temperature. Drunkenly she unzipped her dress and let it fall to the floor around her ankles. She stepped out of the puddled material and lurched toward the terrace's edge. Naked except for her thong panties and stockings she leaned on the railing to steady herself.

"You jumped, Lou," she cried out loud, "I know you jumped and I can't blame you!"

Standing on tip toes she leaned over the railing and measured the nine story drop. Sobbing she wished she had the guts to join Tim the way Lou joined Dana. Tears blinded her as she turned back toward the terrace door.

"You're a spineless bitch, Emily Hoyle," she slurred the words as she staggered back toward the living room.

Bending down to pick up the Valentino dress she almost fell. She scooped up the silk material and fought to regain her balance. Suddenly she wheeled around and ran back toward the railing.

Emily tossed the couture gown over the edge; leaning over she watched it float to the ground. It looked as small as a handkerchief when it finally reached the pavement below.

She cried out like a wounded animal, her shriek pierced the winter air. Shaking she stood at the railing and wept; with all her heart she wanted to jump but she couldn't muster the nerve.

Emily turned and ran toward the living room; she hurled herself face down onto the couch and she cried until she had no more tears. Robotically she sat up and reached for the Jack Daniels. She looked down at the tattoo on her lower abdomen as she gulped from the bottle. The good luck got really good, but the bad luck got really bad.

Emily's mind drifted to her first week back in New York.

Two days before Tim's funeral she had visited a dermatologist who specialized in tattoo removal. The man had taken one look at the Buena Suerte body art and refused to hit the metallic ink with the laser. Two other specialists expressed the same trepidation and refused treatment.

One recommended a fading cream. Emily tried every product on the market to no avail; oddly the tattoo appeared even more vivid after the application of the ointments.

Emily felt like crying but no tears came; she drained the bottle of bourbon. Once again she rose abruptly to her feet. The adwoman strode toward the kitchen; she was remarkably steady considering her massive intake of alcohol. She selected a steak knife from the wooden block on the counter.

In a second she was up the stairs and standing before the full length mirror in the master bathroom. Emily eyed her almost naked body. She had loved the image of the Raven but now she more than feared it. Taking the sharp knife she pierced the skin in a U shape around three sides of the tattoo. Blood ran down her shapely leg: surprisingly she felt no sting.

She placed her fingernail in the corner of the cut and tried to peel the skin back. Blood gushed from the wound and burning pain sobered her.

"Oh my God!" she shrieked out loud. Her voice echoed in the granite tiled room; panicked Emily dove for a towel to suppress the bleeding. She had never felt more insane. The pain was becoming unbearable.

A wave of nausea overtook the lanky brunette; she barely made it to the toilet in time to vomit uncontrollably. Blood soaked the towel she held to her abdomen as she knelt by the commode. Tears ran from her eyes.

Emily knew she had to call 911. She began to heave thinking of admitting what she had done. Again she vomited and dizziness enveloped her. I have to get to the phone she reasoned. Shakily she got to her feet though the room was spinning. Finally she focused on the bathroom door and quickly took the first step toward it.

Her foot hit the puddle of blood at the base of the toilet. Emily flew into the air; the adwoman was parallel to the ground. Her head came down first clipping the commode as she fell; she heard a cracking sound as her skull hit the granite floor.

Distantly she heard herself moaning; more vomit rose in her throat. Emily felt a searing pain in her chest.

70

Edward Comstock sat on the edge of the canopy bed in the Royal Suite at the Burj Al Arab. Slipping on his black Prada loafers he smiled; he was glad the bed couldn't talk. It was a rotating bed in the finest suite in the world's finest hotel; he shuddered at the tales it could probably tell!

The New Yorker's smile grew broader as he walked down the marble and gold staircase. He and his young wife had certainly added to the bed's history; so far the celebration of their first anniversary had been everything he'd hoped for and more.

He could hear Afton on the phone when he entered the plush living room. She looked like a fine porcelain statue curled up on the overstuffed burgundy and gold couch. The oil baron was proud to admit that she was one third his age; a better trophy wife than Afton couldn't be found.

By her part of the conversation he could tell she was talking to their housekeeper at the condo in Manhattan. The oil man went to the wall of windows and gazed at the spectacular view of the Arabian Gulf. From the twenty-fifth floor the azure water blended seamlessly with the clear blue sky.

The Burj Al Arab is the world's tallest hotel, world renowned for unparalleled luxury. It occupies a man made island directly off the coast of Dubai; it is considered an engineering marvel. When Sheikh Mohammed bin Rashid Al Maktoum revealed his ambitious plan most engineers considered the project impossible; yet there the hotel stood, built against all odds.

Edward smiled. That's why it was the perfect place for the Comstocks to spend their first anniversary. No one thought their marriage would last, yet here they were, against all odds!

The oil man turned and took in another beautiful view. Afton was a stunning woman in everyway; she looked even more alluring in this opulent setting. Everyone assumed she married him for his money and he married her for her looks; actually people couldn't be more wrong.

He fulfilled all her dark sexual fantasies and she reveled in the desires he had been afraid to admit to any of his previous wives or lovers. They were a match made in the blackest part of heaven; perfect in their secretly perverted union.

He joined her on the sofa as she hung up the phone, "What's going on?" he asked, his wife had a funny look on her face.

"Elena said the building is crawling with police," Afton sounded breathless, "last night some lady killed herself. Real messy too! Supposedly she mutilated herself and bled to death in her bathroom!"

"Did we know her?" Edward was clearly surprised by the news. Most of their neighbors in TriBeCa were pretty quiet.

"No," Afton shook her head, "it was the new lady that moved into the back penthouse; the one in advertising."

"The widow?" he sounded shocked.

"Yeah, do you believe it?" her big blue eyes were wide.

"Maybe she couldn't live without him," Edward offered softly.

"I couldn't live without you, Big Daddy." Afton's voice was like silk.

The oil man grinned. It was good to hear and he loved the names she called him in private.

"Have you given any thought to the tattoo idea, Baby?" Edward asked his pretty wife.

"Anything you want, Daddy Bear. Like always," she said slyly.

Edward grinned even more broadly; Afton was always up for anything; once again the oil baron was glad the bed upstairs couldn't talk.

"I do have three stipulations though," the lady went on.

Her husband's eyebrows shot up in surprise. Despite Afton's public persona, with him she was never demanding; in fact, especially in their private moments she was the polar opposite. Afton was a true and talented submissive and Edward loved every inch of her.

"What are your stipulations?" the billionaire was more than curious.

"I don't want anything too big," she looked down as she added, "or too revealing."

Ah, he understood her uncharacteristic trepidation. The Comstocks had been at underground parties where they had seen people with the word slave tattooed in two inch letters on their backs. Many submissives at these events sported tattoos on their bottoms or chests declaring the names of their owners.

When Edward laughed she looked up in surprise.

"Don't worry, Baby," he assured her, "I wasn't thinking of anything insane."

The young socialite looked relieved.

"How about we get matching little tattoos of this hotel?" Edward suggested. "It'll always remind us of our first anniversary and this great vacation; plus it is a beautiful building."

The Burj Al Arab was a unique hotel in many ways. The structure was designed to resemble a dhow, an Arabian sailing ship. A high tech cloth membrane made up the buildings exterior; it gave the impression of billowing sails. Standing offshore on its island the hotel looked like a giant sailboat coming into port. Stunning colored lighting made the Burj Al

Arab even more impressive at night. The distinctive hotel helped make Dubai the seaside playground for the jet set and the world's elite.

As she always did Afton agreed to his plans.

Edward Comstock was excited. The oil man had been intrigued the minute their private butler told him about Dubai's first tattoo parlor. Tattoos are forbidden for Muslims, so the opening of such a place in the United Arab Emirates was slightly taboo. Edward always loved anything that flew slightly under the radar of propriety.

The butler also said that the tattoos were most unique; they had the look of 24 carat gold. This really piqued the billionaire's interest. Edward had laughed out loud at the last thing the butler told him; it was rumored that the golden tattoo would bring good luck forever. He forgot to tell his beautiful wife that part.

"Guess what else the butler said about these tattoos?"

She looked at him curiously as he answered his own question.

"He said once you get one, you'll have good luck forever!"

Now it was Afton's turn to laugh out loud, "Oh, Daddy, that's so crazy!"

He laughed along with her; Edward picked up the house phone and called their butler.

"Yes," he told the servant, "please have the car ready right away to take us to Buena Suerte. If we need an appointment, make one for me and one for my wife."

Afton loved watching her powerful husband give orders. A Spanish tattoo parlor in the Middle East she thought, life was never dull around Edward Comstock.

The billionaire cradled the house phone and rose from the couch. He moved toward the suite's safe to fetch his wallet. Suddenly he remembered Afton's earlier words, she said three conditions.

"Baby," he said turning back toward her, "what's your other stipulation?"

The stunning Mrs. Comstock picked up a brochure from the mahogany end table. She held it up so her husband could see the writing on the front; the headline read: Gold and Diamond Park on Sheikh Zayed Road.

"I want to stop here on the way," she said, "I want a new diamond bracelet…and not a little one."

Again Edward laughed out loud, "Baby, when have I ever bought you a small diamond?" he feigned offense.

"Never, Daddy," she used that soft sweet voice that got him hard.

"Baby," he promised her, "I'm gonna buy you a diamond bracelet so big and heavy you won't be able to raise your arm! Get ready to go."

Smiling she rose from the couch and headed up the marble stairway to change. Afton eyed her wrist; she could picture her new bauble. The lucky tattoo was already working.

71

The Comstocks went shopping after Richard learned of Buena Suerte's nocturnal hours. True to his word the oil man took his wife to Dubai's best gold and diamond souk. Souk is the word for a market in an Arab city; today many souks are specialized, selling only specific merchandise.

Richard rejected the first offering at Gold and Diamond Park; he told the salesman the $10,000.00 bracelet looked cheap. Immediately the Comstocks were ushered into a private area where the store's manager joined them.

Without delay the supervisor began displaying far more expensive jewelry. Afton pointed to a bracelet made of four rows of diamonds in a white gold setting. After first securing her husband's permission, the man placed the bauble on Afton's wrist.

Mrs. Comstock smiled; Richard's earlier prediction was almost true. The bracelet was not too heavy to allow her to lift her arm but at one hundred fifty two grams it was weighty and certainly impressive. The seller told Mr. Comstock that the wristlet contained seventy carats of round, prong set diamonds and was priced at 551,250 Dirham or $150,000.00 US.

The oil man didn't bat an eye as he extended his black American Express card. The diamonds were stunning next to Afton's creamy skin and she was worth every penny.

The New York couple went on to Dubai's fabulous Mall of the Emirates. Unbelievably they spent the rest of the day skiing. The Middle East's first enclosed ski slope, Ski Dubai is cooled to 30 degrees and features 22,000 square meters of year round snow. Warm clothes and equipment are provided with a slope pass. Expert skiers the Comstock's thoroughly enjoyed the world's only indoor black diamond run; it was even more thrilling to ski in the middle of the desert.

After a much needed rest and late dinner back at their hotel Richard called for the car to take them to Buena Suerte. It suddenly seemed quite the adventure to go out at midnight to be tattooed. As they entered the hotel's complimentary Rolls Royce the butler explained Buena Suerte's one at a time policy.

He assured the Comstocks that they would wait in the comfort of the car while he and another servant reserved the couple's place in line. Because of the late hour, traffic was relatively light driving to one of the city's oldest sections.

Primarily a residential area, Karama houses much of Dubai's expatriate middle class. Peppered among the low rise apartment buildings were stores boasting the best deals on furniture, discounted designer clothes, bags and watches. The Comstocks had not visited this section of Dubai. Wealthy tourists usually bypassed the area, known for the surreptitious sales of counterfeit goods and lesser quality merchandise.

The chauffeur eased the Rolls Royce next to the curb in front of Buena Suerte Tattoos. Two Asian men were already standing in line. Afton and Richard peered through the window at the store front as the servants exited the car's front seat and joined the queue.

"Look at that painting, Af," Richard sounded surprised, "the ocean looks real."

Afton agreed. The storefront painting was very impressive.

Glancing at the sign above the seascape she giggled. Buena Suerte meant good luck in Spanish; Richard followed her gaze and laughed as well. The couple still found it amusing that people actually believed that a tattoo could bring good fortune.

Afton returned her eyes to the painting: the little square structure atop the craggy rock face had a familiar look.

"Know what?" she turned to her husband. "It looks like Tulum, remember that Mayan ruin in Mexico we visited on the Caribbean Cruise?"

Richard scrutinized the painting more closely. Afton was right; he remembered that beach and the ruins on the cliff above.

They watched as the store's ornate screen door slid open allowing the first Asian man to enter. Richard turned to his wife, "I'll go first," he suggested "I don't like this one at a time thing…I'll talk them into letting me go in with you."

Afton smiled; she leaned her head close to her husband's ear and whispered,"Thank you, Daddy Bear."

Richard grinned salaciously; she never used his private name in public, even in hushed tones. He passionately kissed his wife. Distracted, neither of the Comstocks heard the chauffeur disembark. When the car's rear door opened it startled them both.

Quickly exiting Richard headed toward the building's entrance. With a small wave toward Afton he disappeared through the opening.

The oilman stopped dead in his tracks right beyond the door; the claustrophobic lobby was totally unexpected. Now the New Yorker noticed the décor.

"Wow," he said out loud eyeing the relief sculpture on the room's front wall.

It resembled the carving they had seen at the Mayan ruins, but here it looked brand new! The room's tile work was unparalleled.

"Please, sir," Bartolomeo's voice rang out, "please fill in the card."

Richard approached Tolo; now the billionaire stared at the mosaic calendar behind the counter man.

"Are you guys Mayan?" the New Yorker asked curiously glancing over his shoulder at the giant Ildefonso.

"Yes," Bartolomeo answered holding up the brown index card, "please, sir, your information."

Richard slowly complied; then turned back toward Fonso. Before he could ask any more questions the previous customer re-entered the lobby; the billionaire watched the big man slide the screen door open and point toward the opening.

When the customer spoke to the huge doorman in Japanese Richard was shocked to hear the Mayan responded in the same language.

Turning to Richard, Ildefonso pointed toward the archway and now spoke in English, "This way, sir, please enter."

Convinced that this was the weirdest tattoo parlor he had ever seen, Richard Comstock entered the tiled walkway.

72

"Woooo!" Richard whistled as he entered Buena Suerte's main studio.

The billionaire was no stranger to elaborately decorated rooms but this place was right up there with the best of them. The mosaic night sky on the ceiling was unlike anything he had ever seen.

When Itzi approached both men exchanged shocked expressions. Richard was astounded by the High Priest's stature; Itzamna was surprised to see an American.

Operating nearly two months in the Middle Eastern emirate the Cenotes brothers had not seen one customer from the USA. In the present day nearly 90% of Dubai's residents are foreign nationals. The brothers had tattooed a huge assortment of Asians and Europeans. The tourists represented pretty much the same mixed demographic; the brother's joked that Chac had certainly found a variety of flavors all in one place.

"I have a drawing for you," Itzi told the American gesturing toward the tattoo area along the room's left wall.

Following the little fellow Richard began to extract a paper from his pocket; he had brought a line drawing of the Burj Al Arab that the hotel featured on some of its literature. The oil man stopped dead in his tracks when he spied the volume open on the stainless steel table. An oil derrick was drawn there, with golden oil spraying up like a first strike. Richard pointed toward the illustration.

"I'm in the oil business," the billionaire was floored, "did someone tell you?"

"No one tells me," the little artist explained, "I draw what I feel. I actually drew this for you."

Itzi offered the American a paper. The oilman's eyebrows shot up in sheer amazement. A bear stared back; not a cute cuddly bear, a fierce brown bear standing aggressively on his back legs. Shining gold highlighted the animal's fur and wove into a gleaming aura around the beast. No one knew the name that Afton called him in private, no one!

The idea of matching tattoos of the Burj Al Arab flew right out the window. Now the oil man felt torn between the two images. Richard held up the drawing of the bear and pointed toward the oil derrick.

"Could I get both," he asked the little artist, "this and that?"

"If you wish," Itzi replied gesturing toward the leather chaise. "Shall we start?"

The billionaire removed his shirt as he headed for the chair. He requested that the bear be put on his chest, on his right pectoral muscle. He wanted it near his heart for Afton.

"Could you put the oil derrick here?" Richard asked indicating his left shoulder.

"Anywhere you like." Itzamna answered as he prepared the stencil of the bear.

By the time the little artist finished the first tattoo the oil man was nearly crying. Nothing had ever hurt like that; the burning was so intense the billionaire felt like he was hit with scalding water.

Itzi held up the mirror and Richard stared at the reflection, the body art was everything he hoped for. The realistic bear looked ready to leap from his skin and the gold ink definitely gave the tattoo the promised look of jewelry.

"It's beautiful," Richard said softly.

"Shall I start the second tattoo?" Itzi asked.

The oil man shook his head. He didn't want to appear timid, but the pain was far too great to endure a second application.

"No, perhaps I'll come back another night," the billionaire suggested.

"As you wish," Itzamna smiled as he applied the anti-bacterial cream and bandage.

The High Priest was not surprised by the customer's refusal of the second tattoo. Though many clients initially asked for two images, in over a thousand years not one person had gone through with the plan.

Itzi gave the American the instructions for the body art's initial care as he pulled the brown card from the cash drawer. Richard was as surprised to see his card as most clients were.

"How did that get in there?" he asked unabashed by his curiosity.

"It's automated, Mr. Comstock," The little man read the name then quoted the price, "that will be 165 dirham…or $45 US."

Richard was shocked by the cheap price; everything in Dubai cost three times as much as anywhere else. The oil man wondered how they afforded to stay in business with such inexpensive rates; the artwork alone in this place had to have cost a fortune.

The billionaire peeled off a hundred dollar bill and handed it to the tiny Mayan. "Keep the change, you're totally worth it," as an after thought the oil man added, "you ought to charge more. You have a unique product. People will definitely pay more, especially here."

Itzi thanked the man for the tip and the compliment. Walking the American toward the exit the High Priest laughed inside as he mentioned he would consider the oil man's advice on pricing.

"Buena Suerte, Mr. Comstock," Itzamna smiled, "Buena Suerte."

73

When Mrs.Comstock entered the lobby both Ildefonso and Bartolomeo were taken by surprise. They'd seen very few women as customers since opening in the Middle East and this lady was exceptionally beautiful. Tolo eyed the girl with interest until he noticed her huge engagement ring and matching wedding band.

Afton approached the counter and filled in the card as soon as she was asked. When Richard Comstock re-appeared in the lobby the lady wheeled around at the sound of his voice.

"Affie, wait till you see this place," the oil man sounded thrilled, "it's amazing. I didn't get the tattoo of the hotel. Let the artist draw something for you; I think he has ESP!"

"Sir, thank you for coming."

The Comstocks turned toward Ildefonso; both were shocked to be interrupted.

The big man pointed toward the front door and reiterated the sentence looking directly at Richard. The billionaire reached for his wallet as he approached the giant doorman.

"Look," the oil man held out three one hundred dollar bills as he spoke, "my wife is a little nervous to go in by herself. I'd like to go in with her."

Fonso shook his head and made no move to take the cash.

"Only one at a time, sir." the big man intoned.

Richard was surprised. Reaching into the wallet again he doubled the bribe and spoke more forcefully, "I'd really like to go in with her."

Again Ildefonso refused. The oil man was astounded; reaching up he practically stuck the money in the giant Mayan's face.

"One at a time," Fonso repeated totally ignoring the currency under his nose.

"Unbelievable!" Richard's was clearly flabbergasted at the third refusal.

"I don't need your money." Ildefonso sneered.

The arrogance of the ultra rich disgusted Fonso; he was ready to throw the ignorant American out on the sidewalk. The big man was sure the lady suffered no nervousness; the asshole was unwilling to leave his trophy wife alone.

Bartolomeo spoke up before the situation turned ugly.

"Please, sir, only one at a time. Spectators distract our brother from his artistry."

Afton looked over her shoulder toward Tolo's calm voice then took Richard by the arm as she spoke, "Let's just go."

Richard Comstock appeared ready to take his beautiful wife and leave; oddly Bartolomeo wished he would. The family genius was shocked by his feelings; it was the first time he ever hoped a customer would avoid Chac's grasp.

"Affie, the tattoo really does look like gold," Richard looked at his wife, "It'll look stunning on you. Go in. Get whatever strikes your fancy. Put the tattoo wherever you want it. Go ahead; the artist is very nice. You'll be fine."

Though his final words were still directed at his wife Richard glared at Fonso as he finished, "I'll wait right here for you."

The warrior in Ildefonso surfaced. This obnoxious American would not get his way; not here. The big man narrowed his eyes and motioned toward the open door.

"Exit here. Thank you for coming, sir."

Afton waited for Richard to explode; to her utter amazement he turned and kissed her tenderly on the forehead.

"Go in, Affie. I'll be right outside."

The billionaire turned and strode through the door. By the sour look on his face it was clear he was not used to losing. Afton looked up at Fonso quizzically; she had never seen any man get the best of Richard in any situation.

Before she stepped under the archway toward the main studio, she turned her pretty head toward Bartolomeo and thanked him.

Tolo felt like the words pierced his heart. For a second he wondered what Itzi would say if he stood up and told the lady to run the other way. Thankfully the point was moot as she disappeared quickly through the passageway.

Now Tolo turned toward his younger brother, "Fonso, are you crazy?" You almost picked a fight with that guy."

"Fuck him," Ildefonso spat out the words. The big man raised the pitch of his voice and imitated his brother, 'Spectators distract our brother from his artistry'...where'd you get that bullshit, Tolo?"

"I was trying to keep you from knocking his block off!" Bartolomeo was clearly annoyed.

The one at a time policy had evolved over the centuries to get people in and out of Buena Suerte quicker. Spectators greatly lengthened the process plus it was easier to keep the lord's tally of twenty per night.

"Are you sure you weren't trying to save your little girlfriend?" Fonso grinned sardonically, "I saw the way you looked at her. Mmmm...she was quality."

The big man licked his lips.

"Shut up, Fonso," Tolo sounded disgusted, "You're an animal."

Ildefonso grunted in agreement as he opened the door.

74

Afton was totally shocked by Buena Suerte's interior; she had never seen such lush flowering plants indoors. Seeing no visible way to let natural light into the room, she wondered how the plants thrived. She found the paintings of the pyramids exquisite and the ceiling indescribable.

Itzi approached. The High Priest smiled broadly; this woman looked like the porcelain dolls in the old French markets.

Afton relaxed; the little Mayan seemed very exotic; she was barely taller than him. Immediately she noticed his muscular body; he was very cute. She motioned toward the fresco on the right.

"The Temple of Kulkulkan; a breathtaking rendition."

Itzi grinned. He was pleased she called the pyramid by its Mayan name rather than its Spanish one: El Castillo.

"I have a drawing for you," Itzi led her toward the steel table.

Straight off she liked his voice; it sounded like music.

Seeing his illustration she gasped in surprise; her Persian cat! Itzi had skillfully drawn the animal using fine black lines to suggest shadows under the fluffy white hair. Gleaming gold lines rendered light shining through the soft fur.

Stunned, the socialite examined the artwork more closely; it was portrait like, even the face looked exactly like Lionette. Every detail was correct down to the spoiled pet's emerald collar.

"Lionette!" Afton exclaimed, "it's my cat; my cat at home! How did you draw this? How could you draw such a perfect picture of Lionette?"

The High Priest shrugged; it was hard to explain how he saw the pictures in his head. One night, early in their new life in Chac's service, Itzi doodled in the large parchment book during a lull in between customers. When the next person arrived the man stared at the book in awe. Itzamna had drawn a violet, the name of the man's newborn baby daughter.

After that Itzi drew in the books, and later on papers for each customer before they arrived in his studio. Having a design ready had also greatly sped up the tattoo process and it amused Itzi to see the customers so mystified.

"My husband said you had ESP!" Afton was breathless.

Itzi tilted his head. Husband? The High Priest was slightly disappointed as he put two and two together. Two Americans…the bear; that old man was this fine young woman's husband. The little man sighed; some unions seemed so unbalanced.

"Would you like this drawing as a tattoo?" he asked the beautiful lady.

Afton readily agreed; the socialite anticipated his next question. With a mischievous look she put her hand down by her crotch, "Could I get it down here?"

"Wherever you like," Itzi was again intrigued by this woman.

He pointed toward the leather chaise and began making the stencil. The High Priest brought the embroidered modesty blanket when he approached her. When she raised her cocktail dress Itzi was surprised to see she had removed her panties. Beneath her outerwear she was totally naked and completely hairless. She was pointing toward her shaved vulva.

For the first time Itzi realized she wanted the tattoo right above the vagina; where her pubic hair had been. Oddly it was High Priest's turn to be amazed; he had never put Chac's mark on anyone's private part. By the look on the little man's face Afton feared he would refuse.

"Does it bother you to touch me there?" she asked curiously.

"No, no it doesn't bother me…" he removed his gaze from her lower body and looked directly into her eyes, "I'm afraid it will be very painful."

"Good."

Itzi's amazement escalated to astonishment; she relished the possibility! "All right," the little man replied with a slight shake of his head, "then I'll begin."

Afton reclined. She giggled when the High Priest applied the stencil; it felt cold and slimy. Though it came on slowly the burning became intense soon after Itzi started the tattoo's outline.

Many times, at her request, Richard had dripped hot candle wax on her naked body. It burned in a delicious way; but this…this was a whole new level. The pain was indescribable; she was totally aroused.

The buzzing of the tattoo gun became mesmerizing; she could feel the vibration inside and outside her vagina, then all the way back through her buttocks. The socialite intertwined her fingers behind her head. This mimicked her favorite sexual position; Afton Comstock loved to have sex with her hands tied over her head.

She moaned. Itzi's eyebrows shot up in surprise. When the lady moaned again he fought to concentrate on the tattoo. As Itzi finished the final gold highlights he felt her shudder. Unmistakably, she had climaxed.

The High Priest shut the gun, sat back and gazed at his client. She had her eyes closed and was breathing slowly and deeply. Oddly, the tattoo looked stunning on her private area; the reclining cat with his lion like mane beautifully topped the perfect symmetry of her vagina.

THE FLAVOR OF HEARTS

Itzi looked away. Lying there so creamy white with her dress up; she was beginning to look too good to him. He picked up the mirror to divert his thoughts. "Are you all right, Madam?" he asked softly, not wishing to startle her.

Her eyelids slowly opened; her aquamarine eyes glistening, "I'm very much fine," she answered contentedly.

She gasped with delight when she saw the reflection of her new body art, "Ohhhh! Lionette looks soooo beautiful. Unbelievable! It's amazing!" She took her eyes from the mirror and gazed directly at Itzamna, "You are amazing."

The little man nearly blushed at the way she said it. Most women spoke exactly that way after he bedded them. This was definitely the wildest work night of all time.

Itzi prepared the bandage with the bacterial cream. He gently placed it over her private area; then quickly rose and headed toward the cash drawer. Yes, she was definitely looking too good to him.

Reciting the instructions for the tattoo's initial care he retrieved her card. A pang of disappointment crossed his heart; she had signed her name "Mrs. Richard Comstock".

Strangely, he wondered what her name was. Suddenly her mismatched union with the old man made a little more sense; she used her husband's full name to invoke power for herself. Looking up Itzi was glad to see she was dressed again.

"That will be 165 dirham...or $45 US, Mrs. Comstock."

Afton extracted the money from her Gucci bag. As she offered the Dubai currency she took a long look at the little man. Oddly she wished she was single again.

"What is your name?" she asked curiously.

"Itzamna."

She repeated it perfectly; the name sounded magical falling from her mouth. Though tempted, Itzi did not ask hers; the High Priest thanked the lady and moved toward the exit. Gratefully, he ended the encounter as he always did.

"Buena Suerte, Mrs. Comstock." Itzi said, "Buena Suerte."

Afton walked through the arch then abruptly turned back and hugged the little man. For the third time the High Priest fought arousal. Itzi shook his head in amazement; he couldn't wait to tell Ildefonso about this. Fonso will love this story, the High Priest thought with a chuckle, he's such an animal.

75

Richard was glad to see Afton emerge from the strange tattoo parlor. The socialite was surprised to see at least fifteen people waiting to get in. The oil man escorted his wife to their waiting car and peppered her with questions as soon as they were alone in the back seat.

"What did you think of that place? What did the midget draw for you?"

Afton hadn't thought of Itzi that way.

"Do you think he was?" she sounded puzzled, "a little person?"

"Af," Richard laughed, "he was barely four feet tall."

"He didn't look like one," she was picturing Itzi's perfect body and exotic handsome face, "little people have that look, you know what I mean."

"They're many forms of dwarfism," suddenly Richard could hardly believe the turn of the conversation, "Af, what did he draw for you? What did you get for a tattoo?"

Afton wore an impish look and said slyly, "Take me back to the hotel and I'll show you."

Richard checked his watch, "It's two o'clock now; we have to wait two hours to take off the bandages."

"Why?" Afton looked disappointed, "let's go back and I'll show you mine and you show me yours!"

Richard was adamant; he warned his wife how bad it could get if infection set in on a fresh tattoo. Because the Buena Suerte body art was so unique the billionaire was sure they should follow the artist's instructions to the letter.

Richard told the driver to take them to the Bahri Bar; a jazz club located in a hotel near their own. He instructed the driver to return for them at 3:00 when the club closed.

"We'll have some drinks," he told his impatient wife, "then we'll go back and show and tell."

By the time they returned to their room in the Burj al Arab it was nearly 3:30. When Afton headed immediately to the dressing room on her side of the bedroom Richard spoke in a mock stern voice, "Don't touch that bandage for another twenty minutes, Affie!"

"Whatever you say, Daddy Bear," she called over her shoulder.

Richard grinned; she got him hot just talking.

Shortly she re-emerged and joined her husband on the suite's round bed. She wore a champagne colored silk teddy and matching thong panties. Now she made the billionaire hot without talking.

He lifted her nightie and began kissing her tight stomach. Suddenly he reared his head back; in her revealing negligee Richard realized he saw no bandage. His became clearly visible to Afton when he had removed his shirt.

"Affie, where'd you get the tattoo?" he was ultra-curious.

She smiled wickedly when she lowered the panties in front. She laughed out loud at Richard's shocked expression.

"That little midget had a hold of your snatch, my Little Pussy?" Richard was amazed and appalled at the same time.

"Oh Daddy Bear, he wore the rubber gloves!" Afton was thrilled at her husband's obvious jealousy. She was glad to hear his pet name for her; it would be even cooler when she revealed her tattoo.

The socialite pointed to her husband's watch.

"Let's see yours, Daddy Bear," she extended her hand toward the bandage on his chest. Ever the submissive in private she asked his permission, "Can I take it off?"

He nodded in agreement and watched her face as she saw the body art.

"Oh Daddy Bear! It's the most awesome thing I have ever seen!" in a more sultry voice she added, "It's scary and beautiful; like you, Daddy Bear."

Richard was immediately hard; seeing his reaction Afton slid down his body and took his throbbing penis in her mouth. Nobody had ever pleased the billionaire like his young trophy wife.

After he climaxed she laid her head contentedly on his chest, staring at the tattoo.

"I love this, Daddy Bear." she purred.

Immediately he remembered her tattoo. He lifted her head and stared into her eyes; in the stern voice she loved he chastised her.

"I'm still not happy that artist had a hand on you down there, My Little Pussy. I think you should get over my knee for a serious spanking!"

"Oooooh thank you, Daddy Bear," Afton replied as she obediently placed her buttocks over his lap.

Richard slapped her bare rear crisply until both her cheeks glowed a hot pink. The lady moaned in pleasure as the heat built up on her exposed seat. When he finished she laid submissively in the spanking position so he could admire his handiwork.

Richard rubbed her tight blazing buttocks; then fingered her wet vagina. A rousing spanking was always the best foreplay for Afton Comstock.

He smacked her rear again as he spoke in his stern Daddy voice, "Now you get up and show me your tattoo and you better hope I'm pleased." he added in a sexier voice, "or else you'll be back over my knee for more, My Little Pussy."

Afton grinned with delight as she rose to her knees on the bed facing her husband. Sexily she lowered her panties to her mid-thighs. She looked directly at her mate's face as she peeled away the bandage then laughed out loud at his astonishment.

"Lionette! It's Lionette!" he looked up at her face incredulously, "he drew it just like that?"

When Afton nodded in agreement Richard whistled in surprise. He moved his head toward her for a closer look. The body art was more than stunning on Afton. Her pale taut skin was the perfect canvas; the metallic gold gleamed.

"He even had the collar?" the billionaire pointed toward the emerald choker Afton had purchased for the cat on its last birthday.

"Yes, he had the drawing just like you see it," Afton's voice was tinged with wonder, "He had the bear ready for you, Daddy?"

Richard recounted his time in Buena Suerte; he told his wife of the oil derrick and his refusal of the second tattoo. Hearing the tale she was wide eyed with amazement. Knowing his wife's thirst and tolerance for pain he asked about her experience.

"Did you enjoy the burning, My Little Pussy?"

Afton lowered her eyes as she answered demurely, "Yes, Daddy Bear."

She decided to leave the whole story for another time; she would tell Richard of her climax on the artist's table when she wanted a severe paddling.

"Take your clothes off," he ordered, "I want to see you in nothing but Lionette!"

Immediately she complied. He produced a silk scarf from under the pillow and tied her hands. Roughly he threw her down on the plush mattress and pinned her tied wrists over her head. The couple made passionate love until long past dawn.

76

The Comstock's final week in Dubai passed as quickly as a single day. Though both were sad to leave the luxurious Burj Al Arab they were glad to be heading home.

Richard left for the office early on their first day back in New York. Afton woke to a gift on his unoccupied pillow. She was thrilled with the gold pin formed like the famous sailboat shaped Dubai hotel.

Richard's card read, "Thanks for a great anniversary vacation. Here's a memento of that great place and our wonderful time there. I love you, Affie. DB"

The socialite grinned; Daddy Bear could be so romantic.

Afton couldn't wait to get to Jazzercise; she had eaten far too many rich meals on vacation. Waiting for the elevator she heard a muffled techno beat. Turning her head she saw the neighbor's granddaughter approaching; the teenager had her iPod on so loud Afton could hear the music bleeding from the ear buds three feet away.

Afton and Richard had seen this kid around the building before they left for Dubai. She dressed like a prostitute and wore more makeup than a circus clown. Richard said she looked like a dropped on grandma, starved for attention product of a broken home.

The music sounded even louder in the insulated elevator. Afton was appalled; surely the teenager would be deaf by the time she finished puberty. The socialite was thrilled when the youngster bolted through the elevator doors as soon as they opened.

Crossing the lobby Afton saw a glint of pink and silver on the floor; the junior street walker had dropped her keychain. Spying the youngster just outside the glass door Afton hurried through the building's opening. Knowing words were useless she tapped the young lady on the shoulder.

The teenager's sullen look turned to shock when she saw the keychain. Without a word of thanks she snatched the keys from Afton's hand and took off running down Vestry Street.

The doorman apologized as he opened the rear door of Afton's waiting Town Car, "I'm sorry, Mrs. Comstock," he grimaced as he motioned down the street, "that kid…that kid is--"

Afton waved off his polite regret and finished the sentence for him as she climbed into the backseat, "--the very reason I never want to have kids."

The ride to Jazzercise was short; it was barely ten blocks to the studio on Duane Street. Afton joined her friend Pamela near the bench in the studio's locker room.

"How was U-Buy? What did you get?" Pam sounded totally excited.

Afton grinned at their rhyming nickname for Dubai. The abundance of high end malls and duty free designer shops made the Middle Eastern emirate a haven for shopoholics; re-christened "U-Buy" it was aptly named.

"Five pairs of Prada, three Valentino gowns, a Kenzo; I got the greatest Yamamoto dress," Afton began changing her clothes as she went on, "Richard bought me an enormous diamond bracelet, 70 carats!"

THE FLAVOR OF HEARTS

"Ooooh," Pam whistled, "I gotta see it!"

"You gotta see something else, Pammie," Afton leaned over and whispered in her pal's ear, "I got a tattoo."

"No! You? You got a tattoo?" shock was all over Pam's pretty face.

Afton nodded as she lowered her panties; the Persian cat gleamed.

"Wow, Lionette! I've never seen anything like that," Pamela looked closer at the body art, "is it gold? I've never seen a gold tattoo!"

"Me either," Afton agreed, "Richard said he never heard of a gold tattoo 'til we got these. The store was new in Dubai, it was called Buena Suerte. You would love it...full of Mayan carving and artwork."

Pam had a million questions. An archeology major, she collected pre-Columbian art and had always been interested in the ancient sun cultures. Her curiosity would have to wait though; the girls hustled into the main studio when they heard the warm-up music begin.

Afton had not ignored her exercise regimen while on vacation; the Burj Al Arab boasted many fitness related amenities in its Assawan Spa. The socialite had attended regular aerobics sessions, but none were as strenuous as the advanced Jazzercise she regularly practiced at home in TriBeCa. The first day back was enjoyable but harder than expected and Afton was glad the class was nearing the end.

A loud pop punctuated the music; the odd sound was disconcerting. Out of the corner of her eye Afton saw her friend Pamela crumple to the floor.

"It hurts, God, it hurts!" Pam was cradling her foot; the ankle was bent in a most unnatural way.

"Give her room, give her room!" the instructor was pushing through the other dancers already crowding around their fallen classmate.

When she saw the damage up close the teacher gasped; a baseball sized swelling was growing around the injury.

"Pam, that looks broken. I'll call 911 and get an ambulance."

"No...No. Affie, help me up." Pamela looked up at her gal pal standing horrified beside her.

Afton knew of her best friend's aversion to ambulances. As a teenager Pam suffered a burst appendix and nearly died in one; the poor woman still had regular nightmares about ambulances.

"Affie! Help me up!" This time it was a panicked command.

"I'll go to the hospital," Pamela insisted to the instructor, "but Affie will take me."

Despite everyone's advice to the contrary, Afton offered her arm and helped her friend to stand. Hopping along on one leg and leaning on Afton's shoulders, Pamela made it to the couch in the lobby.

"Wait here, don't move. I'll get our stuff and call for my car," the socialite barely finished the sentence when she turned to run through the studio to the dressing room.

With much haste she opened both lockers and fetched their coats and bags. In less than half a minute she ran back toward the lobby. Afton pushed through the crowd of women now clustered at the entrance; she stopped dead in her tracks when she saw Pamela standing.

"What are you doing, Pammie?" the socialite practically screamed, "sit down! Are you crazy?"

"Look, Affie, look!" Pam had a wondrous look on her tearstained face, "I'm fine, check it out!" She elevated to the ball of her foot and did a full turn.

Afton stared slack jawed; even the swelling had disappeared. Pamela continued to dance in the lobby; everyone gasped when she did a leap and landed on the wounded foot.

"I'm fine...do you believe it? I can't believe it, I'm fine!" Pam sounded ecstatic.

Afton couldn't comprehend it. Every onlooker wore the same stunned expression; nobody could understand this turn of events.

"I think you should go to the hospital and get checked out anyway," the instructor suggested. Her voice was shaky; she was too astonished to easily form words.

"Why? I'm fine," Pamela insisted, "Look! Check it out!"

She placed her feet together; no difference could be detected in Pam's legs or ankles.

Puzzled the instructor shook her head; she was sure Pamela's injury was serious.

"Well, you do what you think is right, Pam." she turned and addressed the group, "I guess that's enough excitement for today…I'll see everyone on Friday."

The crowd dispersed and headed for the locker room; murmured comments of disbelief were overheard.

"Let's go get lunch," Pam suggested brightly.

"Are you sure you're all right?" Afton stared at her friend; worry still clouded the socialite's voice.

When Pam did a double pirouette on the allegedly injured foot Afton smiled, "Okay, okay…you don't have to show off!"

77

Richard was glad to be back at the office. Since marrying Afton he was far less the workaholic he had once been but he still relished running his company.

Comstock Allied Energy had started as a small oil business but had grown under Richard's direction to a huge multinational conglomerate. All forms of power: solar, natural gas, wind, nuclear and bio-fuels were represented under the umbrella of the successful corporation. Comstock Allied Energy was on the forefront of modern research finding viable alternatives for fossil fuel.

Richard entered the private elevator from his penthouse office to descend to the 18th floor. The CEO was sorry he'd scheduled a budget meeting his first day back; the bean counters were usually so mind-numbing.

Entering the conference room on the financial floor Richard was immediately approached by his right hand man Christopher Halsey.

"How was Dubai?" the young man warmly greeted Richard, "Did Afton buy the malls out?"

"Almost," Richard smiled, "but I think I avoided bankruptcy!"

THE FLAVOR OF HEARTS

The CEO took his seat at the head of the empty conference table. Many executives made a grand entrance at meetings once all their underlings had assembled; Richard preferred to be waiting for his employees.

Christopher began placing files in front of his boss; pointing out the main issues on the meeting's agenda. Once Richard had a solid idea of the business at hand the assistant retreated to a chair directly behind the CEO.

The billionaire began poring over the budget allotted for the research on mold related biofuel. Richard had never agreed with the idea of converting food sources to energy; his company had been one of the first to investigate processing non-edible plants and algae into fuel.

The billionaire rubbed his eyes; the financial report seemed endless. Once again the CEO regretted calling a budget meeting on the first day but he refocused his attention on the accountant's report.

Eyeing a column of figures nearly a page long a number burst into Richard's head: $751,851.00. He looked to the subtotal: $751,851.00.

With barely a glance at the numbers on the next page a sum again appeared in his brain. Diverting his gaze to the bottom line the oil man blinked; the tally perfectly matched his mental number.

Sure he noticed the total subconsciously; he turned to the following sheet. Richard covered the bottom before he stared at the numerical column. $371,097. Lifting his hand he almost gasped, his mental total was correct!

He did the same thing with the four remaining pages of figures. With barely a glance at the numbers he knew the sum. Richard shook his head back and forth; he tried to shake off this weirdness like a dog shakes off water.

"Chris," the CEO turned toward his assistant, "do you have a calculator?"

The young man fetched one immediately from the credenza along the conference room's back wall. Richard punched random numbers into the machine, eyeing them as they flashed on the display. When he paused a figure clearly appeared in his head: 298,876. The oil man was floored when he hit the calculator's equal button: 298,876!

The CEO stared straight ahead. For a moment he wondered if he was dreaming; still lying in his comfy bed with Afton in TriBeCa.

"Is everything OK, Richard?" The assistant hoped there were no mistakes in the report's calculations; Richard Comstock had a very low tolerance for sloppy mistakes.

"No, no, it's fine." the CEO assured the young man.

The assistant furrowed his brow; though his boss's words were positive in nature Christopher could see his boss's whole demeanor had changed. Both men became distracted by the arrival of the accountants and financial officers.

One by one they greeted the CEO and took their places at the conference table. After two scientists appeared to represent the biofuel research department Richard called the meeting to order.

It was as the CEO expected; a tedious litany of expenses and future expenditures. Though the scientists appeared concerned over the monies allotted Richard was quick to approve anything they needed. Though known for his frugality the oil man was sure the future of Comstock Allied Energy rested squarely on the discoveries of the biofuel lab.

After an hour every item on the agenda was covered; thankfully the CEO called the meeting to an end. Immediately he rose from his chair and circled the table heading toward the scientists.

Richard smiled as he paused before the researchers; accountants were a pretty nerdy lot but these guys brought geekiness to a whole new level. Amused he watched the head scientist shoving papers into an overstuffed binder. The man shot up from his chair as soon as he realized the CEO was standing next to him.

When Richard held out his hand the skinny man wiped his own palm on his pants before accepting the CEO's handshake.

THE FLAVOR OF HEARTS

"I'm proud of the work you're doing," Richard released his grasp; he could feel the man was practically shaking, "the video you sent me was absolutely amazing."

"I'm glad you thought s-s-s-so," the scientist pushed his heavy glasses back toward his unibrow. Richard laughed hearing the man's next words, "Jesus, he must think I'm a stuttering idiot."

"Not at all," Richard answered immediately.

The scientist stared in shock; Richard suddenly realized the man hadn't spoken the self deprecating sentence.

"Well, keep up the good work," the CEO ended the awkward encounter by moving toward the conference room door.

Richard shook his head in the elevator. He was sure he heard the man's voice, yet now he was positive the scientist hadn't spoken the sentence out loud. Chalking it up to intuition the oil man entered his office and sat in his chair.

Spotting the calculator on his desk he suddenly remembered the earlier weirdness with the financial report. The billionaire punched random numbers into the machine. For a half hour he got every total correct, down to the decimal point. He stared out the window in disbelief; in a strange way it was funny.

With a glance at his watch Richard decided to go home a little early; he couldn't wait to show Afton the calculator trick.

Richard was disappointed when his wife was not at their apartment. The maid said Mrs. Comstock would return around six from a meeting at her AIDS charity. The billionaire was proud of the volunteer work Afton was involved in; she worked tirelessly for a multitude of worthy causes.

After a shower he planted himself in front of the wide screen TV and became engrossed in ESPN's Sports Center. True to the maid's prediction Afton joined him right after six.

She stared wide eyed when Richard showed off his new found ability.

"What's the trick, Daddy? How are you doing that?" she grabbed the calculator; sure he had set up the numbers previously.

When he correctly added, subtracted and divided the numbers she punched in at random Afton was slack jawed, "You're the Rainman, Daddy!"

Richard grinned; he had thought of the movie about the autistic savant earlier.

Abruptly Afton's amazement turned to worry; another movie popped into her mind. In "Phenomenon" John Travolta's character had developed amazing mental powers and by the end he died from a brain tumor.

"Daddy, I want you to go to the doctor and get a check up," the socialite said seriously.

Richard's eyes opened in surprise; he assured her of his perfect health.

When she steadfastly explained her new concerns, he realized his wife's anxiety might be warranted. Maybe this oddity was a little more ominous than he originally thought. He promised to make an appointment.

78

Fonso slid his boat into low gear and slowly cruised around the crescent surrounding Palm Jumeirah. He was still totally amazed by the huge man made island. Shaped like a palm tree and nestled in the Arabian Gulf directly off the coast of Dubai, the island's trunk and seventeen fronds had doubled the amount of the tiny Emirate's beachfront property.

The opulent villas and luxury residences on Palm Jumeirah were highly sought after by the world's elite. The gleaming modern hotels and the plethora of duty free designer boutiques drew tourists in droves.

Fonso inched his boat into its slip in the Anchor Marina. Immediately two attendants appeared to catch the lines and secure the yacht. The level of service in Dubai still impressed Ildefonso. The beauty of the Arabian Gulf and the abundance of fish thrilled the giant Mayan as well. He disembarked and headed for the Marina Residences.

Entering the fourth of six looming high rises Fonso was immediately relieved by the cool air; breathing a sigh of relief he crossed the magnificent lobby.

"Mama certainly got her way when she wished we'd arrive somewhere warm." the big man thought as he stepped into the elevator.

Born in the Yucatan Ildefonso was no stranger to sticky weather, but it was stifling hot in the United Arab Emirates. Summer had been unbearable; temperatures had regularly soared to 110 degrees and beyond; now even in December it was a balmy 83.

On the top floor Fonso opened to the door to their apartment and smiled at the three huge suitcases lined up at the door. Even Itzi had bought a ton of clothes in Dubai.

Ildefonso walked through the ornate entrance hall to the sprawling living room and dining room. Turning to his left he opened the massive glass door to one of the apartment's three terraces. It was no surprise to find the High Priest there; the view of the sky and the Arabian Gulf from the penthouse apartment had captivated the little man from their first night there.

Fonso grinned; Itzi's sunglasses were a sure sign the High Priest was barely awake though it was almost sundown.

"Some night?" he asked his tiny brother.

The evening before had been a real party; three Swedish stewardesses had kept the Cenotes brothers busy until nearly dawn.

Itzamna grinned from ear to ear, "Swedish women…very energetic."

Fonso laughed slyly; he readily agreed. His girl had taught him a few new tricks; quite the feat considering his sexual history spanned centuries.

The big man slid into a lounge chair beside his brother and admired the view. Though they had lived nearly a year in the Marina Residences on the Trunk of Palm Jumeirah, Ildefonso had never tired of watching the giant orange sun slip into the Arabian Gulf.

Itzi motioned toward the setting orb, "It's really beautiful here."

Fonso again agreed, "This place would be heaven on earth if it wasn't for the heat and some of the rules."

Itzamna nodded. Though Dubai was easily the most tolerant of the Muslim governed Middle Eastern countries, the

THE FLAVOR OF HEARTS

laws governing alcohol consumption, women's dress and displays of public affection between the sexes were hard to get used to.

"I'm afraid, after all these years, we've become modernized," Itzi commented, "I'm still surprised how much the heat bothered me here this summer. It was hot in the Yucatan, it's been hot a lot of the places we've been through the years, but this summer…"

The High Priest's voice trailed off.

"Remember, Itzi, the last time we were in this neck of the woods, there was no such thing as air conditioning!"

Thinking back Itzamna realized his brother was right; the family hadn't lived in the Middle East since early in the sixteenth century.

"We have become used to modern conveniences," the little man admitted wryly.

"Yeah, modern conveniences, Fonso grinned "how did we live without 'em?

Itzy laughed. Fonso saw no nobility in discomfort.

The brothers sat in silence watching the sun paint the Arabian Gulf. Spectacular reds and oranges bounced on the surface of the aquamarine sea.

Muted lamps automatically lit the opulent residence as sensors read the decreasing daylight. The penthouse apartment had every electronic bell and whistle; it was 4200 square feet of elegant extravagance and Fonso loved every inch of it.

Itzi too had grown fond of the luxury apartment on Palm Jumeirah; so much so that he had suspended his infamous Rule of 1964. The High Priest set the official return to Chac's house to one day before the Move. It was hard to believe how quickly that day had arrived.

"Did Tolo already leave?" Ildefonso asked.

"Yes," the little man nodded, "He went to help the girls move their stuff from Mama's house."

The family had purchased a stunning beachfront villa on the fronds of Palm Jumeirah for their mother; she and the girls had never been happier there. Their private beach, swimming pool and stunning view of the Arabian Gulf made it seem like a year long vacation. The amenities on Palm Jumeirah were unrivaled.

"I told him we would pick up Mama though." Itzi went on, "she's sad to go."

Fonso nodded; he too was reluctant to leave the plush accommodations they enjoyed this past year.

"What do you say we leave?" Itzi spoke glancing at his watch.

The Rolex looked huge on the little man's wrist.

"We need to go to Chac's house," Itzamna continued, "double back to the broker, and then pick up Mama."

Ildefonso nodded as they both stood; traffic was outrageous in Dubai and it was always prudent to leave plenty of time to make an appointment.

The big man hefted Itzi's three suitcases and laughed. Fonso was reminded of his brother's weighty luggage the night they left the Yucatan.

79

The streets were packed all the way across town; by the time the brothers reached the city's Karama section travel had slowed to a crawl. Fonso nearly sighed with relief when they inched down Al Kuwait Street and spotted their familiar sign.

The big man hit a button on his keychain. The painted seascape that occupied half of Buena Suerte's façade rolled to the right, revealing a slightly declined ramp to a garage area. After the car entered the hidden door rolled shut.

Stopping the Jaguar in its space Ildefonso pushed a second button on the keychain. The automobile turned on a revolving apparatus to face the ramp; Fonso appreciated Bartolomeo's inventions more and more each year.

It was Tolo who first suggested trying to store a car inside Chac's house. The family genius suggested cutting the tattoo shop's existing lobby in half and storing the automobile on the other side. First the hidden door was manually operated but shortly after Bartolomeo designed the motorized version. Fonso really loved Tolo's further revision: the turntable that allowed the car to always enter and exit the garage frontwards.

Since 1903 the Cenotes family made the yearly Move with a car; having a vehicle on hand greatly helped them ease into each new location. In the early days their auto caused quite a stir in some of the places!

The brothers exited the re-positioned Jaguar. Fonso extracted Itzi's luggage from the trunk and the back seat. The big man was thankful for another of Bartolomeo's innovations; Fonso loaded the suitcases into the elevator and the brothers rode it to the third floor.

Following the High Priest, Fonso deposited the bags just inside the bedroom door. He leaned against Itzamna's oversized bed as the little man approached the stone boxes carved with Chac's glyph.

"It's been a long time since I've seen the lord's chests," Ildefonso mused out loud.

He was still no less than amazed when Itzi lifted the lid on the smaller of the two; as always the sparkling gold and gems nearly overflowed.

"This place is really expensive to live," the High Priest commented, "we have gone years without even touching this box."

Through the centuries the Cenotes family had amassed a sizable fortune selling the items from the chest they called Chac's Treasure. Their impressive wealth was stored safely in Swiss banks. The two properties they had purchased in Dubai had put a dent in their accounts; multi-millions had been spent on the marina apartment and Mama's villa on Palm Jumeirah.

The High Priest laughed, "The girls have gone through a small fortune just shopping here."

Fonso nodded; he was guilty of some intense spending himself. Every major designer had stores in Dubai and the big man realized he had probably purchased a whole new wardrobe.

As if he read his giant brother's mind Itzi laughed again, "I've bought more than a few things myself," the High Priest admitted while rooting through the treasure.

Fonso watched his brother select at least twenty huge diamonds from the cache and place them in a felt drawstring bag. Ildefonso eyed the larger of the stone chests; seeing

Chac's two containers that first night in ancient Rome Fonso had originally been more impressed by the smaller of the two. Who wouldn't be amazed by a box of riches that magically replenished itself? As the years rolled into the modern age, he had become more spellbound by the second chest; the one the family called the lord's Other Box.

Remarkable paperwork magically appeared there for each new locale: passports, driver's licenses, birth certificates, even license plates and registrations for Fonso's car, once it was stored in the house and moved with their belongings. The documents always passed any official scrutiny. Sometimes the articles Itzi pulled from Chac's Other Box were mystifying. One thing was certain; whatever the item was, its use would be revealed over the course of the year.

The big man's gaze wandered around the room; it was probably twenty years since he had been in Itzi's room in Chac's house. Time was suddenly flying by.

Fonso's eyes rested on the glass display case along one wall; he approached the cabinet for a closer look. Seeing the High Priest's jade breast piece brought on a wave of nostalgia; Ildefonso easily pictured his tiny brother conducting the religious ceremonies on the Temple Pyramid in Uxmal. It had been more than a thousand years since he saw Itzamna holding a beating heart up to the great god but the mental image was as vivid as if it happened yesterday.

Fonso stared at the axe Chac had given his brother so many centuries ago; of all the modern miracles the ancient warrior had seen in the contemporary world, he had still never been more floored than when Itzi first brought out that axe. A voice broke the big man's reverie.

"Do you want anything from in here, Fonso?"

The High Priest was pointing toward the lord's Treasure Box.

Fonso crossed the room and rejoined his brother near the chests. Spotting a huge gold ring the big man was drawn to its design; gold tendrils lined its circumference then expertly joined in front to form an undulating sun.

Having followed his larger brother's gaze Itzi extracted the ring and handed it to Ildefonso. The family giant slipped it on his left middle finger; as was expected, it was a perfect fit. Fonso thanked his older brother.

"All thanks to our great lord Chac," Itzi answered.

Fonso repeated the sentence.

Before he replaced the lid Itzamna removed a handful of rubies. He dumped them in a clear glass vase sitting on the nightstand next to the chests. Ildefonso's jaw dropped; the vase easily held three hundred rubies, some as large as strawberries! Itzi grinned.

"I like the red ones," the High Priest said as he picked up the drawstring bag and headed toward the bedroom door.

Fonso laughed out loud as he followed; the High Priest sounded like a kid with a collection of marbles.

Traffic was heavy on Sheikh Zayed Road but the brothers made it to the broker's office near the gold and diamond souk right on time. By the time they made the transaction and confirmed payment with their Swiss bank it was nearly eight o'clock. Itzamna eyed his watch as they left the brokerage.

"Let's go back to Mama's house and take her out to dinner. What do you think," the little man looked up at his younger brother, "do we have time before we meet Tolo for work tonight?"

Now Fonso checked his own Rolex. Allowing for traffic back to Palm Jumeirah and getting to Mama's villa out on the island's fronds he calculated the time needed to eat and get back to Al Karama to open the tattoo shop by midnight.

"I think we could do it," the big man laughed out loud again, "if we can get Mama to leave in less than an hour!"

80

Early the next morning Itzi placed the lord's sacred stones on the four cardinal points inside Chac's house. One went in the lobby of the tattoo parlor, another on the opposite side of the first floor near Fonso's car. The remaining two were placed toward the rear of the building near the kitchen and in the main tattoo studio. Itzi used a gold compass to set the stones exactly North, South, East and West.

There was always a slight tension in the air on the night of the Move. The family gathered in the dining room right before sunset for a light meal. Over the centuries it had become a tradition to eat lightly and discuss the changes in store.

"Do you think we should keep these two properties, Itzi?" Tolo asked.

The High Priest shrugged. It seemed less necessary to decide the fate of the family's new real estate with 2012 only three years away. The little man turned toward Ildefonso.

"What do you think, Fonso? Do you want the apartment?"

"Let's keep it at least until after the Move," the big man suggested, "if we have to come back to sell the boat, we'll stay there."

In the modern era, on the first days in a new location the family re-claimed some of their belongings from the place before. Waykan and Ixkeem usually took a commercial flight to the old locale and brought the family's private jets to the nearest airport.

If it was geographically possible the men sailed the boat to the new city on the first of their days off. If the new place was too far away from the old, or in a landlocked location, Tolo flew to the old locale and sold the vessel.

"I hope we're somewhere near Wildwood," Ildefonso speculated, "I really liked the boat we had there."

The big man had taken a chance the year before and put the yacht in dry dock storage, hoping to eventually arrive close enough to use it again.

"Well, let's keep both houses," Itzi decided knowing how much his mother liked the beachfront villa.

Besides, the little man thought helping himself to another serving of Mama's delicious Mediterranean salad, undeniably Chac's journey was nearing its end. Since the family's fate was so unsure, it seemed useless to worry about real estate.

"Don't eat too much, Itzamna." Mama warned her oldest son as she placed a fruit salad on the table for dessert, "you know how the Move can be."

Reluctantly the High Priest agreed. Though his huge appetite was hardly satisfied his mother was right. They had all learned the hard way how unpleasant Chac's transition could be on a full stomach.

After clearing the table the family assembled in the living room.

"I hope we land someplace warm," Mama said that every year since she suffered through her first frigid winter.

"Mama, you complained of the heat all summer!" Ixkeem laughed out loud, "I was thinking you might want to go back to Russia or Finland!"

The boys smiled. Their mother hated anyplace that had a lot of snow. The rest of the family had learned to enjoy the winter weather; all of them were expert skiers and ice skaters. Recently Itzi and Fonso had become avid snowboarders; this past year they were regulars at Dubai's indoor ski slope.

THE FLAVOR OF HEARTS

"I hope for America," Tolo spoke up as he laid his laptop computer on the coffee table. The family genius opened a leather case and extracted a GPS unit. It was so easy in the modern world to discern their new location.

Fonso eyed his Rolex and took a deep breath. It was close to nine o'clock. The Move usually happened between nine and ten. The big man tried to relax; it wasn't that the Move was painful, but one could hardly consider it pleasant.

A slow vibration became apparent from the floor accompanied by a buzzing in all their ears.

"Here we go," Ixkeem closed her eyes as did their mother.

The sensation built, like a pulsation from an approaching train. In a minute the quivering escalated to earthquake like shaking. The house shook violently bringing a nauseating feeling to the pit of everyone's stomach.

The living room blurred in and out of focus; though it remained dry, it appeared that water streamed down the walls. A burning smell filled the air as the electric lights flickered off and on. The acrid odor became so heavy it became a taste in the mouth.

Fonso almost laughed. The horrid scent was faintly reminiscent of the burnouts he did to warm the tires on his drag racing car. The Move smelled like burnt rubber times twenty.

The big man braced himself for the part he considered the worst. The vibrations became almost ultrasonic; Fonso no longer heard it as sound; he felt his lungs throbbing inside his chest. Crackling sounds filled his ears, softly at first then louder. The noise intensified; his eardrums popped like firecrackers inside his skull.

With a whooshing sound the air was literally sucked from the big man's lungs; Fonso felt his body flatten. He broke out in a cold sweat as the air was violently blown back in, re-inflating his lungs like a bellows.

The flickering lights suddenly burned steadily at twice their usual brightness. The shaking stopped so abruptly the stillness nearly knocked them all from their seats. In an eerie quiet the lights returned to a normal level.

Gasps of relief were heard from the girls; even Fonso let out a deep breath. The family warrior heard his tiny brother moan beside him.

"Itzi, are you OK?" the big man asked the High Priest first every year.

When the little man nodded; Fonso looked toward their mother. She was still sitting with her eyes closed in her favorite Lazy Boy recliner.

"Mama, are you all right?"

"I am fine," she assured her children opening her eyes. She was always grateful and annoyed at their concern for her.

Waykan stood and stretched her legs, "What a rush!"

She was the only family member that relished the physical sensations of Chac's Move. Itzi grinned. He was always amazed by his sister's reaction.

"Where are we, Tolo?" the High Priest turned toward the family genius.

Bartolomeo looked up from his GPS unit and smiled broadly.

"USA...Florida! Key West!" he announced jubilantly.

The family hooted and hollered; even Mama wore a broad smile. They had lived in the Keys before; once in the 1920's and a year in the 80's.

"Let's celebrate," Waykan fetched a bottle of Dom Perignon, "a year in paradise!"

81

Richard Comstock sat in his doctor's office. Today hopefully he would get a clean bill of health and allay Afton's persisting fear that he suffered from a brain tumor. Sure it was hard to explain his new found ability with numbers, but finally they would rule out any dire physical conditions.

The doctor arrived and greeted Richard as he took a seat behind the desk. Golfing buddies, the men had been friends since college. Dr. Flynn pressed the intercom and asked his medical assistant for Mr. Comstock's test results.

"Good help...you know," he offered in way of an apology for the added wait.

Shortly a stunning young woman appeared in a white uniform. Richard gazed at her pretty face as she placed the file in front of the doctor. Her pierced eyebrow caught Richard's eye.

"I hope he gets this guy out of here quick so we can get to the hotel."

No one spoke but Richard clearly heard a female voice in his head.

The doctor thanked his assistant and she responded, "Anything else, Dr. Flynn?"

Richard sat with his mouth agape. It was the exact voice he'd heard in his mind. The oil man stared at the woman's blue eyes then back at the piercing at the front of her eyebrow.

"Say no so we can get out of here."

It was impossible; Richard clearly heard her voice though she hadn't spoken. The billionaire felt a little woozy; maybe there was something wrong with him.

The doctor assured the assistant he had everything necessary and flipped the folder open. Richard watched him perusing the test results. The billionaire's gaze started at the top of the physician's balding head and moved downward; when his eyes rested near the bridge of the doctor's nose Richard held his breath.

He could hear the doctor reading!

"Glucose normal, cholesterol good...blood pressure low...low?"

"Have you been taking your blood pressure medication as prescribed?" the physician asked as he looked up. The doctor did a double take; Richard Comstock was white as a ghost.

"Richard, are you all right? Is something wrong?"

Fearing an emergency Dr. Flynn quickly stepped around the desk and took his patient's wrist; the oil man's pulse was racing.

"I...I'm fine," Richard didn't sound fine.

Dr. Flynn immediately placed his stethoscope on the billionaire's chest; the heartbeat was elevated but normal in its rhythm.

"Richard, talk to me," concern was apparent in the physician's voice, "you're pale and sweating. Do you feel pain or pressure anywhere?"

Richard shook his head negatively and insisted he was fine. He hardly wanted to admit that he was hearing people's thoughts. The numbers thing was weird enough, but this...

"Richard, look at me directly."

The billionaire followed the order and looked into the doctor's eyes. Dr. Flynn did a quick examination of Richard's face and eye coordination.

THE FLAVOR OF HEARTS

As soon as the oil man rested his gaze between the doctor's eyebrows the physician's thoughts were again audible.

"Jesus, I hope this isn't the start of a mini-stroke."

"I'm not having a stroke," Richard replied to the thought.

Dr. Flynn stared thunderstruck., *"He's reading my mind?"*

Again Richard responded to the thought, "I guess I am."

The doctor sat on the edge of the desk; he needed to sit before he fell.

"Richard, what the hell is going on here?"

Reluctantly Richard told the truth, he explained his recent savant like ability with numbers and this newfound weirdness. Dr. Flynn stared as if an alien had suddenly burst from his patient's chest. This was the craziest thing he had ever heard, especially considering the source. Richard Comstock was one of the most sensible men Joe Flynn had ever met; the physician feared his friend was having a nervous breakdown.

Richard again responded to the unspoken sentence, "I'm not having a nervous breakdown."

Over the recent months Richard had more than a few experiences suddenly knowing a person's thoughts. It was only now in this very office that he realized they weren't random occurrences; today, thanks to the nurse's eyebrow piercing, he figured out how it worked.

He was sure if he focused his eyes between a person's eyebrows he would hear their thoughts. He aimed his gaze at the doctor.

"I could use a drink myself," the oil man laughed at the physician's mental need for a shot of scotch.

"Richard, you're an old friend," Dr. Flynn sounded stymied; "this is crazy."

"It may be," the billionaire agreed, "but it's happening."

Richard told the doctor to get a calculator. Dr. Flynn went back behind the desk and complied. He threw numbers at Richard like Afton did; the oil man got every calculation correct. Next the billionaire tried a new trick.

He told the physician to think of a word; uncannily Richard repeated every word every time. Silently Joseph Flynn extracted a bottle of scotch from the desk's bottom drawer. Cracking the seal he put a shot in a paper cup and put it in front of Richard; he took the same for himself.

He stared across the desk as he drank the welcome alcohol. Richard sipped from his cup. Though it was a great relief to tell somebody of the weird happenings, the billionaire felt guilty that he burdened his old golfing buddy. Clearly Joe Flynn was shaken up. The physician took a deep breath and looked back at the test results. There had to be a rational medical reason for all of this.

"I doubt it," the billionaire again answered the doctor's thoughts.

"Get out of my head, Richard!" Joe waggled his index finger at his friend.

Both men burst out laughing; the laughter definitely eased the escalating tension.

"I don't see anything abnormal in the full body scan. Everything looks normal, but I want you to have some brain scans. I really need some detailed pictures of your head to be sure. Afton is right you know," the doctor sounded grim, "an oddity like this…the first thought is a tumor or blood clot."

"I feel great," the billionaire objected.

"I'll feel great when I rule out all the possibilities," Dr. Flynn was adamant.

The old friends shared another shot of the doctor's Glen Livit.

"I was hoping to give Afton my clean bill of health and finally put her fears to rest," Richard said ruefully. "I'm half sorry I said anything."

"I'll tell you what," Joe Flynn offered, "I'll give you the results of your full body scan to show Affie. It says you're healthy as a horse! I'll do it on the condition that you go to the tests I set up for you." The physician took on softer tone, "after all, at this point there's no reason to upset her further."

Richard readily agreed. On his way from the office he turned to his friend, "We'll keep all this between us. Right, Joe?"

THE FLAVOR OF HEARTS

The doctor assured his old golfing buddy that the surreal events of that afternoon would forever remain their secret.

That night over dinner at La Cirque Richard gave Afton the test results. She was overjoyed. The billionaire decided not to mention his second uncanny ability; surely news like that would get her all revved up again.

82

Afton decided to stop for a coffee and a piece of cake after her manicure. She walked two blocks down Chambers Street, bought a New York Post and entered the Blue Spoon.

Over a delicious latte and an enormous cupcake the socialite perused the New York newspaper. Intrigued she read the headline on a story spanning two pages: "An Angel in Manhattan". Underneath it said, "Doctors Stymied by Miraculous Healings Citywide."

Afton stared at the first of three photos accompanying the article; it was the neighbor's granddaughter! The caption said that Deborah McKinley was mysteriously healed of Leukemia.

Quickly Afton scanned the text for the girl's name. The article said the teenager was staying with her grandmother in TriBeCa for treatment at Sloane-Kettering. Doctors there were thrilled but mystified over her case. Overnight the teenager showed no traces Leukemia before undergoing chemotherapy. A hospital in her home town of Albany confirmed the diagnoses and the incredible cure.

Afton shook her head; she had a slight twinge of guilt for thinking badly of the sick teenager. The socialite read on: three local men had been totally cured of AIDS; Afton was stunned when she saw their names. She knew all three! In fact she had recently seen them at the meeting of her favorite charity: the American Foundation for AIDS.

Next the article mentioned a manicurist from Elegante Nails on Chambers Street. The socialite gasped audibly; she had just come from that place, her regular salon. It said Tomika Curasco was battling breast cancer; radiation treatment was not successful and her doctors had recommended a mastectomy. Inexplicably the illness disappeared in one night!

Slack jawed Afton started at the beginning and slowly read the whole article. At the end the reporter wrote that he was still investigating any connection between the incidents; but as of yet no clear association was apparent.

Afton stared straight ahead. Of the ten people it mentioned she definitely knew six of them. Her stomach was churning. How could it be? Suddenly she remembered her friend Pam's wild recovery at Jazzercise; laughingly they had called that a miracle.

For a brief second she considered the possibility it had something to do with her.

"Impossible, me an angel? I don't even believe in God!" she argued with herself. Her reverie was interrupted by her cell phone.

"Affie," Richard's voice sounded strangely comforting, "guess what I got today? An invitation to a party this Friday at Jazmina's!"

Jazmina Fortesque was also a prominent New York socialite with a secretly kinky life. Her parties were legendary among a select group of New York's upper crust. It was the only place the Comstocks and those of their social stature could practice their fetishism without fear of repercussions.

"Really? That sounds great…" Afton's voice trailed off.

"Are you OK, Affie?" Richard was suddenly concerned; his wife sounded very strange.

She promised her husband she was fine and told him she was excited to attend the party. Hanging up the socialite stared into space; clearly she was still disturbed by the newspaper article.

Ready to call for her chauffeur to take her home she abruptly changed her mind. Stepping out on to Chambers Street Afton hailed a cab. Shakily she told the cabbie to take her to St. Vincent's Hospital.

After assuring the taxi driver it was not an urgent situation she settled into the back seat for the short ride down Hudson Street. Pausing before the entrance to the emergency room she berated herself.

"What the heck am I doing here? What am I going to do, wave my arms around and yell abracadabra?"

Ignoring the impulse to turn around and go home she entered the ER. Scanning the packed waiting room she saw a young man at the nurse's station. He was cradling his wrist and begging for attention.

The nurse told him a doctor would be with him as soon as possible and instructed him to return to his seat. Grimacing he complied; Afton watched him lay his injured wrist on his lap and close his eyes.

Silently she approached and took the seat next to him. Eyeing the man from the corner of her eye she waited. When nothing immediately happened she berated herself again.

"What was I expecting?" she thought feeling ridiculous, "That he would jump up and down and yell hallelujah?"

Oddly, she suddenly wondered if she had to touch the person. Though feeling even more ridiculous she decided to do what she had come here to do; test her crazy suspicion and be done with it. Turning she tapped him on the shoulder.

"Have you been here long?" she asked when he opened his eyes.

"An hour," he answered grimly motioning toward his injured wrist, "it's killing me, like they give a shit."

Immediately the young man apologized for his bad language. Afton assured him she took no offense. Relieved she told him she hoped they would treat him soon and rose to head toward the door. Later she regretted her next action; before exiting she turned and took a last look at the injured gentleman.

Her legs turned to jelly. The man was turning his injured wrist in circles with a wondrous look on his face. Afton charged through the door fearing she would throw up her cake and coffee.

Outside she leaned against the building and gulped air. Frantically the socialite took off running down the street. Almost unconsciously she made the turns and sprinted toward home; halfway down Hudson Street she stopped and leaned on a street sign.

"It can't be," she thought recovering her breath, "I never touched the Leukemia kid."

Immediately the teenager's sullen face sprang into Afton's mind; the keychain, that day in the lobby! Afton remembered tapping the youngster on the shoulder. Finally overwhelmed the socialite turned and vomited into the gutter.

83

Late Friday night the Comstocks entered their limo for the ride back to TriBeCa. For some reason neither of them had enjoyed the party as much as they usually did. As always both took full advantage of Jazmina Fortesque's well appointed dungeon; Richard hung Afton from her favorite apparatus: a suspension bar with padded handcuffs. He lifted her off the ground with her hands manacled above her head and ploughed her. More often than not the young socialite was on the verge of climax as soon as her arms supported her body weight, but this night she did not reach orgasm until her husband did.

Usually when Richard paddled her backside red and made violent love to her while she was strapped in a leather sling Afton Comstock experienced multiple wavelike orgasms; this night she climaxed, but only once. The socialite was puzzled by her strange reactions.

Silently the couple rode home from the Upper West Side. Richard had never been more tempted to use his newfound talent and probe his wife's thoughts. Up until then he had totally resisted the temptation; he was afraid to discover any hidden feelings. He knew he would suffer devastation finding his wife's professed love for him was only lip service.

He gazed at his beautiful partner from the corner of his eye; she wore such a strange expression he abandoned his reservations. Focusing between her eyebrows the billionaire curiously listened to her thoughts.

"What the heck is wrong with me? It's this angel thing...it's gotta be this angel thing. I'm some angel and now I can't find pleasure? What the fuck is happening to me?"

Richard immediately looked forward. Afton never used obscenities; he was totally surprised to hear she thought that way. I'm some angel; he greatly wondered what that meant. The billionaire was sorry he had invaded her private thoughts; it certainly left him with more questions than answers.

"Af, is everything OK?" he asked softly.

She turned to him and smiled wanly. When she assured him that everything was fine he resisted the urge to probe her mind again.

Up in their apartment both went their separate ways to change clothes. Richard sat shirtless in silk pajama bottoms on the leather couch in their bedroom; he flipped on the TV and pretended to watch it. Most nights after one of Jazmina's parties they collapsed exhausted into bed; this night the billionaire felt more than restless.

Afton joined her husband on the couch and snuggled up to him. He put his arm protectively around her. She smelled so good; Richard had never loved her more. Suddenly he feared Afton's strange mood was his fault; he had never kept a single secret from her. Maybe she sensed the second strange talent he kept hidden.

"Af," he started reluctantly, "I gotta tell you something."

She backed up and stared at him. Instantly she feared her lack of reaction that evening had caused a rift between them. "I'm sorry about tonight, Daddy Bear, I'll be better next time, I promise," she sounded half panicked; "I swear I will!"

"Oh, Baby, it's not that at all!" Richard was shocked by her words.

Slowly he told her what happened at Dr. Flynn's. She listened wide eyed when he revealed the additional tests and brain scans he had taken. Afton sighed with relief to hear that they showed no abnormalities in her husband's head.

She was further amazed when Richard did the same word trick with her that he did with the doctor. Her husband even repeated the French words she thought of, even though he had no idea of their meaning!

When Richard apologized profusely for keeping a secret from her, Afton decided it was time to come clean herself.

"Daddy, I have something to tell you."

The words sent a shudder through him; immediately he feared she found a younger man. Richard was totally surprised by her first words.

"Did you hear on the news about the Angel of Manhattan?"

Since the first newspaper article appeared earlier that week, thirty more people had come forward with stories of amazing healings. It was all over the media; everybody was talking about it.

"It's me," Afton sounded on the verge of tears, 'I don't know how, but it's me."

"What?" Richard was flabbergasted, "what makes you think such a thing, Affie?"

It was the billionaire's turn to stare wide eyed as she told of her interaction with many of the miraculously healed. He was speechless when she recounted her experience at St. Vincent's Emergency Room.

"Wow," he barely uttered the one syllable word.

Oddly he felt no need to argue the point; his recent tests had shown he was never in better health. Dr. Flynn had been mystified too. Out of the blue Richard's blood pressure and cholesterol levels were normal; the billionaire no longer needed his previous medications. Even his arthritic knees hadn't bothered him in what seemed like ages.

Richard tried to remember the last time he took pain pills for his knees; it was probably in Dubai, after the last time he and Afton had skied indoors. He told his wife of his improved health and tears streamed down the young socialite's face.

THE FLAVOR OF HEARTS

"What's wrong, Affie? You're upset I'm better?" he asked quizzically.

"No! No, Daddy, I'm thrilled you feel so good. I want you to feel good."

She buried her head in his chest and sobbed out the rest of the sentence, "What is happening to us? I'm afraid, Daddy. All these strange things...what happened to us?"

Richard shook his head and tried to think of something to comfort her. No words came to mind so he hugged her tightly as she cried on his chest.

"Affie, Affie..." finally the billionaire spoke, "don't cry. What's really that bad? Maybe we'll never be sick...and the way I am...nobody will ever get one over on us! What's the down side? I can't see a down side."

He tried his best to sound optimistic. She lifted her head and stared into his eyes; desperately she wanted to believe his positive words. Her gaze lowered to the tattooed bear on his chest muscle; she traced the gold aura around the animal with her index finger.

"I love you, Daddy Bear." she said, her voice was still shaky from crying.

"I love you, My Little Pussy," Richard had never meant it more.

She laid her head back on his chest; and they sat in silence. Oddly they were both thinking along the same lines; exactly when did all this weirdness begin?

Suddenly Afton bolted upright and stared at her husband, "Daddy, maybe it's the tattoos!" she pointed at the bear standing on his chest, "all this started as soon as we got home from Dubai. The thing with Pam, it was the first day we got back!" Her expression was pop eyed; like she had seen the Loch Ness Monster or the Yeti.

At first Richard wanted to pooh-pooh her theory; but in his head he knew the timing was right. He had traced his weird powers to their first day back too.

The billionaire shook his head. It sounded so crazy; could this be the luck that the butler swore by? A tattoo caused these things? Richard felt like a lunatic even entertaining the idea.

"I can't say the timing isn't right," he shrugged, "that place was pretty weird and that little guy…he did have some strange talents."

Afton pictured Itzamna; it was totally amazing how he drew the pictures in advance. Then there was the golden look of the tattoo; both the Comstocks agreed that no one who saw the body art had ever seen such a thing.

They finally made a pact to keep these thoughts to themselves. Afton told Richard she had already been avoiding touching anyone. Richard too admitted he was very selective where he used his newfound talents. He laughed when Afton gave him the first order in their married life:

"And you better stay out of my head too, Daddy Bear! You will totally ruin Christmas!"

84

It was a mild day for early spring so Afton decided to drink her afternoon tea on the terrace. A few things weighed on her mind and the socialite hoped the fresh air would improve her pensive mood.

She had been approached by a reporter the day before at a benefit luncheon for the American Foundation for AIDS. The man said he was investigating the still unexplained New York healings. Though he didn't seem to suspect Afton he asked about any new members of the organization. Apparently he felt a cluster of the miraculous recoveries were centered on the local charity.

Afton did her best to deflect him, explaining that the group's membership roster was confidential. As an officer of the Foundation she was not allowed to reveal the names. She feigned surprise at the ten names he listed as mysteriously healed.

The socialite shook her head. Though she had vowed to be conscious of physical contact with people it was harder than she thought. It was instinctual to shake hands.

Then there were the ones that really tugged at her heart strings. When she visited the children's hospital with the national president of AMFAR Afton could not resist returning on the sly and helping the sickest kids.

She didn't regret that, even now, but the reporter had definitely scared her. She could just imagine the commotion if she was labeled the Angel of Manhattan. With a shudder she thought of the throngs of paparazzi that used to hang outside their old apartment building aggressively stalking the celebrity residents.

"I'll have to be more careful," she promised herself, "no matter how sorry I feel for any one!"

Sipping the raspberry tea Afton mulled over the second thing eating at her. Her weekly phone call with her mother in Florida had been disturbing; her father was diagnosed with prostate cancer. The doctors thought he should start treatment with a round of radiation. Her mother's last sentence played over and over now in Afton's head.

"Maybe we should take a trip to Manhattan;" her mother had said half jokingly, "maybe the Angel would heal your Dad!"

Afton fought tears; she had been very close to her parents most of her life. The announcement of her engagement had caused a slight rift in her family. Though her parents liked Richard as a person they made it apparent that they wished their only daughter had chosen a spouse closer to her own age. After their wedding her parents treated Richard more than cordially but Afton still sensed their disapproval.

It was also troublesome to hear that the news of the Angel of Manhattan had made its way to Florida. Her mom said she first heard about the miracles on television; but it had been in the West Palm Beach newspapers as well.

The socialite had cringed when her mother asked if Afton knew any of the people healed. A devout Lutheran her mother sounded absolutely thrilled over the New York phenomenon.

Again Afton recalled her Mom's desperate half-joking words, "Maybe the Angel would heal your Dad!"

Afton picked up her cell phone and hit the speed dial.

"Mom," she could tell her mother was pleasantly surprised by a second phone call, "I'm gonna take trip down to see you this weekend. Is it OK? I'd like to visit with you and Dad before he starts the treatment." Afton could tell that her mother was thrilled.

"Mom," the socialite almost hated to ask, "Is it all right if Richard comes too?"

"Oh, Affie, of course it's OK, he's your husband."

"Are you sure? Afton was concerned, "it won't stress Dad out more?"

"I'm sorry we ever acted strange about Richard, Affie," her mother's voice softened, "he's a good man and your dad and I both know how happy you've been. Forgive us for the things we said before you married. You deserve to live your life the way you want."

Afton's jaw dropped. Her mother sounded so sincere; the gulf between them was dissipating.

"I love you, Mom," Afton's voice cracked.

"I love you too, Affie."

The ladies cried together long distance; great joy was apparent on both ends. Afton promised to call with their time of arrival. Yes, Mom, Afton thought as she hung up the phone, for sure the Angel of Manhattan will heal Daddy.

85

Early Saturday morning the Comstocks took their limousine to Teterboro Airport. Richard had been thrilled to hear of Afton's latest conversation with her mother. It had always bothered the oil man to be the cause of discord in his wife's close family and he had always hoped Afton's parents would eventually fully accept him.

Traffic was fairly light from Manhattan to New Jersey. The Comstocks arrived at the hangar and boarded their private jet in a little over 30 minutes.

When the pilot greeted the couple he reported that the weather looked clear all the way down the coast and they could expect to land at Palm Beach International in a little over two hours.

Richard stowed the bag of New York delicacies Afton purchased as gifts for her parents then strapped himself into the leather seat beside her for take off.

She looked so happy his heart soared. Though he felt some trepidation imagining the consequences of the events about to happen he refused to put any kind of a damper on his wife's upbeat mood

"So what if they suspect Afton is the Angel." Richard mused.

THE FLAVOR OF HEARTS

The oil man was sure her parents wouldn't spill the beans and bring the press down on their own daughter. Anyway, Afton's dad was a great guy and he deserved a break. The billionaire knew he would do exactly the same thing if he had the power to remove the man's cancer.

"Besides," Richard reasoned, "Affie will be back in New York by the time the hospital examines her dad and finds him healthy." The billionaire pushed the worry from his mind; silently he swore to protect his wife with all his resources if she was discovered.

A little while into the flight the co-pilot appeared, "Mr. Comstock," he requested, "could you and Mrs. Comstock put your seatbelts on? We see a storm up ahead. It's wasn't on the weather charts. We're gonna try to fly above it."

Afton looked up from her magazine. She looked worried but complied with the request.

"Is everything okay?" Richard asked.

The co-pilot assured his boss the pilot had everything under control but they might hit turbulence closer to the storm.

"I knew I should've taken a valium," Afton grimaced.

"Don't worry, Baby." Richard tried to sound positive as he adjusted his seatbelt.

The couple felt the aircraft climbing. The oil man put his arm protectively around his wife. They could hear the approaching thunder; it shook the jet's body.

"What do you make of this?" the co-pilot sounded more worried in the cockpit than he had in front of the Comstocks.

"I've never seen such a thing," the pilot sounded shaky.

The storm ahead was huge; it stretched as far as the eye could see in all directions. The clouds were blacker and thicker than either aviator had ever seen. Lightning and thunder shook the craft.

"Radio down to Atlanta tower," the pilot told his partner, "ask them how big this thing is."

The radio cracked and the signal seemed weak. The co-pilot stared at the pilot in amazement as they both heard the tower's reply, "We have no indication of a storm in your area, Challenger N6743N. Confirm your altitude and your heading."

"No storm? Listen to this!" the co-pilot practically shrieked as thunder rocked the fuselage. He repeated the jet's altitude and heading.

"We see no storm in your area. All clear, Challenger N6743N." the tower replied, "your signal is weak. We suggest a change to this frequency..."

Thunder shook the jet so violently the co-pilot could barely make the requested change to the radio's controls. Lightning bolts five inches thick surrounded the jet. An eerie blue light appeared with each strike.

"Jesus, help us," the pilot screamed over the din, "I've never seen such a thing!" Unworldly vibration shook the fuselage; the jet's avionics became erratic.

"Arm the emergency locator," the pilot fought to maintain altitude.

Unbelievably the lightning grew bigger. The eerie blue light turned green, then bright orange; it enveloped the fuselage and filled the cockpit with odd luminosity. Thunder cracked so loud it pounded their ear drums; the pressure became unbearable.

"Radio a distress signal." the pilot shouted through clenched teeth.

Afton screamed at the top of her lungs. Richard fought the urge to do the same. The thunder roared so loud it buried her voice. It was like a nightmare; she shrieked with all her might but couldn't hear a sound coming from her mouth.

Crackling lightning shook the aircraft; unnatural orange light filled the cabin. Richard put his arms tightly around Afton's head and pulled her face into his chest. He felt her sobbing as the plane nosedived.

THE FLAVOR OF HEARTS

The orange light turned brighter as the jet descended; a fireball enveloped the craft as it hit the ground. No one survived.

86

Itzi stared out over the harbor. He eyed the sun moving slowly across the sky. Shaking his head he pondered the speed at which time was suddenly passing.

As a Mayan High Priest he was considered a Master of Time; using the sky Itzi tracked and measured the days and nights to the nanosecond. His calculations were more accurate than modern atomic clocks. Often he had heard people say that time flew, but for him it never had. That is until recently.

The previous year in the Florida Keys felt as if it passed in a week. Looking back it seemed like a blur; an enjoyable blur, but a blur nonetheless.

Itzi focused on the Eastern Harbor gleaming before him. How surprised he had been last December when the family landed again in Alexandria. It was the first time in Chac's journey they had lived in a city twice. Often they crisscrossed through an area; they would arrive in a familiar country but always in a new town and most times at least decades apart. Now another year had passed in a blur.

Itzi opened the first of the leather volumes he had brought with him that day. Since the family's first Move the High Priest drew landscapes of the places they lived; at first to hone his drawing skills for Chac's tattoos then later for fun and relaxation.

On his first time in Alexandria he had created many drawings of the famous harbor. That afternoon he had walked along the concrete promenade surrounding the modern harbor to find the exact spot he had sat centuries before.

Much had changed in Alexandria since 953CE; the most obvious difference was the absence of the lighthouse on the Eastern Harbor's upper left side. Many modern scholars debated the look of the ancient Pharos; some had even questioned its existence. In the fall of 1994 a French scuba diving expedition had found huge stone blocks on the floor of the harbor, proving to the world that the ancient wonder did exist.

Itzi grinned at his depiction in the oldest sketchbook; the lighthouse had been a stunning sight both in the day and at night. Rising nearly 400 feet its marble façade gleamed in the sun.

Much speculation was made in the modern world about the beacon. Itzi easily remembered the amazing light. The keepers started the huge bonfire with grease covered timbers and stoked the flames with oil soaked animal dung. They amplified the blaze with buffed brass mirrors and a bank of huge polished quartz crystals.

The light was definitely visible 30 miles out to sea. In 953 the High Priest spent many nights out in the Mediterranean charting the stars; he and Fonso, along with many ancient mariners, had greatly appreciated the beacon when navigating into Alexandria's harbor.

Rumors abounded then and now regarding the Pharos; some ancient writers claimed the light could be used as a weapon to concentrate the sun and set approaching enemy ships on fire. As with many tales, the wild speculation was based in some truth.

The ancient light keepers could aim the beacon at will by tilting the huge mirrors, during times of war they used the light and the magnifying crystals to scan the horizon; enemy ships could be spotted miles out to sea approaching Alexandria. Hence, most unfriendly vessels were destroyed by the formidable Egyptian navy long before they reached the harbor.

Itzamna opened the second of the leather volumes. Drawings he had made over this last year covered the pages. The Fort of Qait Bey had been built in 1480 on the site of the ancient lighthouse using some of its ancient foundation. Itzi had created some beautiful drawings of the fort, a modern tourist attraction.

The High Priest compared his two versions of Alexandria's Harbor; he was a much better artist now than he was in 953. Itzi grinned; his drawing skills had improved with over 1000 years practice!

Ildefonso walked along the Corniche, the modern name of the concrete promenade encircling Alexandria's modern harbor. He spotted his tiny brother up ahead sitting on the concrete wall with his leather sketchbooks. It was a sight the big man had seen in many places over the years; the volumes always looked huge on Itzi's tiny lap.

Fonso slid his feet over the wall and sat next to the High Priest. "Wow," he commented when he saw the book open to Itzi's drawing of the famous lighthouse. "I was just thinking of that! It looks so different here without it!"

"A lot has changed," Itzi agreed.

The four lane highway packed with cars behind them was another definite difference. "It's odd to be in a city twice after all this time," Fonso commented.

Itzamna nodded; many things puzzled the High Priest as 2012 rapidly approached. The sun itself seemed unusually quiet, since 2008 solar activity had been very minimal. Not one to worry, Itzi hoped the sun was storing power for the upcoming union with first mother on the winter solstice a year from tomorrow.

Furrowing his brow he tried not to think of the fate of his loyal family. In the last few years Itzi dreaded the annual Move; they were flying toward the uncertain end of Chac's journey. Ildefonso sensed his tiny brother's uneasiness.

THE FLAVOR OF HEARTS

"Let's go to the Havana," the big man suggested

The Havana was Itzi's favorite Alexandrian bar. The High Priest readily agreed. He could use a few beers and he hoped the delicious roast pigeon was on the menu.

87

The following night the family gathered in Chac's house. Itzi checked his Rolex before he placed Chac's sacred stones: 8 pm, December 22, 2011. After the customary light dinner the High Priest joined his brothers and sisters in the family living room.

At first it was an almost somber gathering; all of them knew the significance of the upcoming year. Itzi looked uncommonly grave. He worried the mighty Chac would take his family's hearts this year, maybe this very night. Itzamna suddenly feared life alone.

Mama appeared from the kitchen with a bottle of aged cognac and her finest Venetian glass snifters. She filled one for each of her children as well as one for herself.

"We will not serve our lord Chac with such long faces. For all he has given us, we will give thanks and celebrate."

The spirit woman looked directly at her oldest son when she finished, "We will not act as children who have decided that what they have been given is not enough."

The words stung Itzi; he smiled wanly. Leave it to his mother to easily discern his true thoughts.

They drank in silence at first; waiting for the darkness to descend and the house to shake. Mama's French porcelain

THE FLAVOR OF HEARTS

clock ticked away the seconds; it sounded unusually loud from the mantel.

Waykan turned to Fonso, "I'll bet you a thousand dollars we land in Europe." She opened her purse and laid ten crisp 100 dollar bills on the coffee table.

"Europe's too big." Ildefonso was always sensible in his betting. Reaching into his right jeans pocket he extracted a wad of bills easily three inches thick.

For the last century on the day of the Move each family member filled their pockets or purses with U.S. currency. Ready cash greatly helped a quick adjustment to most new surroundings. In the modern world American money was easily converted just about anywhere.

"Pick a country," the big man said as he peeled off ten hundreds and placed them next to his sister's, "closest one wins the money."

Tolo perked up, "I'll take a piece of that. Canada." he smiled as he threw his money down; of all the family he probably was the biggest gambler.

"I'm in too," Itzi grinned, "I take Brazil."

One by one they called out a country and anted up. By the time the house began to tremble the coffee table was littered with 100 dollar bills. Half of them were on the floor by the time the building was finally still. The acrid smell was still heavy in the air when the roaring died down.

All eyes turned to Tolo as he consulted his GPS unit, "It's California! Yountville!"

Fonso had never been so happy to lose a bet. Yountville was the closest town to their ranch and vineyard in the Napa valley. They could live in their beautiful farmhouse and commute less than 20 minutes each night to the tattoo parlor for work.

Itzi grinned. Everyone had made the Move safe and sound and Napa Valley was definitely one of the family's favorite places.

88

Fonso halted his stallion just over the crest of the hill. He eyed the vineyard below and filled his lungs with the clean air. Ildefonso had loved the Napa Valley from the family's first visit there 123 years prior.

Back in 1888 the Cenotes family had landed in San Francisco. Even then the Napa Valley was a popular tourist destination. San Franciscans eager to escape the city's damp foggy weather were drawn to the valley's Mediterranean climate and the abundance of mineral hot springs in the area.

In Chac's service, as the god had commanded, the family opened the tattoo parlor for fifteen straight days and then took five days off. In the summer of 1888 the Cenotes family boarded the train to Napa on one of these five day vacations; they were immediately enchanted with the rural community. Ildefonso suggested buying a two hundred acre farm offered for sale by a descendent of one of the area's original pioneers, George Calvert Yount.

Mama and the girls spent most of the rest of 1888 in the Napa Valley and the men joined them for all of their remaining days off. Before the Move that year Ildefonso hired a local man, Juan Ortiz, and his family to oversee the property and care for the fledgling vineyard. Whenever possible the Cenotes family returned; so long removed from the Yucatan they began to consider the Napa Valley their home.

Fonso saw a cloud of dust cutting across one of the side roads near the vineyard. He still wanted to laugh every time he saw Itzi drive the Yamaha Rhino. His tiny brother looked almost comical in the little all terrain vehicle. The whole family was surprised to see how much Itzi seemed to enjoy driving it.

Though Itzi knew how to drive a car the High Priest had never shown much interest in it; he seemed content to let his brothers and sisters take him anyplace he wanted to go. Maybe the little Rhino is more his size, Fonso thought watching Itzi cut a path toward their house.

The big man checked his watch; it was close to one in the afternoon. Surely the High Priest was headed back to the house for lunch. Ildefonso gently spurred his horse and did the same.

It was at least twenty minutes before he unsaddled and brushed his beloved stallion. By the time he left the horse safely in the paddock and jogged to the family's home the big man was surprised to find Itzi sitting on the porch.

Mama was like clockwork; on their days off she had lunch on the table promptly at one and Itzamna was never one to be late for a meal. The big man eyed his watch as he joined his tiny brother; it was 1:20.

"What's going on?" Fonso was more than curious, there was no way Itzi ate his fill in twenty minutes!

"Mama's asleep." the High Priest sounded puzzled.

"Asleep?" Fonso was shocked.

"Yeah," the little man looked up at his younger brother, "she's in her recliner sound asleep."

It was easy to hear the surprise in his voice; frankly Fonso was surprised himself. In all their years he could not recall their mother sleeping during the day.

"What do you make of that?" Ildefonso asked.

The High Priest shrugged, it was more than unusual. He retrieved a box of Ring Dings from the floor next to his chair and offered it to Fonso. The big man waved off the chocolate snack cakes.

"Mama didn't make lunch! She's in her LazyBoy chair asleep!" Bartolomeo appeared from the house sounding perplexed. Both men shrugged as their middle brother slid into a chair beside them.

"What's going on? That's not like Mama at all!" Tolo also refused when Itzi offered the box of Ring Dings.

"I guess she's tired." the High Priest's statement of the obvious made it seem all the more unusual.

The Cenotes men sat in silence; each mulling over the odd turn of events. Itzi's stomach growled so loudly it broke their reverie; it sounded like the little man had swallowed a lion. All three men burst out laughing.

"I'll go make you a sandwich, Itzi." Fonso offered.

"I can do it." the High Priest countered.

"I got it," Fonso insisted standing.

Quietly the big man entered the house; eying their mother still sound asleep in her favorite chair he tiptoed toward the kitchen. Easily he found half a roast beef left from last night's dinner, some Swiss cheese and a loaf of French bread.

Fonso cut the long loaf and fashioned three sandwiches, loading extra meat and cheese on his tiny brother's. Though he was the smallest Itzi definitely had the biggest appetite of all of them!

Ildefonso wrapped the sandwiches and three napkins in a dish towel and tucked it under one arm. He grabbed three Heinekins from the fridge and quietly rejoined his brothers.

"She's still asleep," he informed them before they asked.

He doled out the food and beer and the brothers ate in silence. As they polished off the impromptu meal all three of their heads turned in unison as they heard the screen door opening and their mother appeared on the porch.

"I fell asleep!" she sounded as surprised as her sons had been.

At first the brothers stared wordlessly then Fonso spoke, "It's good to take a little nap." It was obvious he tried to sound like it was no big deal.

She gave him a sour look. For the first time she noticed the beer bottles and the Ring Ding box at Itzi's feet.

"I didn't make lunch! You ate cake and beer for lunch?" she sounded appalled.

"Fonso made us some sandwiches, roast beef sandwiches," Tolo spoke up.

She shot him a semi-sour look but seemed slightly appeased. Sensing she was annoyed at herself Itzi spoke, "Mama, you don't have to make us lunch every day when we're off. I think you work too hard for us."

"Hmmph," she snorted, "don't talk about me like I'm the family mule!"

"Mama," the High Priest said gently, "I meant nothing of the sort."

"Well, be on time for dinner," she stormed through the screen door before she barely finished the sentence. The brothers eyed each other quizzically as they listened to her banging things around in the kitchen.

"She looks tired," Fonso whispered. Itzi nodded in agreement.

"I was going to offer to take us all out for dinner tonight," the little man smiled as he added, "but I was afraid she would find something to throw at me!"

89

"It's cold," Waykan zippered her jacket as she and Fonso left the Calistoga Jiu-Jitsu Institute.

The big man eyed his sister with amusement. It was at least fifty degrees; it could be colder in the Napa Valley this time of year. Sensing he was about to tease her Waykan spoke again, "I know," she laughed, "I sound just like Mama."

"At least it's dry today." Fonso commented; February was a notoriously rainy month there. They climbed in the Jaguar parked near Grant Avenue and Fonso drove toward the St. Helena Highway. It was about a half hour ride back to their house near Yountville.

"You looked good today, Waykan." Fonso complimented his sister.

Through the years they had both studied a multitude of martial arts. Highly accomplished in Japanese and Brazilian Jiu-Jitsu they took private instruction at the studio in nearby Calistoga.

"Thanks," Waykan appreciated the praise from her warrior brother; he was easily the most formidable fighter she had ever seen in all her years.

"You are better than anyone at that dojo, Fonso," she added.

"Gene is good," Fonso laughed, "he'd be better than me if he had all the years I have in it!"

Waykan nodded. Sometimes it was easy to forget that she and Ildefonso had over a thousand years practice in the martial arts and they had studied with some legendary masters.

"Fonso," Waykan decided to take this private time between them to get something off her chest, "does Itzi look any different to you?"

"Itzi?" Ildefonso was taken aback, "Like how?"

Some discussion had taken place among the Cenotes men regarding their mother; but Fonso had never noticed anything overtly different about their oldest brother.

"He looks tired and he seems quiet," Waykan's voice was tinged with concern.

"I know he is worried about Mama," Ildefonso admitted, "I think he is worrying about all of us."

"Itzi is worrying?" she sounded shocked, "he's always been so against that. You know, trust our god…"

Suddenly Fonso's last words sunk in.

"All of us?" her voice rose in pitch, "why is he worrying about us?"

"He's wondering what's going to happen," Fonso stole a sideward glance at his sister, "at the end of the Great Cycle this December."

A Mayan Great Cycle is 26,000 turns of the sacred Ha'ab; a section of their three part calendar based on the movement of the sun. In the modern world a Great Cycle is roughly equivalent to 26,000 years.

All of them had gone to school as children in Uxmal. They were taught by the priests that at the end of each Great Cycle the world was torn down and reborn. Mayan history recorded three such previous events; the upcoming winter solstice marked the end of the fourth Great Cycle. Back then none of them had ever expected to live to see this upcoming point in time. It was apparent that Waykan remembered the teachings of the priests.

Again her voice rose slightly in pitch, "What does Itzi think will happen?"

It was so unlike Waykan to seem afraid; she was easily the bravest woman Fonso had ever come across. The big man decided to spare his sister the High Priest's theory on the great god taking all their hearts.

"He doesn't know our fate," Ildefonso knew that was basically the truth.

Entering Yountville the big man decided to make a stop and hopefully end this line of conversation.

"I'm gonna get some cake," he pulled the car into the parking lot of the Bouchon Bakery, "you want anything?"

Waykan declined the offer and decided to wait in the car. She mulled over her giant brother's words. She and Ixkeem had noticed that their mother had been sleeping later and going to bed a little earlier. It was a surprise to hear that her brothers had noticed changes in their mother's behavior. It was also a surprise to hear that Itzamna was in the dark about something; all her life she was sure her venerated oldest brother knew everything about everything.

Fonso selected three loaves of French bread and asked for a dozen of the bakery's signature cakes, Chocolate Bouchons. Itzi loved the brownie-like treats; the High Priest had been known to eat five or six of the moist chocolate cylinders in one sitting!

"Make that two dozen Bouchons," the big man decided.

Fonso paid the bill and headed for the exit; he held the door for an elderly lady approaching the bakery. When she looked up to thank him, a flash of recognition lit up her face. "Ildefonso? Ildefonso Cenotes?" Suddenly confusion clouded her visage, "You...you look exactly the same…"

Fonso immediately recognized her voice. Looking past the years that changed her appearance he easily remembered her. He had met Mary Jane in 1964; when the Cenotes family was officially living up the coast in Scotia, California. He had felt quite a spark for Mary Jane Atkinson, she was half the reason

THE FLAVOR OF HEARTS

he had selfishly ignored his duties at the tattoo parlor that year. The lady mistook his silence for misunderstanding.

"I'm sorry," she stammered, "You look so much like someone I knew long ago. Of course it couldn't be...by chance, would your last name be Cenotes?"

Fonso wanted to turn and run; but he felt he owed the lady more.

"Yes, yes it is. My name is Ildefonso Cenotes," quickly thinking he added, "the second. Perhaps you knew my father?"

Suddenly the strange situation made sense to her, "I was beginning to think I was having another of my 'senior moments'," she beamed. "I thought my mind was really playing tricks on me!"

Fonso nodded sympathetically; he was glad to see she seemed less disturbed.

"How is your father?" she sounded very curious.

A little too curious for Ildefonso's comfort so he informed her that his father had passed on. Before she could ask any more questions the big man made a move to take his leave. Re-opening the bakery door for her he expressed his pleasure to meet a friend of his father's and explained he was late for an appointment.

She smiled and conveyed the same pleasure in their meeting. The big man felt her eyes on him as he practically ran toward the Jaguar.

"A little old for you, isn't she, Fonso?" Waykan teased.

"She wasn't the first time I met her," he grimaced, "I knew her in the sixties."

"Did she recognize you?" his sister's curiosity was piqued.

"She remembered my name!" Fonso declared. "I almost broke out in a sweat."

The big man gunned the accelerator and practically sped down Washington Street.

"What did you tell her?" Waykan had never seen her warrior brother so close to being rattled.

"I told her she knew my father."

Waykan burst out laughing and in a few seconds Fonso did the same.

"It's barely funny. It wasn't when I recognized her!" the big man was slowly recovering his composure.

"It's odd," Waykan mused, "I would think that kind of thing would've happened more often, don't you think?"

"Mmmm, I guess it is weird." Fonso speculated. "A few times I've seen people giving me a second look, you know, like they might know me…but I've never run into anyone like tonight, where I knew them right away and I felt the need to spout out some bullshit story."

"I've had lot of people ask me and Ixkeem how we keep our youthful look," Waykan offered.

"What do you say?" Ildefonso asked curiously.

"We tell them its magic."

90

"I wish there was someplace to go after work," Fonso lamented as the Cenotes brothers approached the Jaguar parked in its hidden garage inside Buena Suerte.

Itzamna nodded. Living in the bigger cities when the lord's work was finished he and Fonso often prowled after hours clubs till past dawn. The absence of ultra-late night action was the only drawback to the Napa Valley.

The area had many wonderful restaurants and bars but most closed around midnight; none stayed open past 2am. Over the years the brothers had devised a highly efficient system for marking Chac's twenty people; each customer was barely in the shop fifteen minutes; still most nights Buena Suerte closed around four in the morning.

"We could take the helicopter to San Francisco," Fonso suggested as they drove toward their house.

"No," Itzi looked at his watch, "by the time we get there it'll be too late. We'll go when we're off."

Fonso and Itzi had spent their last two periods off in San Francisco. It was funny; most times they headed for Napa anytime they could during their free days. In their first months living full time near Yountville they never left the Valley but toward the summer they began craving wilder nightlife.

Fonso steered the Jaguar slowly up the driveway to their house.

"Come upstairs," Itzamna suggested to his giant brother and they exited the car, "I have some nice wine Juan gave me. You want some Tolo?" Their middle brother declined. As usual he preferred to hole up in his room with his books and experiments.

"I'll be right up," Ildefonso promised quietly heading toward the kitchen, "I'll get us something to eat."

The big man took the stairs to Itzi's quarters on the third floor. Just as they had built into Chac's house, when they designed the family's new farmhouse they put a whole floor up top for Itzamna. He had a nice bedroom, bath and sitting room with a huge terrace for his observations of the sky.

Fonso joined the High Priest in the sitting area on the rooftop patio. Itzi grinned when he saw the huge bowl of fried chicken Ildefonso brought from the kitchen.

"I didn't heat it," the big man said as his tiny brother reached for a drumstick.

"I like it cold," Itzi barely got the sentence out before he tore into the food.

"Good wine," Fonso commented as he sipped from the glass his tiny brother had poured.

"Juan said it was our grapes."

Ildefonso pictured the younger Juan; the man was covered in tattoos.

"Do you ever worry that since we're in Yountville somebody we know might show up at work," he asked, "you know, to get tattooed?"

Itzi nodded.

"It's crossed my mind," the little man looked almost sad, "I would have to mark them. Between you and me, I'm glad it's never happened."

"That kid, he's the original Juan's great great grandson, right?" Fonso was referring to the first caretaker of the family's property.

Generations of the Ortiz family had watched over the Cenote's farm and vineyard since the late 1800's, when Fonso hired the man he now called the original Juan.

"I think you better add another great to that," Itzi grinned as he finished the calculations in his head, "the original Juan is his great great great grandfather!"

"Plus," Itzi added practically laughing out loud, "You can hardly call that Juan a kid…I think he's close to thirty years old."

"Wow," Fonso shook his head, he felt downright ancient.

"Itzi, do you ever wonder why they never seemed curious about us?" Ildefonso wore an odd expression, "we've been coming here for generations. Even the original Juan and his wife, they never seemed to notice that we never aged…they never said anything."

"They thought we were angels," Itzamna spoke so matter-of-factly; Fonso nearly fell out of his chair.

"Angels?" to say the big man was astonished was an understatement, "are you kidding me? They told you this?"

"Maria, the original Juan's wife…she told me."

"When?" the big man barely got the word out.

"When we returned after Juan's death…sometime in the 1930's," again Itzi calculated the time in his head, "I think it was 1934. Yeah, we had the tattoo shop in San Diego, remember?" Fonso nodded.

"I stopped in to visit her and give my condolences." Itzi continued, "She said that they had always thanked God for sending us to save them. It turns out they were in pretty dire straits that winter. Prospects were so bleak Juan was about to leave the valley."

Ildefonso was shocked. Juan Ortiz had been born in the area; his family went back many generations there on both sides, as did his wife's. No man loved the Napa Valley like the original Juan. The big man found it unbelievable that his old friend had ever considered leaving.

"She told me," Itzi went on, "that Juan had begged his god for a miracle to allow them to stay here. Ten minutes later you met him outside the general store and offered him the job as our caretaker. She said at first they joked that we were angels but later their god proved it. I'm assuming," the High Priest finished, "the proof was our strange longevity."

"I can't believe they thought that." Fonso was truly astounded.

Itzamna shrugged. "It's not too far from the truth," the little man reasoned, "in their beliefs an angel is a servant of their god. We are servants of the great god Chac...it seems many religions have different names for the same basic things."

"Itzi," Ildefonso almost laughed, "you don't believe we're angels?"

"That is just a word, Fonso," the High Priest stated, "We are what we are."

Itzamna looked up; dawn was approaching. Ildefonso stood to leave; he could tell his venerated brother was ready to commune with the sky.

"I'll see you later, Itzi." the big man decided to welcome the day his favorite way, "I think I'll go and ride my horse."

The little man was already at the telescope by the time Fonso reached the stairway that led down to the second floor. Lately the High Priest had been more interested in studying the sun than the stars. As all ancient Maya, Itzamna believed the offering of the heart and the sacred blood fueled K'inich, the life giving sun. Lately the flaming orb had been very quiet; the High Priest had witnessed very few flares even fewer sunspots over the last three years.

Itzi adjusted the telescope's filters then watched as K'inich rose to its full glory. He was glad to see two small but significant sun spots; he hoped it was a sign that the sun was burning stronger.

The High Priest recorded the solar activity in his pik hu'un along with the date. With the aid of his powerful telescopes he had put many modern calculations in the ancient Mayan book. Itzi reread his account of the transit of Venus that occurred two months earlier in June.

It had been highly exciting to clearly watch the planet pass in front of the sun. The Maya revered Venus as the companion of the sun, both as the morning star, Ah-Chicum-Ek' and as the evening star, Lamat. In some ways they considered Venus, Chak Ek' more important than the sun itself. Wars were planned by the position of the planet in the sky as well as other vital events.

Itzamna fondly remembered some of the priests in ancient Uxmal. Ah, the little man thought, how much they would have enjoyed the modern telescope. Itzi eyed his watch; it was nearly 9:30. He closed his ancient volume and headed down the stairs to have coffee with his mother.

91

Ildefonso took a nice long ride, nearly encircling the family's property. He stopped the horse near a stand of trees overlooking the main vineyard. The vines were heavy with fruit; there was sweetness in the air from the maturing grapes. It was a beautiful sight that the big man never tired of; often in other remote locations he pictured the Napa Valley in August. His cell phone broke the morning silence.

"Fonso," Tolo sounded breathless, "are you still out on your horse?"

Before the big man could answer his middle brother went on, "Come home, we need you at the house."

"Is something wrong?" Ildefonso had never heard his brother sound this way.

"Come right away, Fonso," Tolo choked on the last words and hung up the phone.

The family warrior immediately spurred his horse and galloped toward the farmhouse. All kinds of scenarios flashed in his head. The last time Bartolomeo sounded any where near that panicked it was 1974; Waykan had crashed the family helicopter and she and Ixkeem were in a hospital.

Fonso thanked the great god he was nearer to the house that he had been earlier that morning. He leapt from the

THE FLAVOR OF HEARTS

saddle, quickly tied the reins to the porch railing and charged through the screen door.

He followed the sound of what seemed like sobbing and found his family in the kitchen. The sight before him made his heart beat faster; the girls were seated at the table openly weeping; Tolo was pale as driven snow.

"What's going on?" Ildefonso's warrior training belied his own panic.

"Fonso," Itzamna spoke from near the kitchen's other doorway, "Mama has died."

At the words said aloud the girls wept more loudly. Tears streamed down Bartolomeo's face; and Itzi's as well. Ildefonso stood rooted in the same spot; he felt paralyzed. The words sunk in and he brushed the tears back that sprang to his own eyes.

"Mama?" the big man lowered his head and let the water roll down his cheeks.

The big man felt Itzi's hand on his shoulder; leaning down Fonso hugged his tiny brother.

"I'm not sure what we're supposed to do," the High Priest said softly when Ildefonso released his grip.

Fonso took out his cell phone and dialed Juan Ortiz, the current caretaker. In five minutes the young man appeared. He immediately offered his condolences and told the Cenotes brothers he had called for the sheriff.

Shortly the law officer arrived followed by an ambulance. The family watched from the porch as the EMTs gently loaded their mother's body into the emergency vehicle. The sheriff too offered his condolences and then gave Itzi the card of a local funeral home. He told the bereaved little man to call the mortician to make arrangements for Mrs. Cenotes.

Before leaving Juan Ortiz offered his family's support and assistance. Once again Ildefonso expressed gratitude and watched the departure of the sixth Juan Ortiz that he had considered a friend. The big man rejoined his family now sitting on the porch.

They sat in stunned silence for almost an hour until Waykan finally spoke, "How could this happen, Itzi? How could the great Chac let Mama die?"

"Our god did not promise us eternal life," Itzi answered softly. "He promised we would age one tun for every baktun,"

Waykan argued, "Mama was not old, not physically, she should've had many years left!"

"We can't predict the length of someone's life," the little man replied, "not by their age or their health or anything else."

Again the family sat in silence; now each of them seemed to contemplate their own mortality and that of their siblings.

Remembering the teachings of the priests from her childhood, Ixkeem suddenly began worrying over their mother's fate. The Maya believed the soul lived on after death. Anyone who died of natural causes immediately entered Xibalba, the Nine Level Underworld, to be tricked and tortured by the malevolent gods there.

A more noble death assured a Mayan an immediate journey to peaceful place in the sky. Those who died in human sacrifice, in battle or during childbirth went directly above to a thirteen level paradise surrounding the heavenly Ceiba Tree, the Tree of Life.

Oddly, even a Mayan who called upon Ixtab, the goddess of suicide and ended his or her own life by hanging went directly to the paradise above. Mama had gone to bed and not woken up; it was not a noble death by Maya standards.

"Itzi, Mama is in Xibalba!" Ixkeem began to wail, "It isn't right, Itzi! Make the lord Chac protect her, make the lord help her find her way to the sky!" She began to sob uncontrollably.

Itzamna rose from his chair and went to stand before his sister. He was the perfect height to put his arms around her as she sat before him.

"Ixkeem. Ixkeem, don't worry about Mama. She is under the Ceiba tree I'm sure. She is looking down on us I promise." She pulled back and eyed him quizzically. "Are you sure, Itzi?" fresh tears streamed down the girl's face, "She died in her bed!"

THE FLAVOR OF HEARTS

"She was taken by the great god Chac." the High Priest spoke empathically, "Our hearts became his that night on the hill when we left Uxmal. I guarantee Mama will rest under the Ceiba Tree."

Ixkeem was relieved. Relief was on each of their faces.

"Itzi," Tolo asked curiously, "what will we do about the funeral?"

"Could we get a tomb for Mama, something grand like the one we got for Dorcas?" Waykan asked suddenly.

Through the centuries they had seen to quite a few burials: Anita's husbands and children, Fonso's wife and his beloved son, and the family's first brush with the death of a loved one, the funeral of Dorcas. After twenty years the Roman woman had become part of the family, when she died in Vienna they gave her a funeral worthy of an Austrian queen.

In all those instances they let the customs and technology of the time and area dictate the burial rituals; however this situation was different. Their mother had been a revered spirit woman and healer in Uxmal and the Maya had some very specific customs in the burial of their dead.

"I will take everything into consideration," Itzi promised his brothers and sisters, "let me think on this."

Ixkeem offered to make lunch. It was close to noon she had never seen Itzamna go so long without craving food. They were all surprised when he declined and announced he would go up to his room for awhile.

Even Itzi himself was surprised by his lack of appetite; though he could understand why, it was strange not to feel his usual ravenous hunger. Stretched out on his king size bed behind closed eyes Itzi pictured the funeral rites in Uxmal. As High Priest he had presided over the burials of much Mayan nobility. In his mind Mama deserved no less.

Itzamna had personally painted the body of the ruler of Uxmal upon the king's passing; Itzi could still remember the smell of the red sulfide and the cinnabar. To the Maya the color red signified death and rebirth; they painted the dead red to aid in their journey after life. Itzi shook his head; he could imagine a contemporary mortician presented with the ceremonial needs of the ancient Maya.

Falling into a fitful sleep, he dreamed of the funeral of his father. Itzi's mind replayed the priest painting his father's body and the wrapping of the red corpse in the white cotton blanket. Through a dream haze Itzi watched Fonso as a young warrior helping to put the body in a hole beside their house; his father's contemporaries, the elite of Uxmal's army filled the shallow grave with dirt. Dreaming the high pitched wailing of the women the High Priest bolted awake.

Itzi shook his tiny head, the dream felt so real. He remembered digging his father's body up three years later and carefully cleaning the bones. Going back centuries he recalled the ceremony placing his father's bones in the tomb with their ancestors.

In Maya tradition, a family cares for the bones of their relatives. Once all decayed soft tissue is removed the cleaned skeletal remains of whole families are laid together in one place.

"One thing is sure," Itzi thought, "I must think of a way to properly care for and honor Mama within the modern customs."

The little man headed toward his well appointed bathroom; he showered, donned fresh clothes and went down to find his brothers and sisters. They were in the spacious living room; several bottles of wine were on the coffee table along with a plate of bread and cheeses.

It was nearly six in the evening. None of the family had ever seen their tiny brother go so long without food. "It's been hours since you've eaten, Itzi! Did you eat anything upstairs?" Ixkeem sounded worried.

Itzamna smiled. She sounded like their mother.

"No," he admitted, "I thought we would all go out to dinner before work tonight. We should all eat a good meal I think." The little man let the rest of his thoughts go unspoken, *"and most sadly Mama is not here to cook it for us."*

92

Since no one had a preference Fonso drove the family to Napa for dinner. He headed down Main Street to the Historic Napa Valley Mill. The old converted building housed some of the town's most exclusive shops and eateries.

Ildefonso chose Celadon for the family's meal; it was a place they often ate, but rarely with their mother. Ever practical, Mama eschewed the fine restaurant's delicious but pricey selections. Silently each of them appreciated Fonso's choice; avoiding their mother's favorite places made it easier to temporarily pretend that Mama was home in her favorite chair watching her beloved DVD movies.

After the main course Itzi ordered two bottles of 2000 far niente 'dolce'; the late harvest wine beautifully complemented the hazelnut and chocolate mousse bars the family shared for dessert. They sipped the soothing alcohol as the High Priest alleviated some of his brothers and sisters growing curiosity regarding their mother's burial.

"I have made some decisions for Mama," he stared slowly, "I think Waykan is right; Mama must have a tomb of great proportions; one showing her stature as a favored servant of our lord Chac. We will build it in the cemetery here in Napa."

All the Cenotes children nodded. Tolo raised his glass and they silently drank a toast to the proposal. Itzi continued.

"I think outwardly the tomb should look like the finest ones found in the cemetery. Though I would like Mama to rest in a replica of our temple pyramid, I fear it would quickly become a tourist attraction. We will subtly suggest our heritage on the outside and have all the proper marking on the inside. After work tonight I will draw some ideas."

Itzamna looked around the table and noted the nods of approval of his siblings.

Turning toward Barotolmeo the little man asked, "Could you have some money wired from our Swiss account to the Bank of Napa to place a down payment on the construction of the tomb?" Tolo nodded.

"Also," Itzi went on, "would you draw the glyphs of Mama's name and the glyphs of the dates of her birth and death? We will have a mason carve them in stone for us."

"I would be honored to draw the figures for Mama, Itzi." Tolo paused, thinking how to phrase his question, "do you want Mama's real name or the name the lord has given us?"

All eyes turned toward Itzamna. After the first Move the family had found a paper for each of them in Chac's Other Box. Their original Mayan family name had been replaced with Cenotes.

At first Itzi had been totally perplexed by the lord's change of their surname. Later as they crisscrossed the Mediterranean in the of start Chac's journey it became apparent the name was more natural in the strange locations; people immediately assumed they were Spaniards. An ironic assumption as history played out; after the family left Uxmal Spanish soldiers and missionaries all but decimated the Maya civilization in the Yucatan.

"Do it both ways, Tolo," Itzi decided, "Put Mama's original name and then her birthdate then the Cenotes name with the date of the first Move. Follow that with yesterday's date."

Again they all nodded in agreement.

THE FLAVOR OF HEARTS

"As far as the rest of the arrangements for Mama," Itzamna spoke more candidly than he ever had, "I'm not sure what we should do." His siblings stared; their great brother had never voiced uncertainty and their expressions showed their shock.

"Tomorrow we will go to the cemetery," the High Priest smiled wanly at their reaction to his honesty, "I promise I'll have it all worked out by then. I will stay at Chac's house tonight after work; I need to find few things from there for Mama."

Immediately Tolo offered to spend the night in his room above the tattoo parlor; and Ildefonso did the same. On the way from the restaurant Fonso offered to drive his sisters back to the farmhouse; he was secretly relieved when they declined.

"We'll stay at Chac's house with you guys," Waykan said looking toward her sister for a nod of agreement.

Ildefonso smiled. He knew Mama would be glad they all stayed together; he clearly remembered her words from the hilltop in Uxmal.

"We are a family and we will stay a family."

93

A little after four in the morning Itzi retired to his room on the top of Chac's house. His brother's and sisters had seemed a little worried when he declined their offer of food; especially pizza, one of his favorite foods.

Itzamna too was puzzled by his feelings. It was not only by the absence of his usual insatiable appetite at mealtimes; he was astounded by his overall uncertainty. Guided by the great lord Chac, the High Priest had never been unsure in any decision; today he felt cast adrift.

Itzi sat on the edge of his king sized bed and rubbed his eyes. One thing was certain, he must do enough of the right things to care for Mama and assure her rebirth and safe journey to the sky.

It was hard to decide how to follow the ancient Maya customs. The family had become modernized in so many ways and some traditions were downright impossible to accomplish in their new existence. There was no way to bury Mama near their house and be in the same spot three years later to exhume her body and clean her skeleton. They had no place where her bones could be laid with her ancestor's bones.

THE FLAVOR OF HEARTS

Everything seemed so wrong. The High Priest shook his head; he turned toward the cabinet along the wall of his bedroom and eyed his belongings from Uxmal.

Approaching the glass door he began removing objects. In a minute he had donned his Mayan loincloth and his most sacred jade regalia; the High Priest had not worn his ceremonial dress in nearly eleven hundred years.

Next Itzi removed a small container made from a turtle shell with a snake skin covering; it was highly decorated with jade and glyphs. Last he took two square bark papers and headed for his rooftop terrace. He palmed a box of matches and a small pile of kindling from near his outdoor fireplace and moved to an open area of the patio. Facing north Itzamna began his ceremonial prayers to their patron god Chac.

Kneeling, the High Priest unhooked the snake skin and revealed the turtle shell's contents. Though Chac had required none of the old rituals in their new life, Itzi was now sure he was on the right path to end his uncertainty. For the first time in one thousand sixty two years Itzamna prepared himself for one of the Maya's most sacred ceremonies; a blood letting ritual.

The offering of blood was the ultimate form of worship. Human blood and the beating heart were the ultimate commodities in the Maya universe. The most precious possession a Mayan could offer was the very thing that sustained life. The blood of a High Priest or a Mayan king or queen was highly sacred and held much power.

Itzamana selected a bone sharpened to a point and highly decorated with carvings. He reached for a rope woven from linen fibers six inches long and as thick as a finger. It surprised him to find the cord was supple after all these years. Itzi attached it to the bone's end. He laid the first bark paper in front of him.

After reciting a prayer for the opening of his ears, Itzi prayed to hear the voice of the great god Chac and pierced his earlobe with the bone's sharp point. He continued with prayers for understanding as he drew the cord through his flesh directing the flow of blood onto the bark paper.

He pulled the cord back and forth through his earlobe until the blood painted the white bark paper completely red. Now he reached inside the shell for a tiny strip of the bark of the bakalche' tree; again he was surprised by its miraculous freshness. The High Priest rolled the thin strip and placed it in the piercing in his earlobe. The bark's medicinal properties stopped the flow of the sacred blood.

Lighting a match Itzi ignited the kindling. The High Priest dropped the blood soaked paper on the fire when the flames were at their highest. The smoke rose straight up to the sky without a ripple; Itzi was pleased to see the great Chac readily accepted the offering of his High Priest's blood.

Itzamna leaned his head back and assimilated the revelations of the great god. Finally sure of the method of the necessary rituals for his mother the little man recited the prayers of thanks for the wisdom received.

Itzamna placed the second of the square bark papers in front of him. He now recited prayers asking for the words to speak the things he had heard from the great god Chac. The High Priest took the bone and pierced his tongue, again directing the flow blood to the bark paper. As with his earlobe, Itzi drew the cord back and forth through the pierced hole until the paper was crimson.

Again he used the bakalche' bark to stop the flow of blood, relit the fire and burned the second red stained paper. He said the prayers of thanks for the words to express Chac's instructions.

The High Priest felt comforted; the uncertainty had dissipated with the smoke of the sacred offerings. He knew the steps to take to straddle the rift of the ancient and the modern. Itzamna felt assured of their mother's safe passage to the sky.

The High Priest lay down to rest and regain his physical strength. The patio tiles felt cool on his bare back. He closed his eyes remembering the ceremonies in Uxmal; there were times so much of his sacred blood was sacrificed he was carried unconscious to his home atop the temple pyramid to awaken two days later.

Itzi fell into a deep and peaceful sleep.

94

When the High Priest awoke it was fully daylight. By the position of the sun it seemed close to noon. For a split second Itzi had been surprised by the blue sky above and his ceremonial dress.

A feeling of peace washed over him as he stood. He remembered the instructions of the great god Chac. Returning to his bedroom the little man carefully removed his loincloth and jade adornments. He placed them reverently in the glass cabinet then removed some objects for Mama's ceremony.

Itzi selected a fine pottery vase beautifully painted with Chac's glyphs and the patterns suggesting water, thunder and lightning. Next he chose a wooden whistle intricately carved in their patron god's likeness. Itzi grinned at the little noisemaker; the artisans in Uxmal had made it to the High Priest's exact specifications. Chac looked exactly as he had appeared in the flesh that night on the pyramid, down to his little pointy teeth and the axe in his gnarled hands.

Itzamna took his obsidian knife and cut a jade bead from his ceremonial headdress. Closing the glass door he went across the bedroom to Chac's Other Box. Lifting the lid he was sure he would find the last object he needed.

THE FLAVOR OF HEARTS

As expected, a single piece of dried Indian corn rested exactly in the center of the stone container. Itzi removed the tiny morsel and laid it on the bed with the other objects.

He showered and dressed in one of his favorite sweat suits. Fetching his sketchbook the High Priest sat in his recliner and began to draw. He started with a base of nine small step platforms, the sacred way nearly every royal Mayan tomb was constructed.

Atop the ninth level he drew a rectangular building surrounded by graceful fluted columns; he patterned the design after the Greek Parthenon. Though the famous structure was already in ruins when the family had arrived in Athens all of them had been extremely impressed with its majesty. Mama especially had been awed by its beauty; in fact she had a replica model of the ruin in her room in Chac's house.

Itzi sketched feverishly for two hours. He drew the marble tomb from two different angles. Under the peaked roof in front Itzi drew Chac's sacred glyph with their family name in English below it. Below the word Cenotes he sketched the Mayan glyphs that represented the family's original name and the symbol for the word dzonot, the Maya translation of Cenotes.

The High Priest added instructions for the placement of the building; the front must face exactly north, the way to the Maya heavens. He notated that the crypt be made large enough to accommodate the whole family; and also requested a spot be designated inside in memorial to their long departed older sisters.

Next he began some sketches for relief sculptures. Itzi created a three part landscape to be carved on the tomb's outer walls, behind the freestanding columns. He illustrated the flora of the Yucatan rainforest as it appeared during the rainy season: thick and lush. From memory Itzamna peppered the trees and bushes with all sorts of local beasts, birds and insects: butterflies, spiders, howler monkeys, peccaries, iguanas, tapirs, turkeys, Yucatan parrots and the Maya's sacred animal, Ek Balaam, the black jaguar.

For the inside carvings Itzi drew two scenes of Uxmal: the elliptical temple pyramid and a precise drawing of Mama's thatched roof house. He made some illustrations of Maya crops: corn and tomato plants, then squash and melon vines. Itzi depicted the sacred Ceiba tree. He imagined this rendition of the modern cottonwood tree cast in bronze for the door of the vault.

He would ask Tolo to draw the glyphs for the thirteen gods who ruled the Maya paradise in the sky; they should line the tops of the inner walls in Mama's resting place. The High Priest made a drawing of a three dimensional carving of Chac. He would request that four of these be made and placed in the upper four corners of the inner mausoleum. Lastly Itzamna sketched his ideas for the inside ceiling: he drew the sun in alignment with the dark center of the Milky Way, the Union of First Father with First Mother.

Satisified with his work Itzamna took his drawings and went looking for his brothers and sisters. The little man realized he was hungry; he hoped to find some leftover pizza as well.

Fonso was waiting sprawled on the couch in his own bedroom; he was relieved to hear his older brother coming down the stairs from the third floor. Itzi appeared in the doorway and held up his papers.

"I have some ideas for Mama. Let's go down to the kitchen," Itzi suggested, "I'm starving. Is there any pizza left? Is everyone home?"

Ildefonso was thrilled to hear the High Priest's appetite had returned. The big man immediately rose and followed his tiny brother.

"The girls are in the living room," Fonso answered, "Tolo's here."

The big man banged on Bartolomeo's bedroom door as he and Itzi passed.

"Tolo," Fonso bellowed, "come downstairs. Itzi has some drawings to show us."

THE FLAVOR OF HEARTS

The Cenotes brothers and sisters congregated in the kitchen. Itzamna immediately tore into the cold pizza Fonso took from the refrigerator.

"Itzi, at least let me heat it for you!" Ixkeem grabbed the box then grinned sheepishly, "I sounded like Mama!"

They all smiled; it was a welcome reminder. As Itzi feasted on the warmed pizza they all marveled over his drawings and his ideas for the family mausoleum. The High Priest explained his plans for the funeral rites and asked his sibling's help in some aspects.

Tolo immediately agreed to draw the symbols of the thirteen gods of the paradise above. He showed the family the completed drawings of Mama's name and the dates Itzi asked for the night before at dinner.

"Would you girls decide what Mama should wear? I'm afraid I'm hardly qualified in that department," the High Priest admitted.

"We already looked in her room and found a few things," Waykan said. The sisters went through the door to Mama's bedroom suite off the kitchen.

When they returned Ixkeem held up a silk padded hangar; it held a turquoise blue evening dress, elegantly beaded around the neck and sleeves. "This was Mama's favorite dress, when she got dressed up," her voice cracked toward the end of the sentence.

Waykan spoke, unzipping the garment bag she held. "This is Mama's best outfit from…from home," she bravely continued though her voice slightly faltered, "Which do you think, Itzi?"

It had been a long time since Itzamna had seen the clothes his mother wore on the night of the first Move; her elaborately woven linen dress and ceremonial jade breast piece brought tears to his eyes.

"Perhaps she could wear both?" Tolo spared his venerated brother the anguish, "the fancy blue dress with her breast piece…they match."

Waykan removed the jade and hung it over the evening dress; all of them nodded in agreement. The new with the old...it felt right.

"Well, I think we're pretty much ready to go to the cemetery," Itzi stated, "there are a few things we'll bring with us to put with Mama on the day of...on the day. I have a nice vase upstairs for the food offering and a beautiful whistle of our lord to put in her hand."

Mayan people often placed a container of food with their departed loved ones and many times buried their dead with whistles or noisemakers to help scare the bad spirits away on the afterlife journey.

Bartolomeo offered to call the cemetery for an appointment. Fonso retrieved the business card Itzi left with him and they all listened as Tolo settled on a time.

As they separated to prepare for the meeting Ixkeem called out, "Wear something nice."

It was something Mama often said.

They all laughed at Itzi's reply in their Mayan tongue, "He'ele', dze'na'."

He said, "Certainly, little mother."

95

Later the family loaded into the Jaguar and headed down the St. Helena Highway toward the town of Napa. After a stop at the Bank of Napa, Fonso took the Silverado Trail to Coombsville Road and easily found the entrance to the Tulocay Cemetery.

They were instantly struck by the beauty of the grounds; it comforted them to think of Mama's body laid to rest in such a peaceful place.

With a hint of nervousness they entered the funeral home's office. Immediately the director put the Cenotes family at ease, ushering them into the office and giving them all seats. After offering his condolences on the passing of their mother Mr. Manasse explained that Tulocay Cemetery was Napa's oldest and finest; he informed the Cenotes brothers and sisters of the Endowment Fund that would maintain the upkeep on the property long into the future.

"Did Mrs. Cenotes have any specific wishes in her will or perhaps in a pre-need agreement?" the funeral director aimed the question at Itzi.

It was easy to see by the way the family seated themselves around him and the deference they showed the tiny man that he was clearly the head of the family. Itzamna admitted they had no previous arrangements, but explained they had a few specific requests.

"First," Itzi started, "we would like to build a family mausoleum, if that is possible here. We would consider this a down payment if necessary."

The High Priest removed a cashiers check from the inside pocket of his suit jacket and placed it on the desk in front of Mr. Manasse. The funeral director did his best not to react in a surprised way to the thirty million dollars Itzi laid down so nonchalantly. He assured the tiny gentleman that a family mausoleum could be accommodated on the grounds.

They discussed the projected size and Mr. Manasse indicated on a map where they could place the memorial in the cemetery's newest section. He warned the family due to the scope of such a project, Mrs. Cenotes may have to be temporarily interred, perhaps in the cemetery's main mausoleum until the completion of the family's memorial. Itzi easily agreed to the plan; the funeral director promised to arrange an appointment with the area's finest stone masons and sculptors.

"Now, as to the service," the director went on, "if any, did you have any particular religious affiliation?"

"We are Maya," Itzi answered.

Again the funeral director tried to hide his first reaction; but answered honestly, "I'm afraid I have little experience with a Maya service, perhaps if you inform me of some of the particulars I could provide for your needs. Would you need a priest?"

"Our brother is a priest," Fonso answered gesturing toward Itzamna, "he will say the prayers for our mother."

"Ah, very good," the funeral director again directed his gaze toward Itzi, "Then you will conduct the service?"

The High Priest nodded.

The family chose to have their mother embalmed in the modern way, with an open casket wake after a private service. The funeral director began showing the family photos of the finest caskets; he dispensed with the more economic selections after seeing the size of Itzi's check.

"You can see samples of these in our showroom," the mortician offered.

"There are a few things we need for our mother in addition to your standard services and the things you have shown us," Itzi started. "We would like the casket to be red."

Mr. Manasse turned the sample book to a different page and suggested a reddish brown ornately carved cherry wood casket.

"No," Itzi shook his head emphatically, "It must be bright red. Red is a sacred color for us. Perhaps one could be custom made or painted."

For the third time the funeral director hid his surprise; "Of course," the funeral director answered evenly, "I will check with our supplier and arrange that."

Itzi removed the piece of dried corn and the jade bead from his suit jacket and placed the objects on the funeral director's desk.

"We need these placed in our mother's mouth. Is that possible in your process?"

"Ah...yes, of course," The mortician sounded so perplexed Itzi explained the Mayan custom.

"The corn is a symbol of the food our mother will need in the afterlife. The jade will help her pay her way through any obstacles in her journey."

"That is very interesting," Mr. Manasse nodded his head thoughtfully as he placed the objects in an envelope and slipped them in the family's file folder.

"She must also be wrapped in a white cotton blanket," Itzi requested.

The funeral director showed the family pictures of some natural cotton shrouds, asking if any were appropriate.

Immediately the girls selected an ornately decorated one, covered with tiny white embroidered flowers. Itzamna agreed when he was assured it was pure cotton. Mr. Manasse went on with the plans.

"Would you need music for the service? We have an organ and piano, also musicians are available. Anything you may have on a CD could be played through our sound system. Once again," the funeral director sounded apologetic, "I regret that I am unfamiliar with your religious needs."

"I didn't really think of the music," Itzi turned toward the girls and Bartolomeo at his left.

At many Mayan funeral rites loud drum music was played with accompanying melodies on wooden flutes; the Maya believed loud sounds kept Au Puch, one of their gods of death, away from the living.

"I'll make a CD," Tolo suggested, "I'll use some of the modern versions of the traditional Yucatec music we gave Mama for her birthday. Maybe we could play some of the Viennese waltzes she liked so much."

Itzi agreed. Through the centuries their mother had grown to love many forms of music; she especially loved the waltzes of Johann Strauss and the rousing marches of John Phillip Sousa.

The High Priest turned to the funeral director.

"We will supply a CD of some of our mother's favorites. One thing though," Itzi instructed, "The music at the very end of the service must be played very loudly; much louder than is probably your custom here."

"How loudly?" now the funeral director could not hide his curiosity, "You have a religious specification for the volume of the music?"

"Yes," Itzi explained with a slight smile, "it is our belief that loud sounds will keep malevolence from our mother and also from the living in attendance. Perhaps the last two songs could be played as loud as, let's say, the music in a dance club."

The mortician assured the family any requests would be accommodated. Mr. Manasse smiled inside; he had not been asked for loud music since the untimely death of a heavy metal musician a few years earlier. Personally the funeral director highly preferred hearing a Viennese waltz at maximum volume than the riotous death metal music at the young guitar player's service.

The family tightened up the last details: they picked some striking floral arrangements and signed all the necessary papers. Ixkeem gave the funeral director the garment bag with the clothes they had chosen; the man was most impressed with Mama's ornate ceremonial breast piece.

"This is the most beautiful thing I have ever seen," the man was sincerely taken aback. He found the Mayan customs and the jade ornamentation very interesting.

"Perhaps, "he said to Itzamna as he walked the family to the car, "we could meet in the future at a less painful time. I would like to learn more of the customs and beliefs of your Maya religion. It seems very fascinating."

Itzi had liked the mortician upon their initial handshake; now he appreciated the man even more. His frank curiosity and kind manner had greatly put the family at ease. The High Priest agreed to a future meeting and suggested a dinner together; the little man was greatly relieved to leave Mama in the hands of such a fine gentleman as Mr. Manasse.

96

Mama's funeral went smoothly. It was hard on her children to see her laid lifeless before them, though she looked peaceful in her beautiful dress and jade breast piece.

To a background of traditional Mayan drums and flutes Itzi said the Maya prayers for the dead as Ixkeem placed the food offering in the casket. Earlier she had filled the vase Itzi provided with some of Mama's favorite foods: Belgian chocolates, strawberries and a small package of Italian coffee. Ixkeem also added a tomato, a small zucchini and a fresh ear of corn. Out of respect to the body of the departed, the Maya never brought meat as a food offering.

That morning Waykan had carefully dug a cornstalk from Mama's garden and replanted it in an earthenware flower pot. She placed it with the flower arrangements; life sustaining corn was sacred to the Maya. Waykan also laid Mama's snakeskin bag of dried medicinal herbs at her mother's feet so the spirit woman could practice her ancient healing arts in the afterlife.

Tolo put Mama's favorite porcelain coffee cup beside her and Fonso laid her most watched DVD movie, The Sound of Music next to it. After the final prayers Itzi placed the whistle carved in Chac's likeness in his mother's hand.

Mr. Manasse then opened the service to friends and well wishers. The Ortiz family came in full force. The father of their current caretaker Juan Ortiz made a rare public appearance. Though he was only 59, Juan Ortiz V walked with great difficulty; he had been injured in the last great flood in the Napa Valley. By his heroics on New Year's Eve 2005 their homes and the vineyard were spared the devastation of many of the neighbor's properties.

The Cenotes' lawyer from Napa and the president of the bank also came to offer condolences. After two high volume Strauss waltzes Bartolomeo invited all the people in attendance to a lunch in Mama's honor at Piccolino's Cafe, their mother's favorite local Italian restaurant. There they all celebrated Mama's life with her favorite Italian dishes and much local red wine.

97

Itzi sat on the back of the farmhouse's wrap around porch watching Fonso and his two sisters harvesting vegetables from Mama's garden. The little man had offered to help; horrified, his siblings had requested that he watch from the porch.

To them it was bad enough Itzi had started weeding Mama's garden after her death. In ancient Maya culture a priest would never be expected to do physical work. A High Priest was venerated as a god on Earth; it was unforgivable for a Mayan to allow a High Priest to do any form of manual labor.

In truth Itzi enjoyed his work in the garden; he felt close to his mother caring for the plants she loved so much. In ancient Uxmal every household had a vegetable garden; to this day many modern Maya continue this practice on Mexico's Yucatan and throughout rural Belize, Guatemala and Honduras.

It was ingrained in their mother to grow vegetables; immediately after the first Move she had planted her edibles in the Roman atrium, then in later years, in pots on the roof of Chac's house. Itzamna loved eying the sky from the rooftop surrounded by his mother's corn, tomatoes and squash.

In the modern era, often living away from Chac's house, Mama planted a large garden wherever possible. It was something she especially had loved about living that year at the farmhouse near Yountville; the rich soil and wealth of sunshine had allowed her to cultivate one of the finest vegetable patches ever.

Ixkeem took a seat next to Itzi on the porch; laying a bulging basket of zucchini down at their feet. "Mama would have loved these," she said pointing to the dozen squashes, "I'll make them for lunch. Would you like them breaded and fried, Itzi? Or fried with gravy?"

The little man eagerly chose the Italian version. Dorcas had taught the girls the Italian preparation of zucchini: fried in olive oil with garlic, tomato gravy and Romano cheese. Itzamna had been known to consume pounds of fried squash accompanied by multiple loaves of Italian bread! The High Priest gratefully thanked his sister; she had done her best to fill their mother's shoes during the men's five days off; Ixkeem had faithfully made lunch every day and each night offered to make dinner. Itzi had spared her the duty of the evening meals; but was grateful to have the lunch he had grown accustomed to. She politely waved off his thanks but her heart was touched by his words.

A loud thud and a smashing sound took their attention.

"What the heck?" Ildefonso was shocked; he felt the juice of a tomato dripping down his bare back.

Though it was late September it was close to 80 degrees. The big man had removed his shirt as they picked the vegetables in the noonday sun.

The second tomato hit him in the buttocks just as he assessed the situation; hearing Waykan's raucous laugh Fonso charged in her direction. With a ballet leap she soared over two rows of tomatoes exiting the garden. Though her jump was worthy of a gazelle she barely avoided his grasp.

"You are dead, Waykan," the big man bellowed.

In one motion he grabbed two ripe tomatoes, flinging the first one as he moved toward his sister. Laughing hysterically, she easily side stepped the first red missile; the second clipped her arm as she moved in the opposite direction.

Fonso's long legs cleared the space between them as she avoided the projectiles; in a second he had her in a Jiu-Jitsu hold.

"Stop that," Ixkeem started to rise from her chair.

Grinning Itzi put out an arm and stopped her, "Let them go."

The High Priest knew the family warriors needed relief; he was confident they wouldn't really hurt one another. He often marveled at the different martial arts they practiced together; Fonso often extolled his youngest sister's athletic prowess.

Itzi and Ixkeem watched amazed as Waykan countered Fonso's move and slipped his grasp. "Hah," she yelled sprinting down the garden's edge.

Her speed was remarkable but her bigger brother's long legs and legendary quickness were no match. He grabbed her from behind, taking her to the ground and locking a hold around her neck.

Surprisingly, she again slipped his grasp; they went back and forth with holds and counter holds. With every move they rolled closer and closer to the garden; finally Fonso secured a solid choke hold on his slippery sister. She tapped in submission and Fonso let her loose.

When he stood he kept her in his sight; as he expected, quick as a cobra, still lying on her back she reached for a tomato and hurled it in his direction. She was already on her feet when the soft red orb reached him; he let it hit him to be sure he grabbed her cleanly.

Using one arm he pulled her back to his front and sat down; taking her to the ground. With his free hand Fonso grabbed two tomatoes from the plant next to him and smashed them on her head. Juice and seeds rolled down her shining black hair.

"Truce, truce!" she screamed now laughing, "Truce!"

THE FLAVOR OF HEARTS

"No more; and you wash my clothes! Yourself!" he squeezed her tightly.   Knowing his strength and the limits of his patience she swore.

"I will wash your clothes. Myself!" she yelled before they both rose.

Fonso retrieved the t-shirt he'd previously hung on the porch railing and wiped the tomato seeds from his back and jeans; he threw the shirt toward Waykan so she could clean herself.

"And no tricks," he said as they joined their siblings, "no itching powder in my pants or shrinking my shirts to Itzi's size!"

"Well it's been awhile since I washed clothes myself," she answered coyly as she took the chair beside her sister, "I hope I remember what to do."

Through the years the Cenotes family had grown accustomed to the pleasure of much domestic help; Chac's Treasure had given them a fine lifestyle.

"No tricks," Ildefonso growled.

"No tricks." she answered grinning.

"She had the better of you for a few minutes, Fonso" Itzi said deviously.

"Are you kidding?" Ildefonso was appalled.

"Yes," Itzi succinct answer made them all laugh.

Shortly, Waykan turned to her sister, "Did you ask him?"

With Ixkeem's negative shake of the head Waykan turned toward Itzamna, "Itzi, would it be all right if Ixkeem and I went to Los Angeles for awhile? We'll come back for your next days off. Is it OK?"

The girls too had become antsy for later nightlife and the days at the farmhouse seemed very empty without their mother.

"Of course," the little man agreed, "Maybe we'll join you there after this work cycle."

Waykan hugged her tiny brother. Itzi too felt their Napa home's emptiness: he hoped the beach and the wilder nightlife would help his loyal sisters to overcome their grief. As they all went into the house for lunch he asked them to call when they reached Los Angeles.

98

Itzi stared at the paper before him. It was probably the first time in a thousand years a picture didn't immediately come to mind for the next of Chac's customers. The High Priest gazed again at the blank paper. All he could see was the last customer's picture; a nosegay of miniature pink and red roses tied with a gleaming gold ribbon.

For inspiration he thumbed through a leather book of his drawings; every time he was pulled to the same page of flowers. Maybe I'm tired the little man thought shaking his head. In the last years time had been flying by, but the last thirteen days felt like a century.

Maybe I can't get that girl out of my mind Itzi mused. The last customer had certainly been beautiful. A French tourist visiting Napa; the young woman's accent was alluring and her beauty remarkable.

Itzamna sighed as he heard footsteps from the studio's entrance. As he moved toward the archway to greet customer number nineteen he decided to have the person suggest the design or choose from the books.

The High Priest's jaw dropped in surprise; the French woman was back!

"You wish another tattoo?" Itzi was rarely surprised but shock was more than evident in his voice.

She laughed. She sounded like an exotic bird.

"That was my sister before me. You tattooed my sister!"

It was the same voice, the same accent, the same breath taking beauty.

"You are twins?" Itzi asked the question like a declaration. That could explain the lack of a fresh image in his head.

"No," she answered to Itzi's utter surprise. "We are triplets," she went on, "Our other sister is waiting."

Itzamna grinned; he liked the way she said treeplets. This certainly explained the odd absence of his usual premonition. The High Priest marveled at the similarities in the women; Maya people regarded multiple births as sacred occurrences.

She answered his first question before he asked, "Could I have the same tattoo as my sister? It is amazing you drew such a thing before meeting us. You saw our family name first, did you not? Perhaps on the card?"

Her friendly but challenging tone captivated Itzamna.

"No," the High Priest insisted, "I drew the roses before I saw your sister's card."

"Hmmph, perhaps you are, what is the word? Magical!" Smiling, she pointed toward the huge painting of Uxmal's Temple Pyramid, "Perhaps you are the Magician, yes?"

"Perhaps I am." Itzi grinned slyly.

"Hah!" she laughed again, "Well, Monsieur Magician, I would like the same tattoo as Christiane, on my lower back as well."

Itzamna motioned toward the leather table. It greatly pleased him that she recognized his temple and knew its modern name, The Pyramid of the Magician. Earlier her sister had been floored when Itzi showed her the nosegay of roses he had drawn; their family name, Chambre de Rose, meant House of the Rose.

As Itzi made the second stencil from the drawing she spoke.

"You are brothers, no? You and the two men outside?"

THE FLAVOR OF HEARTS

"Yes." Itzi answered as he approached her.

"Umm, I like that, a family that works together. We work as a family too. Ah, that is cold..." She shuddered when he applied the stencil to the small of her back.

Itzamna asked her not to try not to move as he started the outlines. She buried her head in her arms until he completely finished the tattoo.

As he had done with her sister, Itzi invited her to the full length mirror to see her new body art. He held the large hand mirror so she saw her back clearly. The High Priest wanted to laugh out loud; like déjà vu she responded exactly as her sister before her.

"Magnifique! C'est beau!"

She too followed immediately when Itzi asked and allowed him to cover the tattoo with the bandage and bacterial cream. As Christiane had before her she listened attentively to the instructions for the body art's initial care and checked her diamond studded watch when the High Priest mentioned keeping the covering on for two hours.

Curiously Itzi pulled her card from the drawer: Christelle Chambre de Rose.

A beautiful name, the High Priest thought. Surreptitiously he checked her slender finger for a wedding ring. Though he had never made a move on one of Chac's chosen Itzi seriously considered asking this woman to have a drink with him after work.

"That will be $45 dollars, Mademoiselle Chambre de Rose."

She was surprised by his perfect French pronunciation. She was also surprised to see her information card.

"You did see our name!" she exclaimed pointing her finger accusingly.

"I assure you of my truthfulness," Itzi insisted. "I drew the roses before seeing your sister's card."

"Hmmph," she narrowed her eyes and stared.

The handsome little gentleman had more than piqued her interest.

"Ah yes, I forgot," she said playfully, "you are the Magician!"

Itzi laughed as he accepted the payment she took from her Louis Vuitton bag. "I'm afraid you have me at an advantage, Monsieur Magician," she said flirtatiously, "you know my name but I do not know yours."

"Forgive me, I am Itzamna Cenotes."

He kissed her hand and she blushed. Christelle eyed his perfectly formed hands. She stared curiously at the huge golden skull ring with the lightning bolts for eyes on Itzi's right hand. She noted the absence of a ring on his left.

"You are not married, Monsieur Cenotes?" she asked coyly.

The High Priest smiled and replied negatively as he walked her toward the exit. Peals of birdlike laughter echoed through the archway from the lobby. Snatches of friendly conversational French could be overheard.

"It sounds as if my brothers are quite taken with your sisters," Itzi commented.

"Yes," she spoke knowingly, "it seems so. Perhaps you would like to have a glass of wine or a bite to eat with me when you finish tonight?"

Itzi readily agreed. He put his arm around her waist and accompanied her to the lobby. Fonso and Bartolomeo hardly seemed surprised at Itzi's sudden appearance.

"Itzi," Tolo said, "this is Christine Chambre de Rose, our last customer for tonight."

"The girls have invited us to have a bite at their hotel," Ildefonso announced, "What do you say, Itzi?"

"Itzi? They call you Itzi. I like that," Christelle said seductively.

"Fonso, lock the front door, since we have our last customer," Itzamna said smiling, "Tolo, maybe you could get us all something to drink from the kitchen. Let's bring the girls back to the studio. I'll finish with Christine's tattoo and we'll take it from there."

99

Ildefonso's eyes popped open. He glanced at the clock on his nightstand; it was almost eleven in the morning.

It was barely three hours since he walked the Chambre de Rose triplets back to their car. The big man rolled over and tried to go back to sleep but slumber became elusive. Fonso savored the memory of Christiane Chambre de Rose. He could still faintly smell the scent of her perfume on his sheets.

Ildefonso was still surprised that Itzi had suggested entertaining the girls in Chac's house. Out of respect for their mother the Cenotes siblings had always kept their sexual liaisons away from the family home. Fonso sighed. Life was so different without Mama.

The big man returned his thoughts to Christiane lest sadness overwhelm him. He pictured the French woman straddling him; her blond hair flying around her beautiful face. Ah, Fonso thought breathing in her sweet lingering scent, she rode me like a wild bronco.

When his cell phone rang he hoped it was Christiane looking to take another ride. Eying the digital display the big man was disappointed; it was not the number she had given him earlier.

"Fonso?"

Ildefonso's eyebrows rose in surprise; very few men called him by his nickname and this man's voice was totally unfamiliar.

"Yes?" Before the big man could ask the caller's identity the voice went on.

"Are you by chance related to Waykan Cenotes?"

"I am her brother. Who is this?"

"Sir, this is the California State Highway Patrol. Are you also related to Ixkeem Cenotes?"

"Yes, they are both my sisters," Fonso was now fully awake and sat up in his bed.

He immediately suspected that Waykan had been arrested again; too often she took full advantage of her Lamborghini's legendary horsepower. Ildefonso had bailed her out twice that year; the last time she was caught near St. Helena going 164 miles per hour. The judge had threatened her with a jail sentence on her next offense.

Itzi is going to flip the big man thought.

"Sir, I'm afraid I have some bad news. Your sisters were killed in an accident on I-5 North early this morning."

"What?" Fonso heard the words but human nature made him ask the policeman to repeat the sentence.

"Your sisters were killed in an accident on I-5 North early this morning. They hit the guardrail on the West Side Highway near Bakersfield at about 3:45 am. Both your sisters were declared dead at the scene."

Fonso felt like he was kicked in the stomach.

"I'm sorry to give you this news over the telephone, sir," the police officer's voice took on a less official tone, "the local police in Yountville said you were not at your place of residence and they couldn't locate you. We found your phone number in your sister's cell phone."

Numbly Ildefonso retrieved a pen and took down the information the policeman provided. When he hung up the phone the big man fell back on his bed and let his eyes well up.

"Itzi was right," the big man thought darkly, "one by one the great god is taking us."

THE FLAVOR OF HEARTS

He suddenly realized he must now be the bearer of this bad news to Itzamna and Bartolomeo. Dreading the scenario Fonso went to shower first and dress; he decided to let his brothers have at least another hour of peaceful sleep.

Later climbing the stairs to Itzi's room Fonso was reminded of the day their father died. He recalled walking woodenly to their mother's house in Uxmal to deliver the devastating news; today he felt the same heaviness in his chest as he did that day so long ago.

Itzamna's bedroom door was open; the big man almost smiled at the sight before him. The High Priest was so tiny in the king sized bed he was almost obscured by the folds in the sheets. Fonso approached quietly and gently shook his older brother's shoulder.

"Itzi. Itzi, wake up. I have some bad news..."

Later they both broke the news to Bartolomeo.

After the police investigation was complete, the Cenotes brothers had their sisters' bodies sent to the Tulocay cemetery in Napa. Itzamna decided on a private family service and they made no public announcements. With the help of Mr. Manasse they made pretty much the same arrangements for the girls as they had for their mother.

Bartolomeo procured a copy of the coroner's findings and the official police report. Both deaths were ruled accidental. No traces of drugs or alcohol were found in either girl's body. The autopsy showed Waykan had suffered a massive heart attack while driving. The coroner called it an unusual occurrence for a woman of Waykan's age and physical condition. She died instantaneously while behind the wheel, causing the Lamborghini to strike the guardrail. The police report said the car was traveling in excess of 100 miles per hour. Ixkeem died immediately as a result of the impact.

On the day of the funeral Bartolomeo brought two Venetian glass vases with the food offerings. The girls had purchased the glassware on their first visit to the Roman market place; all three men remembered how fascinated the family had been by the transparent glass.

After Itzi said the Mayan prayers for the dead Ildefonso placed the girls' iPODS and their beloved cell phones with them. Itzi put a jade whistle in Ixkeem's hand. The men had to smile at the noisemaker the High Priest had chosen for their youngest sister; a brand new Aerosol Air Horn.

In the 1970's Waykan found her first one in a marine supply store. She tortured the family that whole summer; startling them with the ear shattering sound when they least expected it. Ever the prankster, the air horn had remained Waykan's favorite tool for mischief; surely she would be the scourge of the malevolent spirits of the afterlife armed with it.

Tolo had changed the last music to suit his sisters' tastes: he chose two selections by the rock band Pink Floyd to be played at high volume. *The Dark Side of the Moon* was a favorite album of all of them; even their mother had enjoyed the British band's orchestral rock music. After the song *Eclipse* the service ended with a later song, *On the Turning Away*. A line of lyrics echoed in the minds of all three Cenotes men: "*Feel the new wind of change, On the wings of the night.*" Things had certainly changed and all of them felt bigger changes coming; not only for them but for everyone.

Before the brothers left the cemetery they went to check on the status of their family mausoleum. They were glad to see progress had been made; the marble base of nine graduated steps was nearly completed.

"I'm next, you know." Bartolomeo said it so matter-of-factly, the words hung in the air.

Itzamna and Fonso stared silently at their middle brother.

"The lord will leave you to protect Itzi, Fonso." Tolo predicted. The big man nodded; it seemed logical; Bartolomeo was always thinking.

"That may be so," the High Priest spoke gently, "if it happens that way then you will find Mama and the girls before us. Tell them we have missed them here."

All three nodded. Itzi sensed increased tension in Bartolomeo.

"Don't fear, Tolo." the High Priest, "you have been on the journey before. You will easily remember the way." All Maya trusted in the cycle of life and death; they believed that every Mayan was dead before they were born.

"Don't worry, Tolo," Fonso added, "When you leave...we'll be right behind you."

100

"Look at that guy," Ildefonso sneered, "I'd like to run over him."

Fonso pointed out the window of the Jaguar as he drove down Washington Avenue. Itzi eyed the sight that so disgusted his warrior brother.

It was a skinny, disheveled looking man in a long dirty robe. He waved a sign at the cars passing. It said December 21, 2012…THE END OF THE WORLD.

"Twenty days," he was screaming, "repent before the end! Twenty days!"

In the last year it was hard to watch television or read the newspaper. Everywhere you looked were shows and articles quoting a multitude of prophetic sources: Edgar Cayce, the Oracle at Delphi, the Sibylline Oracles of Rome, Nostradamus, the Hopi Indians, Mother Seton and of course their own culture the ancient Maya. It was odd how so many sources had dire predictions centered on the same point in time.

Many people totally believed the bleak prophesies; psychiatrists reported a rise in business as people tried valiantly to deal with impending doom. Churches of all denominations experienced increased attendance. Real estate agents noted a marked rise in property sales away from the coasts; people were building underground shelters and stockpiling survivalist supplies in caves.

On the other hand, much of humanity seemed to laugh in the face of the impending disaster. Bars and nightclubs were hosting "End of the World" parties. There were Doomsday Sales offered in stores: people were encouraged to use their credit cards with no billing until the unlikely arrival of 2013!

"Look another one!" Fonso pointed to a man three blocks from the first.

He wasn't as dirty as his compatriot; but he stood in front of the Methodist Church with a sign that said: The End Is Near! Come Inside…Be Forgiven!"

Ildefonso grunted, "I'm really sick of this shit."

"I'm surprised how modern people have misinterpreted the end of our Great Cycle," Itzi mused, "no writing exists from our culture that literally calls it the end of the world, yet that's what they believe."

"People want to believe the worst," Fonso suggested. "They quote the priest Chilam Balam."

Ildefonso spoke of an ancient book of prophesies attributed to a Mayan oracle that lived in the Yucatan in the late fifteenth century. Chilam Balam made predictions for each katun, twenty year periods in part of the Mayan calendar. Because the Maya calendar rolls in continuous cycles, the katuns repeat themselves over different time periods.

"I have read those books," Itzamna remarked, "many prophesies attributed to Chilam Balam were made long before, some even predate our time in Uxmal. Most of his predictions for each katun are broad and much can be read into them. Though, I will admit, some of his words have eerily coincided with modern events."

"I would think modern people would be more concerned about the asteroid Apophis," Itzi continued, "that's a real threat to the earth as we know it. That old man should change the date on his doomsday sign to April 13, 2036."

"What do you mean, Itzi?" Ildefono asked curiously.

"An asteroid, a big one, passed very close to Earth in 2004." Itzamna explained, "Calculating its orbit, this asteroid will pass by Earth again on April 13, 2029. At that time, it will come close enough to be seen in the sky with the naked eye. It'll actually be closer to Earth than our communication satellites!"

Itzi continued, "If this asteroid touches a certain band in our atmosphere it could hit a gravitational keyhole and the earth's gravity would draw it closer. Saying that happens, on its orbital return seven years later this asteroid will hit the earth. The odds of this thing hitting the planet are pretty high."

"They calculate the possible day of impact as April 13, 2036," Itzi finished. "They estimate it would hit somewhere in the Pacific off the coast of California."

"Can they really predict this, Itzi?" Fonso was astonished, "They can figure it out down to the actual day?"

"It's a matter of mathematics," Itzamna answered, "Plotting the orbit of a celestial object with its rate of speed they can estimate its future position."

"What would happen if this thing does hit the Earth?" Ildefonso asked.

"You know how they say an asteroid wiped out the dinosaurs 65 million years ago? Well this asteroid, the one they named Apophis, could do the same kind of damage," Itzi said knowingly "If it hits, it will cause devastation to parts of the Earth."

"And scientists know of this?" Fonso was floored to learn of this event.

"Yes, many astronomers are tracking it. NASA has published information on it; they call it Asteroid 99942. There's an American astronaut...what is his name?" Itzamna scanned his memory, "Schweickart, that's it...he's been warning of this asteroid for years. There's talk of sending a manned space craft up toward it. Supposedly there's a committee in the United Nations to decide who should pay for such a mission."

"Why is this not in the news more, Itzi?" Ildefonso was incredulous.

"I don't know," the High Priest shrugged, "but I have seen this asteroid myself and scientifically it is certainly more of a threat to this planet then the upcoming alignment of the sun with the center of the galaxy."

Fonso parked the car near the Bottega Ristorante. He entered the popular Napa eatery and emerged almost immediately laden with four huge bags of take out. Since the death of their sisters and mother the men had become accustomed to buying prepared food in large quantities; even restaurants that didn't ordinarily offer food to go succumbed to Ildefonso's impressive bribery and always accommodated the Cenotes brothers.

As he approached the Jaguar a girl offered Fonso a flyer advertising a Mayan End of the World party at a local club. It mentioned a prize for the best Maya costume.

Fonso showed Itzi the party announcement.

"We ought to get dressed in our old clothes." the big man laughed, "and scare the shit out of them!" Itzamna shook his head in disbelief; it was hard to fathom the varying degrees of panic and partying.

When they returned to the house Fonso called up the stairs for their brother. "Tolo, come and eat." the big man yelled.

He and Itzi went to the kitchen. Fonso put two bags in the refrigerator for after work and began unloading the contents of the others onto the table.

As Itzi tore into the take out, Ildefonso went back to the stairway.

"Tolo, what are you doing?" the big man bellowed, "Come and eat." Fonso sighed in exasperation; sometimes Bartolomeo was in his own world with his books and theories. The family warrior took the stairs two and a time and burst through his brother's bedroom door. Ildefonso was surprised by the vacant workbench and computer desk. He turned toward his brother's bed.

"Tolo, come and..."

Fonso stopped dead in his tracks; for a second time he felt like he was kicked in the stomach. Again he regretted being the bearer of bad news to Itzi.

101

Ildefonso took an undershirt from the drawer. Looking up he was startled to see Itzi's reflection in the dresser's mirror.

"I didn't mean to sneak up on you," the little man apologized.

"No problem," Fonso smiled as he pulled the undershirt over his head.

Itzamna had barely let the big man out of his sight since Bartolomeo's funeral. Tolo's funeral had been hard. The two men had felt very lonely at Bartolomeo's service. Their family of eight had finally dwindled down to a pair.

Donning his shirt and tie Ildefonso chided himself for not hearing Itzi's approach. I must be losing my skills, the giant warrior thought.

"Can we stop at the bank before we go to the lawyer?" Itzi asked as Fonso finished dressing, "I want to put these in a safe deposit box." The High Priest held up the impressive vase of rubies he'd kept on his nightstand.

"No problem." the big man agreed, "Let me take it."

Again Fonso chided himself, this time for his lack of attention to detail; he hadn't even noticed the vessel in Itzi's hands. The big man relieved his brother of the container and was shocked by its weight.

"We better find something less conspicuous to put these in," Fonso suggested, "we'll be the talk of the town walking around like this."

It wasn't everyday you saw a crystal vase nearly a foot high loaded to the brim with rubies. There was probably over a million dollars in gems in the clear container. Fonso took the briefcase that held the papers Itzi wanted to take to the law office and poured the rubies into it.

As they approached the Jaguar Itzamna eyed his giant brother; in his suit with the briefcase Fonso looked very professional.

"You look like a lawyer!" Itzi laughed out loud.

Fonso laughed too. The laughter felt good; since Tolo's death they had felt pretty somber. Work at the tattoo parlor had been really weird without Bartolomeo; Ildefonso functioned as the doorman and had the customers sign the cards. Even knowing the work cycle was their last, the big man had been glad to see it end.

Both Ildefonso and Itzi had been disturbed reading their brother's diary; though Tolo had put on a brave face it seemed he greatly feared death. They cringed reading that Bartolomeo "hadn't had a good nights sleep since Mama died." Oddly, the coroner had determined the cause of Tolo's death to be sleep apnea, a condition that caused a person to stop breathing while asleep.

Though it was hard reading some of Tolo's words, something he had written made Itzi plan that day's trip to the lawyer. Bartolomeo had mentioned a desire to set up a charitable foundation to fund future scientific research. Itzamna realized that a lot of good could be done with the money from Chac's Treasure when they were all gone.

The brothers entered the Bank of Napa. After leasing a safe deposit box Fonso poured the rubies into it. Itzi pocketed the key and they went on to their appointment with the lawyer.

Coombs & Dunlap is the oldest law firm in the Napa Valley. They had handled the trust account for the care of the family's farm and vineyard since the late 1800's.

THE FLAVOR OF HEARTS

Malcolm Mackenzie was glad to see the Cenotes brothers. Immediately he offered his condolences on Bartolomeo's passing. The lawyer had great sympathy for the two men before him; he wondered how they coped with the loss of most of their immediate family in such a short space of time.

"I would like to make a will," Itzi started, "and set up arrangements for three charitable foundations."

The attorney was thrilled to hear this news. Napa was small community; rumors abounded in the small town. Tongues had wagged incessantly after the death of Mrs. Cenotes about the wealth and the assets of the family. Though Peter Manasse had remained steadfastly close mouthed many local people speculated on the cost of the lavish mausoleum the Cenotes family was constructing at the Tulocay Cemetery.

The attorney had also heard the recent gossip regarding Bartolomeo Cenotes. Apparently the young man had died without a will, leaving an account in the Bank of Napa in excess of three hundred thousand dollars.

Itzi removed an envelope from the inside pocket of his suit jacket and handed it to Mr. Mackenzie.

"That is a printout of my account information at UBS AG, my bank in Zurich." the High Priest said.

The attorney opening the envelope and tried not to look astonished; the local scuttlebutt had far underestimated the wealth of the Cenotes family. The Swiss account held more than a billion dollars.

"Because some of the requests I am about to make require a great deal of administration into the future," Itzamna stated, "I was hoping you would agree to function as the paid executor of my will and the chief administrator of the charitable trusts."

The High Priest offered Mr. Mackenzie an extremely generous payment package for these duties. The Cenotes brothers were both relieved when the attorney agreed; he had been a friend to them and they had great faith in his honesty and reliability.

Itzi asked that three charitable foundations be created; the first two in Bartolomeo's name to fund scientific research and to grant scholarships to needy students for higher education.

"The third charitable foundation must be the largest," the High Priest stipulated, "I would like this foundation created for betterment of the Maya people. I want to fund housing, health care, education, business grants, land purchase…frankly, anything needed to improve the lives and advance the status of the Maya people of the Yucatan, Belize, Honduras and Guatemala."

They discussed and agreed on the division of the assets for the charitable trusts.

Fonso removed a stack of property deeds from the briefcase and laid them on the attorney's desk.

"These are my real estate holdings," Itzi explained, "I would like these properties sold with the proceeds placed in the fund for the Maya. All except for the farm and vineyard here in the Napa Valley," the High Priest continued, "I would like that deeded to Juan Ortiz VI, our present caretaker."

Malcolm nodded as he leafed through the stack of property titles; it was an amazing real estate portfolio, the Cenotes family had assets in some of the most desirable locations in the world.

Itzi asked that fifty million dollars be donated to the Upkeep Endowment at the Tulocay Cemetery. The little man removed the safe deposit key from his jacket pocket and laid it on the lawyer's desk.

"There is a safe deposit box at the Bank of Napa. It holds a collection of gemstones I have amassed over the years," Itzamna said, "I would like its full contents given to Peter Manasse personally."

Since the death of their mother Itzi had struck up a friendship with the funeral director; the High Priest was impressed with the man's sincere interest in the Maya culture and his kind and generous nature.

"Oh," Itzi added, "and in the last two cases, I would like to place money aside to pay any taxes that Juan Ortiz or Peter Manasse may incur inheriting these assets."

Itzi turned to his brother, "Did I forget anything, Fonso?"

"The time frame, Itzi," the big man answered cryptically.

The High Priest was surprised at himself; with his lifelong proclivity for tracking the months and years down to the second, the little man was amused that he forgot his will's stipulation regarding time.

"I have two concerns dealing with the time frame of my will. I need the documents drawn up as quickly as possible," Itzi requested, "It is important that I sign the papers and everything is legal by December 20th." I apologize for not coming sooner to take care of this matter."

The attorney consulted the calendar on his desk,

"Today is the seventeenth, which would give us two days..." the attorney knew the time frame was tight but the Cenotes family had been one of the firm's original clients, "I will have your paperwork ready by the nineteenth."

Suddenly the attorney's curiosity was piqued. Here was a Mayan man putting his affairs in order for the day before the media hyped doomsday; maybe there was some credibility in the dire predictions. Immediately Malcolm Mackenzie's legendary logic kicked in. Why would the little man want a will if the world was ending?

"You may consider this last request strange, "Itzi started slowly, "but it is very important..."

The attorney again became curious.

"If you do not receive a visit from me at this office by January 31, 2013...I would like the necessary steps put in motion to declare me legally dead and my will executed as soon as possible."

The attorney stared in surprise; up until this point he considered Itzamna Cenotes a very intelligent and rational man.

"Mr. Cenotes, there are some very specific laws regarding death in absentia." The attorney tried to address this situation in everyday language, "first, seven years must elapse during which time all efforts must be made to locate you or your remains. After that time we must prove to a court that there is a higher likelihood that you are deceased than that you are alive..."

Itzi raised his hand and stopped the man. The High Priest suddenly realized the modern legalities were highly problematic; the last thing he wanted was Tolo's research fund or the help for the Maya stalled in legal quagmire for seven years or more.

"Could the things we discussed as part of my will be put in place while I'm alive?" the little man asked. "Is it possible to make legal documents to accomplish these things regardless of my life or death?"

Mr. Mackenzie stared; now he was utterly shocked.

"You would like to donate nearly three quarters of a billion dollars to charity? The rest of the bequeathed items could be considered gifts..." the attorney was floored at this turn of events, "Mr. Cenotes, I must advise you as your attorney to keep some of your assets for your future."

Itzi shook his head; he was sure he had very little future to worry about.

"I would like these things set in motion immediately," the High Priest was resolute, "Is it possible to have all the necessary paperwork drawn up by the 19th?"

"It is possible, Mr.Cenotes, however," Malcolm Mackenzie was adamant, "in all good conscience as your attorney, I must advise you not to dissolve all your assets. Please, please consider your future!"

The lawyer sounded so concerned and so disturbed Itzi felt the need to put the good man's mind at ease.

"I'll tell you what I'll do," Itzmana suggested, "This afternoon I will take a million dollars from my Swiss account and place it in my account at the Bank of Napa. I live a very simple lifestyle, Mr. Mackenzie; this sum will easily provide for my future."

Itzi grinned broadly, "Will this put your mind at ease?"

"Yes," Malcolm Mackenzie smiled and breathed a sigh of relief, "I would feel better knowing your great generosity did not leave you destitute in your later years."

The attorney agreed to establish the three charitable trusts as of December 19, 2012. He would arrange an immediate fifty million dollar donation to the Tulocay Cemetery's Endowment fund. Finally he would draw documents up outlining two gifts: the Napa property to Juan Ortiz VI and the gem collection to Peter Manasse.

"Do I have everything correct?" the attorney asked.

"Could the trusts officially begin on December 22, even though I sign the papers on the nineteenth?" Itzi asked.

It seemed much more appropriate to the High Priest that the lord's good works begin at the start of the Mayan Calendar's Fifth Great Cycle, rather than at the end of the fourth.

The attorney noted the date; he was curious if the little man picked the day after the supposed doomsday on purpose. Finally the lawyer suggested reworking Itzi's will to state that any assets left upon his death be donated to the Maya trust. Itzamna agreed. Mr. Mackenzie was glad the little man had abandoned the will's stipulation concerning death in absentia.

Before the brothers took their leave the lawyer scanned his notes.

"One last thing," he asked, "the trust for the Maya people, would you like that named for your brother Bartolomeo also? Perhaps after your family?"

"You should name it after you, Itzi." Fonso suggested.

The High Priest shook his head, it seemed wrong to take the credit for the fortune the lord Chac had given so generously.

"We will call it, 'U Siihbil Chac (Chac's Gift)'" Itzi decided.

102

At 12:01 am much of the globe breathed a collective sigh of relief. The doomsayers who waited for instantaneous disaster on December 21 watched the minutes tick by; nothing bad happened.

People poured into the streets from their End of the World parties. They high fived and danced on the sidewalks and intersections; car horns honked, fire crackers went off, people laughed and sang. It was a celebration worthy of any New Year's Eve; humanity had avoided the predicted cosmic knock out punch.

Fonso eyed Itzi as the rowdy celebration started in Yountville. They could hear the ruckus from their vantage point on the High Priest's rooftop terrace.

"Morons," Ildefonso scoffed.

Itzi smiled; since most of the gloom and doom predictions were based on their ancient calendar it was surprising how ignorant modern people really were about Maya time keeping. Mayans calculate a new day at the rising of the sun; technically it was still the day before. The predicted alignment was still hours away.

THE FLAVOR OF HEARTS

Ildefonso threw another log on the outdoor fireplace. He uncorked two more bottles of wine and handed one to his tiny brother as he rejoined the little man on the couch.

"Do you think we'll die right at dawn?" the big man asked nonchalantly.

Itzi grinned. Fonso was truly the greatest warrior Uxmal had ever produced; the man had no fear.

"Hard to say," Itzi answered, sipping from his bottle, "I kind of hope not...after all these years I'd like to see the alignment."

Ildefonso nodded as he sipped his wine, "You deserve to see it, Ah K'uhun."

Itzi's eyebrows rose. At his request, no one in the family had addressed him by his official religious title since their first days in ancient Rome. Having left his temple behind, even at his god's bidding, Itzi had become uncomfortable being addressed as a High Priest. It was odd to hear his title after all these years; but strangely it felt right.

"Fonso," Itzamna looked up at his giant brother, "thank you for everything, thank you for all you've done in all these years. I couldn't imagine a better brother and friend."

"Thank you, Itzi." Fonso answered in a rarely serious tone, "You are the wisest and finest man I have ever known; I have always been honored to be your brother. Because of you we lived amazing lives...for the things we've all seen and done...thank you."

"Thanks to our great god Chac." Itzamna added.

Fonso repeated the sentence wholeheartedly then grinned maniacally, "We had some fun, huh, Itzi?"

The big man clicked his bottle on Itzamna's. The little man laughed out loud and agreed as they both sipped the delicious local wine. Ildefonso stoked the fire and the brothers waited for the dawn.

103

All night the Maya people had streamed into the cities of their ancestors; tourists also crowded the entrances to the ancient ruins at Chichen Itza, Uxmal, Tulum, Palenque and Tikal.

Just before dawn the holy men extinguished the ceremonial fire and began the prayers of the New Fire Ceremony. They broke ritual clay pots then lit a blazing new fire. The people smashed old drinking cups and drank balche from new drinking vessels.

As one calendar cycle ended and a new one began, all was made new; debts were forgiven and trespasses forgotten. Especially on this morning, throughout much of Mexico and sections of Central America the Maya welcomed Fifth Great Cycle with much celebration.

Arianna Rosenberg went around her apartment and removed the plugs from all her electrical outlets. Entering her kitchen she took a glass from the cabinet and wrapped it in a dishtowel. She took a new glass from its box and a bottle of wine and went back to her living room. Extinguishing the candles she had lit earlier, she opened her curtains and waited for the sunrise.

In the last year the California woman had become fascinated with the Maya culture. At first all the television shows on the Mayan doomsday had scared her; but as she studied the beliefs and history of the ancient culture she had become more and more impressed.

When the rays of the sun streamed through her Los Angeles apartment the young woman lit new candles. She smashed the old glass in the dishtowel and filled her new glass with wine. Arianna toasted a new beginning for herself and all mankind. In her own modern way she had tried to replicate the spirit of the Maya New Fire Ceremony and oddly she had never felt more at peace.

Itzamna extinguished the fire in the terrace's fire pit. Though they hadn't expected to live past the dawn the brothers had prepared for the ceremony to welcome the Fifth Great Cycle. They smashed the ceramic bowls Ildefonso had brought to the rooftop. Itzi said the proper prayers to the Mayan gods and relit the fire.

As the brothers watched the flames grow, Fonso threw the bottles they had been drinking onto the fire and uncorked two new ones. The men toasted the Fifth Great Cycle and their highly unexpected survival.

The High Priest headed toward his beloved telescope and watched the long awaited alignment of First Father with First Mother. When the sun was at its full glory the little man joined his brother on the couch in the sitting area.

"What do you think is going on, Itzi?" the warrior was totally perplexed, nothing seemed different. The little man shrugged.

Itzamna had always been doubtful of worldwide devastation at the end of the Great Cycle; he was sure if the sun rose strong enough the earth would avoid such a fate. All along Itzi had hoped, as many Maya holy men did, that earth would receive a spark from the galaxy's center during the alignment and humanity would rise to a new state of consciousness. Frankly, the High Priest saw no obvious change in the sun and he felt the same as he always had.

"I have no idea what's going on." he frankly admitted.

Fonso flipped on the television they had installed in an enclosed corner of Itzi's terrace. The news showed celebrations all over the globe. People were planning survival parties and screaming, "I told you so," at the doomsayers.

"I know one thing," Itzi stated, grinning, "I'm hungry."

Ildefonso laughed out loud; some things never changed!

They drove to Itzi's favorite café and had a huge breakfast. All over town people were in a festive mood. Returning home the men settled in the living room in front of the TV. Merriment was still all over the news; worldwide people celebrated the dodging of the cosmic bullet.

The brother's night long vigil, six bottles of wine and full bellies brought on drowsiness; before long both men dozed off on the comfortable sectional couch. When Fonso awoke he was startled by Itzamna's close proximity and intent stare.

"What's going on?" the big man asked.

"Nothing, I just woke up myself," the High Priest's odd gaze and weird tone unnerved the family warrior.

"Hey, stop looking at me like I'm a dead man walking!" Fonso declared.

Both men burst out laughing. Ildefonso eyed his Rolex; it was almost seven; the house was dark other than the light cast by the huge TV.

"Are you going to place the stones, Itzi?" the big man wondered.

"Frankly, I'm not sure what to do," the High Priest answered, "I guess I should."

"Maybe the lord will take us during the Move." Fonso suggested.

Itzamna nodded; perhaps this time when the air was sucked from their lungs it wouldn't return. As he had on every winter solstice since 951CE the little man retrieved Chac's sacred stones and placed them on the four cardinal directions inside the house. Rejoining his brother in the living room, the High Priest laughed.

Fonso had a GPS unit in one hand and a bottle of Jack Daniels in the other. Ildefonso was always prepared for anything! The brothers drank shots and waited.

At nine o'clock the familiar buzzing started. The Move proceeded as it had for the last 1060 years. Ready to welcome death they were both utterly shocked to feel their lungs re-inflate. The brothers stared at each other in astonishment when the house stopped shaking.

"We're alive." Itzi said it more like a question.

Fonso grabbed the GPS unit; uncharacteristically the big man's hand was slightly shaking as he started the machine's location calculation.

"It's Merida," he said astonished, "we're back on the Yucatan."

104

Itzamana looked up at his warrior brother.
"I want to go to my temple," the High Priest said quietly.
Fonso nodded; that felt right. There could only be on reason they made this Move to the Yucatan; to finish where they had started.
Ilefonso checked his Rolex. It was just after 11 pm.
"Uxmal is a tourist attraction now, Itzi," Fonso warned his older brother, "It's closed at this hour, but I don't doubt we could make our way in somehow. Do you want to try sneaking in there or wait till it opens tomorrow and walk in with the tourists?"
"What do you think?" the little man was willing to take his warrior brother's advice. "You've been there as it stands in the modern world."
In 1975 Fonso, Bartolomeo and Waykan had traveled back to the Yucatan for the inauguration of Uxmal's sound and light show. It was a highly publicized event designed to increase tourism; the Queen of England had attended as an invited guest. Unwilling to see his city in ruins Itzamna had refused to make the trip.
After the fact Itzi wished he had attended. At the end of the inaugural multi-media show a prayer to the rain god Chac

was broadcast over the loudspeakers; though it was the height of the dry season, a downpour had soaked the dignitaries!

"All things considered," Ildefonso suggested, "I think we should wait for daylight. During the day we could enter Uxmal with the tourists and see what's what. We could take cover when the site closes and then probably do whatever you want." The big man suddenly got a better idea.

"Let me get my laptop," Fonso went on, "we stayed in a hotel right near Uxmal when we went in the 70's...if we take a room nearby that would give us someplace to put the car too."

Itzi nodded in agreement. Ildefonso easily found a website for local accommodations; there were now many hotels near the ancient Maya cities. The brothers were highly amused by the website's name: Mayaland.

"Look at this place, Itzi!" Fonso said excitedly, "It's called The Lodge at Uxmal. It says they have a private entrance to the archeological site."

The High Priest looked at the map of the hotel and its proximity to their old city; it was surreal seeing the aerial photos of his temple pyramid.

"Call them and see if we can check in tomorrow, OK, Fonso?"

The big man readily agreed.

"Then see if you can fine us someplace to eat." Itzi laughed. "I'm starving."

105

The Mayan decorations at the Lodge at Uxmal pleased both the Cenotes brothers; however it felt strange to see how their culture had become so commercialized.

"Get ready, Itzi," Fonso warned his older brother as they approached the entrance to the ruins of Uxmal, "It's pretty different."

Fonso paid the admission fee and eyed his tiny brother closely as they entered. The High Priest stared at the souvenir shop, the snack bar, and the modern rest rooms. The brothers walked silently through the exhibits in the site's museum.

"Most of it's wrong," Itzamna grimaced as they exited.

Fonso nodded. During their visit in the 70's Bartolomeo had been highly disgusted by the modern interpretations of their city and lifestyle.

Ildefonso wondered what Itzi was thinking as they overheard guides telling the tourists that the Pyramid of the Magician was built in one night by a mystical dwarf that was hatched from an egg. In truth, much backbreaking labor over decades created the impressive temple. Both Itzi and Fonso cringed when tour guides called the ruler dwarf's mother a witch.

The big man felt the intense stares of tourists and the employees as he and Itzi approached the temple pyramid; people usually eyed the mismatched Cenotes brothers with interest but here they were causing quite a stir.

At first Fonso presumed the legend of the dwarf magician who ruled Uxmal was fresh in people's minds and, other than his modern dress, tiny Itzamna certainly looked the part.

Ildefonso realized it was a little more when the crowd parted as Itzi moved toward the pyramid's base. There was an aura around the little man that was palpable: eerily, the people reverently stepped aside to allow the High Priest to walk right up to his temple's front steps.

Itzi pointed to a sign in two languages that prohibited climbing to the structure's summit. He and Fonso joined the bravest of Uxmal's visitors and ascended the steep stairs to the base of the pyramid's second level; there a guard blocked the way to the two higher sections and refused the tourists admission into the upper interiors.

Along with the rest of the height defying explorers the Cenotes brothers sat along the top of the first level and admired the view.

"There's a lot they haven't uncovered," Itzi said quietly.

Fonso agreed. Uxmal was a far larger city than was evident from the present day ruins reclaimed from the jungle. Itzi looked up over his shoulder to his former home at the temple's apex.

"I want to go to the top," the High Priest sounded determined.

Ildefonso knew there were only two ways to do something prohibited: stealth or bribery. The former warrior eyed the park employee guarding the stairs to the summit; bribery certainly seemed a possibility but definitely not with all these people around.

Stealth was probably a better option, the big man reasoned. Fonso wasn't sure what Itzi planned to do in his former home but privacy seemed necessary.

"I think we should sneak in later," the big man suggested, "either tonight or just after daybreak."

Itzi agreed. The Cenotes brothers descended the stairs much more confidently than the tourists around them. Many people climbed a Maya pyramid without much difficulty but found the return to the ground a dizzying and terrifying trip!

The brothers spent the rest of the day walking the grounds; it was sad and comforting at the same time. Entering a structure on the northern side of the area labeled The Nunnery Quadrangle; they navigated the building's double rooms to a particular set. Fonso was floored to stand in his old quarters. It was ironic the Spaniards thought this place resembled a nunnery; this building had housed Uxmal's finest and most fierce warriors.

Standing on the ball court Itzi remembered every ball game he had ever presided over as High Priest and ruler of Uxmal.

"Let's try to find Mama's house." Ildefonso suggested.

The brothers walked past the south side of the Pyramid of the Magician and into the trees. This section of Uxmal was unexcavated; it seemed much of what the men remembered as the city's residential sections were as yet unclaimed from the jungle.

The brothers found the approximate spot but found no remnants of their mother's actual home; that was not unexpected after all the years. They both pictured Mama's wooden house with its thatched roof.

"It still feels good to be here," Itzi reminisced.

Fonso agreed; many good times had been had in their family home in Uxmal. Heading further south through the trees they stumbled upon the buildings the tourist map called The House of the Witch. It described the structure as the home of the adopted mother of the mystical dwarf that magically built the pyramid and came to rule Uxmal.

"Strange how they're almost right, but not right. Mama's house wasn't far from here." Fonso mused out loud.

"Do you remember what this building really was?" Itzi asked his younger brother.

"I don't remember this place at all." Ildefonso shrugged.

Itzi's stomach growled and the little man grinned, "I wish we could walk through the trees and find Mama roasting a turkey in banana leaves!"

"That makes two of us!" Fonso spoke wholeheartedly, "Let's go back to the hotel. We'll eat and make some plans for getting up on your temple."

The men headed north on the walkway toward the site's entrance. They passed a group of local vendors. Immediately an old woman left her display and approached Itzi. She bowed her head and held out her open palm. She offered a small stone carving of the rain god Chac on a leather cord. "Cha'e, Ah K'uhun." she said, "Ka'ah Chac kalaanteech."

Fonso's eyebrows rose in surprise. The lady addressed Itzmana as a High Priest. She asked him to take this necklace of their god, and she asked Chac's protection for the little man.

Itzamna accepted the lady's gift and she smiled when he immediately put the cord around his neck. He took her hand and blessed her, "Ka xi'ik te'ex hatz'utzil, nohoch xunaan." Itzi said. It meant, "May all go well with you, great lady."

It was easy to see Itzi's words immensely pleased her. Fonso wanted to give the old woman money, but he knew she would consider it an insult.

As the brothers walked on they heard her call from behind, "Tun taal le xaman ka'ano'. She said, "The north wind is coming."

Itzi turned and responded, "Haah, nohoch xunaan," The High Priest told her it was true, change was in the air.

Right before they left the site Fonso asked if Itzi would wait near the exit. The little man was not surprised to see Ildefonso trot back along the walkway toward the Mayan vendors. Fonso selected a small souvenir from each stand and insisted the merchants accept his hundred dollar bills.

In their brief time in the modern Yucatan the Cenotes brothers had both been disturbed to see their proud people treated as the lowest rung of society. Seeing the situation with their own eyes had made the men even gladder that they had made the trip to the lawyer before the Move.

As Ildefonso rejoined his tiny brother Itzi grinned, "You're a good man, Fonso."

"I take after my brother," the big man smiled.

106

At the break of dawn Itzi and Fonso headed back toward the archeological site. They veered off the walkway before the park's entrance and headed into the trees. It was easy to navigate through the jungle during the dry season; and their foray into the forest the day before had given them both a good idea of the direction needed to surreptitiously enter Uxmal.

Emerging on the park's east side the brothers paused near the tree line and scanned the area for any movement. Sure they were alone; they easily approached the Temple of the Magician and climbed to the top.

Itzi stood in the center of his old home. The High Priest relived his visit from the lord Chac; he easily recalled the water dripping from the great god's hands and soaking the floor.

Fonso watched his tiny brother eye each wall. The little man imagined the area lushly furnished with his belongings; now the space seemed large and empty. Itzamna approached the northern wall and knelt down; the little man removed a string of jade beads from the pocket of his jeans and laid it on the floor. Next he removed a carved piece of bone from his pocket; and pierced the fleshy part of his palm below his right thumb. He squeezed the wound until his sacred blood dotted the jade beads.

Fonso watched as the High Priest made his offerings and said the prayers to their lord Chac. The big man vividly remembered the beautiful jade carvings and ceremonial altar that used to occupy that space.

Itzi rose and spoke, "Let's go to the temple below."

Fonso paused by the door and scanned the grounds surrounding the pyramid; Uxmal was still quiet, almost eerily so. Ildefonso led his brother down the steps and into the area the guidebooks called the Chenes Temple. They paused just inside the entrance; it was dusty and dark. The big man shuddered; much sacrifice had taken place there.

Itzmana made a move to go further into the interior.

"Wait, Itzi," Fonso retrieved two small but powerful flashlights from his jeans pocket. Giving one to his tiny brother Ildefonso lit the second and scanned the space. Some small stones had fallen from the ceiling and were haphazardly strewn along the floor; it was easy to see why they prohibited tourists from exploring this area.

The High Priest headed straight for the Northern corner. "They never found the way inside!" he said excitedly.

Fonso had suspected as much; none of the guidebooks or the exhibits had ever mentioned the tombs of the royalty inside the temple pyramid. The big man watched as Itzi pushed a succession of stones. In their day the corner pivoted open and revealed a stairway along the pyramid's inner side wall.

The corner moved slightly but not enough to allow passage. Itzi leaned on the hidden doorway but it didn't budge.

"Let me try it," Ildefonso offered. With some effort on the big man's part the concealed door finally swung open. A blast of air enveloped the brothers; it was dusty and dank. If time had a smell this is it Fonso thought.

The former warrior knew it was futile to try to convince the High Priest not to enter the temple's hidden chambers but he hoped his tiny brother would allow him to take the lead.

THE FLAVOR OF HEARTS

"You've never been down there, Fonso," Itzi countered his giant brother's request, "I know the way."

It was true; this was an area totally off limits to any of Uxmal's citizens. Only the High Priest and his immediate underlings were allowed access into the tombs in the temple pyramid. Ilefonso agreed to follow.

Dust blanketed the stone stairs; even slowly descending the hundred winding steps the men shook up a cloud of powder. Finally they reached the bottom where a dozen arched doorways lined a long corridor.

Ildefonso followed Itzi through the first one. The big man gasped when he saw the room's contents. A highly adorned human skeleton was ceremonially laid on a carved stone funeral slab; an exquisite jade mask covered the face. Matching jade bands covered the bones of the forearms and shins; the skeleton wore a stunning breast piece of carved shells, stones and beads and a decorated loincloth. A huge ceremonial headdress circled the skull.

Highly decorated ceramic containers, jade artifacts and belongings of every description filled the small room. Other than the absence of gold, it was reminiscent of the intact tomb of the Egyptian pharaoh Tutankhamen.

"Hun Uitzil Chac Tutul Xiu," Itzi said reverently, "his priest, Napuc Ten is in the chamber across the hallway."

Ildefonso was speechless; the former warrior had never in his life expected to view the remains of the legendary founder and first ruler of Uxmal.

One by one they entered more of the chambers hidden in the pyramid's base. The High Priest showed Fonso the resting places of many of Uxmal's former High Priests and ruling elite.

Entering a room close to the end of the long hallway they were at first surprised to find the carved funeral slab bare and the chamber empty. Itzi aimed his flashlight on the highly carved walls. Ildefonso sucked in air; though he was rusty reading the old Mayan script he easily recognized their original family name.

"Yes," Itzi said quietly, "this tomb is mine."

The tiny High Priest approached his funeral bier and rubbed away the dust with his hand. To his surprise Itzi found carvings on its flat surface and read the inscription aloud.

"It has the date we left Uxmal," the little man said in amazement, "then it says Itzamna K'ak'nal Ajaw Xiu left Uxmal and has not returned. It is believed the High Priest has joined his ancestors in the sky. It says this space is reserved for the god if he decides to return."

Itzi hopped up on the funeral slab and stretched out flat.

Ildefonso stared in shock. The spooky surroundings had begun to eat at the big man but this…this was too much.

"Itzi, get off there!" Fonso yelled.

The High Priest laughed. "Are you telling me what to do, Ildefonso?" the little man asked impishly.

"Yes, I am! Get off there right now!" the warrior ordered his venerated brother.

"I've returned," Itzamna said slyly, "and this is my space."

"I'm telling you," Fonso barked out the sentence in a no-nonsense tone, "get off there right now!"

When Itzi mischievously refused Fonso quickly approached the stone slab; he intended to grab his tiny brother and drag him bodily out of the pyramid. Itzi roared with laughter as he sat up and dodged Ildefonso's grasp. "Calm down, Fonso," the High Priest said catching his breath.

A hissing sound distracted the brothers; looking up they saw a thick column of dust falling from above. With a sudden rush of air a massive building block dropped from the ceiling; instinctively Ildefonso threw his body over his brother's but the stone's weight was immense.

Chac claimed their hearts simultaneously.

107

"Damn," Russell Reebenaker said aloud as he stopped at the red light. He eyed the sun rising and looked at the clock on his truck's dashboard, "I'm gonna be late."

The last two days had been murder at the construction site where he was foreman. Half the workforce had been scared of doomsday and not shown up; everything was behind.

Boom!

Russell was jostled by the sudden impact. The foreman realized that his truck had been hit in the rear. Exiting the vehicle and seeing the smashed back bumper Russ was surprised at his calm reaction. Normally if anybody breathed too hard on his beloved pick-up he wanted to knock their block off.

Approaching the driver of the van who hit him Russ was taken aback by the guy's shell shocked expression. "That lady, that lady…" The man was pointing and mumbling.

Russell shook his head back and forth. He must've been hit harder than he thought, this guy sounded really weird. The foreman followed the van driver's gaze. Man, I really must've been hit too hard, Russell thought rubbing his eyes in disbelief.

There was a woman flying, she was up by the second story of the building on the corner. She changed directions and flew over them to the other side of the street. Drivers across the intersection exited their vehicles and stared in total shock.

A girl near a red Toyota lifted off the ground. "I can do it too!" she hollered.

Her voice echoed across the open air in the weirdest way. People were collapsing in panic and alarm. Sirens could be heard from a block away; it was pandemonium.

Hearing a scraping sound Russell looked toward his left. A teenage girl was staring at a soda can moving around in circles on the sidewalk at her feet. She was laughing out loud. Suddenly she looked at Russell and the soda can landed at his feet. "Try it, Mister!" she was roaring laughing, "Make it move!"

The foreman shook his head; her voice was so weird! It sounded like they were in a cave. He was home in bed dreaming; he had to be, either that or he was having the worst nervous breakdown imaginable.

"Make it move," she yelled again.

Numbly Russell decided to kick the can back but before he moved his leg the can shot back in her direction.

"That's it," the teenager laughed her echoing laugh.

"Hah," Russell felt irrational, "if this is a dream, then I'm gonna fly too."

The foreman had wanted to fly from the first time he ever saw Superman. He imagined the air below his feet and felt his body lift off the ground. It was unbelievable! Russell felt the air rushing by his face as he soared over the streets; there were cars all over the city stopped in haphazard patterns. People were screaming and pointing. The foreman flew toward his house; it felt so real!

"For sure," Russell yelled at the top of his lungs, "This is the best dream I ever had!"

108

Harriett Donaldson woke up to the sound of raucous screaming. She was glad the sounds of the children next door had not awakened her husband; he had much less patience with the neighborhood kids than she did. Exiting the bed she quietly donned her housecoat. Hoping her husband would continue to sleep she went to the kitchen and made the morning coffee.

The shouting from the yard next door grew louder. Maybe Joe is right, she mused, thinking of her mate's constant complaints about the local youngsters, maybe we should've bought that house in the retirement community.

Mostly Harriett liked the sounds of the children at play but this day the kids seemed exceptionally boisterous. Hoping they weren't up to mischief the old lady opened the kitchen curtain.

Her mouth dropped open in shock; the little neighbor flew by the window! Not running, the little girl flew six feet off the ground! Young Victoria sailed ten feet down the side yard and landed gently on her feet.

Harriett gripped the edge of the kitchen sink. She was positive she was awake but the old woman feared she had suddenly lost her mind. With a loud yell Victoria's nine year old brother Jacob rose from the ground and followed her; landing gently on his feet. Mrs. Donaldson turned from the window to run for her husband. She was startled to see him in the doorway.

"What's going on? What's all that noise?"

She heard his voice but he didn't speak!

"Joe, come here," she barely choked out the words, "I've lost my mind!" Her voice sounded loud and strange; it seemed to echo off the walls.

"What? What do you mean?" her husband approached. His voice also sounded exceptionally loud and strange. He gasped when he saw the view from the window. He and his wife stared slack jawed as the children soared around the yard next door.

"What the hell is going on?"
"Maybe we're dead."
"We're not dead, Harriett!"

Suddenly the Donaldsons stared at each other; they were having a clear conversation without actually talking. The phone rang and startled them both. Harriett walked numbly across the room to answer the call.

"Hello," her voice was shaky, but again, when she spoke aloud her voice was odd and echoed.

"Mom, are you and Dad OK?" their daughter Tricia sounded worried.

Harriett immediately thought to reassure their daughter but before the old lady got the words out Tricia replied, "Good, some really weird stuff is going on. They say on CNN that it's happening everywhere. You and dad stay in the house, OK? I'll be right over."

"OK, honey, we'll wait for you."

Harriett thought the words and Tricia definitely heard them!

"Good," their daughter replied, "I'll be right there."

The old lady turned toward her husband. *"Tricia's coming."* she aimed the thoughts at her mate, *"She says weird things are going on all over; she saw it on CNN."*

THE FLAVOR OF HEARTS

Joe turned toward the TV set on the kitchen counter. The power switched on by itself!

"Did you do that, Joe?" Harriett shrieked aloud, her high pitched tone careened off the walls and ceiling. *"I think I did!"* he sent his words to her through the air.

Aiming a thought at the television the old man turned the power on and off three or four times. Grinning he turned to his wife; she was frozen in utter shock. *"Try it, Harriett. Think about it and it'll happen."* he said without speaking, *"Try it! See if you can do it!"*

At first she was afraid, but curiosity got the better of her. She did as he asked and turned the TV off from across the room. She staggered toward the kitchen table and sat down. *"This is more than weird, Joe."*

Even though her voice only appeared in his head, Joe Donaldson could tell by his wife's tone that she was on the verge of fainting. He joined her at the kitchen table. This day he did not take the chair across from her as he had for the last thirty years. He sat in the chair beside her and pulled the seat closer to his shaking wife.

Tenderly he put his arms around her. When she buried her head in his chest he held her tightly. A warm feeling filled him from head to toe; he realized it had been years and years since he had really hugged his loyal partner.

"I love you Harrie," he said it out loud, so she would know for sure she wasn't imagining the words. Harriett Donaldson pulled back and stared at her husband.

"You haven't said that in years." she was astonished.

"I should've said it every day. You are the best thing that ever happened to me," Joe sent the thoughts to her but he meant every word as much as if he yelled it from a mountain top.

"Oh, Joe!" Harriett began to cry.

"Don't cry, Harrie. Let's have coffee," the old man was sure they should do something normal. Before she could move he jumped up from his chair and took two cups from the cupboard. Filling them at the coffee maker he returned to the table placing one before his wife.

Again Harriett stared amazed. She couldn't remember the last time Joe poured her a cup of coffee; it might have been when she had their daughter forty years ago! When Joe noticed the shocked look on her face; guilt washed over him. He suddenly realized Harriett had been the perfect wife for over fifty years. Sure, he had provided for her and their family, but she practically waited on him hand and foot.

"Harrie, thank you for everything you've done for me and the kids. I'm gonna do more for you," again he said it out loud so she'd know the words weren't just in her head.

"I love you, Joe. I love you," tears streamed down her face. He hugged her tightly again.

"Let's have the coffee, before it gets cold," he sent the thought to the top of her head. She pulled back from him and they sipped from their cups.

"It sounds weird when we talk out loud," she thought toward him, *"it sounds more like your real voice when you think the words to me!"*

"I know," he agreed silently, *"it's like Star Trek!"*

He was grinning widely. Suddenly living like his favorite TV show Joe Donaldson looked twenty years old again. Harriett laughed out loud; her laughter sounded rich and musical bouncing around the room. When Joe joined in, their combined mirth sounded like an airborne symphony.

Joe suddenly had an idea; if he could turn the TV off and on with a thought... he turned toward the silk flower arrangement at the center of the table. A daisy rose from the vase and floated toward Harriet!

She gasped, but smiled broadly when she reached out and plucked the flower from mid air. Again they laughed; the musical sound of the laughter was indescribable.

"Try to move something, Harrie!" Joe thought toward her.

She looked toward her coffee cup and imagined it moving across the table. They both gasped in surprise when it did; and they both grinned when she called the cup back to her. Joe turned toward the coffee maker and the half filled coffee pot floated toward the table. When the urn landed he picked it up and filled their cups. The old couple roared laughing.

"It's like Bewitched!" now Harriett was reminded of her favorite old TV show.

"Do you think we can fly, like the kids?" Joe stared wide-eyed at his wife.

"Don't, Joe!" she thought back, *"remember your hip!"*

The doctor had warned the old man the year before if he got another fracture he might need a hip replacement. Joe Donaldson couldn't resist. He pictured his body rising off the chair; to his disappointment nothing happened.

"Maybe it only works with small stuff," he thought toward her.

She was relieved; she didn't even want to imagine her husband floating around the kitchen.

"Mom! Dad!" their daughter's voice sounded really loud from the front hallway. When she appeared in the kitchen Tricia Donaldson's worried expression turned to relief.

"You're OK!" her sentence appeared in both of her parent's heads.

"We're fine." Joe immediately reassured their daughter.

"Do you want some coffee, honey?" Harriett sent the question to her daughter. Tricia stared. It was something her mother asked on every visit; yet never quite this way. The young woman grinned and thought a sentence back.

"They say on CNN it's a worldwide phenomenon. Everybody can talk without speaking! Some people can move things with their minds, and some people can fly."

"The neighbor kids can fly!" Harriet said telepathically, *"we saw them."*

"I saw some people doing it on the way over here," Tricia answered, *"I couldn't do it."*

"I couldn't either," Joe said ruefully, *"maybe we'll be able to figure it out.*

Simultaneously the ladies mental sentences echoed each other, *"You better not!"*

They all laughed. The amazing sound of the laughter made them laugh even harder. Tricia joined her parents at the table and they marveled over their new found abilities. All of them could converse without speaking and all three could move objects; but try as they might they could not lift their bodies.

"It's wild how you can both hear me when I think the sentence," Tricia commented mentally.

"Yes," her father agreed excitedly, *"it's amazing. You don't seem to hear someone's thoughts...just what they would have said!"*

They tried to test his theory.

"Think of a word, Harriet," Joe suggested, *"just think of it and we'll try to guess it."*

He and his daughter tried to no avail to hear the thought.

"What word were you thinking?" Tricia asked curiously.

"Refrigerator," her mother replied silently.

They shook their heads in amazement. It was a mystery how they could converse mentally, but not hear one another's thoughts.

"Well, I don't know how that works, but it's a relief," Harriett smiled, *"I wouldn't want half the people at church knowing what I really think of them!"*

Their melodic laughter bounced around the kitchen.

109

Leaders and representatives of every nation in the free world stood shoulder to shoulder at the United Nations Headquarters in New York City. Television cameras panned up and down the rows of men and women then paused at a podium in the center.

A voiceover announced: Ladies and Gentlemen, the President of the United States.

"Citizens of the World, I have been asked to speak tonight on behalf of my colleagues from the Emergency Summit on Global Transformation. In the last two days we have experienced sudden and unprecedented changes in our world. I will explain the current scientific theories on these changes and will announce some guidelines we feel must be established for worldwide public safety.

As you have all seen and experienced, people have developed the ability to converse without speaking. This ability, known as mental telepathy, has been documented worldwide.

Rest assured it is not the ability to read another person's mind. As it has been explained to us at the Summit; human beings have suddenly developed the power to zero in on the section of the brain that initiates speech. In essence, you are hearing the intended message from the speaker's brain before the words are formed by the vocal chords in the throat. All people in all corners of the globe are now endowed with this power.

As you may have noticed when people speak out loud; it echoes. Scientists theorize that this resonance is caused by a Doppler effect; put simply, the listener hears the same information twice a second apart; first from the speech center of the brain and second from the vocal chords.

Tonight my voice is being altered by sound technicians so I can speak out loud and sound normal to you. It was decided that until we are all accustomed to this new wordless way of speaking it would be less distracting for you to see my mouth moving and hear the words as you always have.

Some people have developed the power of telekinesis. This is the ability to move objects with the mind. Though people worldwide are exhibiting this amazing ability, it is not a global change. We estimate fifty percent of the world's population have developed this capability. It also seems that the people who display this skill have varying degrees of strength; simply, some can move larger objects than others.

Research will continue on this amazing ability. Frankly, scientists have not settled on a clear theory on how this works and why only a percentage of the population is affected, but rest assured, we will continue to find answers.

As you have probably seen, a very small percentage of the world population, approximately ten percent, have developed the astounding ability to levitate and fly. As with the telekinesis, scientists are unclear as to how this levitation works or why such a small percentage of people can accomplish it. Much research will be done on this unbelievable talent.

This is probably the most dangerous of humanity's sudden new found abilities; both for those who can defy gravity and the rest of us. Too many deaths and injuries have already been reported.

From this night, there is a worldwide martial law in effect regarding unaided human flight. No human being with the ability to fly is allowed over six feet, or two meters, from the surface of the ground. Any person found disregarding this rule will be arrested and immediately jailed.

A collision of two people flying within the permissible height will be treated as seriously as any vehicular accident, with the same penalties in effect. In a case of a person flying within the permissible height who collides with a non-flying human: it will be considered aggravated assault and severe penalties will be assessed. These laws regarding unaided human flight will be enforced worldwide by local authorities to assure public safety.

Lastly, all of you must be wondering what happened to cause this sudden transformation in human capabilities. The first scientific theories are centering on the earth's magnetic field. According to preliminary research; two days ago, when our sun aligned with the center of our Milky Way galaxy, the magnetic field that surrounds our planet was increased by a third. Though we can not be sure this was the cause of what scientists are now calling spontaneous evolution, it is the first step toward an explanation of the unprecedented events of the last two days.

As more research is done and clear answers are discovered news reports will be issued to keep you informed. For now, let us all revel in our new abilities and this unexpected step toward a bright new future. Let us work together to insure a safe and secure future for all mankind."

110

Over the next weeks additional changes were detected in the people of Earth. These transformations were more subtle; but no less astounding.

Though many originally feared the crime rate would soar as people learned to take advantage of their telekinetic and levitational powers, exactly the opposite happened. The crime rate dropped to unprecedented levels; in many areas crime was nonexistent. People were more patient and caring; an era of sharing and selflessness dawned.

Overnight the most affluent suddenly realized the ridiculous waste of frivolous spending; suddenly it felt ludicrous to spend thousands of dollars on a pair of shoes while other human beings went hungry. Philanthropy became widespread; people instantly showed a genuine concern for one another.

It wasn't only revolution in the hearts and spirits of humanity; people's minds took a huge leap forward.

Early on the morning of December 23rd scientists entered their labs and easily found answers to the problems that had hindered breakthroughs in all forms of research. It was as if blinders were removed; the solutions became instantaneously apparent.

Doctors at the Harvard Medical School in Boston announced a protein that inhibited the growth of all cancer cells. That same week their colleagues discovered a way to reprogram a patient's skin cells; these pluripotent cells would cure a multitude of illnesses. Overnight Parkinson's disease, Multiple Sclerosis, Alzheimer's and a host of other debilitating conditions became a thing of the past. Cases of crippling paralysis were easily reversed with the infusion of a patient's own pluripotent cells.

So many diseases were cured in the last weeks of 2012 the medical journals fought to keep up with publication; they were forced to plan multiple volumes to chronicle the scientists' amazing findings.

The technicians at the Sandia National Laboratories announced an advance of amazing proportions in the field of cold fusion. People marveled at the reports of the new form of energy; it promised safe, unlimited and virtually free power for the planet.

The media extolled the New World; it was a welcome change after the previous year of gloom and doom predictions. People suddenly wondered why in the past it had seemed easier to embrace something bad rather than something good.

111

Edwardo Xiu Martinez walked briskly through the entrance at Uxmal. Admission was free on Sundays and the modern Mayan holy man often started his day off at the ancient city of his ancestors.

Approaching the Pyramid of the Magician he was surprised to find no guard at the structure. Taking full advantage of the situation the holy man climbed to the top. He admired the view and breathed the cool air; it was such an unexpected pleasure to be at the pyramid's apex. He had always been proud to be distantly related to the people who had built this structure and ruled this legendary city.

Moving toward the northern side of the House of the Magician Edwardo immediately began prayers to the god Chac. He thanked Uxmal's patron deity for the recent changes everyone had experienced in the world.

Oddly the holy man felt the urge to say the Maya prayers for the dead. At first he resisted the thought, superstitiously fearing this action would bring death toward him or his family. The feeling became stronger; finally he succumbed to the irresistible urge and began the prayers.

When he finished with the words for the veneration of his ancestors the holy man felt a drop of rain. He stared at the sky; there were no clouds; the rainy season was months away! Edwardo held his hand open; he was shocked to see two huge raindrops hit his palm.

Immediately he recognized the sign from Chac, the Maya god of rain and thunder. The holy man wasn't sure who had died in need of the funeral prayers, but he was now positive he had done the right thing.

Edwardo offered words of gratitiude to the lord Chac. He thanked the god that the sun had risen with enough power at the end of the Fourth Great Cycle to avoid the feared destruction of humanity. The holy man finished with a prayer of personal appreciation to live in the lord's Golden Age.

As Edwardo descended the pyramid's steps a feeling of peace washed over him. The holy man smiled. He blissfully anticipated his family's delicious Sunday dinner and a wonderful afternoon playing with his grandchildren.

ABOUT THE AUTHOR

Carol Milazzo lives in New Jersey.
She works as an artist and copywriter.
This is her first novel.

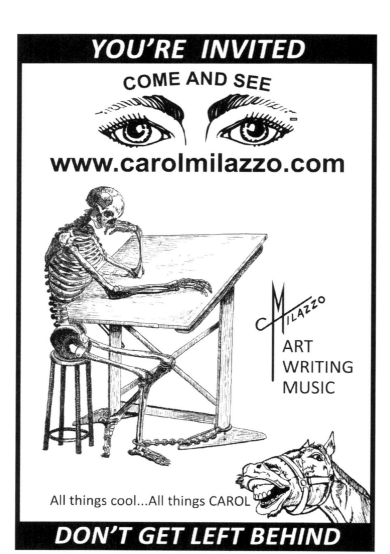

Made in the USA
Charleston, SC
29 June 2012